THE CHESSMAN

A Jack Haldean Mystery

Dolores Gordon-Smith

Severn House Large Print
London & New York

This first large print edition published 2016
in Great Britain and the USA by
SEVERN HOUSE PUBLISHERS LTD of
19 Cedar Road, Sutton, Surrey, England, SM2 5DA.
First world regular print edition published 2015 by
Severn House Publishers Ltd.

British Library Cataloguing in Publication Data
A CIP catalogue record for this title is available from the British Library.

ISBN-13: 9780727894328

Severn House Publishers support the Forest Stewardship Council™
[FSC™], the leading international forest certification organisation. All
our titles that are printed on FSC certified paper carry the FSC logo.

MIX
Paper from
responsible sources
FSC   FSC® C013056
www.fsc.org

Typeset by Palimpsest Book Production Ltd.,
Falkirk, Stirlingshire, Scotland.
Printed and bound in Great Britain by
T J International, Padstow, Cornwall.

Dedicated to Helen and Lucy.
Two sharp-eyed and enthusiastic readers!

One

Alan Leigh shuddered in relief as he heard the key turn in the lock of the front door of the flat. Simon! At last. He'd been a hell of a long time. Hell. His hell.

'Simon!' he called as the door to the sitting room opened. There was a catch in his voice. 'Simon, where've you been?'

He trailed off, staring as a man entered the room. The man looked like Simon, but he wasn't Simon. He was older for a start, a big, middle-aged, muscular man with high cheekbones and vivid blue eyes. Alan swallowed hard and, with an effort, spoke. 'Who are you? Where's Simon?'

The stranger looked down at Alan slumped helplessly on the sofa, then nodded slowly, as if unsurprised by what he saw. 'So you're Alan Leigh.'

It wasn't a question. His voice was oddly soft for such a large man. Soft but with power and the hint of menace.

'Where's Simon?' asked Alan once more. He knew his voice was breaking. 'Simon said he'd . . . he'd . . .'

He broke off as the man opened the briefcase he was carrying and took out a small glass bottle full of colourless liquid. 'Simon said he'd give you this?'

Alan made a grab for the bottle, then fell back

1

with a little cry as the man, with an amused laugh, put the bottle in his pocket.

'Later, Mr Leigh. We have a matter of business to discuss.'

Alan clenched his fists together and breathed deeply, fighting for a measure of control. There was a veiled threat in the words. Alan had come across many men who not only threatened, but enjoyed carrying out their threats. That's why he'd been so grateful to Simon. Simon had protected him, looked after him, helped him, and now, here in Simon's flat, this scary man with the vivid blue eyes and the quiet voice had tracked him down.

There was a time – not so very long ago – when Alan wouldn't have been scared. He'd been a fighter once. A little flicker of courage flared. He didn't want to show how afraid he was.

'Who are you?'

The man sat down in the chair opposite Alan.

'I am Sir Matthew Vardon. You probably know my name. I'm Simon's father.'

Alan tried to make sense of the words. 'Simon's father? But . . .?'

'He's told me all about you, Mr Leigh. You're Stamford Leigh's nephew.'

He reached in his pocket and, taking out the little bottle, placed it on the low table between them.

Alan gave a whimper. He couldn't help it. The tiny bottle seemed to grow in size, until it filled his entire vision.

'I knew your uncle well. As a matter of fact, he was a cousin of mine.'

What did he care about his uncle? His uncle was dead.

'You're Stamford Leigh's heir.'

Alan blinked in irritation. He knew he'd *been* his uncle's heir, but what did that matter? He'd run through his uncle's money long since and there was nothing left. He didn't care. All he cared about was that bottle on the table in front of him.

Despite himself, he reached out for the bottle.

The man – Simon's father – moved with light-ning speed for such a big man.

'Naughty,' he murmured, his mouth curving in a smile. He held the bottle between his thumb and forefinger so the light shone through it. 'You can have this, Mr Leigh, when we've had a little chat.'

Alan felt as if his insides were being wrung together. He fell back into the sofa, his hand covering his eyes. 'What d'you want?'

'Your uncle left you quite a lot of money, didn't he, Mr Leigh?'

'It's gone.' His voice was a whisper.

'So I understand. He also left you a portfolio of shares, most of which, if I understand your affairs correctly, have been sold.'

Alan hardly registered the words, but nodded dumbly.

'You do, however, have one block of shares which you have not been able to sell. A block of shares in Antilla Exploration Limited.'

'For God's sake, tell me what you want, damn you!' It was a weak, futile, defiance.

The man raised his eyebrows and laughed. 'I want those shares, Mr Leigh.'

Alan could hardly make sense of what the man said. 'Why?'

3

The man grinned. 'Call it a whim.' He held up his hand. 'I know they're worthless. But, Mr Leigh, I'm feeling generous. I am prepared to pay you twenty pounds.'

Alan wasn't capable of much emotion apart from the desperate desire for the little glass bottle, but he was conscious of a flicker of surprise when the man took out his wallet and, opening it, laid four white five-pound notes on the table.

'There's this, too,' said the man, holding up the bottle. 'I'll throw this in as a gesture of goodwill.'

Alan nearly sobbed. 'Yes! Damn you, yes. Have anything you like.'

The man took a legal-looking form from his briefcase. 'I need you to sign this form, Mr Leigh.' He laid the form on the table and took a fountain pen from his jacket pocket. 'Sign it!'

There was a jag of menace in his tone.

Alan took the pen and, hand trembling, managed to sign his name at the bottom of the form.

'Very good,' said the man, with what was virtually a purr of approval. 'Very good indeed.'

He reached into the briefcase once more and, taking out a flat black case, opened it and, removing a hypodermic syringe, unscrewed the top. Lips pursed, he poured the contents of the bottle into the syringe. He attached the needle to the end and handed the syringe to Alan. 'Yours, I believe, Mr Leigh.'

Sir Matthew swirled the brandy round in its glass and sipped it with satisfaction. 'It's damn good brandy this, Simon.'

'I'm glad you like it,' said Simon absently. He looked across the room to Alan's slumped body on the sofa. His mouth twisted. Alan's arm was flung over the side of the sofa, the syringe on the floor beside him where it had fallen. 'I hope he's going to be all right.'

'He'll be fine,' said Sir Matthew easily. 'Don't you worry.'

Simon ignored his father, crossed the room and stooped over his friend. 'Alan? Alan, can you hear me?' he asked gently. There was no answer. Alan's eyes were open but his mind was far away.

Simon glanced at his father. 'Did he have the entire bottle?'

'Why shouldn't I give him the entire bottle? He wanted it badly enough.'

Simon ran a hand through his fair hair. 'It was a very pure solution. I told you as much. I said it should be mixed with glycerine.'

Sir Matthew laughed dismissively. 'He didn't want glycerine. I just gave him what he wanted. Why shouldn't I? Think of it as a last kindness.' He paused and looked quizzically at his son. 'Don't tell me you're worried about him. I wouldn't believe it, Simon. You haven't got a compassionate bone in your body.'

Simon faced him squarely. 'Perhaps I inherited that from you. You don't seem to understand. If he does croak, what am I meant to do?'

'Get rid of the supplies in the bathroom for a start. The police would be very interested in them.'

Simon's eyes narrowed. That cupboard was locked. Or had been locked. He didn't know his

5

father had rummaged round the flat. 'Are you threatening me?'

His father shrugged. 'You're a grown man. If you want to stuff yourself with dope, that's your lookout, but you're a fool.' He jerked his thumb at Alan. 'I wouldn't want you to end up like that.' He snapped the lock shut on his case. 'Look at him. What a useless wreck.'

'He saved my life on the Somme.'

'And I'm sure you were very grateful to him. What use is he now? I must say, m'boy, I very much appreciate your part in the deal. Your friend Mr Leigh reacted exactly as you said he would.' He clapped his hands together and rubbed them enthusiastically. 'All I need now is that final block of shares from Castradon and the sky's the limit.'

Simon looked at Alan and laughed cynically. 'Excuse me for not fainting with delight.'

'There's money to be made.' Sir Matthew drew the words out with lingering pleasure. 'A lot of money.'

Simon looked at him sharply. 'What are you going to do about Castradon? What if he won't sell you the shares? I've never met the man but, from what I've heard, he's a stubborn devil.'

Sir Matthew nodded. 'Castradon's stubborn and, in my opinion, unstable.'

'It's probably shell shock,' said Simon thoughtfully. 'He was badly shot up in the war, wasn't he?'

'Yes, he's our very own war hero with the scars to prove it. I think it's affected his mind. He walks round, muttering to himself, and he's got a filthy temper. He's an ugly devil, too. Why his wife stays with him, I can't guess.' He looked at his son with a glint in his eye. 'His wife, I may say, is a very beautiful woman. She's wasted on him.' He paused. 'You could have a lot of fun, getting her away from that husband of hers. I'd do it if I was twenty years younger.' He grinned. 'I might yet.'

Simon drew back in disgust. 'What about my mother?'

Sir Matthew grinned. 'She's a very tolerant woman. But, perhaps you're right. You really ought to try your luck. I certainly would've done at your age.'

Simon gave a sudden crack of laughter and sat back in his chair. 'Are you seriously suggesting that I should come down to a one-horse hole in the country for the sole purpose of charming the village belle? I think you've been away from London for too long. Besides that, considering you want Castradon to sell you his shares, committing adultery with his wife is probably not the best way for me to set about helping you.'

'There is that about it,' conceded Sir Matthew. 'It's perhaps just as well that you feel so straight-laced.'

'I'm not straight-laced. I've got a certain amount of sense. How are you going to get Castradon's shares?'

'He's got a great sense of family pride. Don't forget, I knew his father, Mike Castradon, very well indeed.' An odd expression, half-shifty, half-defiant crossed Sir Matthew's face. 'If I do a little bit of digging into the past, who knows what I might come up with?'

Simon looked at his father with sudden interest and sat down on the arm of the chair. 'You've got something in mind, haven't you?'

Sir Matthew hesitated. 'There was an incident. It was long ago, when Stamford Leigh, Mike Castradon and I were in Peru. Things got a bit lively one night and, to cut a long story short, a woman died.' Simon's eyebrows rose expressively. 'Don't look at me like that, boy!' growled Sir Matthew. 'You'd be a lot better off if you took your pleasures like a real man, rather than messing around with filthy chemicals. She was only an Indian woman, one of the natives. She didn't matter, but Castradon cut up rough about it. He blamed me.'

'Were you to blame?' asked Simon quietly.

His father shrugged. 'It was her own fault. If she'd have kept quiet there wouldn't have been any trouble. It wasn't as if Castradon was a plaster saint,' he added, more to himself than to his son. 'He could be a dangerous man. From then on Castradon wanted nothing more to do with me. I was just unlucky. It could have happened to anyone, but he was very peculiar about the whole business.'

Simon stared at his father. 'Peculiar, you say? That's an interesting choice of words. Were there any witnesses?'

'A couple of natives,' said Sir Matthew with a shrug. 'I squared them easily enough, but I could never make Castradon see sense. I always resented that.' He gave a sudden, wolfish grin. 'It would be very sweet indeed to tell his son about that incident.' He laughed. 'With a few minor alterations, you understand.'

'But won't Castradon know the truth?' demanded Simon.

'I doubt it!' Sir Matthew grinned once more. 'He got very respectable in his old age, did Mike Castradon. He won't have told anyone, especially his precious son.'

Simon sat back thoughtfully. 'I'm your son,' he murmured. 'You don't seem to mind telling me.'

'I give you enough credit for knowing which side your bread's buttered on, boy. You're safe enough. Besides that, you *are* my son. We're pretty alike, you and me.'

Again, Simon said nothing for a while. 'Maybe,' he conceded eventually. 'Have you told Tom? My brother?'

Sir Matthew's lip curled dismissively. 'Thomas? He wouldn't believe it.'

Simon moved impatiently. Tom probably wouldn't believe it. Tom was a good man, decent, straightforward and honest. Simon suspected his father resented that. Tom would never credit how much the old man had relished telling that story.

From the sofa, Alan Leigh gave a sudden groan and threw out his arm in a convulsive gesture.

Simon rapidly crossed to him and felt under Alan's shirt for his heart. 'Oh my God!' He turned his head to his father. 'I'm going to call the doctor. He's in a bad way.'

'Why on earth are you so upset?'

'I just am,' said Simon tightly. 'I don't want him to die.' He smoothed back the hair from Alan's forehead, looking anxiously into his eyes. He was rewarded with a flicker of recognition.

9

He made his voice deliberately calm. 'Alan, I'm going to get help.' He caught hold of the trembling hand. 'I'm going to get a doctor.'

Alan Leigh made a little noise in his throat. 'Simon? Simon . . . help.'

'I will. Don't worry.'

Sir Matthew Vardon looked on in surprise as Simon picked up the telephone and, getting through to the exchange, demanded the doctor.

'I'll leave you to it,' he said. 'Maybe we're not as similar as I thought.'

The great Lanchester swept up the drive and, with a scrunch of gravel, drew up outside the front door. Ryle, the chauffeur, got out and opened the door for Sir Matthew.

From the window of the drawing room, a frown of disapproval creased Lady Adeline Vardon's plump face. She disliked Ryle intensely. He did *not* show the deference she expected from a servant.

Adeline Vardon had been brought up to observe the most rigid divisions between employer and employee. She was the daughter of a wealthy Stoke-on-Trent pottery manufacturer and his wife, who saw their daughter's marriage as a definite step up the social ladder. Adeline had been dazzled by the prospect of a title and bowled over by the big, handsome man with his dashing manners. Her parents' enthusiasm was increased, if anything, by the fact he was a widower with a young son – it seemed so *respectable* – and had only been slightly dampened by the discovery that Sir Matthew had no money to speak of.

As she watched, the chauffeur inclined his head towards Sir Matthew. Sir Matthew threw back his head, laughing, then clapped the man on the shoulder. Ryle, grinning broadly, pushed his cap back and, hands in pockets, replied.

The sunlight caught his face and, for a few brief seconds, the two men looked exactly alike. Adeline Vardon blinked and the likeness was gone.

She must have imagined it. After all, Ryle was a thin cringing whippet of a man, with a dreadful Cockney accent and her husband was a powerful, well-built, masterful man, who still retained those handsome looks she had been so charmed by. Adeline Vardon hated the way Matthew allowed Ryle to be so familiar. She must speak to him about it. She was not going to allow any servant – and especially Ryle – to get above themselves.

Ryle picked up Sir Matthew's bag and the two men walked up the drive together.

Adeline Vardon's frown deepened into frank disapproval. She went into the hall and out onto the drive. Ryle looked up, smothered a grin and touched his cap in what seemed to Adeline Vardon to be a very off-hand way.

'You can put the car away, Ryle,' said Sir Matthew. 'I won't need it again today.'

'All right,' said Ryle in that Cockney twang she hated, adding, as a seeming afterthought and with a glance at Lady Vardon, 'sir.'

Adeline Vardon waited until she and Sir Matthew were in the house. 'You allow that man to be far too familiar.'

'Nonsense, my dear,' he said, kissing her.

'There are other chauffeurs, I suppose.'

'There aren't any other chauffeurs who worked for Ned Castradon.'

She was frankly puzzled. 'Why does that make any difference?'

'Because I want to know as much as I can about that gentleman. Don't ask me why, Adeline. It's a matter of business.'

She tossed her head impatiently. 'I don't understand anything about business.'

He laughed delightedly. 'I know, my dear. And a very proper attitude it is, too. Simon seems well.'

All her irritation vanished in a flash. 'Simon?' Her voice softened. 'Oh, Matthew, I'm so glad you've seen him. I've sometimes thought you don't appreciate dear Simon enough.'

That, thought Sir Matthew, was probably true. It would be virtually impossible for anyone to appreciate Simon as deeply as his mother thought he should be appreciated.

'Is he coming here?' she asked eagerly. 'I do wish we saw more of him. Why, he's hardly been home since the war ended.'

'There's nothing for him here, Adeline. You go up to town often enough. You see him then.'

'It's not the same,' said Adeline obstinately. 'Did you ask him to the county ball? I'm sure he'd enjoy it.'

Sir Matthew's mind went back to the scene in Simon's flat. The idea of discussing something as refined as a county ball in the presence of that drug-sodden wreck of a human being, Alan Leigh, struck him as very funny indeed.

'As a matter of fact, I didn't, my dear,' he said with high good humour. 'We had other things to talk about. Talking of the county ball, I must arrange to get your diamonds out of the bank.'

Lady Vardon glanced down at her nails. 'I don't know if I want to wear my diamonds, Matthew. What I really want are pearls.'

'You've got pearls, my dear.'

Adeline sighed. Men just didn't understand these things. 'I've got a pearl *necklace*, Matthew, but I can't wear that to the ball. I need a rope of pearls. Really good pearls. Everybody has pearls.'

'You wear your diamonds, Adeline. They can outshine any pearls in the county.' He looked at her petulant expression and grinned. 'If my little bit of business comes off – and it will – you can take a trip to any jeweller you fancy.'

'I don't see why I should have to wait. I want them now.'

'You'll have them. All in good time.'

Two

Isabelle Stanton glanced up in surprise from the breakfast table to where the window overlooked the drive. 'Arthur, Sue Castradon's here. I wonder what she wants so early in the morning?'

Arthur put the newspaper down and, pushing his chair back, stood up to greet Sue as Mabel, their maid, showed her into the room.

'I'm sorry to disturb you at breakfast,' said Sue,

13

taking the chair Arthur pulled out for her, 'but I wondered if you'd heard the news.'

'No,' said Isabelle, pouring out a cup of coffee for her friend. 'What's happened? It's not Ned, is it?' she added with a tinge of anxiety. Arthur liked Sue's husband, Ned Castradon. Isabelle wasn't so sure. She felt sorry for Ned – he'd had a tough time in the war – but there was no getting around it, he was moody and bad-tempered and, thought Isabelle, very difficult to live with.

'No, it's nothing to do with Ned,' said Sue, picking up her coffee. 'This is *news*. I simply had to tell you. Our maid, Rose, got it from the fish boy. I imagine your cook, Mrs Jarvis, will be full of it too. You know Lady Vardon's diamonds?'

'The ones she was wearing at the county ball?' asked Isabelle.

'Yes, that's right. It happened last night. Lady Vardon was attacked and her diamonds stolen.'

Isabelle and Arthur stared at her, then Arthur let out a long whistle of surprise. 'Attacked? Good Lord! Is she all right?'

Sue nodded vigorously. 'She's all right, but in an awful state. The thief got clean away.'

'How on earth did it happen?' demanded Isabelle. 'She doesn't keep her diamonds at home, does she?'

'No, she doesn't, but they'd been taken out of the bank for the ball. They should've been sent back today, but she decided to wear them last night at dinner. There was only her and Sir Matthew at home, so it's silly in a way for her to get all dressed up.'

14

'If I had diamonds, I think I'd want to wear them whatever the occasion,' said Isabelle. 'Especially if they're usually in the bank. So what happened?'

'As far as I can make out, she went for a stroll on the terrace with Sir Matthew when the thief jumped out. He was armed with a cosh. He stunned Sir Matthew and chloroformed Lady Vardon. When Sir Matthew came to, he found Lady Vardon senseless beside him and the diamonds gone.'

Arthur and Isabelle gaped at her. 'Good grief,' said Arthur eventually. 'Do the police know?'

'They're at the house now, apparently, but I don't know what they can do. Sir Matthew caught a glimpse of the man, but he had a scarf over his face. All he really knows is that he was a big, powerful man. Lady Vardon didn't see the man but she's convinced one of the servants must be to blame.'

'That's rotten for them all,' said Arthur with a frown. 'What does Sir Matthew say?'

'He says it must've been a professional thief who'd been waiting his opportunity, but he thinks they're in league with the servants, too.'

'It doesn't sound much fun for the servants,' said Arthur dryly.

'No, that's what I thought. My Rose was very indignant on their behalf.' Sue idly ran her finger round the rim of her cup. 'Isabelle, doesn't your cousin, Jack Haldean, solve mysteries and crimes and so on? I wonder if he'd be interested? After all, those diamonds must be worth thousands.'

Isabelle shook her head. 'I don't think this is

Jack's sort of problem. He doesn't solve mysteries for a living, you know. What he actually does is write detective stories. He just happens to have been caught up in various cases.'

'That's right,' said Arthur. 'Jack only gets involved if he's interested or if someone appeals to him for help. If one of the Vardons' servants were wrongly accused, say, then I could see Jack pitching in, but not otherwise.'

'That's right,' Isabelle agreed. 'Beside that, it does help if he likes the people involved and I'd be very surprised if he took to the Vardons.'

'I don't like them much,' admitted Sue, 'and Ned can't stand them. There was some sort of history between Ned's father and Sir Matthew. There's no love lost between them, that's for sure.'

'Your Aunt Catherine warned us not to get too friendly with the Vardons, didn't she, Arthur?' said Isabelle. Arthur managed Aunt Catherine's estate. 'She's always kept on good terms with them, because she says life's impossible in the country if you don't get along with your neighbours, but she doesn't care for them at all. She thinks Sir Matthew is far too harsh with his tenants and she hates the way Lady Vardon treated Sir Matthew's eldest son, Thomas. I must say I felt very sorry for Thomas.'

'Why?' asked Arthur, puzzled. 'I thought Thomas Vardon had done very well for himself.'

'He's done very well indeed,' said Sue. 'He lives in Hollywood and married a film star.'

'A film star?' repeated Arthur in surprise. 'Is she famous?'

Sue pulled a face. 'I don't know. She's called Esmé Duclair. I must say, I'd never heard of her.'

'So why d'you feel sorry for him?' asked Arthur. 'He seems a lucky sort of beggar to me.'

The two girls looked at each other. 'It's the way Lady Vardon treated him,' said Sue. 'I had this from Mrs Dyson, the vicar's wife, and you know what a dear she is. She'd never be nasty about anyone who didn't thoroughly deserve it. Thomas is Sir Matthew's son by his first wife and, when she died, Sir Matthew married again.'

'That's right,' put in Isabelle. 'As soon as Lady Vardon had a son of her own – he's called Simon, I think – she resented the fact that Thomas would inherit the estate.'

'I wouldn't have thought the estate amounted to much, however much Lady Vardon resents him,' said Arthur. 'He'll be far better off in Hollywood. The diamonds weren't part of the estate, were they?'

'No,' said Sue, shaking her head. 'They were a wedding present from Lady Vardon's father. Lady Vardon received a very generous marriage settlement from her father. Not that it's done her much good,' she added darkly.

'What on earth d'you mean?' asked Arthur. 'And how the dickens d'you know all this?'

'Mrs Dyson again,' said Isabelle with a grin. 'Sir Matthew hasn't been lucky with money.' She looked up as the door opened and Mabel, their young and very bright maid, came in with a tray to clear the breakfast things.

'Have you heard about the robbery at the Vardons, ma'm?' asked Mabel, loading up the tray. 'The fish boy's just told us. The police haven't got a clue who did it. The thief got clean away and left Lady Vardon and Sir Matthew senseless. Lady Vardon suspects the servants as being in league with the villain, but that doesn't seem right, to go saying that sort of thing without any proof,' she added with a censorious sniff. 'And that's not all,' she added, her eyes bright.

Isabelle hesitated. She knew she shouldn't encourage Mabel to gossip but . . . 'What else has happened?' she asked.

'It's Sir Matthew,' said Mabel. There was no doubt she was enjoying being the bearer of news. 'He's been took mortal bad. It must've been the shock. He was acting queer this morning – he didn't seem to know where he was or where anything should be – and then he keeled over. Dr Lucas was sent for and he says as how Sir Matthew's been struck down with apoplexy. He's been struck bad,' she repeated with emphasis.

Arthur, Isabelle and Sue stared at her. 'Apoplexy?' said Arthur. 'A stroke? Is it . . . I mean, will it be fatal, does anyone know?'

'Folk do recover from apoplexy,' admitted Mabel grudgingly. 'My mum says she's heard of those who you'd expect to be measured for their box to get up, bright and lively, and to shake it off as if nothing had happened, but from what I've heard, this is a real bad one. Cook says as how it's a judgement.'

There was no mistaking the relish in Mabel's words. 'Cook says he might linger for a while, but it sounds like there's not much hope. By all accounts he was beside himself last night, ranting

18

and raving and carrying on at the staff. He threatened to sack the lot of them and Hester Drewitt – she's nice, Hester – says she's never been spoken to like that in all her born days. I agree with Cook,' continued Mabel, warming to her theme and stacking the plates onto the tray, 'I say it's a judgement, but time will tell.'

Time did tell. Despite Adeline Vardon's protestations there was nothing seriously wrong, over the next three weeks Matthew Vardon's condition worsened.

In Sir Matthew's bedroom, Dr Lucas checked the thermometer and glanced at the wasted body of the once virile man on the bed. It couldn't be much longer.

He wasn't sorry. He wiped the thermometer and put it back in its case before snapping the lock on his bag.

'There's not much hope, is there, Doctor?' asked Nurse Pargetter at his elbow.

'I'm afraid the longer he remains in this semi-conscious condition, the likelihood of him either simply slipping away or suffering another apoplectic stroke is greatly increased. There's very little I or anyone else can do. No,' he added, 'there isn't much hope.'

The nurse looked at him quizzically. There was an odd note of satisfaction in his voice, but his face betrayed nothing but professional concern.

The doctor rubbed a hand through his thinning hair. 'I must speak to Lady Vardon. I'll have to prepare her for the inevitable. I can't say I'm looking forward to it. She refused point-blank to listen to me when I tried to bring the subject up before.' He couldn't keep the brightness out of his voice. 'Still, it can't be helped.'

Lady Vardon dabbed at her eyes with a lace-trimmed handkerchief and blinked at the doctor. 'It's too awful. Poor Matthew.'

Dr Lucas glanced surreptitiously at his watch, noting with surprise that the interview had only lasted ten minutes at the most. It felt like hours. What made it worse was that he believed the woman was quite sincere in her grief. Didn't she have any idea of what the man was really like?

He continued to nod sympathetically while his thoughts ran off at a tangent. He'd have to be careful. Nurse Pargetter was an observant woman and she had looked at him very oddly more than once over the last few weeks. But with Sir Matthew gone he would be free. Life could begin again, but there was danger.

Let the nurse get any idea into her head that his attitude was anything other than completely professional, and it could destroy his career. Rumours were the very devil to counter but it was difficult not to let his feelings show. Even on his deathbed, Sir Matthew was a dangerous man. He suddenly realized that Lady Vardon had asked him a question. A question that brought him up short and suggested Nurse Pargetter had started her rumours already.

He wiped a little bead of sweat from the corner of his mouth. 'I'm sorry, Lady Vardon. I didn't quite catch that.'

'I asked you,' repeated Lady Vardon, twisting

the handkerchief round in her fingers, 'if you had any doubt that Matthew's condition is . . . is *natural*?'

It was like running into a wall. There it was, the start of a ghastly nightmare of innuendo, suspicion and accusation. Danger. Stark danger. This could ruin him.

'Natural?' he repeated. 'Of course it's natural. Your husband suffered a severe apoplectic stroke, a condition sometimes referred to as a stroke of God.' Anxiety made him bluster. 'If you have any doubts about his condition or the course of treatment I am pursuing, I would be more than happy for you to call in a second opinion.'

He gulped. A second opinion would help. It wouldn't help Sir Matthew but it'd help him. With another doctor on the case, it would be impossible for anyone to accuse him of carelessness, of neglect and even, perhaps, something worse.

'I haven't any doubts about your treatment, Doctor,' she said.

Dr Lucas blinked. That was unexpected, if reassuring.

'A second opinion—' he began but she cut him off.

'Matthew likes you, Dr Lucas.'

Did he? That was really unexpected.

'Yes,' she continued, 'I remember him laughing once when your name came up. He said that he did like a doctor without any ideas of his own, who'd do exactly what he was told.'

All Dr Lucas's loathing of Sir Matthew intensified. 'I must insist, Lady Vardon, that you call in a second opinion. I can provide you with a list of suitable names but you are, of course, at complete liberty to choose your own man.'

'I don't *want* another doctor,' she wailed. She held out a piece of notepaper to him. 'I want someone to explain *this.*'

Dr Lucas took the notepaper with a puzzled frown. The message consisted of one neatly type-written line. *I am killing you slowly. You are going to die. The Chessman.*

Dr Lucas looked at the note in bewilderment. 'Who sent this?'

'I don't know! That's the second letter Matthew's had. The first arrived a couple of days after Matthew was taken ill.' Her handkerchief was now a series of inextricable knots. 'Someone's hounding us, Doctor. First I was attacked and my diamonds were stolen and now this! There's a plot, a wicked plot against us! I wanted to show the letters to Matthew, to ask him what I should do, but he's been so under the weather, I can't.'

Dr Lucas wryly thought that *under the weather* was one way of describing acute apoplectic shock, but refrained from comment.

'Anonymous letters are horrible, Lady Vardon. I'd chuck it in the fire and not give it another thought.'

'But who can it be from, Doctor? Who could possibly hate Matthew so much?'

Quite a lot of people, countered the doctor to himself, but he schooled himself into showing nothing but avuncular reassurance. 'Please don't upset yourself, Lady Vardon. I can assure you that your husband's condition is entirely natural.

These letters are probably written by some nasty-minded crank, taking advantage of your husband's illness. They probably make a habit of such things, preying on unfortunate souls such as yourself who are in grave distress.'

'So you don't think these letters really have anything to do with Matthew?' she said slowly. 'That this crank could write to anyone?'

'That's exactly it, Lady Vardon,' said Dr Lucas, rather more heartily than he intended. 'However,' he added, 'I'm afraid your husband is very ill. I would value a second opinion.'

At Dr Lucas's insistence, Dr Jacob McNiece of Harley Street, was called in to give a second – and expensive – opinion that there was little hope.

At twenty past two the following morning, Sir Matthew Vardon died. He was buried four days later.

It was at Sir Matthew's funeral that Simon Vardon first saw Sue Castradon. That's when the rumours started.

Two days after Sir Matthew's death, 5,500 miles away in a white-walled Spanish-style bungalow on Ryder Avenue, West Hollywood, Thomas Vardon came down to breakfast. He took a plate of scrambled eggs and bacon from the dishes on the sideboard – Thomas retained his English breakfast habits – poured himself a cup of tea, then, picking up a paperknife, slit open the cablegram that lay beside his plate on the breakfast table.

'Good God!'

His wife, known to her fairly small public as Esmé Duclair, looked up from her copy of *Motion Picture Magazine*. 'What is it, Tom?'

'It's my father. He's dead,' Thomas said simply.

Esmé drew her breath in. 'Dead?'

'Yes.' He pushed his hair back from his forehead in bewilderment. 'I know Simon said in his last letter he was really worried about him, but I had no idea it was so serious.' He looked at his wife. 'I'll have to go to England, I suppose. Damn!'

He drummed his fingers on the table. 'It could be worse,' he added thoughtfully. '*A Woman's Trust* is more or less finished and I can give *Paris Nights* to Dusselberg.' He paused once more. 'Yes, that should be okay.'

He pushed his chair back from the table. 'I'll sort everything out at the studio but—'

'You don't seem exactly heartbroken,' interrupted his wife reprovingly.

Thomas shrugged. 'You didn't know my father.'

'Had you quarrelled with him?' Esmé knew very little about her husband's relations. She knew he wrote to his brother, but he'd hardly mentioned the rest of his family.

Thomas shook his head. 'Not quarrelled exactly, but we never saw eye to eye.'

A calculating expression came into Esmé's eyes. Although she knew virtually nothing about her husband's family, one fact she was sure of. 'Tom, your father was *Sir* Matthew, wasn't he?'

'Yes, he was.'

'And that's aristocracy, right?'

Thomas sighed. No matter how many times he

explained things, Esmé was convinced that a genuine English title equated to a genuine English aristocrat. 'Hardly. He was a baronet.'

Esmé's eyes glazed over. 'A baronet? It sounds good to me. What's a baronet, Tom?'

'A baronet is one of the landed gentry.' He laughed ruefully. 'Not that there was much land in the estate.'

Esmé shook her head impatiently. 'But you do get the title? I mean, you're Sir Thomas now?'

Thomas laughed cynically. He knew exactly what was in his wife's mind. 'I suppose I am. Which means, Esmé, that you're Lady Vardon.'

'Lady Vardon,' she repeated softly, then said it again, with great satisfaction. 'Lady Vardon. I like it.'

It was quarter past ten on Sunday evening, a fortnight after Sir Matthew Vardon's funeral.

Jonathan Ryle lurched out of the Red Lion and across the green in a state of boiling resentment. He wasn't drunk. He could handle his drink. And, even if he had had a couple, that was what pubs were for, weren't they? If Sir Matthew had still been alive, that swine of a landlord, Brandreth, wouldn't have dared to speak to him like that. He sniffed hard and brushed his sleeve across his eyes, feeling an unexpected tear well up. He missed the guv. The guv had been good to him. It had been all right when the guv was alive. People respected him then.

He looked down the quiet high street of Croxton Ferriers with disgust. Croxton Ferriers was a lousy little dump. If this was the country, they could keep it. Everyone was against him but he'd show them. Once he got his hands on some real money he could get up to London and real life. He'd have some respect, then. He hated bloody Croxton Ferriers and all the bloody stuck-up snobs who lived here.

He walked unsteadily up the road until he came to three large houses. There was the Vicarage, with that stuck-up snob of a vicar, all hale and hearty, with his football and cricket and boxing for young lads. The guv had despised him.

The next house belonged to that doctor, Lucas, and his son. Ryle grinned. Young Lucas was twitching with nerves. The guv showed them, all right. It had made him laugh, that had.

Next door to them was the house that belonged to the worst of the lot. Castradon.

Ryle leaned over Castradon's front gate, looking resentfully at the neat garden with its neat path leading up to the house. Who the hell did Castradon think he was?

Castradon was the ugly bugger who'd thrown him out of a job. Ugly bugger was about right, too. He had an eyepatch and a great ugly scar, the freak.

A little bit of gossip came to his mind and he grinned. Castradon wouldn't like to hear that. My God, he'd like to see him squirm. So why not tell him?

Ryle leaned over the gate. 'Castradon!' he yelled. 'Castradon! Get yourself out here!'

Nothing happened. Ryle threw back his head and shouted again.

Lights went on in the house. The front door

was flung open and Ned Castradon came out. 'Who the devil's making all that noise?'

He saw Ryle and, shoulders squared and fists clenched, marched towards him. 'Clear off, damn you!'

Ryle had drunk a substantial amount of beer washed down with a fair amount of whisky and was spoiling for a fight. A proper fight, a street fight, a fight which ended in giving Castradon a good kicking. He leaned over the gate, grinning. 'Clear off? Make me.'

Castradon stopped dead. 'Say that again and I will.'

'Oh yeah?' Ryle was thoroughly enjoying himself. 'You, with that ugly mug of yours? Let me tell you something, pal. Mr Simon, the guv's son, didn't half fancy your wife and good for him.' He leered over the gate. 'Got places as well, if you ask me. Sweet girl, your missus. Very tasty.'

For a moment Castradon said nothing then, taking off his jacket, he undid his cuffs slowly and pushed his sleeves up his arms. 'You shouldn't have said that,' he said quietly.

His expression was so terrifying that Ryle backed away, all his whisky-fuelled courage evaporated. 'Leave it out,' he said quickly. 'I was only joking. Honest, guv.'

Castradon opened the gate. Grabbing Ryle by the scruff of his jersey, he pulled back his fist to strike.

Ryle twisted away, yelling, and kicked out. His heavy boot struck Castradon on the knee. Castradon, shuddering with pain, relaxed his grip and Ryle punched him on the nose.

Castradon reeled back, then, gathering himself, leapt forward. Grabbing Ryle, he forced him to the ground and the two men rolled over in the dust. There was a confusion of shouts and blows, then Castradon, nose bleeding, ended up on top, kneeling firmly astride Ryle. Ryle reached out and, grabbing a heavy stone, brought it up hard under Castradon's chin.

Castradon fell away. As Ryle scrambled to his feet, he caught hold of his leg, sending him sprawling. Castradon rolled towards him. He raised his fist high. Ryle's face contorted with fear. 'No! No, guv, don't!'

There was the sound of running footsteps behind then, then Castradon's fist was caught from behind and he was forcibly wrenched away.

'For pity's sake, man!' It was Mr Dyson, the vicar. A big man, he pulled Castradon to his feet. 'What the devil d'you think you're doing? The entire village must've heard you!'

Panting, Castradon ignored him, and tried to pull away.

'Stop it!' shouted Mr Dyson, keeping a firm grip on his arms.

'Let me get at him!' yelled Castradon.

'Don't be stupid,' said the vicar shortly.

Ryle rolled over on the ground and got to his feet, backing away. 'He's mad,' he said to Mr Dyson. 'He just attacked me for no reason. He's bloody mad, he is.'

Castradon made another grab for Ryle and, once again, was restrained by Mr Dyson. 'Let me go, damn you!' he bellowed, turning to face the vicar. 'I'm going to kill him!'

'No, you're not, man,' growled Mr Dyson, wrestling to keep his grip. He looked at Ryle. 'Get out of here. Run, you fool!'

Ryle backed cautiously away. 'I'll get you for this, Castradon. So help me, I'll get you for this.'

'Get out!' growled Mr Dyson once more as, muscles straining, he restrained Castradon. 'Castradon, for God's sake, man, will you calm down!'

Castradon dug an elbow into the vicar's ribs and, grunting, Mr Dyson relaxed his grip.

Castradon made a lunge for Ryle. Ryle, with a whimper of terror, dashed across the road to where an open-topped car was parked. With Castradon after him, he dodged behind the car. 'Help!' he yelled. 'Help!'

Mr Dyson ran across the road and planted himself firmly in Castradon's way. 'Leave him be!'

Ryle scrambled into the car, searching anxiously for the self-starter. The engine roared into life and the car jerked forward.

Castradon ducked under the vicar's arm and flung himself at the moving car, grabbing hold of the door. Ryle twisted to one side, flinging out an arm to fend him off. The front wheel clipped the deep ditch by the side of the road and the car lurched to a halt, the wheel spinning in the soft mud. Ryle was jolted over the seat, slithering in a tangle of arms and legs over the smooth leather into the back.

Castradon made a wild grab for him. Mr Dyson caught at Castradon's arm once more, then – Mr Dyson wasn't sure what happened – Ryle gave

29

a shriek and erupted out of the car as if he'd been flung bodily from it.

With Mr Dyson hanging onto him, Castradon leapt after Ryle again, but Ryle had had enough. Feet pounding, he hurtled down the road, yelling, and away from the two men.

Furiously Castradon shook himself free from the vicar. Standing in the middle of the road, he shook his fist after the running man. 'Ryle!' he bellowed. 'If I see you again, I'll kill you!' He spun round to face the vicar. 'What the devil d'you think you're doing, eh? How dare you interfere?'

'I was trying to stop you killing him!'

'I'll murder him the next time he shows up. What did it have to do with you? My God, man, that was a private quarrel. *Private.*'

'No, it wasn't,' retorted Mr Dyson. 'It was a public brawl.' He felt his cheek tenderly where a blow had landed. 'Come on, Ned,' he added, in a quieter voice. 'What if you had injured him? Perhaps seriously? Calm down and don't be a complete fool. You're a lawyer. What d'you think the law would do if you'd managed to land one on him, eh? You might have killed him.'

'It'd be worth it,' snarled Castradon, and, dusting himself down and clamping a handkerchief to his nose, turned away and strode back into his house.

Mr Dyson, breathing deeply, watched him go. His wife, alerted by the noise, was waiting anxiously for him on the garden path.

'I heard what he said to you. Freddy, what are we going to do about Ned Castradon?'

30

'Nothing,' he said wearily. 'Don't interfere, Phyllis. You'll only make things worse. I've got a deep regard for Ned Castradon.'

Phyllis Dyson sniffed disapprovingly. 'I *had,* but his temper's getting unbearable.'

'Possibly,' agreed the vicar uneasily. He was worried about Ned Castradon.

It was only to be expected that the news that the solicitor, Edward Castradon, had been involved in a street brawl with the Vardon's chauffeur should travel quickly round the village.

What was lacking, much to the chagrin of Croxton Ferriers, was any detail.

Why Edward Castradon had brawled with Jonathan Ryle was something that simply couldn't be established. And that was despite it being rumoured that Mr Dyson, the vicar, knew a great deal more about it than he let on.

As Mrs Cunningham-Price, one of the leaders of public opinion in Croxton Ferriers, said in the Palm Tree tea shop to her bevy of listeners the following Tuesday afternoon, Dr Lucas and the Dysons lived next door to the Castradons and could therefore be assumed to have had a ringside seat.

'I really do think the vicar should consider it his public *duty* to openly reprove such behaviour,' said Mrs Cunningham-Price. 'It was utterly *disgraceful.* Mr Castradon's late father, old Mr Castradon, would turn in his grave.'

'Absolutely,' agreed Mary Clegg. 'He would never have countenanced anything of this sort.'

'Well, who would, my dear?' agreed Corrie

31

Dinder. 'It's his wife, poor Mrs Castradon, I feel sorry for. Mrs Castradon is a very sweet girl.'

There was general consent to this proposition.

'She could be a film star,' sighed Winifred Charteris. Miss Charteris was an avid picture-goer and uncritical reader of film magazines. 'She has those *looks*, don't you think? So sweetly pretty.'

'Handsome is as handsome does,' said Mrs Cunningham-Price mysteriously. 'She keeps herself rather aloof, don't you think? She's not what I call an *organiser*.'

'Well, dear, we can't all be as active as you, can we?' said Margaret Hernshaw. Mrs Cunningham-Price looked at her dubiously, detecting a whiff of criticism, then was side-tracked by Corrie Dinder.

'I can't help thinking it is so sad that Mrs Castradon was married so young. She was far too young, in my opinion. Some mothers are far too quick to marry their daughters off to the first man who comes along.'

'I'd hardly say that was the case,' put in Jane Lawson. 'The Castradons were a most respected family. And, say what you will, many people really do think a great deal of Edward Castradon.'

'His *temper*,' opined Mrs Cunningham-Price, 'is, I believe, simply frightful. Once before, when Ryle worked for him, Mr Castradon went for him in the most disgraceful manner.'

A few of the ladies made interrogative noises.

'Did you not hear about it? Mr Castradon had a violent argument with the man. He was heard shouting – yes, *shouting* – in the street at him, and turned the unfortunate man out neck and crop without a reference. Thank goodness, the chauffeur was able to find a position with Sir Matthew and Lady Vardon, otherwise heaven knows what would have become of him. Call me strict, if you will, but I believe it's positively *wicked* to take away a servant's reputation in that high-handed manner. We have a duty to those Providence has placed in a different class of life than ourselves.'

'I thought it was such a shame poor Sir Matthew was taken so suddenly,' sighed Winifred Charteris. 'I did hear,' she said, lowering her voice, 'that Dr Lucas wasn't exactly heartbroken when poor Sir Matthew passed away.'

'Dr Lucas is a most conscientious man,' said Jane Lawson. 'I do hope, Miss Charteris, that you're not suggesting he was careless in any way?'

'Not careless, exactly, but the nurse, Nurse Pargetter, did wonder . . . Apparently he seemed positively pleased that his patient was ailing. She said as much to Nurse Collins, who attended my poor cousin, Cynthia. She was disturbed by his attitude and I have to say that Dr Lucas's son, Jeremy, sometimes strikes me as positively *unbalanced.*'

'We all have our cross to bear,' pronounced Mrs Cunningham-Price, irritated that what sounded like a real item of interest should have escaped her. 'I agree with Mrs Lawson. Dr Lucas is a most conscientious man, no matter how odd his son may be on occasion. I'm sure that his care of Sir Matthew couldn't be faulted. Lady

Vardon, I know, is only too ready to find fault with those she considers to be of an inferior social position.'

The sniff with which she finished this sentence gave a clue to her more observant listeners that Mrs Cunningham-Price had fallen foul of this failing. 'She has nothing to be particularly proud of, for all her airs and graces. Her father was a manufacturer of cheap pots. The title was Sir Matthew's.'

'He was such a good-looking man, wasn't he?' put in Winifred Charteris. She had heard Mrs Cunningham-Price hold forth about Lady Vardon before and was anxious to change the subject. 'I thought his son, Simon Vardon – so handsome – took after him. Didn't I hear he had something to do with *Hollywood*?' She said the word reverently.

'You've got that entirely wrong,' said Mrs Cunningham-Price briskly. 'It's Sir Matthew's other son, Thomas, who's in Hollywood. That's why he wasn't at the funeral. Naturally he couldn't be expected to travel from America in such a short time.'

'Hollywood,' repeated Winifred Charteris in a dreamy voice. '*So* exciting. It's a pity poor Mrs Castradon was married so young. I couldn't help thinking, when I saw her and Sir Matthew's son at the funeral, that they would make a lovely couple. So good-looking, the pair of them.'

Margaret Hernshaw was shocked. 'Miss Charteris, may I remind you that Mrs Castradon is a married woman? Besides that, you shouldn't have such thoughts at a funeral. It isn't seemly.'

'It's quite natural,' sniffed Mrs Cunningham-Price.

She was feeling distinctly put out with Margaret Hernshaw. 'If you ask me, Sir Matthew's son was completely distracted at the funeral. I won't name the cause but others might.'

'I still say dear Mrs Castradon and Sir Matthew's son were like two film stars,' repeated Winifred Charteris with a sigh, her mind still on Hollywood. 'So glamorous. They'd make a lovely couple.'

Unaware his affairs were being discussed in the Palm Tree, Edward Castradon entered his office on Croxton Ferriers High Street.

He opened the door and stopped short.

Simon Vardon was sitting in a chair with his feet on the desk, smoking a cigarette. He was toying idly with a chess piece, a rook, from the set that Castradon kept on the side table, and generally looked the picture of supreme relaxation.

Castradon put down his briefcase. 'Did we have an appointment?' He knew perfectly well they didn't.

Simon put down the rook, swung his legs off the desk and stood up with an easy grace. 'No, we didn't, Mr Castradon, but I wanted to see you. No one was in the outer office, so I popped in to wait. I hope you don't mind.'

Ned did mind, but there was nothing he could do about it. His clerk would hear about this, though. And, he thought grimly, hear at some length.

'It's Mr Vardon, isn't it?' They had never been formally introduced. 'What can I do for you? I would ask you to take a seat,' he added, for he was damned if the man was going to stroll in as if he owned the place without any comment at all, 'but you seem to have made yourself at home.'

Simon's eyebrows rose. 'You sound quite put out.'

'I am, a little. What did you want to see me about?'

Simon flicked his cigarette ash onto the floor. 'You like chess, don't you, Mr Castradon?' he asked inconsequentially.

'Chess?' Castradon was puzzled. 'You didn't come here to discuss chess.'

'No.' Simon Vardon smiled. 'I was just trying to lighten the atmosphere. Social chit-chat, you know. As I said, you sound a little put out.'

'The feeling's growing,' said Castradon curtly. 'What do you want?'

Simon leaned forward. 'It's a matter of shares. Shares in Antilla Exploration Limited.'

Castradon's brow wrinkled. 'Shares in what?'

'Antilla Exploration. I believe my late father wrote to you about the matter.'

Castradon drew back. A little knot of anger began to pulse in his temple. 'So you know about that, do you?'

He knew his father had disliked Sir Matthew Vardon intensely. There were family reasons, reasons which went back a long way, to when his father was a young man and had gone to South America with Matthew Vardon and Stamford Leigh.

Castradon never knew what had happened in Peru. His father had been dead a few years now, so the story was lost, but Castradon had always believed it was something very discreditable to Matthew Vardon.

36

His father and Matthew Vardon had obviously been friends once, but his father wanted nothing to do with Matthew Vardon after they'd returned to England. His father had been a good man. It must have been something really nasty to have changed his opinion of Sir Matthew.

Then, about two months ago, Sir Matthew had written to him, asking for an interview. Castradon's mouth narrowed into a thin line at the memory. Sir Matthew had hinted that he knew something that had happened in Peru, something that would reflect very badly on his father's reputation.

That was enough to damn him. There was a whiff of coercion in that letter, a threat to his father's memory, which set Edward Castradon's teeth on edge.

His first instinct had been to write a curt refusal, but then he decided he might as well find out what foul lie Sir Matthew was nurturing. He agreed to a meeting, but Sir Matthew's sudden illness meant the meeting never occurred. Sir Matthew, he thought with a grim smile, had been silenced for good.

His hands unconsciously curled into fists. If Simon Vardon was here to repeat Sir Matthew's lies . . . Be fair, he told himself. Be fair.

The trouble was, he didn't want to be fair. He had seen the way Sue looked at Simon Vardon during the funeral and Vardon's admiration for Sue had been unmistakable. He might have thought it was just his imagination, if that old harridan, Mrs Cunningham-Price, hadn't come in to fuss about her affairs. She'd mentioned it. He'd been hard-pressed to keep his temper.

'I may say,' said Simon in a drawl that set Ned's teeth on edge, 'that I do have proof of what I'm about to say. There were certain papers in my father's possession, papers that I'm sure you would not want to be made public . . .'

'And really,' said Henry Dinder, to his wife, Corrie, that evening, 'I'd give a lot to know what Mr Vardon said to the boss. I've never seen Mr Castradon so angry. I didn't even know Mr Vardon was in the office. The boss really took me to task about that but I said, I'm sure I didn't see him come in, and nor did the girl. He might have climbed through the window for all I know.'

'Don't be silly, Henry,' said his wife. 'A gentleman like Mr Vardon wouldn't climb through the window. You just missed him, that's all. What was Mr Castradon so angry about? Not that Mr Vardon had come into the office without you knowing, surely?'

'No, it was more than that. We knew someone was in with the boss, because we heard voices and couldn't think who it could be. It started off all right, very polite and so on, but then there were raised voices and Mr Castradon, he was white with anger when he rang for me to show Mr Vardon out.'

'Was it about Mrs Castradon?' asked Corrie, mindful of the conversation in the Palm Tree.

Henry Dinder shrugged. 'It might have been. I heard something about shares, but I couldn't catch what. You've always got to watch Mr Castradon's temper, but I've never seen him in such a state.'

'They weren't fighting, were they?' asked Corrie Dinder breathlessly.

'Fighting?' Henry Dinder laughed. 'Of course not. Mr Castradon's a gentleman. He wouldn't do such a thing, no matter how angry he was.'

'He had a punch-up with Jonathan Ryle in the street on Sunday,' said his wife.

'A punch-up?' repeated Henry Dinder. 'Nonsense.'

'It's true,' insisted his wife. 'Mrs Cunningham-Price said as much in the Palm Tree this afternoon.'

It was quarter to seven on Friday morning. A chilly wind lapped the grey waters of the Ocean Dock, Southampton. Thomas Vardon leaned over the rails of the *Olympic,* waiting for the gangway to be secured. The crowd around him were excited, anxious to disembark. Thomas shivered and thought longingly of California. At least he wouldn't have to face his father. From the towering bulk of the ship, he searched the upturned faces of the crowd. Simon should be there to meet him but he never could rely on Simon . . .

Three

A couple of hours later, Sue Castradon sat down to breakfast. She steeled herself to appear absolutely and completely at ease. It wasn't easy.

Naturally enough, Sue knew her husband had come to blows in the street, but Ned simply wouldn't talk about it. When he had strode back into the house on Sunday night he was in a boiling rage and in no mood for conversation.

His face was cut and grazed, his knuckles were bleeding, his ribs were obviously sore and his clothes ruined, but he curtly refused her aid and rejected her sympathy.

For some reason Sue couldn't even begin to guess at, she knew Ned blamed her. It was so unfair! She hadn't done anything wrong and yet she knew Ned was really angry with her. He was nearly as angry with Mr Dyson. He had, apparently, interfered.

The day after the fight she went to see the vicar. Mr Dyson, a big, kindly man, assured her that he wouldn't tell anyone – especially Ned – that she had been to see him. Sue was sincerely grateful to him. She didn't want Ned to know she had been forced to ask the vicar what her husband had been up to. That would make Ned even angrier.

Having said that, there was little Mr Dyson could tell her. All he really knew was Ned had come to blows with Jonathan Ryle, the Vardons' chauffeur, and he had intervened to stop them. He simply didn't know the reason for the quarrel.

Ned's bad mood lasted all week. On Friday morning, Sue looked across the breakfast table at the barrier of the *Daily Telegraph* and sighed. She knew Ned was using the newspaper as an excuse not to talk. When he was in a good mood, he propped the paper up on the coffee pot and commented on the news.

This was the fifth day Ned had sulked and she had had enough. If he had to fight in the street,

40

that was up to him. What she wasn't going to put up with any longer was being ignored. Sue braced herself and attempted a conversation on what she hoped was a neutral topic.

'I'm meeting Isabelle Stanton this morning. It's our turn to arrange the flowers in church this week.'

Silence.

Sue took a sip of tea and waited. All right, so he wasn't interested in her and Isabelle Stanton's doings.

'How did you get on in Eastbourne the other day, Ned?'

Ned had received a telegram from a client, Sir Arnold Stapleton, summoning him to a meeting that Wednesday. The meeting, so Sir Arnold had said, was urgent.

The paper rustled. 'He wasn't there.'

'What?'

'Stapleton wasn't there. It was a complete waste of time.'

'That seems strange.'

Ned didn't reply. Sue sighed once more and tried again. What else could she talk about? An item of genuine news occurred to her.

'I spoke to Mrs Dyson yesterday. She told me that Sir Matthew Vardon's son – the eldest son, I mean – was expected home from Hollywood today.'

Silence.

Sue sighed and persisted. 'He'll be Sir Thomas Vardon, now, of course.'

Silence.

'Mrs Dyson told me he's married to a film star. It all sounded very exciting. We've never had a film star in Croxton Ferriers.'

41

The silence seemed to become slightly more charged.

Sue, an angry glint in her eye, carried on. 'I wondered if we should invite him and his wife round for dinner or a sherry party. Actually, we could have cocktails instead of sherry. Americans drink cocktails all the time, don't they?'

'Not unless they want to end up in chokey,' grunted her husband grimly, behind the *Daily Telegraph*. 'You must have heard of Prohibition.'

Sue ignored Prohibition. She felt as if she had scored a minor triumph. She couldn't pretend that Ned's tone had been friendly but at least he had spoken.

'Shall we invite them, Ned?'

Ned Castradon impatiently folded the paper and tossed it to one side. 'Do what you damn well like.' He stood up. 'I'm going to the office.'

Sue reached breaking point. 'Ned, will you please tell me what it is I'm supposed to have done? You've hardly said one word to me all week. I've had enough.'

Ned drew his breath in dangerously. 'Enough? Enough, you say? You have no idea what enough is. Invite them round if you want to, Sue. Why not?' His voice was icy. 'After making eyes at Simon Vardon all through his father's funeral, the least you can do is weigh up his brother as well.'

Sue gazed at him, appalled. 'Ned!' she said in a shocked whisper. 'I didn't do any such thing. It was a funeral, for heaven's sake. I hardly noticed Simon Vardon.'

'Didn't you, by George! I wasn't the only one to notice, my girl. That old cat, Mrs

Cunningham-Price, came to see me, fussing about her trust funds. The last thing she said was: "Do give my regards to your wife, Mr Castradon. Why, I believe she quite took young Mr Vardon's mind off his father's funeral." I'll say you did.'

Sue flushed angrily. 'I hardly spoke to him.'

Ned started forward, his hands clenched. Sue knew he had just stopped short of banging his fists on the table. 'Don't give me that! You spoke to him, all right.'

Sue met his gaze squarely. 'What if I did? It was his father's funeral.'

'It's nice you had something to occupy your mind. Good-looking, is he?'

'I don't know! I wasn't thinking about him.'

'Oh yes? I don't believe you. And,' he added bitterly, 'I'm damned if I can blame you. After all, I'm not much to look at, am I?'

'Don't speak like that!' Even as she spoke, she knew how angry she sounded. She wasn't really angry, but she was very hurt. She knew how much his injury and the loss of his looks had meant to Ned, but she loved him. Or had done.

Pushing back her chair, she went to stand beside her husband. She wanted to love him still. She reached out and tentatively touched his shoulder. 'Ned,' she said in a softer voice. 'I wish you'd believe that I really don't mind.'

He shook her off. 'And I wish you'd believe that I really don't care.'

He turned and left the room.

Sue blinked very rapidly. She needed to get out, she needed to get away.

43

I'm not going to cry, she told herself, as she snatched her hat from the hall cupboard. I'm not going to do anything silly like that. I am *not* going to let him know how much he's upset me. I am *not* going to let Ned see me in tears. She picked up her bag and left the house. With enormous restraint, she did not bang the door.

At least she didn't have to face the village street. She went through the back garden onto Coppenhall Lane, which ran along to the church. She should have at least a quarter of an hour before Isabelle was there, which was plenty of time to compose herself. She didn't want anyone, not even Isabelle, to know there was anything wrong.

She turned into the churchyard and, with a feeling of dismay, saw that Isabelle Stanton had arrived before her and was perched comfortably, if sacrilegiously, on an old grey box tomb, a trug of flowers beside her.

Isabelle waved cheerily. 'Isn't it a heavenly day? I'm awfully early, I know. Arthur's going to meet us here. I've asked him to bring some more flowers from the garden.'

She looked happy, thought Sue resentfully. And why shouldn't she look happy? She was married to Arthur, who cared for her deeply. Lucky Isabelle. Her life had turned out as expected. Unlike mine, Sue thought resentfully. When she married Ned she thought the future would be wonderful. It could be, she thought desperately. We could be as happy as the Stantons, if only Ned would let himself be happy.

Isabelle got down and held out her hands. 'Sue, what's wrong? Something is, I know.'

Oh, God, was it that obvious? 'Nothing,' she managed to say.

'Come on, Sue, I know there is.' Isabelle glanced round, then, with a hand on her friend's arm, led her to the bench by the wall of the church. 'Come and sit down. No one can see us here. Now, tell me what's wrong.'

Sue couldn't bring herself to speak.

Isabelle looked at her appraisingly. She hadn't seen Sue for a good few days. In common with the rest of Croxton Ferriers, she had heard the tantalizingly sparse details of Ned Castradon's altercation on Sunday night, but she'd assumed that it had all been greatly exaggerated. Now, she wasn't so sure. Admittedly it was nearly a week ago, but, if the story was true, she could guess how upsetting it must have been for Sue.

'I heard about Ned's row last Sunday,' she said gently.

Sue shook her head. 'It isn't that,' she managed to say, then, to her horror, burst into tears. She groped blindly into her bag for a handkerchief. Hand to her eyes, she turned her head away.

Isabelle put her hand on Sue's arm and waited.

After a few minutes Sue blew her nose and managed a watery smile. 'I'm sorry. I didn't mean to cry.'

Isabelle squeezed her arm. 'What's wrong?'

Sue told her. 'It's so unfair,' she finished. 'Of course I saw Simon Vardon at the funeral. I couldn't miss him.'

'I saw him too,' said Isabelle. 'If you must know, I thought he was very good-looking.'

Sue wriggled guiltily. 'Did you? I'll be honest,

Isabelle, so did I, but that's all I thought. I certainly wasn't making up to him. I wish Ned wasn't so horribly jealous.' She glanced around. The church-yard was deserted. 'Do you think I could have a cigarette? I wouldn't like anyone to know I'd been smoking in the churchyard, but . . .'

Isabelle produced her cigarette case and Sue took one gratefully.

'Thanks.' She closed her eyes and breathed in deeply. 'We can't go on like this, you know,' she said eventually. 'Ned's temper's getting worse. There's no two ways about it, Isabelle, if Mr Dyson hadn't been there, I honestly think Ned might have killed Ryle.'

'What on earth was it about?' asked Isabelle.

Sue shrugged. 'I don't know. Ryle used to work for us, you know. I never liked him. Ned caught him mistreating the dog and they had an awful row. Ned sacked him, but they didn't come to blows.'

'Could Ryle have said something about Mr Vardon?' asked Isabelle, aware she was treading on delicate ground.

Sue shrugged. 'He might have done.' She smoked her cigarette for a while. 'Ryle could have taunted Ned about his injury, I suppose. Ned's desperately sensitive about it. I'm not really allowed to mention it.'

'That must be hard,' said Isabelle sympathetically.

'It's damn nearly impossible,' said Sue resent-fully. 'He broods about it all the time.'

'It must be very difficult for him—' began Isabelle.

With a flash of anger, Sue interrupted. 'It's

difficult because he *makes* it difficult. I wish he hadn't been injured, but for months I thought he was dead. I'll never forget the day I got the telegram to say he was alive. It was after the Armistice. He'd been found in a German hospital. I've honestly never been so happy in all my life, but when he eventually came home, it was awful. He was desperately ill and he'd been half-starved. I thought he was going to die.'

She turned on Isabelle. 'Do you know what it's like to have just a sliver of hope?' she demanded fiercely.

Isabelle nodded her head.

Sue stared straight ahead. 'Then you might be able to guess what it was like. When I thought he was dead, there was a sort of blank end. Nothing mattered, but as soon as I started to hope . . . It was horrible. I couldn't stop myself hoping everything would be as it was before.' Her voice broke. 'And now I sometimes feel that it would be better if he had died.'

Isabelle reached out and squeezed her hand. 'You know you don't mean that.'

'Don't I? When they let me see him for the first time, I knew he'd been burnt and I knew he was scarred and he did look terrible. I was so glad that he was alive, it didn't matter, but now he's convinced I hate the way he looks. I've tried to tell him I don't mind, but he won't *listen*.'

She put a hand to her face and felt for the sodden handkerchief. 'He said he didn't care this morning. Well, if he doesn't care, then neither do I. Bloody man.' She sat upright and gave a very faint and wobbly smile. 'I'd better watch what I say. The vicar would have a fit if he could hear me swearing in the churchyard.'

Isabelle squeezed her arm. 'Well, he can't.'

There was a long pause. Sue brushed her eyes with the back of her hand. 'I must look a real sight.' There was another pause. 'I feel I've made rather a fool of myself,' she added in a small voice.

'You haven't. If you want my advice, you'll finish your cigarette, then we'll go into the vestry and you can have a wash and – have you got your powder compact? Good – you can do your face and no one will be any the wiser. Then we'd really better make a start on doing the flowers.'

Sue gave a guilty start. 'I'd forgotten about the flowers. That's why we're here, after all. I meant to bring some with me.'

'Never mind. I've got lots.' Isabelle pointed to the trug beside the tomb she had been sitting on. 'Arthur's bringing some too, and, if we need any more, I'm sure Mrs Dyson will let us have some from her garden.'

Sue stooped and picked up her bag. 'The trouble with revelations is that they always make you feel so chewed-up afterwards.'

Isabelle gave her an encouraging smile and went to pick up the flowers. 'You'll feel better when you've had a wash.'

She led the way round the bulk of the flint-studded wall of St Luke's. 'I've got the key. I picked it up from Mr Dyson earlier.' She was making conversation deliberately, to try and give Sue something else to think about. 'He's awfully fussy about the key, isn't he? The church in the village I grew up in was always left unlocked during the day.'

'You couldn't do that here,' said Sue, seizing with gratitude on the neutral topic. She waved a hand at the hedges round the churchyard. 'The church is too cut off. We had a lot of trouble with tramps after the war, with the alms box being broken into and so on, so Mr Dyson decided to keep the church locked.'

Isabelle turned the key in the lock on the side door into the church and entered the passage that ran into the vestry, her heels clicking on the stone flags. 'Leave the door open, will you?' She wrinkled her nose. 'It smells a bit musty in here.'

The smell in the passage was actually quite unpleasant. Isabelle glanced up at the window a good ten feet above their heads. An elderly cord was hanging down from it and she gave it an impatient tug. The cord snapped in her hand.

Isabelle sighed and pushed open the door of the choir vestry.

In the corner, by the cupboard containing choir robes, stood a stone sink with a roller towel hanging beside it.

'You freshen up,' suggested Isabelle, 'and I'll go and check the flowers in the church. The greenery should be all right and there's just a chance that some of the other flowers have lasted.'

With relief she escaped down the passage into the church, pausing on the other side of the door to gather her thoughts. She always experienced a feeling of tranquil pleasure from being in the empty church, with its smell of old hymn books and ancient stone mingled with the scent of beeswax polish.

Like all well-loved public buildings it seemed, when quiet, to have an air of contented waiting.

Motes of dust floated in the pools of coloured light from the stained glass window above the altar.

Flowers, she reminded herself. I'm here to do the flowers. She looked critically at the arrangements and, picking up one of the large brass vases, went back to the vestry.

Sue, powder compact in hand, looked up with an enquiring smile.

'The greenery is all right,' said Isabelle, 'but the flowers have had it, I'm afraid. Arthur's going to bring some carnations. We'll need the smaller vases for those.'

'You get the vases from the church and I'll look in the cupboard,' said Sue. 'Are all your flowers long-stemmed?'

'These are. I asked Arthur to bring some short-stemmed ones when he came.'

Isabelle returned to the church and tried to lift the biggest vase from its stand. The brass vase, full of water and last week's flowers, was heavy and awkward.

'Sue?' she called. There was no reply. 'Sue? Can you give me a hand with this vase?'

Again, there was no reply.

Clicking her tongue in irritation, Isabelle went out of the church and back into the vestry. She glanced down the passage and saw Sue at the cupboard door.

'Can you give me a hand with the big vase, Sue? It's jolly heavy.' Sue didn't seem to hear her. 'Sue!' Isabelle called again.

The smell that she had noticed ever since coming into the passage, musty and unpleasant, had got stronger.

50

Sue Castradon still stood rigidly in front of the cupboard in the passage. There was something unnatural in her stillness.

'Sue?' Isabelle called again, starting to get slightly worried. 'Sue? What is it?'

With an effort Sue turned her head. 'Isabelle,' she whispered, 'come and look at this.' Her voice cracked. 'There's flowers,' she said. There was a rising note of hysteria in her voice. 'Flowers. I've found some flowers. Oh my God, *flowers*!'

Puzzled, Isabelle went obediently forward. The bad smell got worse. Much worse.

Then she looked in the cupboard. At first she couldn't make any sense of what she saw.

In the cupboard, where she expected to see nothing but spare flower vases and old hymn books, was the jumbled mass of a tartan rug with handfuls of decaying lilies scattered over the top. Flowers.

The rug was rolled together with a couple of large joints of meat, the sort of joints that were hung up on hooks at the back of a butcher's shop.

Then Isabelle realized what she was looking at, and screamed.

Four

Sue backed away from the cupboard, her hand to her mouth. 'It's an animal,' she whispered. 'A dead animal. A pig or something. It's horrible. Who'd put a dead pig in here?'

Isabelle shook her head desperately, feeling

very sick. 'It's not an animal,' she managed to say. She clutched onto Sue's arm and drew her away. 'We've got to get help. We've got to tell someone.'

She turned her head as she heard footsteps outside. With the sight of that thing in the cupboard before her, she felt panic rise as the door from the churchyard opened. She gave a sob of relief as Arthur, holding a wicker basket of flowers, came in.

He stopped dead as he saw Sue and Isabelle. 'Isabelle? What's the matter? What's wrong?'

Isabelle flung herself into his arms. Her face buried in his chest, she gasped out her story in incoherent sobs.

Arthur, his arms tightly around her, looked over her shoulder into the cupboard. He swallowed hard, then reached out an arm to Sue, who was still standing, rigidly gazing into the cupboard. 'Sue? Come on, Sue. Come with me.'

Like someone in a dream, Sue walked backwards from the cupboard.

Arthur, keeping his own emotions under tight control, realized she was badly shocked. Talking very gently, he managed to get both Isabelle and Sue out of the passage and back into the open air of the churchyard.

Taking Isabelle's hands in his, he gripped them tightly. 'Isabelle, I'm going for help. Stay with Sue. She needs you.'

Isabelle drew a deep, shuddering breath. 'Be quick,' she managed to say. 'Please be quick.'

They seemed to be alone in the churchyard for a long time. The sun shone down and the wind rustled the surrounding trees. Birds sang, an occasional dog barked and then – thank God! – the gate creaked open and Arthur, together with Mr and Mrs Dyson, came hurrying up the path.

'You poor dears,' said Mrs Dyson, her plump, motherly face alight with such kindly concern it nearly made Isabelle cry. She put an arm round Isabelle. 'What a dreadful thing to happen.' She looked at Sue. 'Come over to the Vicarage and we can have a nice cup of tea.'

With Isabelle and Sue safely taken care of, Arthur led the way into the passage.

Mr Dyson looked into the cupboard. He started back with a yelp of horror. 'I hardly believed you, Captain Stanton. I couldn't credit what you said. It's worse than anything I saw in the war.' He put his hand to his mouth. 'It . . . it is human, is it?'

'It looks human,' said Arthur, tightly.

Mr Dyson, very white-faced, reached out a hand to the thing in the cupboard. 'Then we have to treat it with respect.'

'Leave it!' Arthur's voice was sharp.

Mr Dyson turned to him in bewilderment. 'We can't leave it, man. I was going to cover it up. This was a human being, God help him.'

'We mustn't touch anything before the police come,' insisted Arthur.

'The police?' Mr Dyson sounded dazed. 'Yes, I suppose we'd better get the police.'

Arthur took control. It was obvious that Mr Dyson, robust though he was, was absolutely floored by the sight of the thing in the cupboard. 'We have to leave everything exactly as it is,

53

lock the church, go back to the Vicarage and ring the police,' insisted Arthur. 'Not the local man,' he added, seeing Mr Dyson was about to protest. 'This is far beyond him. I'm going to ring Superintendent Ashley.'

Superintendent Ashley of the Sussex Police was, as Arthur explained, first to Mr Dyson, then to Mrs Dyson and finally to Sue Castradon, an old friend.

He was also, as Arthur thankfully reminded himself as he heard Ashley's thoughtful Sussex voice over the telephone, too experienced to waste any time in demanding details and explanations that he could better see for himself.

'You've done exactly the right thing, Captain Stanton,' Ashley reassured him. 'I'll be there as soon as I can. I don't suppose Haldean's there, is he? No? Could you get hold of him? I'd like to know what he thinks about it all. He'll want to see that Mrs Stanton's all right, I know, and, speaking for myself, I'd like to have him involved. This sounds like his sort of problem.'

'Who's Jack Haldean?' asked Mrs Dyson curiously, when Arthur explained he wanted to make a trunk call to London to speak to Jack.

'He's my cousin,' said Isabelle. 'He writes detective stories. Superintendent Ashley knows him. He's come across this sort of thing before.'

'Dead men in cupboards?' asked Mrs Dyson. 'Murder.'

With some difficulty Jack parked the Spyker beside the churchyard wall, squeezing it under the shelter of the overhanging hedge in the line of cars, tradesmen's vans, and carts with patiently waiting horses.

St Luke's, a square, flint-studded Norman building on the outskirts of the village, stood at a crossroads. A black closed van was drawn up to the side of the lichgate. Jack could see policemen in the churchyard and, beside the lichgate, two policemen stood solidly on duty, barring the way into the church to the knots of gossiping spectators gathered on the road.

Jack made his way through the crowd to the policemen. From the murmured comments of the crowd and the expression on the faces of the policemen, Jack knew what they were thinking as clearly as if they'd written it on a banner. Amongst the crowd of fair-haired, blue-eyed Sussex villagers, he looked, with his dark Spanish eyes and olive skin, completely foreign. He could see the surprise in policemen's faces as he introduced himself and they heard his completely English voice.

'Major Haldean?' said one of the men, his face clearing. 'We've been expecting you, sir. Superintendent Ashley asked you to go straight into the church.'

Ashley was standing by the porch, finishing a cigarette. He had first met Jack a few years ago, when an ex fellow officer of Jack's was found dead at the Breedenbrook summer fête. His face lit up when he saw him. 'Haldean! I'm glad you found the church all right.'

'I couldn't miss it,' said Jack. 'It's good to see you again. Thanks for asking me. If Isabelle's going to find bodies, I want to know what's going on. How is she?'

Ashley pulled a face. 'As well as can be expected. The two ladies were completely bowled over, and no wonder. It's good of you to come down from London at a moment's notice like this.'

'That's all right,' said Jack easily. As a matter of fact it had involved some very last-minute change of plans, including putting off a meeting with his editor and scribbling a note to Betty Wingate cancelling dinner that evening, but he didn't see why Ashley should be bothered with his domestic arrangements. 'I haven't seen Isabelle or Arthur yet, but it sounds absolutely gruesome.'

'It is,' agreed Ashley. 'It turned my stomach. How anyone could do such a thing beggars belief. I know you've come across some sights in your time – so have I – but this beats them all. Captain Stanton and the vicar, Mr Dyson, said it was worse than anything they'd seen in the war. What makes it worse is where it is. To find such a thing in a church just seems wrong.' He threw his cigarette away. 'Let's go in.'

He led the way round the side of the church and in through the side door. 'The cupboard's not in the church itself but in this passage,' he explained. The door to the cupboard, Jack saw, had been pushed to. 'I've had everything photographed and fingerprinted, but I didn't want anything moved until you had a chance to see it.' He grasped the handle of the door. 'Here we are.'

Jack drew his breath in.

On the middle shelf lay the crumpled-up naked

body of a man rolled in a Royal Stewart tartan travelling rug. Handfuls of lilies lay scattered forlornly across the corpse.

The face had been horribly disfigured by heavy blows. The hands and feet were missing, roughly severed at the wrists and ankles, and the skin of the left upper arm had been hacked away, leaving it raw.

A dark-stained gash of a stab wound over the heart seemed inconspicuous by comparison, but Jack was willing to bet that was how the man had died. There was no blood on the wood of the cupboard. Those injuries had dried before the body was placed there, which meant, of course, that the poor bloke had been killed somewhere else.

And why put flowers on the body? Those flowers, with their mockery of the dignity of a funeral, sickened him.

'My God,' he said in a low voice. 'This is like something from a nightmare. Have you any idea who the poor beggar was?'

Ashley shook his head. 'No. The local doctor, Dr Lucas, thought the man must be in his late twenties or early thirties, but apart from that, we know virtually nothing. I'm fairly sure he's not a local man, because we've got no reports of anyone who's gone missing hereabouts who'd fit the bill. There is this, though.'

He took a torch from his pocket and, snapping it on, reached forward and lifted one of the body's arms so it was elbow down. 'Have a look at these needle marks, Haldean. Dr Lucas spotted those right away. I don't know if it's a course of treatment or if he doped himself.'

Jack took the torch from Ashley and examined the marks. 'Dope, I'd say. Look at the bruising round the marks. I doubt any doctor would be so careless so often.' He shook his head, puzzled. 'But if he was a dope addict, that's a facer. I wouldn't expect to find a drug addict in a sleepy Sussex village. Mind you, I wouldn't expect to find a mutilated corpse in a church cupboard, either. It doesn't add up, Ashley. If the man's not from here, why bring him here?'

'Maybe the murderer wanted to shock everyone,' suggested Ashley. 'It seems crazy to me and maybe it is.'

'Crazy,' murmured Jack. 'Yes, it does look that way.' He glanced at Ashley. 'It's certainly shocking enough. Have you any idea when the poor beggar died?'

Ashley shrugged. 'He's obviously been dead for some time. I've asked the local man, Dr Lucas, to perform the post-mortem. He'll know more when he's done it, but he thinks that the man's been dead anything between three to six days. He says that there's too many variables for anyone who knows his business to be any more definite than that. I'm hoping to narrow the time down, but I know from experience it can be hard for a medical man to give an accurate time after a couple of days. I've done all the basic procedures, of course, but I can't say they told us much.'

He indicated the stone-flagged floor. 'As you can see, there's no chance of any footprints in here and there's none outside, either.'

'Did you find any fingerprints?'

'Very few. I think the killer was wearing gloves.

The prints we did find belonged to Mrs Stanton, Mrs Castradon, Captain Stanton and the vicar. I matched those up this morning. I must say, I'm not surprised that the murderer didn't leave his dabs.'

'Neither am I,' agreed Jack, shining the torch into the cupboard. 'Everyone knows about finger-prints these days.'

All the things that had been on the shelf – flower vases, a roll of red flannel with *Merry Christmas* embroidered on it, a miscellaneous assortment of old hymn-books – had been thrust roughly to one side.

Jack shuddered. He had seen badly mutilated men in the war, but the pathetic ordinariness of those everyday things surrounding the body stuck in his throat. 'Look at it, Ashley,' he said quietly. 'All those old fête banners and prayer books and things, and slap in the middle of it, a naked man with no hands, no feet and his face caved in.'

'Not entirely naked,' corrected Ashley. 'There's this tartan rug.'

'It doesn't cover much, does it? I think the body was probably wrapped in the rug. A full-grown man's a heavy thing to carry, so the murderer probably used the rug to drag the poor beggar along. Which means, of course, we might be able to find traces of where it was dragged from.'

'I was hoping so, I must say.'

'What about the lilies?' Jack reached forward and picked up one of the lilies and looked at it with distaste. It had a many-leafed stem with a white, trumpet-shaped flower on top. Yellow in the centre and streaked with pink on the outside, it still had the characteristic stringent lily smell that always reminded him of disinfectant. 'I never did like lilies,' he murmured.

'I don't like those, I must say,' agreed Ashley. 'It's a sort of mockery, isn't it?' He shook his head in perplexity. 'I reckon we really are dealing with a lunatic. The way the body's been treated would make me think that anyway, but these lilies are the finishing touch.'

Jack nodded. 'It's nasty, isn't it? Looking at these injuries, anyone would think that we're dealing with someone with several screws loose. On the other hand, it's certainly going to make the body difficult to identify. That's rational enough.'

He leaned forward and pointed to the arm that was slung across the torso. 'The skin's been hacked off on his upper arm.'

'I wondered if that was to conceal some sort of mark.' Ashley turned to Jack. 'I think he had a tattoo.'

Jack nodded. 'I bet you're right. Again, it looks as if the murderer's trying to conceal his victim's identity.'

'So you think the murderer is entirely sane?'

Jack clicked his tongue in dissatisfaction. 'I don't think he's entirely sane. I can understand him trying to conceal who the poor bloke was, but I can't explain the lilies. Perhaps the murderer associated the idea of lilies with churches and funerals. We could be looking for someone with an anti-religious kink, or maybe someone who's got a personal grudge against the vicar.'

'That's an idea,' agreed Ashley. 'I'll ask Mr Dyson.' He stood back. 'I suppose the lilies came from the church? Mrs Stanton and Mrs Castradon were doing the flowers when they found the body.'

'Perhaps,' said Jack absently. He looked again at the flower in his hand. 'Actually, I don't think they did, you know.'

He picked up more lilies and examined the stems. 'Look at this, Ashley. These flowers haven't been cut, they've been picked. Picked very roughly, too, if you look at the stems, as if they've been wrenched out. If they came from the church, Isabelle or one of the other ladies who do the flowers would have picked them, and I can't believe any of them would pick flowers in such a careless way. They'd use secateurs or a knife, surely.'

'I see what you mean,' said Ashley. He rubbed the stem of a lily between his fingers. 'These stems are tough, aren't they? I think it'd take some strength to break off handfuls of these flowers.' He shuddered. 'If the flowers were brought here on purpose, that makes it worse, in a way. I think we're looking for someone who's off their head. It's the only explanation I can think of. They might appear rational enough, but I think there's a big streak of insanity at the bottom of this.'

He stepped back. 'Is there anything else you want to see, or can I have the body taken away?'

'There's just one thing,' said Jack. 'Can you smell something odd?'

'I can smell rather too much for my liking.'

Jack nearly smiled. 'No, I don't mean the body or the lilies. There's another smell, isn't there?'

Ashley breathed in deeply. 'If you say so,' he said dubiously. He put his head to one side. 'Actually, I just caught a whiff of it then, a sort of sweet, sickly smell.'

Jack nodded. 'That's it. It reminds me of the East, for some reason.' He shrugged. 'We might find something to explain it once you move the body.' He stepped back. 'Okay, Ashley. I don't think there's anything more I can add.'

'Right you are. We've got a van waiting outside.'

He walked down the passage and summoned the two uniformed policemen who were waiting by the church door. 'You can take it away now, men.'

'What about the crowd outside the gate, sir,' asked one of the policemen. 'Shall I move them along first?'

'No,' said Ashley. 'Leave them be.' He glanced at Jack. 'I want a look at that crowd. If I see anyone gloating when we take the remains out, I want to know who they are.'

'Good idea,' said Jack. 'I'll keep an eye on everyone with you.'

The policemen, their shapes black against the brilliant sunlight of the open door, walked towards them. They unrolled a stretcher and with a nod to each other, lifted the body out of the cupboard and placed it on the waiting canvas.

Ashley took the torch back from Jack and turned it on, so the light fell on the shelf of the cupboard. 'The knife's not in there, is it?'

'No, but something else is. It's a chess piece.'

Using his handkerchief, Jack reached into the cupboard and picked up the chess piece. It was a black knight with crystal eyes, heavy for its size, carved out of marble. If it hadn't been for the torchlight, they might have missed it. 'This is an interesting find.'

'I suppose I'd better keep it,' said Ashley doubtfully. 'Although it probably belongs to the church.'

Jack shook his head. 'I don't think so. It looks as if it's from far too expensive a chess set to be kept in a church cupboard.' He made a rapid search of the other shelves in the cupboard. 'There isn't a chess set here. There aren't any board games at all. There's no sign of the knife, either.'

Ashley sighed. 'I went through this church with a fine toothcomb earlier on. If the knife's not in the cupboard, I'm fairly certain it isn't here at all. The murder obviously took place elsewhere. If we can trace how the body got here, we might find the knife abandoned at the spot.'

He glanced up at the two policemen. 'Give me and Major Haldean a couple of minutes to get to the gate before you bring the body out. And cover it up, will you? I don't want anyone in the crowd fainting on me.'

They walked down the path and, joining the two policemen who had guarded the entrance to the churchyard, stood either side of the lichgate. The rise in the ground gave them a good view of the waiting knot of onlookers.

The crowd fell silent as the body, its nakedness

now covered by the tartan rug, was carried past. The men, moved by an innate sense of propriety, took off their hats and caps. Jack saw interest, sympathy and decently disguised excitement on the faces around him but nowhere could he see that evil and unholy joy that Ashley had speculated upon. Whoever the murderer was, he was willing to bet they weren't here.

The stretcher was loaded into the van and the crowd fell back as it drove off.

'Move these people along,' said Ashley to the policemen. 'There's nothing more to see. Stay on duty and make sure nobody enters that church until I say so.'

Jack stepped back into the churchyard. In one way it was idyllic, with the sun gilding the old stones of the ancient, hummocky graves and the daisy-rich grass, bright with buttercups, rustling gently in the breeze. However, the churchyard's very air of otherworldly peace, enclosed as it was by high hedges, made it very secluded. *The grave's a fine and private place* . . . The line of poetry ran through his head. The graveyard was a fine and private place, too. You wouldn't be overlooked here.

'Have you searched the churchyard, Ashley?' he asked. 'I wonder if he was bumped off out here?'

'I had the same idea, Haldean. I ordered a thorough search this morning and had a good look round myself. There's no traces whatsoever. I think we can rule out the churchyard.'

'So it wasn't a living man but a dead one who was brought here,' said Jack thoughtfully. 'How did the body arrive? By car?'

'A car's the obvious answer,' agreed Ashley. 'However, I've searched the road and couldn't find a thing.'

He led the way down the path, out of the lichgate. St Luke's stood on a corner plot, with the main road running past the churchyard at the front, with a tree-lined lane to the left. The lichgate opened onto the lane, a broad, dusty corner of road that quickly narrowed into a grassy path with overhanging trees.

The main road running up from the village, with its grass verges and ditches, was wide, its surface of earth and chalk showing deep ruts from farm carts and tyre tracks. It carried, as Ashley said, most of the traffic in and out of the village.

The other road, Coppenhall Lane, widened out at the lichgate of the church, but quickly narrowed into a narrow, pebbly path with grass growing up the centre.

'You can see the problem for yourself,' said Ashley. 'It's been at least three days, perhaps more, and the chances of finding an individual car track, especially after the crowds that have been here this morning, are just about nil.'

'I'm sure if there was anything to be found, you'd have found it,' said Jack. He returned to the lichgate, looking closely at the hawthorn hedge that grew round it. 'There's nothing there that I can see.'

Keeping on the road, he stepped past the entrance of the gate and examined the hedge on the other side, the side coming from Coppenhall Lane. 'Where does this lane go to, Ashley?' he asked.

'It's nothing but a footpath, really. It's fairly wide here, but, as you can see, you couldn't get a car along it. It's a short cut to the village proper. It comes out not far from the Red Lion and the village green.'

Jack crouched down, looking at the glossy green of the hawthorn with its spiky thorns that grew up beside the church wall and spanned the narrow ditch. A thread of red and yellow caught his eye and he gave a little grunt of satisfaction.

'Ashley! Come and have a look at this.'

Ashley looked to where Jack was pointing and grinned. A few red and yellow threads were caught on the thorns. Taking a pair of tweezers from his pocket he detached the threads and laid them flat on the palm of his hand. 'I bet they're from that tartan rug.'

'I bet they are too,' said Jack as Ashley placed the threads in an envelope. He crouched down again, examining the grass beside the gate.

'This grass has been flattened and some of the buttercups have been broken. The grass is dry enough to show traces. If the murderer closed the gate behind him, he'd have to put the body down to do it. Do we think the body was placed here?'

'That seems reasonable enough. Hullo! What's that?' Ashley stooped to where the grass grew in a long fringe under the hedge, parting it with his fingers. He picked up a small square silver box with a flip-top lid. 'It's a silver matchbox. I caught the gleam of it just then.'

Ashley picked up the box by the corners and

held it up to view. 'It's a nice little thing, isn't it?' He held it out so Jack could see. 'There's the initials E.C. engraved on it. It can't have been here long, otherwise the silver would've tarnished.'

'It looks like a nice, solid sort of clue,' said Jack approvingly.

'It could be. As I see it, the murderer put the body down by the hedge and opened the gate. He could've easily have dropped the matchbox then.'

'True,' agreed Jack. He clicked his tongue. 'On the other hand, E.C. could've come out of the gate as a perfectly innocent churchgoer and lit his pipe or a cigarette before heading home. He might not have been into the church at all, but simply stopped for a breather.'

'Fair enough,' admitted Ashley. 'Still, it's near enough to where the threads were snagged to make me want to keep it.' He put the matchbox into an envelope, put it in his bag and stepped back. 'Those threads are on the wrong side of the gate if we're assuming the murderer came up the main road.'

Jack turned and looked down Coppenhall Lane. 'So the implication is . . .?'

'That the body was brought along the footpath, I suppose.' Ashley's forehead crinkled in a frown. 'You couldn't get a car along here. The murderer would have to have some strength to carry or drag the body along the path.'

'I've come across a murderer who moved a body in a wheelbarrow before now.'

And so he had. Figuratively speaking, Betty had been involved with that murder and that wheelbarrow, he thought with a rush of tenderness. It was rum that something that had started so badly should end so well. He was supposed to be taking her out to dinner tonight.

'A wheelbarrow?' said Ashley, recalling him to the here and now. 'That's an idea. Let's have a look along the lane, shall we?'

Coppenhall Lane was flanked by the tall hedges of the church on one side. Across the road was a grass verge, a ditch and trees. In the bright sunshine it was pleasantly shady, but at night it would be pitch black. You could move a platoon of bodies along here at night without being seen, but, on the other hand, you'd have to be very confident of being able to find your way.

They walked slowly along the path, round the corner that led to the village.

About four hundred yards down the path, they came to the low stone walls of the backs of three substantial early Victorian villas, each set in their own large garden.

A vigorous climbing rose, cut back to allow the gate to open, virtually concealed the wall of the first house.

Jack looked at the rose and grinned. 'This is rather nice, isn't it? Are you interested in roses, Ashley?'

Ashley looked to where Jack was pointing. A few red and yellow threads were caught on the thorns. 'I'm interested in those roses,' he said, brightening. Using the tweezers, he picked the threads off and added them to his collection in his bag.

'Who does this house belong to?' asked Jack.

Ashley paused, getting the geography right. 'These houses face onto the village green. This first house is the Vicarage, but I don't suppose the vicar had anything to do with it. Dr Lucas, the doctor who's performing the post-mortem, has the middle house in this row. He uses the front rooms as his surgery. The end house belongs to Mrs Castradon and her husband.' He stopped abruptly. 'I say, Haldean! Mr Castradon's Christian name is Edward. E.C.! Those are the initials on the matchbox.'

'Steady on,' said Jack with a grin. 'That matchbox could be nothing more than a blind alley. I don't really believe in murderers who drop their initialled property at the scene of the crime.'

'You'd be amazed at the mistakes criminals make. However, it could be a coincidence. Come on. Let's see if we can find anything else.'

Despite a careful search, the rest of the lane yielded nothing and, a couple of hundred yards on, they came out onto the village green.

'Well,' said Ashley, 'we're a bit further forward. We know the body was brought along Coppenhall Lane.' He turned and looked at the backs of the houses thoughtfully.

'It's tempting,' said Jack, 'to assume that the body was brought out of the back gate of one of those houses. However, there's plenty of space round the green to park a car. The murderer could've parked here and taken the body along to the church along the lane. On the face of it, that seems to argue local knowledge but really, there's nothing that a ten-minute stroll round the village couldn't tell you.'

'True enough. But that doesn't answer the big question, does it? Why was the body left in the church in the first place?'

'Maybe,' said Jack, 'the vicar will be able to shed some more light on that. Let's go and see him, shall we?'

Five

It was easy to see which one of the three houses which fronted the green was the Vicarage. Mrs Dyson, a stout, friendly-looking woman, was in the garden, with a trowel in hand and a wicker basket beside her. She straightened up and waved them over with a flourish of the trowel.

'Do come in, Mr Ashley,' she said, coming to the gate. She looked inquisitively at Jack as Ashley introduced them.

'Major Haldean? It's a pleasure to meet you. You're Mrs Stanton's cousin, aren't you? I'm so glad her husband was here to take care of her.'

'She was very grateful to you as well, Mrs Dyson.'

'It was the least I could do,' said Mrs Dyson with deep concern. 'She and poor Mrs Castradon were terribly upset, poor things. Frederick and I brought them to the house and I made sure they both had a cup of strong tea with a drop of brandy in it, but really, there was nothing we could *do*. Poor Frederick was very shaken, of course, as we all were, but, being a man, he doesn't like to say as much.'

'Male pride, eh?' said Jack with a grin. 'Anyone would be shaken, after a sight like that.' He took the marble black knight from his pocket. 'Incidentally, Mrs Dyson, we found this in the cupboard. I don't suppose you recognize it?'

She took the chessman from him and, taking off her glasses, examined it closely. 'No, I can't say I do. We do have a chess set and other board games, of course, for the Scouts and Guides and Frederick's Lads' Club, but they're all kept in the parish hall,' she said, handing it back to him. 'This looks as if it's from an expensive set, Major. All our board games are made of boxwood, so they're cheap enough to replace if any pieces get lost.'

'Is Mr Dyson at home?' asked Ashley. 'We'd appreciate a word with him if he can spare the time.'

'I'm sure he'll be glad to see you both,' she said, wiping the trowel and putting it in the wicker basket. 'It seems as if we've got a lunatic at large, but I can't think of anyone who'd do such a thing. There are a couple in the village who are wanting, as the expression is, but they're not mad, just poor souls who are simple-minded.'

She stopped, her naturally rosy face paling. 'What I saw in the church this morning seemed *evil*. That's a strong word, but I don't think I've ever come across real evil before.' She looked at the garden helplessly. 'That's why I came out here. I simply had to find something physical to do to take my mind off it.'

'Of course you're upset, Mrs Dyson,' said Ashley kindly, laying a hand on her arm. 'It's only to be expected, having something like this happen on the doorstep, as you might say.'

'That's the worst of it, Mr Ashley,' she said, leading the way up the path. 'It more or less has to be someone who's on the doorstep. I did wonder if it could be someone so unhinged they've got a grudge against the church or even Frederick, but it really doesn't seem possible anyone would go to such *lengths*.'

'It's funny you should say that, Mrs Dyson,' said Ashley. 'That's more or less what Major Haldean and I wondered ourselves, isn't it, Haldean?'

Jack didn't answer. His attention had been caught by a scrubby bank of white flowers. 'Look over there,' he said quietly.

'By George,' muttered Ashley. 'Lilies. Mrs Dyson, can we have a closer look at your flowers?'

'The lilies?' asked Mrs Dyson, puzzled. 'Yes, of course.'

She walked across the lawn to where the tall white flowers stirred gently in the breeze. 'These are Regale lilies. They have a wonderful smell and they grow even on our chalky soil. I wish you could've seen them earlier in the week,' she added wistfully. 'They looked magnificent, but a dog or something got in and broke down all that centre section. At least, Frederick says it must've been a dog, but I didn't agree. I thought it was much more likely to be naughty children, taking them for their mothers, perhaps, as the flowers weren't trampled on the ground, there was a whole lot of them gone . . .'

She stopped, her voice trailing off. She put her hand to her mouth and swayed. Jack quickly put his hand under her arm. She looked as if she might faint.

'Those were the lilies in church,' she whispered. 'Our lilies.' She turned a stricken face to them. 'Who would do this? Who would use *our* lilies in *our* church. Can there really be anyone who hates us so much?'

'Let's go inside,' said Jack. 'I think you need to sit down.'

Jack liked the look of Frederick Dyson. He was a big, burly, square-shouldered man in his forties, who hurried into the hall at his wife's call. 'Hello, Superintendent,' he began, then broke off as he saw his wife. 'Phyllis! What's wrong?'

'Mrs Dyson's had a shock,' explained Ashley. 'It looks as if the flowers that were scattered on the body in the church came from your garden, sir.'

'They were our lilies, Freddy,' broke in Mrs Dyson on the verge of tears. 'Someone came into our garden and took them.'

Frederick Dyson whistled soundlessly. 'Did they, by George? Phyllis, come into the sitting room, dear. Do you want a cup of tea? No? You need something. You look worried to death.'

Once in the sitting room, he poured his wife a brandy from the decanter on the sideboard and added a splash of soda. 'Now, drink that, and you'll feel better.'

He stuffed his pipe with tobacco from the jar and lit it with a worried air. 'Please smoke,' he said absently to Ashley and Jack. 'Are you sure they were our flowers?'

'I don't think anyone else in the village has

Regale lilies,' said Mrs Dyson, sipping her brandy. 'Besides that, they were damaged in the week. You know they were. They have to be our flowers.'

Mr Dyson patted his wife's hand with clumsy sympathy. 'It seems incredible,' he said gruffly. 'The whole thing is crazy.'

'Actually, sir, distressing as it is, it might work to our advantage,' said Ashley. 'It could help us establish when the body was left in the church. If you can remember when the flowers were damaged, it would be a great help.'

Frederick Dyson looked helplessly at him. 'I really couldn't say.'

'Wednesday morning,' said Mrs Dyson, distantly. She gave herself a little shake. 'That's when I saw the damage. The garden was fine on Tuesday afternoon. The damage must have been done late on Tuesday. I had Guides on Tuesday and I needed to get to the hall early because Corrie Dinder wanted to see me about the river trip. I usually get out in the garden after Guides at this time of year, but I couldn't, because Lucy Palgrove called to see me about more wool for the Mothers' knitting circle. By the time she'd gone, it was time for the news on the wireless. Frederick and I always listen to the wireless together, so I didn't get out that evening.'

'You're sure it was Wednesday morning you noticed the damage, Mrs Dyson?' asked Jack.

She nodded. 'Yes, that's right. I called Freddy out to see what had happened, didn't I, Freddy? You said at first it was probably Charlie Brandreth's chickens that had got in. That's happened before.'

'Charlie Brandreth keeps the Red Lion,' put in Mr Dyson. 'Those chickens of his get everywhere.'

'It's the gate,' explained Mrs Dyson. 'The frost this winter lifted the stones on the path and the gate won't shut properly.'

'If the gate was open, I think you could see the bank of lilies from the road, couldn't you?' asked Jack.

She nodded. 'Yes, you can. People have said how nice they look.' She gulped. 'I was cross about the lilies. I knew it couldn't be chickens and then Frederick said it was probably a dog, but I knew it wasn't, because the flowers weren't just trampled, they were missing.'

She put her hand to the back of her mouth. 'I thought it was Ben and Nathan Halford. They're very naughty little boys, but it wasn't them, was it?'

Ashley shook his head. 'No, Mrs Dyson, it wasn't.' He glanced at Jack. 'If the damage was discovered on Wednesday morning, that means we're looking at Tuesday night.'

'What beats me,' said Mr Dyson, 'is how the feller got into the church in the first place. He could've climbed through a window, I suppose.'

Mrs Dyson shook her head. 'That's not possible, Frederick. The church windows are far too high for anyone to climb through and the windows in the vestry won't open. You know I've complained about those windows before. I've asked Tom Hernshaw – he's the church warden – to see to them lots of times and he always says that he'll "get round to it".' Her voice was steadier now.

'He's been getting round to it for the last three years.'

'What about the window in the passage?' asked Ashley.

Mrs Dyson shook her head. 'That won't open either. It looks as if it should, but it won't. I'm sure all it needs is a drop of oil on the ratchet. I'd do it myself, only I can't stand heights.'

'You leave that window alone, Phyllis,' said her husband in some alarm.

'It doesn't sound as if the windows are a possibility,' said Jack. 'Especially if you think the chap was encumbered with a body to heave about. I don't think he'd be able to climb a ladder.'

'I agree,' said Ashley. 'Which means, of course, that he must've come through the door.' He glanced at Mr Dyson. 'You stated that the church is always kept locked unless there's a service, didn't you, sir?'

Mr Dyson nodded. 'That's right. We had some trouble with tramps breaking open the alms box, so I decided the best thing to do was to keep the church locked.'

'When is it open, Mr Dyson?' asked Jack.

'Sunday is the busy day, of course. We have Matins at half eight and Communion at eleven. Evensong is at five o'clock. During the week, we have Matins every day, again at half eight, and Evensong at five.'

Ashley nodded. 'So you've been in the church, morning and evening, every day this week. Have you noticed anything out of place?'

Mr Dyson shook his head. 'I honestly can't say I have.'

'You haven't found the church open when it shouldn't have been, for instance?'

'No. As a matter of fact, I can't remember that's ever happened.'

Ashley sat back with a frown. 'What happens to the keys when you're conducting a service?'

'I usually leave them on a hook in the vestry. When I'm at home, I always hang them up in the hall. Those are the set I gave you this morning, Mr Ashley. I've got a spare set, which are in my desk, but I hardly ever use those. The keys in the hall are the ones that Phyllis or myself or the girl give to anyone who wants to go into the church. Tom Hernshaw, the warden, has a set, too, but those are for his own use. He doesn't lend them to anyone.'

Ashley took the church keys from his pocket and put them on the table. 'May we see the spare set, sir?'

'Yes, of course.' Mr Dyson walked to his desk and produced a second bunch of keys. 'What are you hoping to find?'

'I really wanted to see they were where you left them, sir,' said Ashley. 'I don't suppose many people know these keys are kept in your desk, do they?'

Frederick Dyson shrugged helplessly. 'I never made any secret of it.'

Ashley nodded. 'Fair enough. What's the procedure for handing out the keys, Mr Dyson?'

Mr Dyson looked vaguely alarmed. 'We don't have a procedure as such. Someone comes to the door and asks, and I, or Phyllis, or the girl, let them have the keys. We always know who they are and what they want them for, of course. In a place like this, everyone does know everyone else and what their business is. It's not like a city parish. And don't run away with the idea that people are popping in and out of church all day.' He gave a sudden smile. 'It's as much as I can do to get them to come on Sunday.'

His face fell. 'I don't know if I can possibly tell you who's asked for the keys this week but I'm certain that they wouldn't be handed out to someone we didn't know.'

Jack picked up the keys and weighed them in his hand thoughtfully. 'Is there a list of parish activities we can look at?' he suggested. 'It might jog your memory.'

'There's the parish magazine,' said Mr Dyson. He went to his desk and took out a copy. Sitting beside his wife, he opened the magazine.

'Cookery hints,' she said, taking the magazine from him and leafing through the pages. 'How to re-model last year's hat, notes of the knitting circle, the Brownies' outing . . . Here we are. The parish diary. Friday is flowers and choir practice in the church and the Ladies' Aid Society meet here, in the Vicarage. That's this evening. We'll have to cancel the choir practice, Freddy. Thursday, church warden's meeting at six thirty.'

'Tom Hernshaw would've used his own keys for that,' put in Mr Dyson.

'Wednesday morning is church cleaning,' continued Mrs Dyson.

Ashley looked up sharply. 'Wednesday morning? That's the morning the damage to the lilies was discovered. Who does the cleaning? I wonder if they saw anything out of place?'

Mrs Dyson shook her head. 'I'm sure they'd have mentioned it if they thought there was anything unusual or untoward. Mrs Clegg and Mrs Howard do the actual dusting and mopping, then Mrs Cunningham-Price and Corrie Dinder do the brasses. They're all most respectable and, indeed, unimaginative women, but they do notice things and comment on them.'

'Mrs Cunningham-Price?' said Mr Dyson, wryly. 'I'd say so.'

'Where's the stuff kept for cleaning the floors and the brasses?' asked Jack. 'They must need mops and cloths and Brasso and things.'

'In the broom cupboard.' She swallowed. 'That's in the passage where the body was found.'

'What about Tuesday?' asked Ashley.

'Nothing happens on Tuesdays or Mondays,' said Mr Dyson. 'No one asked for the keys on Tuesday, did they, Phyllis?'

'No, they didn't, Freddy. Doreen – that's the girl – would've mentioned it if they had.'

Jack glanced at Ashley. 'It looks as if someone waited their moment, got into the vestry and took a wax impression of the key.'

'An impression?' queried Mr Dyson. 'That sounds very elaborate. Why not just take the key?'

'Because the keys are all accounted for, sir, and seem to have been accounted for all week,' said Jack, sitting forward in his chair. 'I think we can rule out anyone who asked for the keys openly. Neither Superintendent Ashley nor I believe for a moment that the murderer turned up at your door and simply asked for the keys.

That really does beggar belief. And yet, as the windows can't be opened and the church shows no sign of being broken into, that means the murderer used a key. Unless the murderer was able to take a key and return it without your knowledge – and, granted the body was left in the church at night, that seems unlikely – they have to have taken an impression of the key. The obvious time to have done that is when it's hanging up in the vestry.'

'They'd have to know the routine of what happens when in the church of course,' said Ashley. 'Mind you, the parish magazine would tell them that. I did wonder if this was going to be a Scotland Yard job, but we're back to somebody local with local knowledge, aren't we, Haldean?'

'It certainly seems like it,' agreed Jack. He looked at the Dysons. 'Talking of local knowledge, I know there's no one who's officially been reported as missing, but can you think of anyone who's not been seen for a few days?'

Mr Dyson clicked his tongue. 'There's no one—' he began, when his wife interrupted him.

'What about that chauffeur of the Vardons, Frederick? No one's seen Jonathan Ryle since that terrible fight at the weekend.'

Ashley hunched forward in his chair. 'Fight? What fight?'

Mr Dyson frowned at his wife. 'Ryle left on Sunday. It's a man who's been missing since Tuesday we're looking for, Phyllis. I'm sure the Superintendent doesn't want to hear about our little local troubles.'

Jack looked at him quickly. There was an odd note of reproof in his voice.

Mrs Dyson had picked up the note of reproof as well. 'You can't ignore what happened, Frederick.'

'It was nothing,' said Mr Dyson. His wife gave a disbelieving snort.

'Let me be the judge of that, sir,' said Ashley, unconsciously slipping into his official manner.

Mr Dyson looked distinctly ill at ease. 'It was something and nothing.'

'It was a great deal more than something and nothing!' said his wife, reproachfully. 'The thing is, Mr Ashley, Frederick thinks it looks bad for one of his parishioners. Although why you should be so sensitive about Ned Castradon's feelings, Freddy, when he couldn't give tuppence for yours, I don't know.'

'Mr Castradon?' asked Ashley. Jack could hear the suppressed excitement in his voice. 'Perhaps you'd tell me what happened, Mr Dyson.'

With some prompting from his wife, the story of the quarrel came out. 'Although what caused it, I've no idea,' finished Mr Dyson. 'I may say that Castradon did not appreciate my interference.'

'The language,' said Mrs Dyson firmly, 'was awful. Ned Castradon was beside himself.'

'Did he threaten this man, Ryle?' asked Ashley.

Mr Dyson didn't answer but Mrs Dyson nodded vigorously. 'He most certainly did. It was only Frederick's intervention that stopped them killing each other.'

'Phyllis,' said Mr Dyson warningly, 'don't exaggerate.'

81

'What did he say?' asked Ashley.

'Oh, Lord.' Mr Dyson took a deep breath. 'I'm sure he didn't mean it.'

'What did he say?' repeated Ashley.

Mr Dyson looked thoroughly unhappy. 'He said if he saw Ryle again, he'd kill him.' He caught a look from his wife. 'All right, Phyllis! He said he'd murder him,' he muttered.

'Did he, by Jove,' muttered Ashley with great satisfaction.

'Good heavens, Superintendent, the two men had just come to blows! You'd expect threats of that nature to be bandied about. It doesn't mean anything.'

Ashley looked up and smiled. 'Perhaps it doesn't. I know perfectly well that a man can let himself be carried away.'

'There's more to it than you realize, Superintendent. Ned Castradon had a rotten time of it in the war and his temper is very irascible. However, he's a well-respected man, as was his father before him. He's honest and straightforward and the very last person to be mixed up in a horrific business like this. He certainly wouldn't allow his wife to be the one to discover the body. He'd never subject her to that sort of ordeal.'

Ashley nodded. 'I appreciate your opinion, sir. It's good to have what you might call an insider's view of the situation.'

Jack admired Ashley's air of complete acceptance of the vicar's opinion. Knowing him well, he could see just how satisfied Ashley was with the information he had gathered.

'I'll keep the keys to the church for the

82

meantime, if I may,' said Ashley, rising to leave, 'but I'll let you have them back as soon as possible.'

Ashley preserved a decent silence until they were out of the front door and well out of earshot. Then he turned to Jack and, with a broad grin, rubbed his hands together.

'How about that? We've got the tartan threads and the matchbox, a violent quarrel with threats being bandied about, a possible identification for the victim and – I really appreciated this point – a man who's got a real grudge against the vicar. Our Mr Castradon obviously didn't like Mr Dyson butting into his fight with Ryle one little bit.'

'Murdering a man and sticking him in a cupboard in the church is a bit of an extreme reaction, wouldn't you say?'

Ashley laughed. 'Come on. You know as well as I do that what seems to be an extreme reaction to an ordinary person is more than enough cause for someone who's unbalanced.' He looked at Jack keenly. 'What's bothering you? Something is.'

Jack shrugged in dissatisfaction. 'Nothing really. I agree that with the lead we've been given, you have to chase up Castradon and see what his alibi's like for Tuesday. After that, it might very well be an open-and-shut case. I suppose what's really bothering me is Mr Dyson's assessment of Castradon's character. He seemed to think it was so utterly incredible that Castradon would kill a man in that way.'

'Parsons are paid to think the best of everyone,' said Ashley. 'I'm a policeman. I'm not.' He glanced at his watch and clicked his tongue. 'I doubt if Dr Lucas will have performed the post-mortem yet. I'd like to know what the results are before we see Mr Castradon.'

'I'd better be getting back to Belle and Arthurs',' said Jack. 'I don't want to be late for dinner and I'd like to see if I can pick up some local gossip. If the local solicitor fighting in the street didn't set everyone by their ears, I know nothing about village life.'

'Can you meet me after dinner?' said Ashley. 'I'd like to know if you've heard anything interesting.'

Six

Isabelle and Arthur's house was on the outskirts of Croxton Ferriers. The house, Jack remembered with a grin, had been the cause of some debate between his cousin and her husband.

Some months previously Arthur's Aunt Catherine had asked him to take over the running of her neglected estate. Arthur flung himself into the task with unbounded enthusiasm and announced that the job came with a house he described as a little Jacobean gem.

Isabelle had mixed feelings about the gem. It was, she said, not to put too fine a point on it, a ruin. Yes, there were walls and a roof, but that was about all. A period of some seriously hard work followed, much to the benefit of the local builders, and, like a phoenix from the ashes, the

house of Arthur's dreams, and to Isabelle's satisfaction, emerged.

Arthur was, thought Jack, a very happy man.
He was also, as they sat in the dining room
together, a worried one.

'I'm afraid it's a scratch meal,' he said, as they
sat down to chicken casserole. 'Poor Isabelle was
completely skittled out this morning and it never
occurred to me to think about meals, so Mrs
Jarvis, the cook, and Mabel, the girl, took over.'

'It just seemed to knock all the stuffing out of
me,' said Isabelle apologetically. 'I do hope
everything's all right, Jack.'

'It's all absolutely fine,' said Jack, 'and this
casserole is delicious. Granted the circumstances,
I was going to stay at the local pub, Belle, but
Arthur insisted I came here.'

'How did you get on today?' asked Arthur. 'I
can't believe we've got a killer – a deranged
killer – in our midst. Do you know when the
poor bloke was killed?'

'We think it happened on Tuesday. Those
ghastly lilies were taken from Mrs Dyson's
garden on Tuesday night.'

'Don't,' pleaded Isabelle. 'Those flowers were
horrible. I could virtually hear the murderer
laughing at us.'

'It seems that way, doesn't it?' said Jack
thoughtfully. 'Ashley's convinced that the killer's
off his rocker. He might be right.'

He crumbled a piece of bread. 'We did find
something odd. When we moved the body, we
found a black knight from a chess set. It was
carved out of black marble with crystal eyes. It

was far too expensive to be from a set belonging to the church. Mrs Dyson confirmed that. All the church board games are kept in the parish hall and the pieces are made of plain old boxwood, not elaborately carved marble. It has to have been left there deliberately. I think it's a message from the murderer.'

'But what's the message?' demanded Isabelle. 'What does it *mean*?'

'Games,' said Arthur softly. 'The killer's playing games.' He gave a long breath. 'What else did you turn up?'

'It looks as if the body was brought along Coppenhall Lane. We found tartan threads from the rug snagged along the bushes. Ashley found a silver matchbox with the initials E.C. engraved on it by the lichgate where the body had evidently been put down for a time . . .'

He broke off at the sight of Isabelle's expression. 'E.C.?' she repeated softly. 'Oh my God, Arthur. *Edward Castradon*.'

Arthur put down his knife and fork and gazed at her. 'Isabelle, you can't honestly suspect Ned Castradon.'

She looked stricken. 'But the chess piece, Arthur! He's a real chess fiend.'

'So what if he is?' He turned to Jack. 'There's a thriving chess club in the village and Ned Castradon is one of their leading lights. They meet in the Red Lion once a week, but you can't base anything on the fact that a man plays chess.'

'I wasn't going to,' said Jack. 'But Edward Castradon's known for his rocky temper, isn't he?'

'He's dreadfully moody,' said Isabelle.

Arthur shot her a warning look. 'Isabelle . . .'

'He *is* moody,' persisted Isabelle. 'I know, just as well as you do, Arthur, that's very different from being nuts, but he's got a shocking temper.' She turned to Jack. 'You heard about the fight he had with Ryle, the Vardons' chauffeur?' Jack nodded. 'That's just one incident. He had a dreadful row with Sue this morning. When she arrived at the church this morning, she was terribly upset. Ned's been in a foul mood all week. He's hardly spoken to her.'

Arthur looked profoundly uncomfortable. 'I don't think we should gossip about our neighbours,' he began, but Jack disagreed.

'I'd rather hear it from you and Belle than anyone else, Arthur. I know you'll be as fair as possible.'

Arthur was unconvinced. 'I don't see what the Castradons' private affairs have to do with the body in the church, no matter how upset Sue Castradon was.'

'Neither do I,' agreed Jack amicably, 'but it's good background knowledge and you can bet your boots I'll hear it from someone sooner or later.'

He very much did want to hear about it. Ned Castradon had a fight with Ryle on Sunday, a fight which was interrupted forcibly by the vicar. Castradon had resented Mr Dyson's interference. On Tuesday the body was put in the church, garlanded with lilies from the Vicarage garden. That really could be seen as an insult or even a threat to Mr Dyson. And Ned Castradon had been in a foul mood all week? Yes, despite Arthur's qualms, he wanted to know the reason for Castradon's bad temper.

'It's so unfair,' said Isabelle. 'It's all about Simon Vardon.' She launched into an account of how village tongues had wagged about Simon Vardon's obvious admiration for Sue at Sir Matthew's funeral. 'The trouble is,' she finished, 'is that Sue's lovely. I honestly doubt if any man could avoid noticing her.'

Arthur nodded vigorously in whole-hearted if rather tactless agreement.

'And Ned,' she continued, 'was badly shot up in the war. I know it's not his fault but especially with Sue being so . . . well, striking, I suppose you could say, it's all a bit like *Beauty and the Beast*. Ned's quite horribly jealous. It's rotten for Sue. It's so unfair.'

'It sounds it,' said Jack. 'But what brought matters to a head this week?'

'It could've been Castradon's fight with Ryle,' suggested Arthur. 'If Ryle taunted him with the village gossip, that could account for it.'

'Yes, it could,' said Jack thoughtfully. 'Tell me more about the Vardons.'

'I don't know much,' said Arthur with a shrug, 'but Sir Matthew Vardon was a nasty piece of work altogether, in my opinion. He died of apoplexy about five weeks ago.'

'I never liked him,' said Isabelle. 'Did you hear the rumour going the rounds that his illness wasn't natural?'

'I did hear something,' admitted Arthur. 'It wouldn't surprise me if someone did want to bump him off, but Dr Lucas would've known if there was anything dodgy going on.'

'Apparently it was Dr Lucas who was under

suspicion. The nurse, Nurse Pargetter, said Dr Lucas was a bit too happy that Sir Matthew showed no signs of a recovery.'

Arthur shook his head vigorously. 'Old Lucas wouldn't do anything to harm a patient.'

Isabelle pulled a face. 'Put as starkly as that, I didn't think he would, either. To be fair, he called for a second opinion, and a doctor from Harley Street came. That proves he's innocent, doesn't it?'

'To play devil's advocate for a moment, it doesn't prove anything of the sort,' said Jack. 'He could've called for a second opinion as a blind.'

Isabelle wriggled impatiently. 'Of course he could, but I don't believe it. I think it's as Arthur said. Because nobody liked Sir Matthew much, when he died, the rumours started. Aunt Catherine warned us to be careful of him. Sir Matthew's son, Thomas – he's the son of Sir Matthew's first wife – will inherit the place. If he's expecting quiet village life, he's got a nasty shock coming, with a murderer on the loose. Mind you, he must be used to excitement. He's worked in Hollywood since the war.'

'Hollywood? Gosh. I bet that's caused some gossip.'

'We've been talking about nothing else for weeks,' said Arthur with a grin.

'It's *interesting*, Jack,' said Isabelle, 'even though Arthur's bored to death with it all.'

Arthur sighed meaningfully and turned his attention to his dinner as Isabelle launched into an account of what had been gleaned in the village about Thomas Vardon's life and career to date. As even that repository of knowledge about all things Hollywood, Winifred Charteris, actually knew very little, there was a mountain of speculation to a molehill of fact.

'And,' concluded Isabelle, after a monologue in which the words *film, Hollywood, picture* and *studio* had featured heavily, 'Mrs Dyson told us that the poor man should arrive today.'

'Why is he a poor man?' enquired Jack, finishing his chicken and putting his knife and fork on the plate.

'Lady Vardon resented Thomas bitterly because he gets the title. He married a film star.'

'A film star?' said Jack with gratifying interest.

'Well, I don't think she's exactly a star. I suppose she's a starlet. Or a starling.'

'Ruddy pests,' muttered Arthur. 'I need to get a shotgun to them.' He glanced up at Jack's snort of laughter. 'Starlings, I mean,' he explained.

'Why don't you tell me all about this star, Belle?' asked Jack. 'Or starling, if you'd rather. You're obviously dying to meet her.'

'Well, I am,' agreed Isabelle. 'Her name's Esmé Duclair. I want to know what Hollywood's really *like.*'

Jack laughed. He couldn't help it. 'You're star-struck.'

'It's all right for you, living in London,' said Isabelle with dignity, 'but we're positively moss-bound here. You wouldn't credit how the smallest piece of gossip becomes news and how satisfying it is to pass it on. If there's some genuine news, we're all agog. Why, the morning after Lady Vardon's diamonds were stolen, Sue Castradon came and told us about it at breakfast.'

Jack's eyebrows crawled upwards. 'It doesn't sound as if you've been lacking for interest recently, village or no village.'

Explanations followed. 'And,' said Arthur, 'what you make of it all, I don't know. Could it possibly be connected with the murder?'

'On the face of it, no,' said Jack thoughtfully. 'They're two remarkable events, though, and I'd count Castradon's fight with Ryle as a third. A professional man is usually more careful of his reputation. Who is Ryle, anyway? I know he was the Vardon's chauffeur, but apart from that, I mean?'

'The person to ask is our cook, Mrs Jarvis,' said Isabelle. 'She'll be able to tell you more than we can. Not that she liked him, particularly. I don't think anyone did much.'

'All right. Apart from Edward Castradon, is there anyone else you can think of who strikes you as a little bit odd? This is just between the three of us,' he added hastily to cut short Arthur's protests.

'I can't think of anyone who strikes me as that crazy,' said Arthur.

'Sir Matthew Vardon's grandfather had to be locked up,' said Isabelle. 'He was as nutty as a fruit cake, by all accounts.'

'Yes, darling, but he's been dead for about fifty years,' said Arthur patiently.

'I *know*. I was just thinking out loud.' Isabelle frowned. 'Jerry Lucas – that's Dr Lucas's son – has seemed very nervy lately. He used to be such a pleasant man but he's been terribly broody for ages. Twitchy, you know?'

Arthur shook his head. 'Jerry Lucas wouldn't

be involved in anything like this, poor chap. He's a bag of nerves.'

'Have there been any other odd events? Particularly anything to do with Ryle. I'm trying to work out possible connections.'

'There is something,' said Arthur after a few moments' thought. 'Aunt Catherine never liked the Vardons, as I said, but she always kept on good terms with them.'

'She told me about Sir Matthew's grandfather,' put in Isabelle. 'He was *dangerous*.'

'And dead,' said Arthur with an impatient sigh. 'When Aunt Catherine heard of Sir Matthew's condition, she asked me to deliver her good wishes to Lady Vardon. When I called at the house, Dr Lucas was with Sir Matthew and Lady Vardon and I was shown into the morning room to wait. The window looks over the back of the house. I heard Dr Lucas leave, so I was surprised to see him walk past. He'd gone out of the front door, you see, and so must have deliberately gone round to the back. He stopped by the outbuildings and waited. Ryle came out of the garage. They were friendly enough at first, then Ryle flared up and started shouting. I don't know what was said, but I did catch something about the war. Lucas was really jumpy and kept looking around as if he were nervous about being seen. He was obviously unhappy, but seemed to give in. Ryle calmed down and looked very pleased with himself. I couldn't understand it.'

Jack whistled slowly. 'Dr Lucas and Ryle, eh? That's a link I'd have never suspected. What happened then?'

'Nothing, as far as I know,' said Arthur with a shrug. 'Lady Vardon came into the morning room, so I had to speak to her.'

'Ryle was shouting about the war?' asked Jack with a frown. 'Dr Lucas wasn't in the war, was he?'

'No, he wasn't. He's been in practice here for a good few years. I like old Lucas. He's a bit pompous but I like him. You haven't met him yet, have you?'

'Not yet. Ryle's name seems to keep cropping up, doesn't it? I'll have a word with your Mrs Jarvis before I meet Ashley.'

'Are you driving to the village, Jack?' asked Isabelle. 'You can give me a lift if you are. There's a Ladies' Aid meeting in the Vicarage.'

'Mrs Dyson won't expect you, surely, Isabelle?' asked Arthur.

'I'd like to go. I'd like to feel that everything was as normal as it possibly can be.'

'If you're sure,' said Arthur dubiously. 'Do you want me to come?'

'It's ladies only,' she said with a smile. 'You'd be very out of place.'

After the meal was over, Isabelle took Jack into the kitchen. Mrs Jarvis was sitting down, keeping a watchful eye on Mabel who was washing up. Mabel was obviously not sorry to have this break in their routine.

'Major Haldean wants to know about Ryle,' said Isabelle. 'I'll leave you to it, Jack. I want to get ready to go out.'

'I think the mistress is doing too much,' said

93

Mrs Jarvis, when Isabelle had left the kitchen. 'There's not many who'd be up and about after a nasty shock like she had this morning.'

Mabel turned away from the sink and dried her hands on a roller towel. 'You told her, didn't you, Mrs Jarvis? You said she should be resting and the doctor sent for, but she wouldn't hear of it.'

'I did,' agreed Mrs Jarvis repressively. 'Not that it's any concern of yours, girl. All the mistress was really concerned about,' she added with a reproving glare at Jack, 'was seeing everything was shipshape for you coming, sir. I told her she shouldn't be thinking of guests, not after what she's been through.'

'It's very kind of her,' said Jack in mild embarrassment. 'I'm very grateful for the trouble everyone's taken,' he added tactfully, including Mrs Jarvis and Mabel with a smile.

His evident sincerity had its effect. 'I'm sure I like to oblige when I can,' said Mrs Jarvis, mollified. 'Excuse me, sir, did the mistress say you wanted to know about Jonathan Ryle?'

'That's right. I keep on hearing various stories about him, such as his fight on Sunday night, and I wanted to find out more.'

Mrs Jarvis pursed her lips disapprovingly. 'In my opinion he's a wrong 'un, if ever there was. He worked for Mr and Mrs Castradon when he first came to the village, but that didn't last long. Everyone's saying as how Mr Castradon shouldn't have been fighting with him on Sunday, but what I say is, what about Ryle? You mark my words, he started it.'

'He started a lot of trouble, Ryle did,' put in

94

Mabel, a sharp-looking girl of about sixteen. 'My mum told me to be careful of him.'

'Your mum told you right, my girl,' agreed Mrs Jarvis. 'I won't hear a word against Mr Castradon, for all everyone was saying he was to blame. He's a good man, Mr Castradon is. He was that kind to our Albert, when Albert had a bit of trouble with the police over those roofing tiles and he said he didn't do it and Mr Castradon knew he didn't do it, and wouldn't charge him a penny piece for proving he didn't do it, and Albert was that grateful. He's been good to a few like that, has Mr Castradon.'

'He's got a right temper, though,' said Mabel dubiously. 'I've heard stories.'

'True,' agreed Mrs Jarvis, with pursed lips. 'But there's worse things.'

'What stories?' asked Jack curiously.

'Well, sir,' said Mabel, with a glance at Mrs Jarvis for support. 'It was all round the village earlier this week about the set-to he had with Mr Vardon when Mr Vardon came into his office, wasn't it?'

Mrs Jarvis took over. 'Bessie Quinn – she's the office girl – couldn't think how Mr Vardon had got in there. It was a mystery, that was, and, even though he had good cause, Mr Castradon took on dreadful, both with Mr Vardon and the staff. Him and Mr Vardon had *words*. It worried Bessie. "Get out and never darken my door again!" shouted Mr Castradon, at the top of his voice.'

Jack grinned. 'Was that exactly what he said?'

'Well, something like that,' amended Mrs Jarvis.

'Have you any idea where Ryle is now?' asked Jack.

Mrs Jarvis and Mabel looked at each other and shrugged. 'I don't think anyone's seen him for a good few days,' said Mrs Jarvis. 'Mind you, he's probably lying low after that leathering that Mr Castradon gave him, but I'd have expected to have seen something of him.'

'Would you recognize him?' asked Jack, 'If you couldn't see his face, I mean?'

Mrs Jarvis gazed at him in bewilderment. 'I don't see how I could, sir, do you? It sounds a right old guessing game, that does.'

'Did Ryle have any special friends?' continued Jack. 'Any particular cronies?'

'Not him,' put in Mabel. 'He thought himself above the likes of us.'

'That's right,' said Mrs Jarvis, put out by Mabel's interruption. 'Not that it's your place to say it, young lady. He was always so hoity-toity, very proud of himself he was, working for Sir Matthew Vardon. He thought himself a cut above everyone round here. Country bumpkins he used to call us.' She sniffed loudly. 'Downright cheek, I call it. He came from London and gave himself no end of airs and graces on the strength of it. As I said, it was Mr Castradon who brought him here. You could ask him about Ryle.'

'Why d'you want to know about Ryle anyway?' asked Mabel curiously.

'Be quiet, girl,' said Mrs Jarvis, shocked. 'It's none of your business what the Major's asking questions for. The Major finds out things about nasty crimes and goings-on, don't you, sir? I've heard the mistress talk about it many a time.'

Mabel's eyes widened. 'Are you finding out

about the man with his head battered in what was murdered in church?'

'I'm hoping to find out something,' said Jack.

'And is that why you want to know about Ryle?' asked Mabel breathlessly, then stopped, her eyes growing, if possible, rounder. 'It is, isn't it? That's why you asked if we'd recognize him if we couldn't see his face. That's because he's been all bashed up, isn't it? It's Ryle. I know it's Ryle. My mum always said he'd come to a bad end.'

'Be hushed,' began Mrs Jarvis once more but Mabel wouldn't be hushed. 'It is him, isn't it? He's not been seen for a week. He's the man, isn't he? This'll be in the papers, won't it, sir? He's been hideously *murdered.*'

'It's too early to tell,' said Jack, but Mabel hardly heard him.

'Murdered,' she repeated with rich if ghoulish enjoyment. 'Ryle's been hideously *murdered.* Wait till I tell Mum!'

Seven

Jack parked the Spyker outside the Vicarage and helped Isabelle down from the car. As he did so, a well-dressed woman opened the gate of the adjacent house.

'Hello, Sue,' said Isabelle. 'Are you coming to the meeting too?'

Jack uttered a silent *Wow.* So this was Sue Castradon. Isabelle had said she was striking, but

97

good grief, she wasn't just striking, she was gorgeous. Unconsciously, he adjusted his tie and pulled his jacket straight. She had pale gold – almost silver – hair and luminous grey eyes. The words *elfin* and *ethereal* came to mind. She was so slight and her colouring so translucent, that there really did seem something otherworldly about her.

'This is my cousin, Jack Haldean,' said Isabelle.

'Isabelle said she was going to ask you to stay, Mr Haldean,' said Sue. 'She said you're good at working out problems. I don't suppose you've got anywhere, have you?'

Her voice was as lovely as she was. She really was a stunner. He wanted to say something memorable and devastatingly witty, but all he could think of was: 'Not yet, Mrs Castradon, but it's early days,' which was hardly worth saying. He tried to make up for the banality of his words with a dazzling smile and a look which betokened enthralled interest when, rather to his chagrin, she turned her head, distracted, as a tall, clean-shaven, brown-haired man came out of the Vicarage gate.

'Hello, Mr Vardon,' she said in surprise.

For a moment Jack, still kicking himself for not making a better first impression, didn't take in the import of what she said. Vardon? The man who there'd been all the gossip about? He was a good-looking beggar, thought Jack, with an alert, intelligent face and vivid blue eyes. If he'd been attentive to Sue Castradon, he wasn't surprised there'd been talk.

Then he realized there was something wrong.

98

Sue Castradon stopped in embarrassed confusion, the colour mounting in her cheeks as the man looked at her blankly.

He raised his hat politely and looked at her with a well-bred stare of puzzlement. 'Excuse me,' he said, 'but I don't think we've met.' He smiled in undisguised admiration. 'I'm sure I would have remembered you.'

'I'm sorry,' said Sue, flustered. 'I really am awfully sorry. I thought you were Mr Vardon.'

The stranger laughed. 'But I am. Or I was, until recently. I think you must have met my brother. I'm Tom Vardon. Everyone says we look very alike, although I can never see it myself. Did you want to see him? He should be here in a couple of days, Miss . . .?'

'It's Mrs,' said Sue. 'Mrs Castradon.' Jack was privately, if uncharitably, amused to see Thomas Vardon's face fall. 'I saw your brother at your father's . . .' She broke off once more in embarrassment. 'At your father's . . .'

'At my father's funeral?' finished Thomas Vardon. 'I'm sorry I couldn't be there but I only arrived in Southampton this morning. Do you live in the village?'

'Yes,' hurried on Sue, obviously glad to have the conversation steered away from the perhaps delicate subject of his father's funeral. 'Yes, I do. We – that's my husband, Ned and myself – were going to invite you and your wife round for cocktails or dinner.'

'That's very kind of you,' said Sir Thomas, 'but my wife won't be arriving for a few days. She's working on a picture and couldn't get away.

99

Excuse me for mentioning it, Mrs Castradon, but I've just spoken to the vicar. You are the lady who discovered the man in the church this morning?'

Sue nodded. 'That's right. And this is Mrs Stanton, who was there with me.' She rapidly completed the introductions.

'It must have been a horrible discovery, Mrs Castradon,' said Thomas sympathetically.

His sympathy, Jack thought, seemed to be directed chiefly towards Sue Castradon. Isabelle, he noticed, had spotted that as well.

'As a matter of fact,' continued Thomas, 'I want to call on the police. Is the station still across the green?'

'Yes, it is,' said Jack. 'I'm going there now.'

With a promise to Isabelle to pick her up after the meeting, ('We'll probably be at the Castradons,') Jack and Thomas Vardon walked off.

Isabelle stood by the Vicarage gate and gave a toss of her head. 'Well! So that's Thomas Vardon.'

'I don't know what he must have thought of me, saying hello like that, and him a perfect stranger, too,' said Sue. 'Then mentioning his father's funeral right away. It was so tactless of me. He doesn't really look that much like his brother, either. Not close to.'

'Don't you think so? I thought they were very alike. He's darker, of course.'

'I thought he was awfully nice.'

'Did you?' said Isabelle, opening the gate. She had enough self-awareness to realize she wasn't used to being quite so thoroughly overlooked and was slightly piqued at the experience.

100

Isabelle tried hard to be fair. It was very petty minded to object to the effect Sue had on men. Look at the way Jack had goggled at her, eyes wide and straightening his tie, the idiot. She was prepared to bet large sums of money that, just for the moment, his beloved Betty couldn't have been further from his thoughts. Sue hadn't noticed. She never did notice.

Thomas Vardon, the handsome Thomas Vardon, had certainly noticed Sue, though, and, as they walked up the garden path to the Vicarage together, Isabelle spared an uneasy thought for Ned Castradon. She hoped there wasn't trouble in store.

'I wouldn't have expected Mrs Castradon to be out and about after her experience this morning,' said Thomas Vardon, as they walked across the green. 'She must be a plucky girl.'

'She must,' agreed Jack. 'So's Isabelle. Mrs Stanton, I mean.'

'Yeah,' said Thomas absently, clearly not remotely moved by Isabelle's fortitude. 'I don't know how she'd photograph.' He obviously wasn't talking about Isabelle. 'Film probably wouldn't do her justice. It'd be difficult to catch that colouring but I'd love to try.' He laughed. 'I can't imagine a girl like that in Hollywood, though. She's too much of a lady. Hollywood calls for a different kind of toughness. Not,' he added, 'the kind that's to be admired.'

'Are you planning to stay in England?' asked Jack. He, too, had spared a thought for Ned Castradon.

'Eh?' said Thomas, recalling himself. 'It depends. I must get the estate sorted out. There's precious little in it, but it needs work.' His voice took on a cynical note. 'My wife, Esmé, wants to live here. She fancies being a real English lady. We'll have to see how it goes. I could make quite a good thing of being a commission agent. There's plenty of people in the movie business who'd pay to use real English locations, but don't know how to find them. I've got the contacts, of course, both here and in Hollywood. I'll have to see how Esmé settles in.'

At least he remembered he's got a wife, thought Jack. 'Is she arriving soon?'

'In about a week.' He half laughed. 'She was looking forward to quiet English life as the lady of the manor. So was I. The quiet part, at any event.'

He stopped and looked around him. The village green in the hazy evening sunshine, bordered by the quietly gurgling Croxton Brook seemed the epitome of peace. Geese waddled along the bank of the stream, pecking at the scrubby grass. A horse and cart slowly clopped over the little humpbacked bridge, the carter hardly needing to hold the reins. A group of boys were playing cricket with a homemade bat, an old tennis ball and a propped up dustbin lid for their wicket, their shouts and laughter softened by distance. Outside the Red Lion, three elderly men sat on a bench, under the shade of a spreading oak tree, pulling contentedly at their long churchwarden pipes and nursing half pints of bitter.

Sir Thomas gave an appreciative sigh. 'I missed this in America. This is what I thought of when

I thought of home. I've been promising myself a pint of home-brewed beer in the Red Lion all the way across the Atlantic, but when I arrived off the train from Southampton I seemed to have stepped straight into the pages of a dime novel.'

He shrugged his shoulders expressively. 'It seemed so unbelievable that I thought my step-mother must be exaggerating, but I owe her an apology. I'd just been to see the vicar, Mr Dyson, to see if it could possibly be true. I gather it is.'

They walked into the police station together. Croxton Ferriers police station, marked out by the blue lamp above the front door, was the front room of Constable Stock's house. Constable Stock himself had been relegated to the nether regions of the tiny sitting room and kitchen, from which issued a smell of frying onions.

Ashley, sitting at the desk, pipe in one hand and pen in the other, glanced up enquiringly.

Jack introduced them and, ejecting the station cat, Ashley pulled out a chair for Sir Thomas. 'You wanted to see me, sir? If it's anything routine, can I refer you to Constable Stock? You'll understand if I say I've got my hands full with this murder.'

'Murder,' repeated Thomas Vardon thoughtfully.

'Do you know anything about it?' asked Ashley sharply.

Thomas Vardon shook his head. 'No, this is something else altogether. It's certainly not routine, though. It's a crime. Or I think it is.' He smiled apologetically. 'It sounds a bit melodramatic, but it might even be murder.'

Ashley paused as he sat down, staring at Sir Thomas. 'Can you explain yourself, sir?'

Thomas ran his thumb round the angle of his jaw. 'I'm not sure where to begin. As you know, my father, Sir Matthew Vardon, died.' He hesitated. 'I don't suppose there were any doubts raised at the time, were there? About it being a natural death, I mean?'

Jack felt the hairs on the back of his neck prickle.

'There's been nothing said to my knowledge,' said Ashley. 'Mind you, I don't know if anything's been said in the village.'

'As a matter of fact, Ashley, there have been rumours,' put in Jack. 'Isabelle – that's Mrs Stanton, Sir Thomas – told me as much at dinner. Both she and her husband thought it was nothing more than ill-natured gossip.'

Ashley tapped his pen thoughtfully on the desk. 'Rumours, eh? Well, all I can say, Sir Thomas, was that nothing was reported officially. His medical attendant ought to be able to reassure you. Who was his doctor?'

'He had the local man, Dr Lucas. I was going to call on him, too.'

'You must have a reason for asking,' said Jack. 'Apart from these rumours, have you any reason to suspect it was anything other than a natural death?'

Thomas Vardon nodded. 'Yes, I have. As a matter of fact, I hadn't heard any rumours. My stepmother obviously doesn't know about them either, or I'm sure she would've mentioned them. No, it's something else entirely.'

From his inside jacket pocket he took out two letters and put them on the desk.

'Before my father died, he received these letters. As you can see from the postmark, they're posted locally.'

Pushing them across the desk, he tapped the uppermost. 'That's the first one. The second arrived a week later.'

Ashley picked up the envelope. The name and address was typed, as were the contents. The letter consisted of one typed line. '"You have been tried in the balance and found wanting. You will die. The Chessman." Good grief!'

Jack drew his breath in. He remembered reaching into that cupboard in the church and pulling out a chess piece. A black knight. A chessman.

Ashley's eyes met his. From his expression, he'd obviously made the connection too. He reached forward and picked up the second letter.

'"I am killing you slowly. You are going to die. The Chessman."'

Sir Thomas looked at them both.

'My stepmother showed those letters – the second one, at least – to the doctor. He told her that they must be the work of some nasty minded individual, some crank who made a practice of writing such things. He advised her to chuck them in the fire.'

'I'm glad she didn't,' said Ashley thoughtfully.

'Excuse me for asking,' said Jack with apparent guilelessness, 'but what do you think of the doctor's theory, Sir Thomas?' He had Arthur's strictures on Sir Matthew Vardon firmly in mind, but wanted to see what his son would say. 'Do you think they're the work of a crank or do you think there's more to it than that? Remember, we didn't know your father. Was he the sort of man who would have an enemy? An enemy who would wish him real harm?'

'Undoubtedly,' said Thomas with a short laugh. 'Look, I don't want to speak ill of the dead. He was my father after all, when all's said and done, but he was not a nice man. It's chiefly because of him that I went to America after the war. I certainly didn't want to come home. My brother, Simon, perhaps got on with him better than I did, but even he knew enough to be careful.'

'Careful?' questioned Jack. It seemed an odd word to use.

'Careful. He would find out anyone's weak spot and exploit it ruthlessly. You really did have to be on your guard with him. He had enemies, all right.'

'Let me get this straight, Sir Thomas,' said Ashley. 'What you're actually asking is if there's any truth in these letters? If the Chessman, whoever he is, could have killed your father?'

'I suppose I am,' said Thomas slowly. 'That's why I wanted to see Dr Lucas. I wanted to know if there was any doubt in his mind that my father died of natural causes. I believe he called in a second opinion, a Dr Jacob McNiece of Harley Street.'

'Dr Lucas must have signed the death certificate,' said Jack. 'If there really was any doubt in his mind, he should've applied to the coroner.'

Ashley shook his head. 'That doesn't always follow, Haldean. A coroner's inquest can be very upsetting for the family. The doctor might be uneasy, but doesn't want to rock the boat on the grounds of mere suspicion. Unless he's certain, a doctor has to be cautious, otherwise his career will be ruined. No one wants to call in a doctor who shouts foul without very good cause.'

He pulled the letters towards him and studied them for a few moments, drawing thoughtfully on his pipe. 'I'll have a word with Dr Lucas, if you like, Sir Thomas. I've got to see him anyway. Rumours or no rumours, these letters need explaining.' He cocked an eyebrow at Jack. 'I don't suppose they suggest anything to you, do they?'

Jack slewed the letters round on the desk. 'Judging by their appearance, they've been well handled. I doubt you'll get any fingerprints off them, Ashley. The paper's Basildon Bond, ordinary letter paper, which you can buy at any stationer. And the typewriter is, I'd say, a Bartlett or a similar machine. It's got a slipping 'e' and an elevated 'd' and the ribbon could do with changing.' He glanced at Ashley. 'I had a Bartlet once. They're small, lightweight machines. It's not a commercial typewriter. Offices tend to use big machines such as Remingtons or Olympias, which means whoever typed these probably typed them at home.'

'There was another piece of mail addressed to my father,' said Thomas. He reached in his pocket and took out a small square cardboard box. 'My stepmother has thrown away the original wrapping, but it arrived some time ago, after the funeral.'

He opened the box. Inside, on a bed of cotton wool, was a chessman. A black king, made of marble with crystal eyes. Jack heard Ashley's smothered grunt of recognition. It was obviously from the same set as the chess piece they'd found in the cupboard in St Luke's.

'I don't like this, Haldean,' muttered Ashley.

It was, thought Jack, downright creepy.

Thomas looked at Ashley. 'I don't like it either,' Thomas said grimly. 'Especially when I tell you this was waiting for me when I arrived today.'

He took out another letter with a typed envelope and pushed it across the desk. It was addressed to Sir Thomas Vardon and had been posted in Croxton Ferriers three days ago. 'Read that. It's from the Chessman.'

Ashley whistled. 'Are you the only person to have handled this letter, Sir Thomas?'

Sir Thomas nodded.

'Then we might get some prints off it.' Ashley took a pair of tweezers from his bag and, extracting the letter, laid it open on the table with care.

As before, the letter was typed on a machine with a slipping "e" and an elevated "d".

Ashley read it aloud. '"A short life and a merry one? Make it merry. It will certainly be short. I'm saving you until the end. The Chessman." Good grief,' he said again, his lip curling in disgust. 'This bloke must be deranged.'

'Are there any fingerprints on it?' demanded Thomas.

108

'Let's see.' Ashley took a bottle of grey mercury powder from his bag and dusted both the surface of the letter and the chessman and its box.

'Well, there are prints,' he said, looking at them through a magnifying glass, 'but I'd say they all belong to the same person. Let me have your fingerprints for comparison, Sir Thomas.'

Thomas Vardon obligingly pressed his fingers first on an ink pad, then on a card.

'Yes, they're yours,' said Ashley, after a brief examination. 'There's nothing there, unfortunately. Whoever typed this is a careful beggar.'

Jack examined the envelope. 'Did you notice this was posted on Tuesday, Ashley?'

'What's special about Tuesday?' asked Thomas, wiping his hands on the cloth Ashley had given him.

'Nothing, sir,' said Ashley blandly. 'It was just an observation. Will you leave the letters and the chess piece with us, sir? I'd like to investigate this matter further. And thank you for bringing it to our attention.'

Thomas Vardon stood up to leave. As he picked up his hat, he hesitated. 'Look,' he said awkwardly, 'I don't want you to think I'm losing my nerve, but I must say those letters have worried me.'

'You leave things with us, sir,' said Ashley reassuringly. 'I may say that anonymous letters are fairly common in cases of this sort. Try not to worry about it unduly, but if you do happen to receive any more letters, or hear of anyone else who does, let me know right away. Can I ask you what your plans are for the next few days?'

'My immediate plan is to see if the Red Lion still serves as good a pint of home-brewed as I remember,' said Thomas with a smile. 'Other than that, I'll be living at the Manor for the next few weeks at least.' His smile faded. 'You'll let me know if you find out more about those letters, won't you?'

'Don't you worry, sir,' said Ashley as he ushered Sir Thomas out of the door. 'You enjoy your pint and don't let this prey on your mind.'

He came back to the desk to find Jack holding the black knight and the black king.

'They're from the same set,' Jack said, placing them on the desk. 'I know you told Thomas Vardon anonymous letters are commonplace, but this seems a little out of the way to me.'

'I had to reassure him somehow,' said Ashley. 'I don't mind telling you, though, that those letters and the chess pieces made a very nasty impression on me. I think we're dealing with a criminal lunatic, but I hardly wanted to tell Sir Thomas that's what he's come home to.'

'No. Especially when he's been told he's in the firing line. So who's next?' Jack demanded.

Ashley's eyebrows crawled upwards. 'Who's next? You want another murder?'

'*Want* is the wrong word,' complained Jack. 'You make me sound ghoulish. *Expect* is, perhaps, better. After all, Thomas Vardon's letter said he was being saved until last. That implies there's more to come.'

'Oh, my God.' Ashley stood stock still, then shook himself. 'Come on, Haldean. We've got to get to the bottom of this. What have we got?'

'Well, to take the events in order, we've also

got two letters from the Chessman to Sir Matthew, threatening murder. Incidentally, the rumour I mentioned originates with a Nurse Pargetter who was Sir Matthew Vardon's nurse. What it amounts to is that Dr Lucas didn't seem exactly heart-broken that his patient failed to recover.'

'I'll bear that in mind,' said Ashley, 'but it doesn't seem much. These letters, on the other hand, and the chess piece that Lady Vardon received, are solid evidence.'

Jack picked up the black king and weighed it thoughtfully in his hand. 'It seems bizarre, doesn't it? We have to take it seriously though, because whoever killed the poor devil in the church is obviously very serious indeed.'

'We know that on Tuesday, the day of the murder, the killer posted a letter to Sir Thomas. Why, Haldean? Why would the killer warn his intended victim?'

'Terror, I suppose,' said Jack. 'I can't think of any other reason. Leaving aside murder committed on the spur of the moment, which this obviously isn't, a murderer who wants to gain something will keep his plans very quiet. However, a murderer who kills for hate or revenge would enjoy seeing his victims squirm.'

Ashley blinked. 'Blimey, Haldean, you're making my flesh creep.'

'Was Sir Thomas worried, would you say?' demanded Jack.

'Of course he was. Anyone would be.'

'And if he knew we'd found a chessman at the scene of that revolting murder this morning? What would his reaction be then?'

'He wouldn't be human if he wasn't scared stiff.'

'Exactly.'

'But who the blazes is this man?'

'He has to be local,' said Jack. 'The body in the church tells us that and, if I'm right about the killer wanting to watch Sir Thomas sweat things out, he'd have to be on the spot to see it.'

'All right, I'll grant he's a local. That's what I thought anyway. But why on earth should he want to kill Sir Thomas? He's lived in America since the war. He can't have any enemies here. He's not been around to make any.'

'No . . .' Jack leaned back in his chair and lit a cigarette. 'We'll know more when we can identify the victim in the church,' he said eventually.

Ashley rolled his eyes upwards. 'Well, I could've told you that.'

'Yes, but who is the poor beggar? I'd guess he has to be some connection of the Vardons. I talked to Isabelle's servants, her cook, Mrs Jarvis, and a very sharp kid called Mabel. Mabel leapt to the conclusion that the victim was Jonathan Ryle. I'm willing to bet,' he added with an apologetic grin, 'that's all round the village by now. Mabel isn't one to keep her opinions to herself.'

'Nothing on earth will stop women talking,' said Ashley morosely. 'Jonathan Ryle, eh? It could be, I suppose. And if it is Ryle, then, to my mind, Edward Castradon is the obvious suspect. He had a fight with Ryle and threatened to kill him, and putting the body in the church can be explained by his quarrel with Mr Dyson. He certainly wasn't best pleased that the vicar intervened.'

'Apparently he's a chess fiend as well,' said Jack absently. 'Dr Lucas is a possible, too.'

'Dr Lucas?' repeated Ashley in surprise. 'You're not thinking about the rumours Nurse Whatsername started, are you?'

'Partly. What's really bothering me though, is that Arthur saw Dr Lucas and Ryle meeting in what you could call a furtive sort of way.'

Ashley looked a question. Jack told him what Arthur had seen. 'And Ryle,' he finished, 'definitely had the upper hand.'

'Ryle,' commented Ashley, 'seems to have annoyed a good few people. But look here, Haldean. I know Ryle was connected with the Vardons. He was their chauffeur, but surely that's not nearly enough by any stretch of the imagination. If the victim is Ryle, it doesn't square with this theory that Sir Matthew Vardon was murdered.'

'No . . .' Jack smoked his cigarette down to the butt and stubbed it out. 'Ashley, let's go and hunt up Sir Thomas. I want to catch him before he leaves the pub. If there are any photographs of Ryle, they'll be at the house. I have a feeling that a photograph of Ryle might be very useful.'

'A photograph of the chauffeur?' said Sir Thomas in surprise. He drained the remains of his bitter and put the tankard on the table. 'My word, that tasted good. I suppose there might be a photo somewhere, although I can't see why my father or my stepmother should keep pictures of the servants.'

'What sort of car did your father have?' asked Jack. 'If he had a chauffeur he must've had a car.'

'He had a Lanchester 21. He picked it up a

113

couple of months ago. He was very proud of it. I prefer something a bit more sporty.' He grinned. 'That Spyker of yours looks pretty good.'

'Thanks,' said Jack. 'To go back to your father's car, if it was fairly new, then he might have a photograph of it.'

Thomas put his head to one side thoughtfully. 'As a matter of fact, that rings a bell. Yes, dammit, you're right. It's on the hall table. I hadn't really noticed it but I'm sure it's there. I can let you have it tomorrow.'

'Could we have a look at it now?' asked Jack. 'I'm sorry to rush you, but it might be important. My car's outside the Vicarage. It won't take long.'

With a certain amount of reluctance Sir Thomas let himself be escorted out of the Red Lion.

Ten minutes or so later they were in the hall of the Manor. There were a few photographs on the table, but it was easy to find the one they wanted. It was a large print in a modern silver frame. The Lanchester, its hood down, was drawn up in front of the house beside the steps sweeping down to the drive. The photograph reeked opulence. Sir Matthew, a big, handsome man, reclined in the back of the car, his top hat pushed to the back of his head. His astrakhan collared coat was open to show the silk lining, and the hand that was negligently draped over the door held a fat cigar. Beside him the chauffeur, in his cap and coat, stood stiffly to attention.

Jack picked up the photo and examined it closely.

'That's my father,' said Sir Thomas, looking at the photograph over Jack's shoulder. 'He looks pretty pleased with himself, doesn't he?'

Ashley took a magnifying glass out of his bag and, taking the photograph from Jack, looked at it through the lens. He glanced from Thomas Vardon to the face in the photo. 'I can see he's your father, sir. There's a very striking resemblance.'

'Yes, both my brother and I take after him in appearance, if not in character, I hope.'

'And this is Ryle,' muttered Ashley, turning the lens on the chauffeur.

'He's worth a second look,' said Jack meaningfully.

Ashley glanced up, puzzled, then studied the photo again. 'Good God!'

'You've seen it, Ashley?' asked Jack.

'It's unmistakable, now you've pointed it out. Well, I'll be damned.'

'Excuse me,' said Thomas with understandable sharpness. 'What on earth are you talking about?'

Ashley thrust the magnifying glass and the photo into Sir Thomas's hands. 'Take a look for yourself, sir. Look at the chauffeur's face.'

Puzzled, Thomas looked carefully at the picture and then stiffened. 'My God,' he breathed. 'This guy Ryle is my father's son.'

Eight

'You knew,' said Ashley as they drove back to the village. 'I'm blowed if I know how you knew, but you knew.'

'It was a lucky guess, really,' said Jack. 'We

were looking for a connection of the Vardons and, in view of Sir Matthew's reputation, I thought it was possible. Thomas Vardon didn't have any difficulty believing it, did he?'

'None whatsoever. D'you know, I can feel sorry for Lady Vardon. Apparently she's not much liked, but I feel sorry for her all the same.'

'Having said that, Sir Thomas didn't think his stepmother had guessed the real state of things. She can't be a very observant woman.'

Ashley shrugged. 'To be fair to her, it doesn't seem to have occurred to anyone. Sir Matthew was a big, well-built man and Ryle wasn't. I imagine it's one of those likenesses which are much easier to spot in a photograph than in real life. After all, when you look at a photo, all you're looking at is the face. That's not the case when you actually meet someone.'

'You're probably right,' agreed Jack. 'So what now, Ashley? The idea that there's a connection between the Chessman and the Vardons seems tenable, at least.'

'It certainly does. It also seems tenable that our victim really is Ryle. We have to identify that body.' He glanced at his watch. 'It's nearly half past eight. Dr Lucas won't have the post-mortem results for me until tomorrow, but I think it's about time we called on Edward Castradon.'

As the doorbell jangled for the second time, Ned Castradon flung down his pen and swore under his breath. Rusty, the elderly springer spaniel, who had been asleep at his feet, raised his head, looked at his master, and woofed impatiently.

116

'Quiet, boy,' muttered Castradon. Where the devil was the maid? Blast that girl! Couldn't she hear the damn doorbell? He'd have to get Sue to speak to her again. Why wasn't Sue here? After the shock she'd had, the last thing he'd expect her to do was to go gallivanting off to meetings, even if they were only next door.

With a guilty start he remembered the last thing she'd said to him was that it was Friday night, Rose's night off, and he'd have to answer the door.

He pushed his chair back and, with Rusty at his heels, strode into the hall.

He should've remembered it was Rose's night off. He really had forgotten. He seemed to forget things so easily these days. He hadn't told Sue, but it worried him. Appointments, meetings, things people had said . . . He'd managed to get away with it so far. No one wanted a legal advisor who couldn't remember where they were supposed to be and what they were supposed to be doing. He didn't think anyone had noticed so far – he was good at covering up his lapses – but it worried him.

He opened the door to find Superintendent Ashley and that cousin of Isabelle Stanton's, Jack Haldean, on the doorstep. His insides twisted. Rusty, with the odd telepathy of dogs, picked up his master's feelings and growled faintly.

'Quiet, boy,' Ned said once more. They must be here about the business in the church. He shrank from the thought of answering a whole raft of questions about times and dates and who had seen who and when. It had been a long day but he forced himself to be friendly.

'Superintendent Ashley? If it's my wife you're

117

after, I'm afraid she's attending a meeting in the Vicarage.'

He hoped it was Sue they wanted to see. If it was, he could say that it was getting late, she would be too tired to answer any questions when she got home, and put the whole miserable business off until tomorrow.

'It's not Mrs Castradon but my cousin, Mrs Stanton, I'm looking for,' said Jack. 'I promised to give her a lift home after the meeting. I'm Jack Haldean. I'm staying with the Stantons.'

Ned brightened. That sounded as if the call might be at least partly social. He didn't mind that so much and maybe Haldean – he wasn't a professional policeman after all – would be able to tell him if they'd discovered anything. He was curious about that.

Superintendent Ashley coughed. 'We were hoping to ask you a few questions, too, sir.' He smiled reassuringly. 'Nothing too searching. It's mainly verifications of times and so on and information we've gathered from your neighbours.'

Ned's spirits sank. So it was official, after all. He stepped back, inviting them into the hall. If he had to be grilled, he might as well do it with as good a grace as possible. 'You're welcome to come in and wait.' He clicked his tongue for the dog to follow. 'I'm expecting Sue back any time now.'

Ashley and Jack followed Ned down the hall and into the sitting room, Rusty waddling behind them.

'This is very kind of you, sir,' said Ashley.

'Not at all, Superintendent. However, you'll excuse me if I say it's been a very long day.' He walked over to the sideboard. 'Please sit down, won't you? Can I get you a drink or is this strictly an official visit?'

'I'd very much appreciate a whisky and soda, sir,' said Ashley.

'And the same for me, Castradon,' said Jack. 'Thank you very much.'

The sitting room was a bright room, painted in cream and sage green. A bowl of red carnations stood on the sideboard, a bookcase filled one alcove and pictures of country scenes hung on the walls. It was a room to relax in, made hospitably untidy by an upturned book on a small table, a newspaper on the sofa, a few records stacked on their side against the radiogram and cushions placed with regard to comfort rather than precision.

A chess set, with a game obviously in progress, stood on a green baize card table, with a newspaper folded back on itself beside it. Lots of people play chess, Jack told himself, but even so, the innocent game pieces seemed to strike a sinister note.

'Do you play chess?' he asked casually.

'Yes,' said Castradon pouring out the drinks. 'I prefer it to bridge. Sue doesn't play, but I tackle the chess problems in the paper and there's a chess club in the Red Lion. We meet once a week. Do you play?'

'Not well enough to give an expert a run for their money, I'm afraid.'

'You should take it up properly.' He hadn't, Jack noted, argued with the implied description of himself as an expert. 'It's terrific mental exercise.'

Jack reached his hand out to the dog. Rusty, wary at first, sniffed his hand cautiously then gave him an approving lick, and settled down with his muzzle between his paws.

'He's a nice old boy,' said Jack, scratching the spaniel behind its floppy ears. Dogs, he thought, were a great way to break the ice. It worked. He could see Ned Castradon's shoulders relax.

'He's getting a bit stiff and creaky now, poor old beggar,' said Ned, handing Jack his whisky and soda. 'He's Sue's dog, really. Her father used to breed spaniels and he's the last of the line. Help yourself to cigarettes, by the way. They're in the box beside you.'

He took a cigarette for himself, then reached down and patted the dog affectionately. 'Look, talking of Sue, can we get the official part over before she returns? I'd rather not go into it all when she's here. She was pretty shaken up this morning.'

'I'm not surprised,' said Jack. 'It would've shaken anybody.'

Without seeming to, he looked carefully at his host. That Edward Castradon had once had a craggy charm was painfully obvious, for one side of his face was untouched, a brown eye showing under a dark brow. The other eye was covered by a patch and the skin running up to it was scarred and discoloured. He had a nervous habit of continually putting his hand to his face as if to cover his disfigurement.

Could he be capable of that horrific murder? It seemed unthinkable and yet, Jack reminded himself, the mere fact that no one had pointed to an obvious suspect meant, in a small village like this, that the murderer had to appear sane.

Ashley cleared his throat. 'There's a suggestion,

Mr Castradon, that the victim was a man called Ryle.'

Castradon looked at him in blank astonishment. '*Ryle?* Good God!' Here was one person at least who hadn't heard the jungle drums of village gossip, thought Jack. 'It can't be Ryle,' continued Castradon. 'He wasn't exactly popular, but to end up like that . . .' He shook his head in disbelief. 'It doesn't make sense. I could well imagine Ryle getting into trouble with a gang of toughs up in London, say, but nothing like this. Why on earth do you think it's Ryle?'

'No one's seen him for days,' said Jack. 'It's a little early to say yet, of course, but no other local man appears to be missing.'

'Why does it have to be a local man?' asked Ned, then stopped. 'I suppose you think only a local would be able to get in and out of the church?'

Jack nodded in agreement.

'That's probably right,' said Ned. 'Mr Dyson keeps the church locked up. I don't think you could get in without a key. But look here,' he added with a frown, 'surely that only means the murderer's a local man. The victim could be anyone.' He shook his head once more. 'I just can't believe it's Ryle. It seems so unlikely, somehow.'

'Ryle worked for you, didn't he, Mr Castradon?' asked Ashley. Ned nodded. 'You said you could imagine him getting into trouble in London. Do you happen to know if he'd ever run foul of the law?'

Ned shrugged. 'I honestly can't say. It wouldn't surprise me if he had. It wasn't the happiest of relationships, to say the least. In the end I had to give him the push. He always resented it.'

'Could you give us a few more details, Mr Castradon?' asked Ashley politely. 'I gather he was a Londoner. Did you know him before he came to work for you?'

'No,' said Ned with a sigh. 'I first came across him quite by chance. I thought at the time it was a lucky break.' His mouth twisted ironically. 'I didn't think it was nearly so lucky afterwards. It was about nine or ten months ago. I'd been to see a client who lives outside Cobden Heath. It's a remote piece of country and as the house is a couple of miles from the nearest train station, I'd decided to drive. As luck would have it, I broke down on the way home. There wasn't an AA scout or a telephone box anywhere in sight and I'm no great shakes as a mechanic. I'd just resigned myself to walking back to Cobden Heath to find a garage, when this chap Ryle happened along. To do him justice, he did know his way around a car, and he had it running in no time. He told me he'd been on the tramp down from London and was heading for this part of the world because he'd been in the Royal Sussex during the war and thought he might run in to some old friends who could do him a bit of good.'

'So he was in the army, was he?' said Ashley thoughtfully. 'I'll be able to look up his records. Go on, sir. Did he meet any old friends, do you know?'

'Not as far as I know. I got the impression that he had some family in the area, but I never heard of any subsequently.'

Jack and Ashley exchanged glances. It

obviously wasn't mere chance that had brought Ryle to Croxton Ferriers.

'Well, as you can imagine,' continued Ned, 'I was properly grateful that he'd fixed the car. We needed an odd-job man, so I offered him a billet. He lasted just over three weeks with me and was on dodgy ground most of the time.'

'What finally led to you giving him the push?' asked Jack.

'He was an arrogant beggar and upset the other servants. I suspected him of petty thieving, too, but I never actually caught him at it. What finally did it though was when I caught him kicking the dog.'

Jack, who had been reaching down to pat the spaniel, looked up sharply. 'Kicking the dog? Why? Surely this old boy wouldn't attack him?'

'I don't know what Rusty had done,' said Ned with a shrug. 'I've never known him go for anyone, but I saw Ryle from an upstairs window laying into the poor brute. I yelled for him to stop, charged downstairs and gave Ryle his marching orders on the spot. He had the cheek to ask me for a reference but I told him he was lucky to escape without a thrashing.'

'You did come to blows with him though, didn't you, Mr Castradon?' asked Ashley.

Castradon sighed deeply. 'You've done your homework, haven't you?'

'What was the cause of the quarrel, sir?' asked Ashley.

Castradon drew his breath in and drummed his fingers on the side of the chair. 'I'd better tell you,' he said at last. 'But I warn you, if Sue comes in, I won't say another word.'

He put a hand to his mouth. 'The truth is, it's damned embarrassing. Last Sunday evening I heard someone shouting at the front gate. I went out to see what the row was about, and it was Ryle. He'd obviously had a fair old bit to drink and was spoiling for a fight. Ryle said . . .' His mouth tightened. 'Ryle made the most offensive suggestions about Simon Vardon and my wife.'

He held up his hands as if to ward off criticism. 'I know I shouldn't have risen to it. He was drunk and I should've told him to go and sleep it off, but the fact is . . . Well, I was jealous,' he added in a rush. 'Sue had seen Simon Vardon at his father's funeral. The thing is, Simon Vardon is a very good-looking man. His brother's a film star or something and you could believe Simon Vardon's a film star, too, judging by his looks.'

Jack could see the resentment in Castradon's eyes. Good looks, he thought, were a sensitive subject.

'Not that,' Castradon added grimly, 'I'm one of his fans. There isn't any question about it, Sue noticed him.'

'Noticed him?' asked Jack with a lift of his eyebrow.

'That's all it was,' agreed Castradon wearily. 'It wouldn't have been so bad, but all the old cats in the village noticed it too. I know there's nothing wrong. Sue's as straight as a die. I know that, but I was needled. I knew there'd been talk and I hated it. I . . . I must have been pretty unbearable ever since the funeral and when Ryle turned up, wanting a fight, I was only too ready to square up to him. To cut a long story short, I lost my rag and took a swing at him. He's a cowardly little beggar and started yelling fit to bust. We were in the thick of it when old Dyson came charging down the path, forcibly wrenched us apart, and yelled at Ryle to run for it.'

He gave a shamefaced grin. 'It's just as well old Dyson did stick his nose in, I suppose, because I'd have murdered Ryle . . .'

He stopped abruptly. Jack and Ashley looked at him in silence.

'I didn't mean that,' said Castradon. 'Yes, I admit, I wanted to give him the thrashing of a lifetime, but that was in the heat of the moment.' He saw Ashley's expression and looked at him in bewilderment. 'You can't honestly think I'd lie in wait for him, carve him up and put him in the church for my wife to find? That's hideous. It's insane. It's a far cry from wanting to thump him.'

'Yes, it is,' agreed Jack. Castradon looked at him gratefully. 'What happened to Ryle after Mr Dyson intervened?' he asked. 'Did he make a run for it?'

'Eventually. There was a car parked across the road that he tried to make off with. He actually managed to get the engine started, but I made a grab for him, he was catapulted into the back, gave a scream like a banshee – I must admit I was trying my level best to scrag him – and went hurtling off down the road. That's the last I saw of him, and good riddance, too. Dyson and I broke off our argument to watch him go, said a few more home truths to each other, and it ended with me coming back in here and slamming the gate on him. I suppose you've had a colourful version of events from the Dysons, haven't you?'

'Mr Dyson was very reluctant to say anything at all about the matter,' said Ashley.

Castradon gave a twisted grin. 'Which means that Mrs Dyson wasn't so circumspect, I suppose.' He leaned back in his chair. 'He's not such a bad chap, old Dyson. I'd better go round and make my peace with him.'

'Simon Vardon came into your office, didn't he?' asked Jack, mindful of the conversation he'd had with Mrs Jarvis and Mabel. 'I gather it was a fairly stormy encounter. Was his visit related to your quarrel with Ryle, by any chance?'

'No, it damn well wasn't,' said Castradon shortly. 'Look, I don't know who you've talked to or what you've heard, but I never laid a finger on Simon Vardon, much as he deserved it. I sent him off with a flea in his ear. To hear him say what he did was more than I could stand. I always thought the world of my father.'

Ashley and Jack looked at each other, puzzled. 'I beg your pardon, sir?' said Ashley. 'How does your father come into it?'

'Vardon made certain accusations,' said Ned. 'My father was a great old boy, a fine man, and to have that swine Vardon say what he did . . .' He broke off broodingly. 'I don't want this to go any further,' he said abruptly. 'To cut a long story short, Simon Vardon was after some shares my father owned. He didn't make a proper appointment, but strolled into my office, cool as be damned. When I came in I found him with his feet on my desk. He'd sidled in without a word to my clerk, and made himself at home.'

126

'That must've been very annoying for you, sir,' said Ashley.

'Annoying? I'll say so. As I said, he wanted some shares my father had left me. I refused to sell and told him pretty curtly to get out.'

Jack flicked the ash off his cigarette. 'What shares were they?'

'Some old mining shares,' said Castradon with a shrug. 'To be honest, I'd virtually forgotten all about them. They've never returned a dividend as far as I know, but they were my father's and I've got no intention of selling them. Matthew Vardon – he hadn't come into the title then – together with my father and a chap called Stamford Leigh had all gone out to South America together. They were all young men and hoping to make their fortunes. This was years ago, in the 1880s. My father rarely talked about his adventures but something happened out there that made him loath – that's not too strong a word – Matthew Vardon for the rest of his life. However, before they quarrelled, the three of them formed a company, Antilla Exploration Limited, and those are the shares Vardon wanted.'

'Were the shares available to the public?' asked Jack.

Ned Castradon shook his head. 'No, it was always a private concern. The shares had been split between the three men and the agreement was that if they hadn't been sold or willed elsewhere, then each party's share would be split between the survivors or their heirs. Apparently Sir Matthew had acquired Stamford Leigh's shares and Simon Vardon fancied getting the rest.

Now if Vardon had asked me to sell him the shares in an ordinary, straightforward manner, I don't say he'd have succeeded, but at least I'd have listened to him. As it was . . .'

He broke off, his face darkening.

'What happened?' prompted Jack.

'What happened is that Vardon attempted nothing more or less than blackmail.' Castradon's voice was icy. 'He said that he knew and, what's more, could prove, that my father had been responsible for the death of a native woman, an Indian, out in Peru.'

'Good God,' said Jack softly.

'He said a great deal more into the bargain,' said Ned, his mouth tightening in anger. 'If I didn't play ball, he would – with the greatest regret – make public the facts, as he called them, about how a well-loved man, a pillar of the local community, had started his career with rape and murder.'

Ashley's face contorted in disgust. 'That's an appalling thing to say.' He hesitated. 'Mr Castradon, you'll excuse the question, but I didn't know your father. You're sure there isn't any truth in Mr Vardon's accusations?'

'No, there damn well isn't!' bit back Castradon. 'I could credit Sir Matthew would do something of the sort, but *not* my father.' He stopped. 'I'm sorry,' he said stiffly, putting his hand to his face once more. 'It's a fair question. But that's the whole trouble with this sort of scurrilous filth, isn't it? To anyone who did know my father, the idea's utterly ridiculous, but to anyone else . . .' His fist clenched and unclenched. 'Well, it might be believed.'

'Can't you do anything?' asked Jack.

'What can I do?' demanded Castradon. 'You can't libel the dead. That's a point of law. Legally speaking, Vardon can tell as many lies as he sees fit and I wouldn't be able to do a thing about it. What I did do was show him the door and threaten to knock the living daylights out of him if he dared to say one word about my father.'

'Man to man, I can't say I blame you for that, sir,' said Ashley.

'When was this, Castradon?' asked Jack.

'Tuesday,' said Ned. 'Tuesday afternoon.'

Jack and Ashley exchanged quick glances. 'Tuesday,' repeated Ashley slowly. 'Would you mind telling us what you did for the rest of the day, Mr Castradon?'

Ned sipped his whisky and soda. 'No. I haven't any objection to that. I went to Eastbourne.'

He lit a cigarette and blew out a long mouthful of smoke. 'And that little excursion didn't improve my temper, either. I received a telegram from a client, Sir Arnold Stapleton, asking for an urgent meeting at eight o'clock on Wednesday morning at his house in Eastbourne. Sir Arnold is the chairman of the board of a joint-stock company. It's principally a City concern but Sir Arnold was an old pal of my father's. There's been a suggestion that when the present company secretary retires, I could take on the post, which would be a big step up, as far as I'm concerned. So I dropped everything, travelled down to Eastbourne, booked into a hotel and showed up bright and early at Sir Arnold's house the next day, only to find Sir Arnold was in London and no one knew anything about the telegram.'

'The telegram was a fake?' asked Jack.

'Exactly,' agreed Castradon. 'I got Sir Arnold's butler to telephone him, to see if there'd been some mistake about where the meeting was supposed to take place, but Sir Arnold knew nothing about it. I'd been had, good and proper, but what the point of it was, I don't know. If it was a joke, it was a pretty poor one.'

'Which hotel did you stay in, sir?' asked Ashley.

'The Grand. I travelled down by the five thirty-two on Tuesday and came back the next day.'

'Have you still got the telegram, by any chance?'

'No, I chucked it in a bin at the Grand. I was pretty sore about the whole affair, as you can imagine.' His brow contracted in a frown. 'Look, what's the point of these questions?'

'It's just a matter of routine, sir,' Ashley said smoothly. 'There's just one last question. Did Ryle ever take drugs, do you know?'

'Drugs?' repeated Ned in astonishment. 'No. I never suspected it, but he may have done, I suppose.'

'I see, sir.' Ashley glanced at the grandfather clock. 'It's past nine. I expect Mrs Castradon will be back soon. You're taking Mrs Stanton home, aren't you, Haldean?'

'That's right.' He smiled apologetically at Castradon. 'I hope you don't mind, but I told Isabelle I'd probably be here.'

'That's all right,' said Ned absently. 'Haldean, you were in the Flying Corps, weren't you?'

Jack nodded.

'Your cousin's told us about you. She said you got the DFC. You were a real crack pilot.'

Jack heard the resentment in Castradon's voice

130

and was suddenly annoyed. He wasn't going to apologize for his record or his medals.

'I was decent enough, I suppose,' he said coolly. 'And lucky.'

'Lucky.' Castradon repeated the word. 'I was in the Flying Corps.' He touched his face. 'That's how I collected this. It was only my second time over the lines. That was in April 1917.'

Jack felt instantly contrite. April 1917 – Bloody April as it was called by anyone who survived it – had left the Flying Corps reeling and nearly broken from the ferocious assault by the better armed and better organised Germans. They had hung on by the skin of their teeth, but the life of any pilot had been measured in hours. Punch drunk and weary from endless fights, he had survived by sheer chance. He felt a rush of fellow feeling towards Castradon.

'That's really tough,' he said quietly.

Ned shrugged. 'I'm lucky to be alive, I suppose. The irony is that I only joined the Flying Corps because I wanted to get married. I'd been in the Artillery for nearly two years and didn't have a scratch to show for it. I thought six months at home in a Flight Training School would be the best start I could manage to married life.' He laughed bitterly. 'It would have been better for Sue if I'd stayed in the army.'

There didn't seem much to be said to this, and it was with a sense of relief that Jack heard the front door open and voices in the hall.

The three men stood up as Sue and Isabelle came in. They both, thought Jack, looked dog tired.

Isabelle still wore her coat and hat. 'Sue asked

me if I wanted to stay for a drink,' she said, 'but I'd really rather get off if you're ready, Jack.' She stifled a yawn. 'It's been a very long day.'

'Ned, we heard the most extraordinary thing at the meeting,' broke in Sue. 'Everyone says that the poor man in the church is *Ryle*. I can hardly believe it.'

'I know,' he said. 'I've just heard.' Sue looked on the verge of tears. 'What's wrong?' he asked gruffly.

'Don't you see, Ned?' she broke out. 'You quarrelled with him. Everyone thinks you're responsible. *You.*'

Castradon drew his breath in. 'That's absolute nonsense,' he said shakily.

'That's what I said,' she agreed eagerly. 'It's nonsense and we can prove it's nonsense. Mrs Dyson said the murder happened on Tuesday evening, but you weren't here on Tuesday evening. You were in Eastbourne. I don't know who sent that telegram or why, but thank God they did.' She turned to Ashley. 'That's real evidence, isn't it, Superintendent? Ned has to be innocent.'

Jack was suddenly aware of how tensely Castradon was waiting for Ashley's answer. 'It's very good evidence,' said Ashley soothingly. 'We'll have to follow it up, of course, as a matter of routine, but I don't think you need worry yourself unduly.'

Castradon closed his eyes in momentary relief.

'Shall we go, Belle?' asked Jack in a deliberately cheerful voice. 'You look all in. Talking of routine, though,' he added, turning to Castradon, 'you run a car, don't you?'

'Yes,' said Ned in surprise. The surprise was

132

mirrored by Ashley. 'I've got a Riley. Why d'you want to know?'

Jack gave Ashley an almost imperceptible wink. 'It's the rug that was covering the body. It looked like a travelling rug, the sort that's kept in a car. It could've been stolen, so we're asking anyone with a car to see if their rug's missing.' Was it his imagination or did Sue Castradon suddenly look very worried?

'That's right, sir,' said Ashley, lying manfully. 'It's just a matter of routine. Do you have a travelling rug?'

'Yes, we do,' said Sue in a low voice.

'You're welcome to take a look,' said Ned. 'Would you mind coming back tomorrow, though? My wife really is very tired.'

'Let's look now, Ned,' said Sue quickly. 'It'll only take a few minutes.'

Castradon shrugged. 'Just as you like. The car's in the old stable block.'

He led the way out of the house and, picking up a torch from the drawer in the hall table, led them round to the old stables. 'I can't see it being ours,' he said as he bent down, lifted up a stone and drew a key out from underneath. 'I keep the stables locked when the car's inside.'

He creaked open the door, and, striking a match, lit the oil lamp on the shelf inside the door.

In the warm light Jack saw the bulk of the car, but he also saw a line of tools hung neatly on hooks on the wall. He nudged Ashley. There were a couple of gaps in the line of tools.

'Are you missing any tools, sir?' asked Ashley, pointing to the gap.

Ned stared at the wall. 'That's odd. My monkey wrench has gone. My axe is missing too. Where the blazes are they? I always put my tools back after I've used them.'

'When did you last use them, sir?'

'I can't remember. Some time ago. I haven't taken the car out for a couple of weeks, so I haven't been in here. Where the dickens can they have got to?'

'Do you keep an outdoor man, sir? Could he have taken them?'

'We've got a gardener who does odd jobs, but he won't have used my wrench. He's got his own tools.'

Sue was standing beside the car. 'Ned,' she said in an odd voice. 'The rug from the car's gone. When I saw that rug round the man this morning, I thought, Isn't that strange – we've got a rug just like that one.'

'Sue!' said Castradon quickly.

'And now it seems as if we had . . .'

Nine

The telephone in the hall rang. After a brief conversation, Arthur Stanton, smiling broadly, came into the morning room where Isabelle and Jack were having breakfast.

'That was Ashley on the phone,' he said, picking up the coffee pot. 'He's been on to the Grand in Eastbourne and I'm glad to say Ned Castradon's got a complete alibi.'

'Thank God,' murmured Isabelle fervently. 'That's wonderful. I knew Ned couldn't be guilty. Do Ned and Sue know? Sue was worried to death last night.'

'Yes, Ashley's told them,' said Arthur, stirring his coffee. 'Apparently Castradon always stays at the Grand and not only is he in the register, the receptionist recognized him, as did the head waiter in the restaurant where he had dinner. He stayed in the hotel all evening. I'm glad to say there's no doubt about it.'

'That's wonderful,' repeated Isabelle. 'Isn't it, Jack?'

'Yes . . .' he said doubtfully, picking up the marmalade.

She glared indignantly at him. 'Jack! Don't tell me you *want* poor Ned to be arrested. What about Sue?'

'Don't get me wrong, Belle,' he said, spreading his hands out pacifically. 'And don't bite my head off. But don't you see? That telegram to Ned Castradon, the one that took him down to Eastbourne in the first place, has to be explained.'

'It was sent by mistake,' said Isabelle dismiss-ively. 'These things happen.'

'Do they? It's remarkable that it happened on the evening Ned Castradon needed an alibi.'

'Ashley said he was going to contact Sir Arnold Stapleton,' put in Arthur. 'That's who supposedly sent the telegram. He wants to confirm that Castradon really did show up at his house on Wednesday morning.'

'He'll have been there all right,' Jack said confi-dently. 'If Castradon did receive the telegram, then of course he'd keep the appointment. If he sent the telegram to himself, then he'd be equally keen to show up.'

'Sent it to himself?' Isabelle repeated blankly. 'Jack, you seem to be determined to make out Ned Castradon is guilty.'

'No, I'm not. I'm just pointing out that the telegram isn't the cast-iron alibi that you seem to think it is.'

Arthur stretched out his hand for the marmalade. 'Castradon can't be in two places at once, Jack.'

'He could've made sure that everyone in the hotel saw him, gone up to his room, then sneaked out and returned here. It's perfectly possible. After all, he was in Eastbourne, not Timbuktu. It's not that far away.'

'But how?' demanded Isabelle. 'There isn't a train at that time of night and he said himself he hadn't taken the car out for over a fortnight.'

'That's what he *said,* I agree.' Jack looked at Isabelle and Arthur's disapproving faces and laughed. 'Don't worry. I'm just pointing out flaws in his alibi. It's a far cry from saying he's guilty. Ashley and I are going to see Dr Lucas this morning to get the post-mortem results. In view of what you told us about the doctor's secret quarrel with Ryle, he's got some explaining to do.'

'For Pete's sake, Jack,' protested Arthur. 'It was a revolting crime. Do you have to accuse one of the neighbours?'

'We worked out the murderer had to be a local man. That means, I'm afraid, that, like it or not, one of your neighbours is guilty.'

*   *   *

136

As arranged, Jack met Ashley at the police station just before ten.

'I've had a busy morning,' Ashley said as they strolled across the green to Dr Lucas's together. 'I've asked the War Office to dig out Ryle's record for me and I've been onto the Criminal Records Bureau. It turns out our pal Ryle has quite a history of thieving and extortion. He got mixed up with a gang running a drugs racket last summer and tried to be clever.'

'Whoops,' said Jack. 'That doesn't sound very clever at all.'

'It wasn't,' said Ashley with a grin. 'He made some very nasty people very angry indeed. He disappeared last September and since then, no one in London's seen hair nor hide of him. Last September was when Castradon picked him up, if you remember.'

'You're not saying Ryle was bumped off by one of the drug gang, are you? It doesn't seem very likely.'

'No, I agree. Mind you, we still don't know that the body in the church is Ryle. I've requested a full search for him and I'm hoping at the very least we'll find someone who saw him after he scarpered last Sunday. It isn't a gang killing, though. Leaving a body in a cupboard in a village church is not how London gangs operate and it doesn't begin to explain this odd business of the Chessman letters.'

'Talking of the Chessman letters, isn't that Thomas Vardon coming out of Dr Lucas's house?'

It was. Sir Thomas shut the gate, turned, saw them and waved.

'I've just been to see Dr Lucas,' he said, catching up with them. 'He hadn't heard any rumours at all about my father's death and was hugely indignant that there'd been any suggestion of foul play. I must say, I found his complete certainty that nothing untoward happened very reassuring. He thinks the letters my mother received can be put down to some crank who had some reason to dislike my father.'

'Did you tell him you'd had a letter?' asked Jack.

'Yes, and he set my mind at rest about that, too. He thought it quite likely, as I've got the title, that this crank would include me in this beastly campaign.' Sir Thomas laughed ironically. 'The title is about all I have got. I've looked at the accounts. There's a mortgage on the estate and it's been running at a loss for years. So, I'm afraid that my poor wife's dream of living a life of ease as lady of the manor will have to wait for a while. I'll have to go back to Hollywood. I can't afford not to.'

'What about the estate?' asked Jack. 'Will you sell it?'

'Sell it? I wish I could, but it's entailed.' He rubbed his face with his hands. 'The only thing I can do is find a trustworthy man to manage it, so the running costs, at least, will be met, and then set about paying off the old debts. It's my responsibility but I want to speak to my brother about it. I don't know if he'd be willing to take on the job of running the place, but he'd be the obvious choice. He hasn't any experience but he is part of the family. I'll have to see what he thinks about the idea when he arrives.'

Jack felt a twinge of sympathy for Edward Castradon. Castradon was under enough of a strain already without Simon Vardon popping up and living permanently in the village to add to his woes. 'When should your brother arrive?'

'He was meant to be here yesterday,' said Sir Thomas with a shrug. 'I did try and phone him but couldn't get any answer. Simon does things in his own time. He'll show up eventually. By the way, I'm glad to have seen you. I haven't told my stepmother about my father's . . .' He paused, finding the right words. 'My father's connection, shall we say, with Ryle.' He lit a cigarette with nervous fingers, his eyes alight with entreaty. 'If it possibly can be kept quiet, I'd be very grateful. It'd only upset her.'

'Don't you worry about that, sir,' said Ashley. 'Unless it's absolutely necessary, your stepmother need never know.'

'That's a relief.' Sir Thomas tipped his hat and walked away.

'I could feel quite sorry for that man, title or no title,' said Ashley as he departed. 'He's had a dickens of a homecoming. There's the murder in the church which has set everyone by the ears, the estate's in a mess and his brother, who doesn't sound anything to shout about, can't be bothered to show up. From what I've heard, his stepmother isn't jumping for joy to see him, and to top it all, he's having kittens that she'll find out that Ryle's her husband's illegitimate son.'

'It's a fair old list,' agreed Jack, mentally adding Thomas Vardon's obvious liking of Sue Castradon to the catalogue. 'Incidentally, Ashley, I was thinking about the link between Ryle and Dr Lucas.'

Ashley looked at him sharply. 'What about it?'

'Drugs,' suggested Jack quietly. 'Doctors have access to drugs.'

Ashley stopped dead. 'Drugs! Dammit, you're right! Of course! Lucas could've been supplying Ryle with dope. *And* the victim in the church was a drug addict.' He rubbed his hands together. 'Well, well. This is growing, isn't it?'

'Steady on,' warned Jack. 'It's only a possibility. We don't know who the victim is yet or where these Chessman letters fit in.'

'We're not doing too badly,' said Ashley enthusiastically. 'Let's see Dr Lucas.'

Dr Lucas, a rotund middle-aged man with a friendly, if rather pompous, manner, had carried out the post-mortem in the basement of his house. Rather to Jack's relief he didn't offer to conduct the conversation downstairs over the laid-out remains of the corpse.

'This house,' said Dr Lucas chattily, as he escorted them into the surgery, 'was built to the specifications of the local surgeon in the 1850's and has always been known as the Doctor's House. I am fortunate in possessing my own facilities with a purpose-built stone table with the sinks, the water supply and the drains and so on that are needed, which means any coroner's work in the district is usually referred to me. However, as I do not possess any storage facilities, the remains will be removed to St Peter's hospital later today until a burial can be arranged. That, I may say, is becoming a necessity, as the corpse is beginning to show distinct signs of decay.'

Ashley winced and took the offered seat. 'Talking of which, Doctor, do you have a more definite time of death?'

Dr Lucas shook his head. 'Unfortunately, no. Between three to six or seven days is the closest I can get with any certainty. Dating a death is trickier than you may suppose.'

'Could he have died on Tuesday?'

'Oh, yes, and perhaps even earlier. Putrefaction as a greenish tinge is clearly visible over the lower abdomen . . .'

'I know. I saw it,' put in Jack, hastily.

'And rigor, which is a very helpful guide, has virtually passed away. Is there any particular reason you have settled on Tuesday, Superintendent?'

'The lilies on the corpse were taken from the Dysons' garden on Tuesday night.'

Dr Lucas's eyebrows shot up. 'Were they indeed? From the Dysons, you say? Why, that's only next door! I heard nothing untoward that evening.'

'Are you sure, sir? There was no disturbance front or back?'

Dr Lucas shook his head. 'None whatsoever.'

Ashley sighed and moved on. 'Tell me, Doctor, the cause of death was the stab wound, wasn't it?'

Dr Lucas nodded. 'Yes. Despite the terrific injuries the corpse sustained, they were not the cause of death. What the victim actually died from was a stab wound to the heart. It was a single upwards blow between the fourth and fifth ribs and death would have been virtually instantaneous. I should say the blade was at least six inches long. There

141

is also another injury to the left upper arm which I am at a loss to account for. The hands and feet were removed rather crudely. I'd say they were chopped off.'

'Chopped with an axe?' asked Jack. Castradon's axe was missing.

'I believe so, yes. Considering the extent of the other injuries, the actual death blow was rather neatly done.'

'Would the killing have required any specialized knowledge?'

Dr Lucas shrugged. 'I don't really know how to answer that, Superintendent. The killer only struck once, so it certainly wasn't a random blow, but all the killer would have to know is the position of the heart, which he could have acquired from any standard textbook. And, of course, since the war, there has been a great increase amongst the most unlikely people of a practical working knowledge of anatomy.'

'Can you tell us anything about the man, Doctor? His age, for instance?'

'I would say he was in his late twenties or early thirties. At one stage he underwent an operation for appendicitis, as is clear from the characteristic scar. He hadn't eaten for some time before he died, but he had been drinking. In fact, there were indications, judging by the state of his internal organs, that he was a very heavy drinker.'

'What about the needle marks on his arm?' asked Ashley. 'You pointed those out when you first inspected the body.'

'Yes. He was certainly in the habit of injecting himself with some substance.'

'So he was a drug addict?' asked Jack.

Dr Lucas shook his head. 'It's impossible to say. Naturally, one's first thought is of a prohibited drug such as cocaine, but that leaves no post-mortem traces. Granted that he was a heavy drinker, though, I would remind you that various cures for alcoholism containing such substances as cocaine, bromides, opium and Indian hemp are sold quite legitimately and frequently cause as much of a problem as the condition they are supposed to alleviate.'

'I bet they aren't injected,' muttered Jack. Something the doctor had said struck a chord. 'Hemp!'

Ashley blinked. 'Excuse me, Haldean?'

'Hemp. I've just remembered what the smell was, the odd smell that hung about the body. It's hemp. I said it reminded me of the East.'

'By jingo,' muttered Ashley. 'You're right.'

Jack turned to the doctor. 'Granted that both Mr Ashley and I smelt hashish, it gives credence to the idea that the man was a drug user, wouldn't you say?'

Dr Lucas blinked. 'Perhaps. Indeed, yes. It is, as you say, suggestive. But who could the man be? I can think of no one in the immediate vicinity of whom I have ever suspected of having a drug habit.'

Ashley cleared his throat, leaning forward in his chair. Now for it, thought Jack. Ashley looked at Dr Lucas squarely. 'There's a suggestion,' he said slowly, 'that he might have been the Vardon's chauffeur. A man named Ryle.'

The reaction was fleeting but unmistakable. Dr Lucas's chin jerked upwards, his eyes bright, then he schooled his face into a look of concern. 'Ryle, you say?'

Despite what Jack was sure was a real effort, Dr Lucas couldn't keep the note of satisfaction out of his voice.

'Did you know him?' asked Ashley.

Dr Lucas looked him very straight in the eye. 'I knew who he was, of course, but he wasn't a patient of mine.' He looked away. 'I never had anything to do with him.'

And that, as Jack would've guessed from his attitude and knew from Arthur's story of seeing Dr Lucas and Ryle together, was a lie.

Ashley knew it too. He sat back and, when he spoke, his voice was slow and his accent reassuringly stronger, a virtual invitation to a clever doctor to put one over on a dim-witted policeman. 'Are you absolutely certain, sir? Naturally we're interested in anything anyone can tell us about Ryle. When did you last see him?'

'I don't really know.' Ashley said nothing and Dr Lucas hurried on. 'I suppose it would have been last week. I called to see Lady Vardon. She suffers from a heart condition which requires supervision and I might have seen him then.'

'Have you ever had what might be described as a private conversation with Ryle?'

'No, certainly not.'

'And yet, Doctor, we have information that such a conversation took place.'

Dr Lucas paled. He gulped a couple of times before he spoke. 'I . . . I might have spoken to him a couple of times, perhaps. When Sir Matthew was taken ill he was worried about his master. In

144

fact, yes,' said Dr Lucas, his confidence growing. 'I believe he did waylay me on at least one occasion to enquire about his master's condition.'

That didn't tie in with what Arthur had overheard them say about the war, but Ashley let it go. 'What was his attitude? Respectful?'

'Yes. Well, no, not always. Ryle has – had, I should say – a very rough and ready manner of speech.' Dr Lucas stopped, wiping his forehead. 'Really, Superintendent, I find these questions very uncomfortable. Someone might have seen me talking to Ryle, but the conversation, if you can call it that, was so unimportant it slipped my mind. And really, I find it utterly incredible that the mutilated corpse I examined could be that of Ryle. He was not very well liked but to inflict such savage injuries on a man calls for some other motive than mere dislike. I cannot believe that the man we found was a local man. It seems too fantastic for words.'

'And yet, sir, to get the corpse into the cupboard in the church required precise local knowledge.'

Dr Lucas looked honestly bewildered. 'In that case, I can only conclude that we must have an unsuspected criminal lunatic in our midst.'

'Is such a thing possible, Doctor? That a criminal lunatic could be unsuspected in a close-knit community such as this?'

Dr Lucas nodded vigorously. 'Unfortunately, although I must say I shrink from the idea, it's perfectly possible. I know little of such matters, but my son, Jerry, is far more versed in modern thinking on psychology than I am. He has discussed cases with me where a man seems perfectly sane in all respects and yet has no real moral sense. I believe the technical term to describe such a man is a *psychopath*. There has been some work on this type of criminal disorder in Germany and, latterly, America. I may say that the motives for the crimes in such cases seem utterly inadequate. Indeed, there may not be any motive that we would recognize as a motive at all.'

The door was suddenly flung back and a dark-haired, nervy-looking man a few years older than Jack erupted into the room. The angle of the door blocked Jack and Ashley from his view and he rushed forward, his hands twitching in agitation.

'Dad! They know the dead man is Ryle!'

Dr Lucas coughed and motioned to where Ashley and Jack were sitting. The man spun round. His eyes widened in dismay as he saw them. 'I'm sorry,' he said uncertainly. 'I didn't mean to interrupt. I thought my father was alone.'

Dr Lucas waved a hand in their direction. 'This is Superintendent Ashley and Major Haldean, Jerry. This is my son, Dr Jeremy Lucas.'

'Pleased to meet you,' muttered Jerry Lucas, looking anything but pleased.

'Who told you the identity of the dead man?' asked Ashley.

Jerry Lucas twisted his hands together. 'It's all over the village. I . . . I thought my father should know. He did the post-mortem.' Jerry Lucas spoke in quick, jerky sentences. 'I thought he'd be interested.'

'Did you know Ryle?' asked Jack. Jerry Lucas's eyes flickered to his father. Dr Lucas nodded his head very slightly.

'Yes. That is, I knew who he was.'

146

'Did you like him?'

'No! I mean . . .' Jerry Lucas pushed his hair back from his forehead.

Dr Lucas moved closer to his son. It was an unmistakably protective gesture. Jerry Lucas stopped, gulped, then plunged once more into speech, his eyes seeking his father's approval. 'I didn't know him well enough to like or dislike him.'

Jack could see the relief in Dr Lucas's face.

'What my son means,' said the doctor smoothly, 'is that Ryle suffered from an unsavoury reputation. If you want further information, you could ask either the Vardons or the Castradons. We know very little about him, don't we, Jerry?'

Jerry Lucas looked at him gratefully. 'Hardly anything,' he agreed. He edged to the door. 'I think I'd better go now.'

'Wait a moment,' said Jack pleasantly. What he really wanted was to get Jerry Lucas on his own, away from his father who seemed to be controlling the conversation like a puppet master, but that didn't seem to be possible. He decided to back a hunch. Whatever the connection was between Dr Lucas and Ryle, Jerry Lucas obviously not only knew all about it but, Jack was prepared to bet, was as involved as his father.

'Surely you knew Ryle better than you say. After all, you met him privately more than once, didn't you?'

It was a guess but there was no doubt of the truth. Jerry Lucas paled and shrank back, his tongue moving over suddenly dry lips. 'How did you know?' His voice was a whisper.

'What did Ryle want from you?'

Dr Lucas intervened. 'There were no private meetings. My son obviously misunderstood your question, Major Haldean. He wanted nothing. Isn't that right, Jerry? Nothing at all. Now, gentlemen, I know you'll excuse me, but I have some more work I must do this evening so if I can show you out . . .'

He attempted to usher them to the door, but Ashley stood firm. 'Not yet, Doctor. There are some questions to be answered.' He glanced at Jack, breathed deeply, and took the plunge. 'We believe Ryle took drugs. He must've got them from somewhere.' He stopped, looking at father and son keenly. 'Did you supply him with drugs?'

Dr Lucas stared at him. 'Did *I* supply him?' he repeated incredulously.

Ashley turned on Jerry Lucas. 'Did you?'

'Me!' Jerry Lucas took a step backwards, stuttering in his anxiety. 'No, of course not. That would be wrong. Really wrong. I don't know why you'd think such a thing. Ryle was a swine, a real swine, but he didn't take drugs. At least, we never gave him any, did we, Dad?'

His manner was so sincere, Jack was certain Jerry Lucas was telling the truth. He could tell Ashley believed him too.

Ashley looked thoughtfully at the young doctor. 'So if you weren't supplying him with drugs, what was the nature of your relationship with Ryle?'

Jack felt honestly sorry for Jerry Lucas. He looked like a hunted animal. He tried to speak, but couldn't.

Dr Lucas drew himself up to his full height. 'Superintendent! I must insist you stop these questions. Apart from a few chance meetings, neither my son nor I had any relationship whatsoever with Ryle. Furthermore, I very much dislike the tone you have adopted. This is, I would remind you, my house and you are here at my invitation to receive a post-mortem report which I have carried out at your request.'

'I'm grateful for the work that you've done, sir,' said Ashley with every appearance of sincerity. 'Having said that, you must see why I'm puzzled. For instance, you've stated that neither you nor your son knew Ryle well, yet Dr Lucas here—' he indicated Jeremy Lucas – 'says that Ryle was "A real swine".'

Jerry Lucas shrank back, his eyes wide. He didn't speak but gave an odd little whimper.

All of a sudden, Jack could hardly bear it. He wanted to shout, 'Stop!' but Ashley couldn't stop. There was no hint of bullying in his voice. He was polite but as implacable as a steamroller. 'You must have some reason to hold such a strong opinion.'

Jerry Lucas shook his head dumbly. The tension in the room stretched like a piano wire.

'Well?'

Dr Lucas gave a snort of impatience and suddenly the tension was gone. 'Ryle had an unsavoury reputation. That was what my son referred to, Superintendent. I repeat; we had no personal connection with Ryle whatsoever.' Ashley stirred and was about to speak, but Dr Lucas ploughed on. 'If you think either my son or myself have a charge to answer, then make your accusation and we will thresh this out in court.'

Ashley held up his hand in a placatory way.

149

'We're nowhere near making any accusations yet, sir. All I'm doing is asking a few simple questions and hoping for some answers.'

'Which you have received. Now, gentlemen, I really think it would be best if you left.'

There was nothing for it but to allow themselves to be shown out.

'What d'you make of that?' asked Ashley in disgust as they walked back across the green to the station. 'I'd love to know what was going on between those two and Ryle. Do you think they were selling him drugs?' he demanded.

Jack clicked his tongue. 'It's hard to tell, but I don't think so. The pair of them seemed astonished by the idea Ryle used drugs. I'd say they were telling the truth.'

'It's about the only thing they were telling the truth about,' grunted Ashley. 'There's something going on and I want to know what. I'm going to get to the bottom of this.'

Ten

The next morning, after dropping Isabelle in the village, Jack visited the police station. He'd had an idea about Jerry Lucas and Jonathan Ryle, an idea he wanted to discuss with Ashley.

Ashley, however, wasn't there. Constable Stock didn't, he said morosely, rightly know when he'd be back.

Strolling aimlessly across the green, Jack decided to take another look at Coppenhall Lane. Although they'd explored it pretty thoroughly yesterday, there was just a chance there could be a few threads from the tartan rug they'd over-looked. If he could find any threads on the village end of Coppenhall Lane, past the Castradons' house, it wouldn't automatically rule out Ned Castradon as a suspect, but it would be a strong presumption in his favour.

He walked up the lane, looking in the ditch, scanning the hedges and paying particular atten-tion to the odd clumps of spiky hawthorn and thorny holly, but there were no red or yellow threads.

He was nearly at the Castradons' when he saw Thomas Vardon coming along the lane from the church. He, too, was studying the hedges carefully.

'Hello!' said Jack. 'Are you looking for something?'

Sir Thomas gave a disarmingly shy smile. 'In a manner of speaking. You'll probably think I'm wasting my time, but I was taking a hand at playing detective. It struck me yesterday how dark this lane must be at night and I wondered if that poor guy in the church was brought along here. I suppose I was hoping to find a clue,' he added with a grin. 'Sherlock Holmes always finds footprints or cigar ash . . .'

He broke off as the noise of a door slamming came clearly from the house beyond the hedge, followed by a man's voice, thick with worry and bad temper. It was punctuated by the higher tones of a woman. Sue Castradon's voice rang out clearly. 'And what about me, Ned? Don't my feelings matter?'

Jack exchanged an embarrassed look with Vardon and, inclining his head for him to follow, walked up the lane in the direction of the village, stopping when he judged them to be out of earshot.

'That guy,' said Vardon, catching up with him, 'deserves to be kicked. If I had a wife the last thing I'd do is spend my time arguing with her.'

Jack looked at him quizzically. 'But you've got a wife, haven't you?'

'And how! I meant if I had a wife like that. Mrs Castradon's a cut above the average.'

For Sue Castradon's sake, Jack hoped that Thomas Vardon's only-too-obvious admiration wouldn't come to Ned Castradon's attention. Sue Castradon had quite enough to contend with without another layer being added to her husband's jealousy. 'Did you find anything in the lane?' he asked, hoping to change the subject. 'Any clues, I mean?'

'Not a thing,' said Vardon with a shrug. 'I don't suppose you and Superintendent Whatsisname – Ashley – found anything, did you?'

'I don't think I should really answer that,' said Jack. 'After all, this is a police case.'

'That means you *did* find something,' said Sir Thomas in triumph. 'I'm glad to know you're getting somewhere. Was it Ryle who was bumped off? Everyone seems to be very sure it was.'

'The honest answer is that we simply don't know, but I must say it's looking that way. After

152

all, he seems to have disappeared without a trace.'

Thomas digested this in silence. 'Ryle's my father's son,' he said slowly. 'I suppose that makes him my brother, not that I can think of him in that way. However, those letters I showed you, the letters from the guy calling himself the Chessman, he said he'd murdered my father and threatened to murder me. My father made a good few enemies in his time. Could this guy, the Chessman, be carrying out some sort of vendetta against my family?'

'He *could,*' said Jack cautiously. It was, he thought, a perfectly coherent explanation but the last he wanted to do was add to Thomas Vardon's worries. 'The Chessman would have to know the connection between your father and Ryle, though.'

Thomas shrugged. 'I can't see why he shouldn't. After all, you spotted it right away, once you'd seen that photograph. It was obvious.'

He bit his lip distractedly. 'I wish my brother was here. He's good at working things out. He can see connections. He's got that sort of mind. I know you and the police are working on the case, but if there is some sort of family feud, then we're the ones most concerned. He might even be able to guess who the Chessman is. Simon knows far more than I do about my father's business dealings.'

'I'd certainly like to get some sort of clue as to who the Chessman is. It'd be worthwhile talking to your brother. I think you said yesterday you were expecting him?'

'I tried to telephone him this morning, but there was no answer.'

Jack was about to reply when the gate to the Castradons' garden swung back and Sue Castradon, holding her hat in her hand and looking, Jack thought, hopping mad, strode out.

She gripped the brim of her hat and, with an angry snort and a gesture far more expressive than any words, rammed it on her head, breathed deeply, then turned down the lane towards the village.

She looked utterly dismayed when she saw them, then with a little shake of her shoulders and her chin held high, she walked towards them.

'Good morning.' Her voice was steady but her eyes had a furious glint.

The two men raised their hats in greeting.

'Hello,' said Thomas Vardon with a brilliant smile. 'I'm in luck. I was going to call on you.'

She stopped, uncharacteristically flustered. 'Sir Thomas? It's not . . . not really convenient. I was just going to the village.'

'I'll walk with you, if you don't mind,' said Thomas. 'I wish you'd call me Tom. Everyone did in the States.'

She forced a smile. 'I'll try to remember.'

Sir Thomas tipped his hat to Jack. 'I'm sure you'll excuse us, won't you, Haldean?' he said smoothly, offering Sue Castradon his arm.

Sue hesitated momentarily, then took his arm and the two of them walked off down the lane.

Jack looked after them with a frown. He couldn't help thinking Ned Castradon had enough problems without finding a handsome rival at his very door. Thomas Vardon, married or not, had a dangerous charm.

*　　*　　*

Sue Castradon was experiencing a guilty pleasure in that charm. And why not? she thought, rebelliously. With a sense of one reaching for forbidden fruit, she set herself out to charm in return. After all, they were only walking down the lane together.

'My wife should be arriving in five days' time,' Thomas said. 'I had a cable from her this morning. So if that invitation to dinner still stands, we'll take you up on it next week.'

Reassured by the mention of the absent Lady Vardon, Sue smiled up at her escort. 'You must be looking forward to that.'

'Maybe.' He sounded doubtful. 'I don't know how she's going to find village life. She's a city girl, you see, and Hollywood's an exciting place.'

'But she'll be with you.'

Vardon gave an ironic smile. 'I don't think that'll be enough to entertain her.' He hunched his shoulders and for a moment looked like a young and unhappy boy. 'Esmé's not like you, you know. Mrs Castradon – Sue – do you mind if I tell you about it? I'm sick of trying to cover everything up and pretend things are fine.' He stuck his hands in his pockets and stared moodily into the middle distance. 'I don't know if you'd understand.'

'I might,' said Sue, quietly.

He glanced down at her. 'Yes, I really believe you would. I'm Esmé's second husband, you see,' he said in a rush. 'I suppose I've been a disappointment to her. I've never measured up. Marriage and divorce seem to be easier in Hollywood. I've tried – perhaps I could have tried harder – but it takes two to make it work.

I'm sorry. I feel a bit of a cad talking like this, but it's such a relief. Let's talk about something more cheerful, shall we?'

She squeezed his arm. 'Not unless you want to, Tom.' She said his name with a conscious effort and was rewarded with a smile. 'I'm fairly good at keeping secrets.'

'Oh, well, there's not much more to tell. Esmé had asked me for a divorce when the news of my father's death came through and all of a sudden she realized she was Lady Vardon. Can you believe it? Some rotten tin-pot title with nothing to go with it and she was over the moon. I was back in favour and all ideas of separation went out of the window.'

He smiled wryly. 'Look, I really am sorry to have burdened you with all my problems. I want you to like Esmé. It'd be easier if she got on with local people. I don't know why I mentioned it. There's just something about you that made me feel I could talk to you, but you don't want to hear about other people's marriages. God knows, I know I'm not alone.'

'No,' said Sue with a sudden surge of bitterness. 'You aren't.'

Without any very definite aim in mind, Jack continued his walk along the lane to the church. St Luke's, he thought idly, dominated the village. It was built on a mound, a great flint-studded monument to ancient faith and local pride, solid and enduring, with its square, hundred-foot stone giant of a three-storied bell tower, brooding over the landscape below.

The lichgate, he noticed, was swung back. Ashley, he knew, wanted to get the church back to normal as soon as possible. Maybe he'd find him here.

He walked up the gravel path between the lichened gravestones. The church door was open. He paused in the porch, took off his hat, and walked into the cool, quiet space, blinking as his eyes adjusted from the sunshine outside to the dim light.

To the front of the church, the doorway to the vestry stood open. He could hear the scrape of furniture being moved. Someone – Ashley or the vicar, he presumed – was in the vestry close to where that ghastly body had been.

He walked past the entrance to the bell tower to get round to the side aisle to the vestry, when a gasp made him turn round.

Jerry Lucas rose up from a pew where he was kneeling behind a squat pillar. His face was ashen. 'You!'

'Hello,' said Jack pleasantly, turning back to him. 'I'm looking for Superintendent Ashley.'

'The police!' said Jerry Lucas in a strangled whisper. He started to back out of the pew. 'No! I know what you think but you're wrong!'

'What's the matter?' asked Jack. He walked towards Lucas. 'I only want to—'

Jerry Lucas gave a yelp and retreated out of the pew. 'No!' he said again, still in that strangled whisper. 'No!' He reached out behind him and his grasping hands picked up a solid hymn book. He held it in front of him like a shield. 'Leave me alone.'

He looked, thought Jack, at the end of his tether. His face was white, his hair dishevelled and there were dark shadows under his eyes. The hymn book trembled in his hands.

'Did you sleep last night?' asked Jack. He didn't look as if he had. Jerry Lucas twitched his head impatiently. 'Why don't you come with me . . .' Jack began.

'No! Leave me alone!'

Jack stepped forward and Lucas hurled the hymn book at him.

Completely taken aback, Jack raised his arm to ward off the heavy book, flung it to one side, and stepped forward to grab Lucas. With a yelp, Lucas evaded his grasp and, flinging out his fist, shot past him to the open door. Jack dodged the blow, whirled round and nearly caught Lucas as he ran.

A man holding a bucket stepped into the porch. 'What's going on?' he asked in a slow Sussex voice.

'Stop him!' shouted Jack.

Lucas veered off to one side, grabbed the door to the bell tower, and wrenched it open.

Jack plunged after him, thrusting his way through the hanging ropes of the bells. 'Lucas!' he yelled. 'Stop, you idiot!'

Jerry Lucas didn't answer but with an odd little whimper, backed across the room, then ran up the narrow winding stairs to the clock chamber above.

Jack followed him, his feet slipping on the narrow, worn stone. 'Lucas!' he called again. 'Stop!'

There was no answer apart from the thud of feet on the stone stairs. The sound hollowed out to a drumming noise as Jerry Lucas gained the wooden floor of the clock chamber.

Jack emerged into the bare, sun-filled space of the clock room. The door to the belfry stood open and he could hear feet racing up the stairs.

'Lucas!' he called once more, then followed him.

The belfry was dark, the light from the louvered windows blocked by the great bronze hanging bells above him. Jack paused, then saw Lucas swarm up a ladder attached to the wall, past the bells, up to the timber cage from which the bells hung.

There wasn't a solid floor up above, just a network of ancient wooden beams forming a walkway. Jack climbed onto the walkway, the bells spread out beneath him.

A movement and a flash of sunlight caught his eye. Jerry Lucas had reached the end of the timber walkway, climbed the short ladder and opened the trapdoor onto the roof.

Jack reached the foot of the ladder. He paused, listening, before he climbed.

Jerry Lucas could easily push him off the ladder as he came through the narrow trapdoor. Then he'd fall, fall onto the vast bronze convex slope of the bells, with nothing to grasp, nothing to hold, nothing to stop him sliding off the bell to be dashed to his death below.

'Lucas!' he called again, trying to make his voice steady.

There was dead silence. Jack clung onto the

159

ladder, blinking in the sunlight streaming through the open trapdoor. Above him was a rectangle of blue with scudding white clouds. Around him, the dust motes danced in the light. From far away came the sound of birdsong and the distant bark of a dog.

'Lucas!' he called again.

For a few moments nothing happened, then Jerry Lucas's head appeared, black against the light.

'I'm coming up,' said Jack firmly, and started to climb.

'Leave me alone!'

Jack ignored him. Lucas drew back, then, as Jack grasped the final rung, hit down hard with his fist on Jack's hand, pushing him away.

It was a stinging blow and Lucas was strong. With a yell, Jack missed his footing, his feet scrabbling into the void. Holding on with one hand, he made a wild grab for the ladder, then Jerry Lucas, unexpectedly but miraculously, caught his flailing arm and pulled him out of the trapdoor onto the stone slabs of the flat roof of the tower.

Jack sprawled out on the stone, then unsteadily raised himself up on his knees. He tried to stand but his knee gave way and he fell back against the low stone wall, clutching his leg.

'What's the matter?' said Jerry Lucas after a difficult silence.

'I injured my leg some years ago,' said Jack through gritted teeth. 'It's still weak.'

This was true. Although he was for all practical purposes recovered, he'd still put enough strain on his leg in the last few minutes for it to let him down.

Lucas slumped down, his back against the low wall, under the crenulations of the tower. 'How did you injure your leg?' he asked awkwardly.

'I came an awful cropper flying.'

'The muscle must've been damaged,' said Jerry Lucas in a different voice. He sounded calm and professional, for all the world as if Jack was in his consulting room and not stuck at the top of a hundred-foot tower after chasing a man who'd first tried to kill him, then save him. 'There's some exercises that would help. Have you tried massage?'

This was bizarre. Jack raised his head and looked him straight in the eyes. 'Why did you run?'

Blind panic leapt up once more in Lucas's face. 'The police were there! You knew!' He pressed his hands against the rough flint of the walls and levered himself upwards. The wind whipped his hair and he glanced nervously over his shoulder to the dizzying drop below. He gulped defiantly. 'I'll do it. I'll jump.'

The knuckles on the hand that grasped the corner of the wall were white. Jerry Lucas was tense to breaking point. Jack knew that the slightest wrong move, the merest hint of aggression, could send Lucas literally over the edge.

He bent his head and rubbed his leg again. 'Don't do that. People care about you.' Lucas gave a snort of dissent. 'They do,' Jack persisted. 'My cousin, Isabelle and her husband, Arthur, like you very much. They told me so. And your father cares for you deeply, doesn't he?'

Despite himself, Lucas nodded dumbly.

'I need you, Jerry. I can't get down those ladders alone. I need you.'

The knuckles on Lucas's hand relaxed and Jack breathed a sigh of relief. 'Come on, Jerry. Let's go down.'

'No!' Panic flared again. 'I can't go down. I just can't. Ryle's *dead*. If you only knew, if you knew about me, you'd know everything. You'd know why I wanted him dead.'

'I don't know if Ryle's dead.' Jack's voice was measured. 'I do know why you'd like him to be dead though.'

He didn't know; he'd had an idea, an idea that explained quite a lot, but he didn't *know*. He had been going to discuss his idea with Ashley, to get some proof that he was on the right lines but he needed to tell Jerry Lucas something. If Lucas thought the game was up there was every chance he'd fling himself over the tower.

Jerry Lucas gaped at him. 'You can't,' he said eventually. 'No one knows. Dad said . . .' He broke off, his eyes fixed on Jack's face.

It was working. Curiosity was keeping Lucas safe. 'Your father said he'd look after you, didn't he?' suggested Jack.

Lucas nodded slowly.

'I know it happened in the war.' Jack knew the war had to come into it somehow. The snatch of conversation Arthur had overheard between Dr Lucas and Ryle told him that much. What happened he could only guess. He just hoped that Jerry Lucas would fill in the gaps in his knowledge.

'The war,' repeated Lucas softly. 'I hated the war.'

162

Jack grinned and leant back against the wall. 'It wasn't the best thing that's ever happened to me, either.'

Lucas looked at him with scared eyes. 'You were brave, though, weren't you? I've heard Mrs Stanton talk about you. You won the DFC.'

This was the second time in two days his record hadn't won him any friends, but he was damned if he was going to apologize for it. 'I think most of the time I was numb,' he said thoughtfully, and that was probably true.

Lucas looked at him with quick understanding. 'Numb? Yes, I think most men were. I . . . I wanted to be numb. I wanted to shut it out, to make it all routine and duty. I wanted to stop *feeling*.'

Jack felt a surge of acute sympathy. He'd seen men with their nerves rubbed raw. There had been times when he'd been one of those men. He remembered, although he hated to remember it, exactly what it was like.

'I know,' he said softly.

Jerry Lucas looked up. 'You do know,' he said wonderingly. 'I wouldn't have thought you would, but you do.'

Jack eased himself back against the wall. Taking out his cigarette case, he lit a cigarette, then slid the case across the roof to Lucas. 'Tell me about Ryle.'

Lucas paused with a cigarette in his hand. 'But you know about Ryle.'

That was awkward. Guesses weren't knowledge. 'I'd like to hear it from your point of view.'

It worked. Lucas shrugged. 'Why not? If you know already, you might as well hear my side of things. I wish it hadn't happened,' he added. 'I've always regretted it.' He sighed deeply. 'As you know, I'd only just qualified as a doctor.'

Jack didn't know, but he nodded in agreement.

'It was the spring of 1918. I was in an Advanced Aid Post, in a shelled-out house in Hooge, only a few hundred yards from the front line. We were all at fever pitch, waiting for the next wave of attacks . . .'

A sound like a giant insect whined overhead. The shelling was getting closer. Jerry instinctively winced and grabbed the table, bracing himself for the explosion. It came in a ground-juddering crump, rattling the surgical instruments on the table. Another piece of plaster fell off the wall, adding to the heap of debris that rimmed the room.

Corporal Harris ducked, then looked up with a grin. 'Blimey, sir, that was nearly a bull's eye.'

Jerry tried to smile and failed miserably. When he was completing his degree, he'd never dreamed that anything resembling medicine could be practiced in the ill-lit, bombed-out ruin, with its dank cellar smells of wet brick dust and earth that was the Advanced Aid Post. He couldn't begin to copy the breezy cheerfulness of his orderlies, with their graveyard humour and seemingly unflinching nerves.

His nerves, as he knew only too well, were shot, but he mustn't let the men know. He couldn't let them know how close to the edge he was. They needed him. He was in charge. That miserable little rag of pride was all he had left to keep going. The only sleep he'd had for the last four days had been in twenty-minute snatches and he was dangerously close to complete exhaustion.

Another shell, and another, whined overhead, nearly drowning Private Simmons' yell of 'Field Ambulance!'

A Field Ambulance wasn't a vehicle, it was men, stretcher bearers, who gathered up the wounded and brought them back to the Aid Post, with the walking wounded following in their wake. It was a beastly journey, through trenches with broken duckboards and over cratered, water-logged ground, where the blast from a shell could knock a man off his feet and into the waiting deep, evil mud that was Flanders.

Jerry, working mechanically, sorted out the casualties. Four men, with massive shrapnel wounds, were nearly dead. Private Connolly gave them morphia and they were laid against the wall to die. More morphia for three men caught in the same shell blast who would probably survive after amputation. They were taken to the rear of the cottage for the Field Ambulance to carry them up to the Main Aid Post. Yet more morphia for a man whose hand and arm was a bloody mess. A bad blast to the cheek and eye, a serious chest wound – fatal? Maybe not. It was worth taking him to the Main Aid Post. Embedded shrapnel accounted for seven more injuries and there were two more possible amputations.

It wouldn't be so bad, thought Jerry, if he couldn't *hear*. Morphia masked the pain but the sound of the wounded would stay with him always.

165

The walking wounded were next. They always presented a challenge. The point of an Aid Post was to get as many men as possible back into the fighting line as quickly as possible. Bandages and iodine solved most problems, and . . .

'What's the matter with you?' he asked a soldier, slumped on the ground.

The man seemed perfectly well, apart from his arm which he held limply by his side.

'It's my arm, sir. It was the shell blast. I can't move it.'

An orderly helped him off with his tunic and Jerry examined the arm. There was a long graze, but he couldn't find anything seriously wrong.

'You're shirking, Ryle,' said the man behind him, whose tunic was stiff with blood. 'You're yellow. You always were. You wanted to duck it. He's just a shirker, sir,' he said to Jerry.

Ryle spun round and let fly with a string of obscenities.

'Cut that out!' shouted Jerry, above another giant whine of a shell. That shell was *really* close. The impact shook plaster from the roof, sending clouds of choking dust into the air. In the haze, Jerry saw Ryle dodge nimbly to avoid the falling plaster, lifting his supposedly damaged arm to shield his eyes.

'Right,' he yelled. 'You – Ryle – get out. There's nothing wrong with you.'

Ryle sullenly squared his shoulders. 'I ain't going. I need a stretcher. Me legs have gone too.'

The pent-up frustration and sheer exhaustion of the last few days struck Jerry like a tidal wave. He let Ryle have it. He hardly knew what he was saying, but the nods of approval and mutters of, *'You tell him, sir'* from the men surrounding Ryle added to his fury. That someone – this shirker – should demand that his men, his men who risked so much, should demand to be carried on a stretcher was the last straw. He saw Ryle's fist – the supposedly injured fist – twitch.

'Go on,' jeered Jerry. 'Hit me. It's a court martial for you if you do. Go on, hit me . . .'

His voice was lost in the biggest insect scream yet.

'Down!' yelled Private Connolly, forcing him to the floor as the shell hit.

Jerry woke up with his mouth full of the taste of cordite and earth, his ears ringing with silence, Connolly's weight heavy on him. He raised his head. He could only have been unconscious for a few minutes. The room was full of dust-hazed light, open to the sky. Ryle was half-buried under a pile of rubble and for a stupid moment, although he couldn't hear anything, Jerry thought he was singing. Then he realized the man was shouting for help.

He had to help. He could move if Connolly rolled away . . . but Connolly was dead. Jerry blinked around the ruin. There were other men, some dead, some also singing – no, *shouting* – for help, their mouths opening and shutting. He groggily got to his feet. He had to help. He stumbled forward, then the first sound he'd heard since the shell burst, a sound like a giant insect, scissored through his head.

He ran. He left his post, he left his patients, he left his men, and ran. He didn't know where he was running to but he had an impression of staring eyes and grime-blackened faces and hands trying to hold him, then an invisible giant's hand picked him up, shook him and kicked him high into the air . . .

Jerry Lucas pulled deeply on his cigarette. 'I ran,' he said flatly. 'I called Ryle a coward, but I was the one who ran. I left my patients and my men and ran. A shell took me off my feet and when I woke up this time, I was in a field hospital as a patient. I ended up being shipped back to England and that was the end of my war.'

'You poor beggar,' said Jack.

Lucas looked at him with haunted eyes. 'You think so? I never told anyone what I'd done. I deserted my post and deserted my patients when they needed help urgently. Men *died* because of me. I could've got help for them, but I ran. I told my father. He knew, but he was the only one. I couldn't forget it, though. I always dreaded the past catching up with me. When Ryle turned up it seemed meant, somehow. He knew who I was, all right. I wanted to apologize to him, to try and make it up somehow, but he wanted far more than that.'

So that was that. Jack had guessed as much. Not the circumstances or the details, but the result. 'Blackmail.'

Lucas sunk his head in his hands. 'Blackmail. Ryle told Sir Matthew Vardon everything and he put the screws on my father. Dad's not a wealthy man. He had savings, yes, but they went fast. I wanted to face the music, to own up to what I'd done, but Dad couldn't bear the idea. Once that

168

story got out, my reputation would be shot.' He paused. 'A doctor needs his reputation. Once it's gone, he's ruined.'

That, thought Jack, was true.

Jerry Lucas lit another cigarette, smoking mechanically. 'Can you imagine the relief when Sir Matthew was taken ill? That damned nurse guessed something of my father's feelings, but Dad was in the clear, no matter what she may have thought or said. He knew Sir Matthew was dying. All he had to do was wait. Ryle, on the other hand . . .'

Jack waited.

'Ryle knew,' said Lucas in a flat voice. 'He was dangerous. My God, I hated Ryle. "Good morning, *Doctor*," he'd say, inviting me to challenge him. I dreamed that he was dead.' Jack looked at him sharply. Lucas's voice had quickened. 'Don't you understand? I wanted to be free. I dreamt of killing him.' His voice took on a hard edge of satisfaction. 'And now he's dead. I got what I wanted.'

In that moment Jack could well believe that Jerry Lucas really had murdered Ryle. It didn't answer all the questions, but it was *an* answer. There was one big question though, that Lucas hadn't touched on.

'What do you know about the Chessman?'

'The Chessman?' Lucas looked puzzled. 'I don't know what you mean.'

With a sigh of relief, Jack reached out his hand. 'Come on, Lucas. Let's go down.'

'What if I did murder Ryle?'

'You haven't murdered anyone.'

Jerry Lucas shook his head, as if to dislodge a fly, and looked at Jack's outstretched hand uncomprehendingly. 'I need a hand,' said Jack.

Reluctantly, Jerry Lucas stood up. 'If I go down,' he said uncertainly. 'I'll have to face all that again. The police think I killed Ryle. You think I killed Ryle.'

'No, I don't.'

Jack could see the battle between doubt and hope in Lucas's face. Lucas slowly reached out and took Jack's hand. 'I've told you what I did. Dad told me never to tell anyone. You could be dangerous.'

Jack decided not to answer. With Lucas's help he stood up, wincing as his foot touched the ground.

'You go first,' he said as if it had been agreed. 'I might fall.'

They got down the ladder and onto the timber walkway. Jack felt Jerry Lucas stiffen as he looked down onto the bells. He suddenly knew he was in great danger. One push from Lucas could send him over, onto the dangerously enticing smooth bronze of the bells, spread out below. The best – perhaps the only – defence was to offer none at all.

'You'll have to help me across the planks, I'm afraid,' said Jack, leaning on him. 'I don't think I can make it alone.'

For a fraction of a second Jerry Lucas paused, then took the weight of Jack's arm round his shoulders. It was a relief when they were across the timbers and on the ladder down to the belfry.

From below came the sound of voices.

'Haldean! Haldean, are you up there?' It was Ashley.

'We're in the belfry,' Jack called back. 'Lucas is here.'

Jerry Lucas froze, then turned and looked at Jack in horror. 'It's the police. You tricked me. I *trusted* you.'

Ashley appeared at the top of the stairs. 'Hello, Haldean,' he said anxiously. He looked at Jack, standing with his arm on Lucas's shoulder. 'Is everything all right? Hernshaw, the church warden, told me he'd seen you and Dr Lucas go up the tower.' Jerry Lucas walked towards him like an automaton. 'You've come for me. I can't stand it any longer.' His voice cracked. 'You know what I've done. Go on. Get it over with. I killed Ryle.'

Ashley looked at him with blank astonishment, then turned to Haldean. 'What on earth's he talking about?'

'Ryle was blackmailing him,' said Jack wearily. 'He thinks we suspect him of murdering Ryle.'

'For God's sake, stop!' begged Lucas. 'Arrest me! Get it over with. I'm going to hang.'

'For killing Ryle?' demanded Ashley. 'Don't be so bloody stupid, man. You haven't killed Ryle, or anyone else, by the look of you. I shouldn't think you'd have the nerve,' he added in an undertone.

The complete assurance in Ashley's voice took Jack by surprise. 'You sound very certain,' said Jack.

'Of course I'm certain. Ryle was arrested in Harwich at nine o'clock this morning on suspicion of theft. He had over six thousand pounds on him. Blackmail will come as a nice addition to the charge sheet. Oh, for Pete's sake,' he added in disgust. For Jerry Lucas had broken down in tears.

Eleven

Jack walked stiffly up the steps to the front door of Lucas's house. Although his leg felt much better, he wouldn't be sorry to sit down.

'You . . . you'd better come in,' said Lucas. Jack followed him into the tiled hall.

Dr Lucas came out of the surgery.

'Jerry? I wasn't expecting you back so soon.' Dr Lucas stepped back in surprise as he saw his son's companion. 'Major Haldean?'

Lucas motioned with his hand, trying to quiet his father. 'It's all over, Dad.' He gestured towards Jack. 'He knows all about it. He knows what happened in the war.'

Dr Lucas sagged and seemed to age visibly. 'I think you will understand, Major, that you are not welcome here.'

'No, Dad!' said Jerry quickly. He looked appealingly at Jack. 'Can you explain? Please stay.'

Dr Lucas shrugged and silently led the way into a drawing room that had a cold, unused air about it. A table like a sarcophagus flanked one wall, its gleaming surface threatening anyone to defile it with fingerprints. A horsehair sofa and two armchairs, all with antimacassars, stood at an exact distance from each other round a Turkish

172

carpet in front of an empty grate. 'Perhaps,' he said quietly, 'you will tell me what you know.'

'He knows about me,' interjected Jerry. 'Sit down, Haldean. That leg must be giving you gyp.' He faced his father. 'Haldean knows Ryle blackmailed us.'

Dr Lucas looked at his son in horror. 'You're talking wildly, Jerry. Goodness knows what you've been tricked into saying, but—'

'Cut it out, Dad,' said Jerry wearily. 'He knows, I tell you.'

Dr Lucas turned on Jack. 'And what business is it of yours, Major Haldean, may I ask?'

'Officially none,' replied Jack, sinking gratefully into an armchair. 'But haven't you realized, Doctor, that both you and your son have been under suspicion of murdering Ryle?'

Dr Lucas stared. 'That's incredible, sir! It's totally untrue.'

'I know,' said Haldean coolly. 'Ryle was arrested this morning which does rather let you out. If he hadn't been . . . well, it was fairly obvious that you were covering something up and it was known that you'd had at least one meeting with Ryle that you didn't want talked about. Things were looking a bit black.'

Dr Lucas sank back in his chair. 'Ryle's alive? That creature is alive?'

'Very much so.'

'But why should anyone think that I – *I* – killed him? What motive could I have?'

Dr Lucas was starting to irritate Jack. 'He had a hold over you. That was clear. The body in the church is obviously that of a drug addict. As a doctor you have ready access to drugs.' He watched as Dr Lucas flushed. 'Ryle had six thousand pounds on him. I don't suppose you gave it to him, did you?'

There was a stunned silence. 'Six thousand pounds?' Dr Lucas stared at him. 'Even if I sold everything I had I wouldn't be able to raise anything like that sum. I'm a general practitioner, not a Harley Street specialist. You can put that idea out of your head, Major.'

Jack nodded. He knew that a doctor in a village or small town usually earned around seven hundred pounds a year, enough to be comfortable but not wealthy by any stretch of the imagination. 'You could've inherited some money.'

Jerry Lucas nearly laughed. 'We used to have some investments, but it's all gone. Ryle's been bleeding us at the rate of thirty pounds a month.' He rested his forehead on his hand. 'I didn't want to pay up, Dad. I never wanted you to.'

'What choice did we have?' demanded Dr Lucas tartly. 'Reputation means everything to a doctor.' He got up impatiently and walked to the window. 'I tried. I went to see Sir Matthew. I thought he'd be shocked if I even hinted what his chauffeur was up to, but he merely laughed. He was splitting the money with Ryle. He was never satisfied. He demanded more and more. I couldn't pay and he threatened exposure.'

He let out a shuddering breath. 'My God! When he was taken ill, I felt as if I'd been let out of prison.' He turned to his son. 'We couldn't let it get out, Jerry.'

174

'What? That I'm a coward?'

'We would've been ruined! Both of us.'

Jack looked at Jerry Lucas. 'It isn't a question of cowardice. Your nerve cracked.'

His voice was firm and carried weight. He knew Jerry Lucas was concentrating intently on his words.

'You were under a terrific strain and everyone has a limit. You reached yours. It's happened to better men than you, Lucas.' Myself included, God help me, he added to himself. 'I know some of them. Nothing's on record. Sir Matthew Vardon's dead, Ryle's under arrest and you're in the clear.'

Jerry Lucas took a deep breath and slumped back in his chair. 'It's over?'

Was it over? Jack looked at Dr Lucas thoughtfully. 'What about the Chessman, Doctor?'

'The Chessman?' Dr Lucas looked bewildered. 'I don't know what you mean. What's chess got to do with anything?'

'Chess?' asked Jerry Lucas. 'Dad plays occasionally but . . .' He trailed off. 'I'm sorry. What on earth are you talking about?'

'I understand Lady Vardon received a couple of letters from someone calling himself the Chessman.'

Jerry Lucas looked interested, but Dr Lucas's voice was rich with disgust. 'Oh, those! They were obviously the work of a crank. I told Lady Vardon as much. I wouldn't waste your time on nonsense like that, Major. I imagine Sir Matthew crossed someone – he was not a pleasant man, by any manner of means – and they took this childish way of seeking some sort of revenge. As Sir Matthew's doctor, I can assure you that the suggestion that he died of anything other than natural causes is absurd.'

And there it was. Dr Lucas *might* have murdered Sir Matthew Vardon but Jack really didn't think he had. And, although it wasn't proof, his reaction to the mention of the Chessman was so sincere, Jack couldn't honestly doubt his complete ignorance of the matter. Ryle, who Jerry Lucas had every reason to want to murder, was alive.

'Is it over?' asked Jerry anxiously.

Jack got to his feet and clapped a hand on Jerry's shoulder. 'Yes, old man. For you, it's over.'

Superintendent Ashley looked at the man on the opposite side of the table from him. 'So you're Mr Jonathan Ryle, are you? Please sit down. Shut the door, will you, Sergeant? We thought you were dead, Mr Ryle.'

Ryle shifted uneasily and shot a covert glance at Ashley. He distrusted polite coppers even more than ordinary ones. You knew they were leading up to something. 'Is that why I'm here?' he demanded. 'For not being dead? Blimey, what a country.'

'We're delighted you're not dead, Mr Ryle, but it does leave us with a problem. You can't tell us who the body in the church belonged to, can you?'

'Here, you can't pin that on me,' snarled Ryle, seriously alarmed. 'I've been in Holland since Monday and I can prove it. What the hell are you charging me with, anyway?'

'Well,' said Ashley smoothly, tapping the suitcase on the table in front of him. 'There is the small matter of this money.' He nodded to the sergeant who produced a key and opened the case. Bundles of crisp white five-pound notes lay stacked within. 'Six thousand pounds is a lot of money to be carrying round with you, Mr Ryle. Perhaps you'd like to tell me how you got it?'

Ryle sniffed and rubbed his nose with his hand. 'That's mine, see? I won it.'

'I think not,' said Ashley quietly. 'You stole it, didn't you, Mr Ryle?'

Ryle flung back his head and for a moment the startling resemblance between him and Sir Matthew blazed out. 'I bleeding well didn't.' He dropped his face on to his hands and the likeness faded. 'I never thieved no money. I never did.'

'We know you didn't get it from blackmailing Dr Lucas. He only paid you thirty pounds a month.'

'I had to split that . . .' Ryle flinched as he realized what he had said and cowered back in his chair. 'Look, Guv'nor, who's been talking? It wasn't blackmail. I didn't want to do it. It wasn't my idea!'

Ashley raised his eyebrows. 'Care to tell me whose idea it was?'

Ryle sat back, thinking hard. 'Give me a fag, Guv, and I'll level with you.'

Ashley pushed his cigarette case and a box of matches across the table and Ryle lit one, holding the cigarette behind the palm of his hand.

'I'd got kicked out of the army. Some stores went missing and the buggers pinned it on me. I did a bit of time, then messed round for a bit, looking for a job. I'd always been handy with cars, but something always seemed to go wrong. Last time my services were dispensed with, as you might say, I decided to see what was doing at home. Mum was dead but my Aunty Bessie put me right. Mum had been in service, years ago, with a posh family in Sussex called Vardon and Aunty Bessie said Vardon was my real father.'

He sucked hard on his cigarette. 'To cut a long story short, I asked a young lady in a library to see if there was a family called Vardon and she gave me their address, so I went to Croxton Ferriers. And a miserable little one-horse dump it is, too,' he added gloomily. 'On the way I ran into that bleeder, Castradon, and got a job with him. I hadn't been there a week before I recognized my father. Well, I'd dropped lucky. He told me to find out what I could about Castradon, then come to him. He liked the idea of having me around.'

God knows why, thought Ashley, and forced himself to concentrate once more.

'My father was all right. I told him about recognizing young Lucas, and he told me to put the screws on to see what happened. It was like finding money in the street. Old Dr Lucas cut up rough with my father but he soon got into line. And then everything seemed to hot up. I told my father I didn't think Lucas could pay any more, but he was screwing them hard.'

'And that's when,' said Ashley, mindful of a conversation he'd had with Jack, 'he got you to steal the diamonds for him.'

'Oh hell.' Ryle lit another cigarette with trembling hands. 'He needed money. God knows why,

178

but he needed a lot of money, fast. He told me when he and his missus would be taking a walk and got me to spring out at them. He said if I swiped the stones he could collect on the insurance and then, later on, when the fuss had died down, I could fence them for him. He knew a place in Amsterdam. He had it all worked out. I hid the diamonds in a petrol can in the garage.'

'He left you in charge of the diamonds?' asked Ashley, disbelievingly.

'Honest truth, he did. He made me sign a paper to say I'd swiped them and then, after I'd fenced them for him, he was going to give it me back with a cut of the take. He said it was foolproof, but he went and croaked. Well, I knew where the paper was but do you think I could get at it? There's a secret drawer in the desk in his bedroom but even when I got up there I couldn't get the hang of the catch. After a couple of weeks I thought, sod this for a game of soldiers, and decided to go to Amsterdam on my own account. It all went fine until you rozzers picked me up.'

'You left Croxton Ferriers in a bit of a hurry.'

'Too right I did. I had Castradon after me. He can't half hit. He's a maniac.' Ryle sniffed self-righteously. 'He needs locking up, that bloke. Bleeding dangerous, he is. I got the diamonds and lit out for Holland as fast as I could. But I don't know nothing about this dead geezer and don't you go laying it on me that I do.' He paused hopefully. 'Can I go now?'

Ashley raised his eyebrows. 'Go? I don't think you're going anywhere for a very long time, my lad.'

'But I've done nothing wrong!'

Ashley ticked the points off on his fingers. 'There's assault, blackmail and grand larceny.'

'But I didn't steal the stones!'

'Oh yes? You've just admitted that you signed a statement to say that you did. I think you're going to be a guest of ours for some time, Mr Ryle.' Ashley turned to the sergeant. 'Take him away.'

As the Atlantic churned green and cold under the bows of the Cunard liner *Mauretania,* Lady Esmé Vardon turned to walk down the companionway. Damn! The man who had been so openly attentive on the train out of Chicago was standing by the rail. She hoped he wasn't going to make a nuisance of himself. She didn't want to start anything, not with Tom waiting for her. The man turned and raised his hat.

'Lady Vardon? I didn't realize we were going to be travelling companions all the way to England. Will you have dinner with me tonight?'

'I think not,' she said coolly. He was attractive, but shipboard romances were a hazard she didn't want to face. Lady Vardon. It sounded kind of nice . . .

'I think I see how this is going to work,' said Ashley, going down on one knee and squinting under the kneehole of the massive writing-desk. 'If we lower the lid – like so – I think we should find another drawer at the back. Now, what have we got in here? Nothing. Can you see how it works, Haldean?'

180

Jack stirred himself from the solid four-poster bed against which he had been leaning and walked across to the huge burr walnut escritoire. Privately he was marvelling at the late Sir Matthew's taste in bedroom furnishings. That anyone should choose voluntarily to sleep in a room that looked like *Act 1 – The Haunted Grange* was beyond his comprehension.

'It would be so like dear Matthew to hide his papers away,' said Lady Vardon with just the suspicion of a sniff. 'Poor Matthew. He was like a boy in so many ways. And so secretive, too, wasn't he?' she added, looking at Thomas. 'I'm going to ask Matthew about it tonight,' she continued.

'You're going to ask *who*?' asked Jack, startled.

'I sit with Mrs Parry-Jones. She's Welsh. She attributes her gifts to her Celtic blood.' Lady Vardon sighed wistfully. 'She has such an insight into the things that are beyond. She has been such a comfort to me since Matthew passed over. He seems so happy in his new existence. Since the veil of illusion has been torn away he has attained real wisdom.'

Jack stooped over the desk, his long fingers searching for the hidden catch. His face was impassive but his dark eyes danced with rich enjoyment. Ashley turned away hurriedly before he could exchange glances and disgrace himself with laughter.

'If I could ask about the diamonds, Lady Vardon,' he said, rather too quickly to be polite. 'They were your own property, were they?'

'Yes, indeed. They were my dear father's wedding gift. Matthew promised to get me some more but he said it would take time to find stones

181

of equal quality. He didn't want me to have second-best. He was always so thoughtful in such unexpected ways.'

'Did the insurance money come to you, Lady Vardon?'

'Oh no. Matthew dealt with all the financial side of things. He had such a head for figures.'

'Have you found that catch yet, Haldean?' asked Thomas.

'I've nearly got it . . . Bingo!' He glanced at the paper before handing it over to Ashley. 'One signed document, as stated.'

'So that's true, at least,' grunted Ashley. He read it quickly and put it in his pocketbook. 'Thank you very much for your time, Lady Vardon. You've been very helpful.'

'Not at all, Superintendent.' She closed her eyes, took a deep breath and sat rigidly. 'I would like to remain here for a few minutes. I feel so close to poor Matthew in this room.'

Thomas turned to Jack and Ashley. 'I'll show you out.'

He ushered them onto the landing. 'You must excuse my stepmother,' he said as they walked down the stairs to the hall. 'I'm starting to get quite concerned about her. This spiritualist nonsense has gone to her head. I didn't even attempt to explain my father's part in the theft. She'd never believe it. Talking of which, Superintendent, what's going to happen to Ryle?'

Ashley sighed. 'Ryle's a ruddy nuisance. He's certainly guilty of conspiring to steal the diamonds, but it'll be nasty for your stepmother when all the facts come out.'

'Why d'you think your father needed money?' asked Jack.

'Search me. I suppose my father's solicitor might help you. He's a chap called Flood of Newson, Harvey and Flood in Gray's Inn. I'm going to see him tomorrow. I need to find out the true state of affairs with the estate.' He paused. 'As a matter of fact, it might be worth your while speaking to Simon. I was going to call on him anyway, after I've seen old Flood, and now we've found out the truth about Ryle, I really do need to see him. He knew far more about my father's shares and investments than I do.'

'Shares,' repeated Jack thoughtfully. The word struck a chord. Edward Castradon had told them how Simon Vardon tried to extort – if Castradon's account was correct, extort wasn't too strong a word – shares in the company that Matthew Vardon and Castradon's father had started.

'I'd like to have a word with your brother,' said Jack pleasantly.

Thomas Vardon gave a disgruntled snort. 'I'd like to have a word with him myself. He was supposed to meet me off the ship, but he didn't turn up. He said he'd come home for a few days, but goodness knows when he's going to arrive. I expected a note from him at least, but I can't get hold of him.'

A suspicion, an only too believable and grim suspicion, crossed Jack's mind. It was possible, yes, but he didn't want to jump to conclusions. 'Does he live with anyone? Anyone who'd know where he was?'

Thomas looked at him in surprise. 'That's a funny question. I suppose someone must know where he is but he doesn't live with anyone. He's got a service flat off the Haymarket. I imagine there's a charwoman, but she doesn't live in.'

'Is he on the telephone?' Thomas nodded. 'Would you mind telephoning him now, Vardon? I really would like to speak to him.'

'Just as you like,' said Thomas in some surprise. 'The telephone's in the hall.'

Ashley drew Jack back a pace as Sir Thomas led them down the stairs. 'What's in your mind, Haldean? What's all the fuss about these shares?'

'It's not shares I'm worried about,' said Jack in a low voice. 'It's the Chessman.' He lowered his voice still further. 'The Chessman's got a grudge against the Vardons. Simon Vardon is *missing*.'

Ashley's eyes widened in apprehension. 'My God,' he said softly. 'I wonder if you're right.'

Sir Thomas picked up the telephone and, after a brief word with the exchange, was put through. After what seemed like a long wait while the telephone bell shrilled, the girl from the exchange came back on the line.

'I'm afraid there's no answer from that number, caller.'

'I knew it,' said Thomas. He turned to them with a wry grin as he hooked the earpiece back on the stand. His grin faded as he saw Jack and Ashley's serious faces. 'What's the matter? Simon's bound to turn up eventually. He always does.'

Ashley drew his breath in. 'Could we have a word with you in private, sir?'

'If you like,' said Sir Thomas, puzzled. 'Come into the morning room.'

The morning room was off the hall. Thomas

led them in and Ashley shut the door firmly behind them.

'Now, sir,' said Ashley. 'I don't want to alarm you unnecessarily, but we do have a murder on our hands.' He paused, choosing his words carefully. 'As a matter of routine, we have to check up on any man reported missing. Your brother . . .'

'My brother?' repeated Thomas Vardon incredulously. He sat down on the arm of a chair and gazed up at them in disbelief. 'You can't honestly think that there's the slightest chance that my brother's been *murdered*.'

'He is missing,' said Jack.

'I haven't seen him, I grant you, but that's not missing. The man in the church can't be Simon. It just can't. Why, he never comes here . . .' His voice trailed away. 'He was here earlier this week, wasn't he? Before I arrived home.' He swallowed hard. 'No. I don't believe it. I just don't believe it. You simply have to be wrong.' He put a hand to his mouth. 'We'll go up to London,' he said after a pause. 'There must be somebody in the flats who knows where he is.'

Ashley cleared his throat. 'There's perhaps a quicker method, sir. As you know, we found the body of a man. I'm afraid the face is beyond recognition but are there any marks or identifying features you could recognize your brother by?'

That, thought Jack, was a tall order. The body was so mutilated there was precious little left to identify. He hoped – hoped very much – that it wouldn't be necessary to show those ghastly remains to Thomas Vardon. The poor beggar seemed to have gone into a trance.

'Sir?' prompted Ashley.

Thomas turned to him with a shudder. 'Simon's about my height but slighter in build.' The two men waited patiently. 'I can't think of anything else.'

Dr Lucas had said the victim had an appendix scar. 'Did he ever have appendicitis?' asked Jack.

Thomas nodded. 'Yes, he did, now you come to mention it.' He snapped his fingers. 'I know! He had a tattoo!' He clapped his hand to his left bicep. 'Here, on his arm. He had it done in Limehouse for a dare. It was a Chinese thing, a charm that was supposed to bring prosperity.'

The body didn't have a tattoo but there was an apparently inexplicable injury to the left arm, an injury that would conceal the fact there'd ever been a tattoo there.

The shocked look in Ashley's eyes told Jack he'd had the same thought. 'I think, sir,' said Ashley, speaking very gently, 'although it'll be very distressing for you, it'd be as well if you took a look at the body.'

Ashley presented their credentials at the mortuary. They were shown into a large room containing a deal table and six chairs, where they were met by a gruesomely respectful attendant. He escorted them through a cheerless brick lobby and down a short flight of steps into a white-tiled room.

Gas lamps showed a human shape shrouded by a thick canvas sheet on a stone-topped slab. The air was cold, cold enough for their breath to show in little puffs of condensation. The smell of chemicals hung bleakly in the still air.

Ashley had asked the attendant to keep the

corpse's head covered. The face was completely unrecognisable and the process of identifying a body was harrowing enough.

Jack stood next to Thomas as the mortuary attendant turned back the sheet. He saw the muscles of his jaw flex. Thomas blinked very rapidly, fighting back tears. He made a little noise in the back of his throat, then wiped the back of his hand across his eyes. He reached out and touched the dead man on the shoulder. He turned to them and tried to speak, but could only swallow.

'Is it your brother, sir?' asked Ashley, quietly.

Vardon nodded, dropped his hand and backed away. 'Yes. It can't be anyone else, can it? Not with that scar and . . .' His voice broke. 'And where his tattoo was.' He stopped, staring at the needle marks on the arm. 'What are those?'

Ashley didn't answer.

Thomas looked at him in bewilderment. 'I've seen marks like those before. In Hollywood. There's a raft of drugs used in Hollywood. Simon didn't use drugs.' His voice wavered and he repeated what he'd said. This time it was a question. 'Simon didn't use drugs?'

'You never suspected your brother of using drugs, sir?'

'No, I . . .' Thomas began, then broke off. 'His letters,' he said softly. 'Sometimes – recently I mean – they were disjointed, incoherent. Then he'd sound all right and I thought everything was okay.' He turned to face Ashley. 'I was uneasy about him. I think that's why I was so keen to see him as soon as I arrived.'

He thrust his hand out, as if to ward off the

187

sight of the naked man on the marble slab. 'For God's sake, let's get out of here.'

'Can I get you anything, sir? A cup of tea perhaps?' asked the mortuary attendant as Vardon strode past him and up the steps.

Vardon waved him away. 'No. God, no. I'll be in the car.'

'Poor devil,' said Jack with feeling, after he'd gone. 'That was a nasty experience for him.'

'It always comes as a shock,' said the attendant as he covered up the body. 'Mind you, it'd shock anyone seeing a cadaver in this condition. We have some nasty cases in here, with traffic accidents and the like, but this is the worst I've seen done deliberately.'

He stood mournfully by the corpse for a moment and then turned to Ashley. 'You'll have to see the mortuary superintendent, now you've got an identification, sir. If you would like to come into the anteroom, I'll tell him that you're waiting.'

It was twenty minutes later before Jack and Ashley returned to Vardon in the car. He lit a cigarette from the butt of the one he was smoking.

'That letter I got,' said Thomas abruptly. 'The one from the Chessman. Did the Chessman do this?'

Ashley had been expecting the question. 'We believe so, sir.'

'So who's next?' demanded Thomas. 'Me? First my father, now my brother. What are you doing to stop this maniac?'

Ashley paused, weighing up Vardon's tense face. 'Do you want an honest answer or a reassuring one?' he asked eventually. 'Because the honest answer is that I don't know who's behind this, Sir Thomas, but I intend to turn Croxton Ferriers inside out until I get them.'

Thomas Vardon sank back on the leather seat. 'I'm sorry. I know you're doing all you can.' He stared ahead blankly. 'We'd better go up to his flat, I suppose. I'll have to sort out all his things. I'll have to tell my stepmother. His mother.'

'I must ask you not to visit your brother's flat without us, sir.'

Thomas looked up angrily. 'What d'you mean? Why the hell can't I go where I want to?'

'Because his flat might contain evidence as to his killer, sir. I'll need to get the Yard in on this, Haldean,' he added in an aside to Jack. 'Sir Thomas,' he added gently, 'I'll need some details from you about your brother.'

'Oh, anything you damn well like,' said Vardon, resting his forehead on his hands. 'And then you'd better take me home.' He shuddered. 'I'll have to break the news to my stepmother.'

Twelve

The next morning, Jack, together with Ashley and Vardon, drove up to London.

Simon Vardon's flat was part of a new building, curved in an elegant bow of brick and glass round Waldeck Court off the Haymarket. Jack was pleased to see his old pal, Chief Inspector Bill Rackham, as ginger-haired and as untidy as ever, waiting to greet them on the pavement outside the flats.

Ashley had telephoned him yesterday and brought him up to date with the events in Croxton Ferriers. Bill, who knew Ashley well, had offered all the help he could give.

'This is Sir Thomas Vardon,' said Jack, introducing him, as they climbed out of the car. Thomas still looked strained. He had been uncharacteristically quiet on the journey up, but tried to smile as Bill shook hands.

'I'm very sorry to hear of your loss, Sir Thomas.'

'I'm still trying to believe it,' said Thomas. 'It doesn't seem possible somehow, that Simon's actually dead.' He looked up at the flats and squared his shoulders. 'I suppose we'd better go in. His flat was number twelve, on the first floor.'

'I know,' said Bill, as they stepped in off the street and into the lobby. 'I've had a word with the porter.' He glanced at Ashley. 'After your phone call last night, I called round and picked up the key. I wanted, not that it'll do any good, to prevent the charwoman going in this morning. Unfortunately for us she's got a reputation as being a very conscientious cleaner and tidier, but it was the least I could do.'

He looked at Thomas. 'The porter was very sorry to hear the news about your brother, Sir Thomas, as you'd expect, but also said that if there'd been any wrongdoing, to find a chap called Alan Leigh. Apparently he's seen a lot of your brother recently. He's stayed here a few times. The porter described him as a very queer customer indeed.'

'Alan Leigh?' said Thomas in surprise.

190

'Do you know him?'

'Leigh? Yes, I know him. He's a distant cousin. We always knew of him, but we didn't get to know him well until the war. Simon, Leigh and I were in the Royal Sussex. Simon was a subaltern in Leigh's company. Leigh was a damn good sort. He saved my brother's life on the Somme. Whatever did the porter mean, by calling Leigh a queer customer?'

'I asked him that. Apparently Leigh's very highly strung and moody—'

'That's true enough,' interrupted Thomas impatiently, 'but as I say, he was a decent sort.'

'I looked up his record,' said Bill flatly. 'After what the porter said, I more or less had to. He's got a conviction for drug offences.'

Thomas froze. 'Drugs?' he repeated in a whisper. 'Drugs?'

There was no mistaking his emotion. Bill, evidently surprised by Thomas Vardon's horrified reaction, gave Jack a puzzled look.

'Simon Vardon took drugs,' explained Jack. 'I'm afraid that was evident from the body. Sir Thomas knew nothing about it.'

'Leigh's to blame,' said Sir Thomas fiercely. 'He must've dragged Simon into his filthy habits.'

'Where's Leigh now?' asked Ashley. 'Have you any idea, Rackham? Granted he knew Simon Vardon well, he might be a valuable witness.'

'I can request a search for him, certainly. The other piece of evidence I've turned up concerns Mr Vardon's car.'

He took out his notebook and flipped it open. 'A car, a 20 h.p. Austin four-seater coupé, number

191

LC 3083, registered to Simon Vardon of this address, was left at London Bridge station last Tuesday morning.'

'That's Simon's car, all right,' said Thomas. 'He bought it second-hand some months ago.' His voice wavered slightly. 'He mentioned it in one of his letters.'

Ashley nodded. 'Tuesday morning? That adds up. We know Simon Vardon visited Croxton Ferriers on Tuesday afternoon.'

Bill unlocked the door of number twelve and they crowded into the hall. A folded-over piece of notepaper, and a few letters, obviously put there by the charwoman, lay unopened on the hall table.

Thomas Vardon picked up the note and read it. '"Wednesday 22nd". That's last Wednesday.'

The day after, Jack thought, Simon had been killed. The same thought clearly occurred to Thomas. He glanced at the note, then thrust it at Jack. 'You read it. I can't.'

'All right. "Simon, where are you?",' Jack read. '"I expected you back last night. I know you said to keep out of it, but I'm going to Croxton. Alan."'

'He went to Croxton Ferriers?' said Ashley. 'No one's seen him, as far as I know.'

Thomas Vardon's chin jerked up, a light in his eyes. 'No one's seen him? Then . . .' He broke off. 'No, forget it. It was just an idea.'

'What, sir?' asked Ashley.

Thomas shrugged. 'I just wondered if the body in the church could be Alan Leigh.'

'You identified the body in the mortuary as your brother's,' said Ashley.

192

Thomas nodded. 'I know,' he said with a sigh. 'It was Simon, all right. I don't *want* it to be Simon,' he added savagely.

He picked up the letters and rifled through them, then stopped. 'My God,' he said quietly, and held it out to Ashley.

The envelope, with its typed inscription, was horribly familiar. Jack felt the hairs on the back of his neck prickle. It was from the Chessman.

Ashley slit open the envelope with a paper knife on the table and held the letter carefully by the corners. 'Listen to this. "If you want to stay alive, keep away from Sussex. Your next visit will be your last."' He checked the envelope. 'It was posted in Croxton Ferriers last Monday.'

'And on Tuesday . . .' Thomas began. His mouth tightened. 'My God, I wish I could get my hands on this maniac.'

Bill nodded sympathetically. 'Maniac's about right, from what I've heard.'

Ashley laid the letter out on the table and, taking a bottle of grey mercury powder from his bag, tested the letter for fingerprints.

'Nothing,' he said in disgust. 'Still, it was worth trying.'

The rest of the letters were mainly bills and receipts, including a bar bill from the Courtland.

'That was his club,' said Thomas.

His club, thought Jack, might be worth a visit.

The only other item of mail was a ship to shore cable sent by Thomas last Thursday from on board the *Olympic*, giving the estimated time of the ship's arrival in Southampton.

'I didn't realize, when I sent this, what I was

coming home to,' was Thomas's comment as he handed it to Ashley. 'If I had, I'd have stayed in America. Poor Simon.' His mouth tightened. 'I was annoyed with him for not coming to meet me.'

'It's a natural reaction, sir,' said Ashley sympathetically. 'Do you mind if we hold on to these letters for the time being?'

'Help yourself,' said Thomas with a shrug.

He wandered gloomily into the sitting room and stood, hands in pockets, looking round. 'There's damn all here. God knows why I came.' He sank down in an armchair, wrapped in his own thoughts.

After a few moments' silence, Bill and Ashley went back into the hall to explore the rest of the flat.

Thomas put a hand to his forehead. 'He's *gone*.' There was no mistaking that ragged raw edge of grief.

Jack stood awkwardly in front of the fireplace. Any words he could say would be inadequate but he wanted, simply by being there, to convey some sort of human sympathy.

Almost despite himself, he couldn't avoid looking round. Thomas was sunk in torpor. Jack crouched quietly down beside the bookcase, trying to get some sense of Simon Vardon's personality.

Simon Vardon had, judging from the pile of papers in the rack beside the sofa, been a newspaper rather than a book reader. There were a few popular detective stories and some reference books. The top of the bookcase was a sort of smoker's corner, with a box of cigarettes, a packet of cigars, a table lighter and a jar of pipe tobacco. A small tin of highly scented, greenish tinged tobacco also contained a packet of cigarette papers.

Jack replaced the lid on the tin thoughtfully and turned his attention to the mantelpiece. Amongst the litter of various oddments were two photographs. One was a flattering studio portrait of a younger Lady Vardon. The other was clearly Sir Thomas together with a man, who, despite his moustache and fair hair, shared that startling, unmistakable family resemblance. Simon Vardon.

He picked up the photograph and examined it closely, trying to get some sense of the character.

'He'd changed,' said Thomas from the armchair. Jack looked round, photo in hand. 'When that picture was taken, he was a light-hearted beggar. Everyone liked him. He was a happy-go-lucky sort of guy. He made quite a bit from stocks and shares, but he earned a very respectable income from acting as a commission agent to high-class gaming clubs. Obviously you have to get on with people very well to make that pay, but he did. I wouldn't like the risk of living like that, but he thrived on it. I always felt protective towards him. He was my younger brother, after all. Obviously, I hadn't seen him for a couple of years, but I'd sensed a change. His letters became more and more infrequent and when they came, he always seemed anxious. They'd become duty letters, if you know what I mean, and the fun had gone out of them. I actually felt slightly anxious about meeting him again.'

Ashley put his head round the door. 'Haldean, can you spare a moment, please? There's something I'd like your opinion on.'

Haldean followed Ashley down the hall and into the bathroom. Bill was standing by the bathroom cabinet, holding a small corked bottle. There were two syringes on the shelf in the cabinet.

'We'll need to get this analysed,' said Bill, 'but I'll bet my boots it's either heroin or melted snow.'

'Melted snow?' asked Ashley, puzzled.

'Cocaine,' translated Bill.

Jack nodded. 'It's nothing more than we expected. In addition, there's a packet of cigarette papers and a tin with some very dubious tobacco in the sitting room. Apparently Simon Vardon acted as a commission agent, introducing clients to high-stake gambling clubs. It's the sort of society where it'd be easy enough to get hold of cocaine. Although I didn't say as much to Sir Thomas, he could make quite a nice income from dope dealing.'

'I wonder if Leigh was one of his clients?' asked Bill. 'After I spoke to the porter last night, I did wonder if Leigh was our killer. If Simon Vardon was supplying him with dope, who knows what quarrel they could have had.'

'If Leigh murdered Vardon on Tuesday, he'd hardly leave a note for him the next day enquiring where he was,' pointed out Jack. 'And I can't see why he'd take Vardon's body all the way to Croxton Ferriers in order to conceal it in a cupboard in the church, no matter how doped up he was.'

196

'No, that's true enough,' agreed Bill.

'That latest Chessman letter was posted in Croxton Ferriers,' said Ashley. 'Our murderer's in Croxton Ferriers all right.'

'Have you any idea who it might be?' asked Bill.

Ashley looked at Jack and shrugged. 'We did have our suspicions of the local doctor and his son. That's when we thought the victim was Ryle. Now the body's been identified as Vardon, it's a different matter. We know Simon Vardon came to Croxton Ferriers on Tuesday. He had a very stormy interview with the local solicitor, a chap called Edward Castradon.'

Ashley briefly recounted the circumstances of the meeting and what they knew about Castradon.

'I see,' said Bill thoughtfully. 'So on Tuesday afternoon, Edward Castradon, who's got a notoriously rocky temper, slings Simon Vardon out on his ear. Not only that, but his monkey wrench and axe, which you suspect was used on the body, is missing, in addition to his travelling rug, which was actually found with the body.'

'To be fair, we don't know it's actually Castradon's rug,' put in Jack. 'It does seem likely, though.'

'Precisely,' said Bill. He cocked an eyebrow at Ashley. 'How come you haven't arrested him?'

'Mainly because of the time we've wasted running round after Ryle.' said Ashley.

'And,' added Jack, 'there's that very inconvenient alibi. Although the telegram that summoned him to Eastbourne was fake, he certainly was in Eastbourne that evening.'

'There's something dodgy going on, all the same,' said Bill.

'Undoubtedly,' agreed Jack. 'What exactly the dodginess is, we're not sure of yet. I want to know more about these shares that Simon Vardon was so keen to get hold of. There's a desk in the sitting room. There might be some relevant paper-work in there.'

They went back into the sitting room. Thomas Vardon was still sitting motionless in the armchair, staring blankly in front of him. He hardly seemed to hear Ashley when he asked for permission to look in his brother's desk. 'What?' he said, when Ashley repeated the question. 'Yes, of course. Go ahead.'

Ashley sighed when he opened the desk. There was a mass of papers, all jumbled up together.

Vardon shook his head. 'You know, Simon was always such a tidy sort of bloke. I can hardly credit these were his things.' He stood up and shook himself impatiently. 'I don't think I can stand this any longer. I need a drink.'

He looked at his watch and groaned. 'I've still got this appointment with the solicitor. I suppose he'll have to know what's happened. God knows what he'll say. It just doesn't seem *possible*.' He looked round the flat and shuddered. 'I'll make my own way home, Haldean.'

After he'd gone, Ashley turned back to the desk. 'Let's get this lot in order. It'll probably be easier without Sir Thomas here. If we split them up into personal, business and private affairs, bills and such like, we'll be able to see what we've got.'

They had been working for no more than a few minutes, when Bill looked up. 'You know your favourite suspect, the solicitor?' He held out a manila folder. Attached to the cover with a paper clip was a note: *Castradon knows!*

Ashley whistled. 'Let me see that!'

They crowded round as he opened the file. There were two lots of share certificates and certificates of ownership in Antilla Exploration Limited. Both blocks of shares belonged to Matthew Vardon. One block of shares, Jack noted, had previously belonged to a Stamford Leigh. The file also contained a geologist's report, a sheaf of receipts and three letters on thin, foreign notepaper. The letters were headed J.B. Crossland, Mining Agent, Jirón Silverio, Huánuco and addressed to Sir Matthew Vardon.

'"Dear Sir Matthew,"' read Jack, picking up the topmost letter. '"I am pleased to report the first consignment of machinery has arrived intact and is being shipped to the Huánuco River workings where, allowing for difficulties with the terrain, I expect excavation will commence within the next month . . ."'

He read on rapidly to the end of the letter, then picked up the geologist's report. He skimmed through it quickly, then sat back, running his hand through his hair. 'They've made a strike.'

'What?' demanded Bill.

'They've made a strike. Antilla Exploration Limited – they've found gold.' Jack jabbed his finger at the report. 'Lots of gold, by the sound of things.'

He stood up excitedly. 'This explains why Sir

199

Matthew suddenly came down hard on Dr Lucas. He wanted more money to finance the mine. It explains why he robbed his own wife of her diamonds and it also explains why Simon Vardon wanted the Antilla Exploration shares from Castradon.'

'Because they'd found gold,' said Ashley, in an awestruck voice. 'A gold mine, Haldean! My God! It could be worth thousands and thousands of pounds.'

'Was Simon Vardon in on it?' demanded Bill. 'He must've been, as he's the one who tried to get the shares from Castradon.'

'That was only last week,' said Jack. 'His father died a couple of months ago. Let's see what else we can gather from this file.'

After quarter of an hour or so, the history of the Huánuco River strike was fairly clear. Following a discovery of gold ore further up river by an American mining company, Sir Matthew had commissioned the mining agent, J.B. Crossland, to assay the land held by Antilla Exploration. In order to exploit the find, however, which was in remote mountainous jungle, money for machinery, transport and workers was needed. Some money had evidently been found; more had been promised.

'That's clear enough,' said Bill. 'I reckon Simon Vardon found this file in his father's papers after his death. We know Simon Vardon tried to bully Castradon into selling his shares but who actually owns this mine?'

Jack lit a cigarette. 'The company, Antilla Exploration, actually owns it, I suppose. The question is, who owns Antilla Exploration? Castradon told us that his father, Michael Castradon, Matthew Vardon and this chap, Stamford Leigh, who has to be a relation of Vardon's pal, Alan Leigh, travelled to South America together. The three men set up the company, but subsequently quarrelled. The shares were divided between the three of them. The agreement was that if the shares hadn't been sold or willed elsewhere, then each party's share would be split between the survivors or their heirs.'

'So that means Sir Thomas Vardon owns two thirds of this gold mine,' said Bill slowly.

Ashley nodded. 'And Edward Castradon owns the other third.' He tapped the notepaper clipped to the folder. '*Castradon knows.*' He sat back in his chair, chin in his hands.

'I think this changes everything,' he said at last. 'Granted the circumstances of Simon Vardon's murder – the church, the lilies, the chessman, the Chessman letters and the threats against the Vardon family – there didn't seem to be any motive apart from sheer lunacy. That's all changed. There was obviously a family feud between the Castradons and the Vardons, but that hardly seemed an adequate reason for the murder. *Castradon knows.* Maybe what he knows is that if the Vardons are dead, he acquires the shares as the last survivor. I'd say the ownership of a gold mine was a very strong motive indeed.'

'Did Sir Matthew Vardon die a natural death?' asked Bill. 'I know your village doctor says so, but there's quite a bit of circumstantial evidence to suggest otherwise.'

201

'The village doctor, luckily for him, called in a second opinion, Dr Jacob McNiece of Harley Street,' said Jack. 'He's worth a visit, Ashley. Now we know there was a gold mine at stake, it all seems a lot more plausible that Sir Matthew was bumped off.'

'*Castradon knows*,' repeated Ashley. 'All I can say is, that if he did know about the gold mine, he was keeping it to himself. All right; let's say, for the sake of argument, that Castradon did kill Sir Matthew Vardon. There was certainly no love lost between them, that's for sure. But why kill Simon Vardon? If Sir Thomas is Sir Matthew's heir, he's the one who should be in the firing line.'

'Maybe Simon was the nearest Vardon to hand,' suggested Jack. 'If Castradon really is the killer, he'd have to bump off Simon Vardon eventually, in order to scoop the pool.' He frowned. 'Where does Lady Vardon fit into this, I wonder? After all, as Sir Matthew's wife, she surely inherited *something*. Could you look into who inherits what, Ashley?'

'Speaking of Sir Thomas,' said Bill, 'I know he seems innocent enough, but leaving Edward Castradon aside, he does benefit. It appears he now owns two thirds of a gold mine.'

Ashley shook his head impatiently. 'Sir Thomas couldn't have murdered Simon Vardon, no matter how many gold mines he owns. For one thing, if he's the heir, he gets the lot, not his younger brother. Why turn to murder?'

'Yes,' said Jack thoughtfully. '*If* he's the heir.'

'I'll have a word with the Vardons' solicitor,'

said Ashley. 'That's Newson, Harvey and Flood of Gray's Inn. Sir Thomas said as much yesterday. All the same, no matter what the terms of Sir Matthew's will are, Thomas Vardon can't be in two places at once. We know he was on the *Olympic* in the middle of the Atlantic when the murder happened. Simon Vardon had been dead for days by the time Sir Thomas showed up.'

'You don't doubt that, do you, Jack?' asked Bill, looking at his friend's expression.

'Call it unnecessary caution,' said Jack with a laugh, 'but I'm going to pay a visit to the White Star Shipping office, all the same. I want absolute proof Sir Thomas was on that boat.'

Thirteen

Edward Castradon walked up the path to his house. It was a lovely evening, just the sort of evening to have tea in the garden or, perhaps, go for a drive. He hadn't been home this early for ages. They could run over to Croxton Magna and have dinner at that riverside place, The Royal George.

It would do them good to get out. He hung up his hat and coat and put his briefcase down by the hall stand.

It was the inquest tomorrow and Sue would have to give evidence. Poor Sue needed to put the whole business to one side, forget about it as much as was humanly possible. Yes, he'd like to take Sue out. He needed, he thought with a twinge of guilt, to talk to her, properly, without quarrelling. It was his rotten bad temper that was at the root of everything. He touched his face before he realized what he'd done. He caught sight of himself in the hall mirror and grimaced. *Sue didn't mind.* She'd told him that dozens of times but he found it incredible. Surely, deep down, she must mind, but . . .

The thought ran through his mind, along the old familiar, well-worn track. He looked at himself squarely in the mirror and forced himself to stop. *Sue didn't mind.*

He walked into the sitting room, looking for Sue. It was a restful room. He picked up a chessman from the board, momentarily distracted with thoughts of the game, then replaced it on the same square. He didn't want to get drawn into a game against a newspaper opponent, he wanted to take his wife out to dinner. He saw the book she had been reading face down on the sofa and smiled. Everything was peaceful and just . . . well, just right, somehow. Home. Maybe she was out in the garden. He let himself out of the side door and then suddenly stiffened. Sue's laugh rang out. She hadn't laughed like that for months. Who the devil was here?

He strode down the path, stopping at the corner. Sue was with a man. For a black moment Ned thought it was Simon Vardon, but Simon Vardon wouldn't bother him again, not after their last encounter. This must be Thomas Vardon. Sue was pointing out the ivy where the sparrows had nested. Vardon said something he didn't catch and Sue turned to him. The sun was on her face and she pushed her hair back with a heart-catching smile.

Ned's stomach turned to water. She used to look at him like that. *Him!* A small angry vein began to pulse in his forehead.

His foot scraped on the path and the couple whirled. Was that guilt in her expression?

'Hello, Ned,' she said in surprise. 'I didn't expect you home this early.'

'No,' he said stonily. 'I can see.'

Sue's face altered. She became tense and wary. Vardon stood by politely.

'Sir Thomas – Tom – has just got back from London,' said Sue. 'He called about our dinner invitation. His wife should arrive the day after tomorrow. How about the day after that?'

He could hear the nervousness in her voice. What was she nervous of? Him? He was suddenly infuriated. Why should his wife be so nervous of speaking to him?

He wanted to strike out, to hurt, to wipe that damn polite smile off Thomas Vardon's face. He couldn't do that. 'I'll go along with anything you've arranged.'

Sir Thomas nodded politely, still with that damn self-satisfied smile. Sue looked so relieved he couldn't help adding a rider. 'You seem to have everything sewn up nicely without me.'

He knew he shouldn't have said it, but it worked. Vardon drew back in shock.

'Oh, Ned,' Sue said softly. She looked at him with a restrained, coping expression, the expression she used when he'd gone too far but she didn't want to lose her temper. She was indulging him, as a mother might indulge a naughty child and it jagged into him like broken glass. He didn't want to be indulged. He wanted the truth.

He put his hand to his face again and felt his scars like raw, ugly ridges. Was it any wonder Sue didn't want him? A beautiful girl tied to a circus freak? He looked at Thomas Vardon's unblemished face with cold hatred.

At that moment he could have killed the man, strangled him with naked hands and rejoiced. His father had loathed Sir Matthew and this was Sir Matthew's son. 'I'll be in the house,' he said and turned and walked away.

After leaving Simon Vardon's flat, Jack, Ashley and Bill paid a visit to Harley Street. Dr Jacob McNiece remembered Sir Matthew Vardon perfectly well.

'An *unnatural* death?' he repeated in answer to Ashley's question. 'Absolutely not, dear sir,' he said with the authority only an upper-class Scotsman can command. 'You can put that out of your mind right away. I know there was some ill-natured gossip, but Sir Matthew had suffered a severe apoplectic stroke. There was no doubt about it – and nothing either I or the local man could do.'

'Could the symptoms have been produced artificially, by drugs, say?' asked Bill.

Dr McNiece shook his head. 'Some, yes, but not all of them. There isn't any question about it.'

'Would an exhumation throw up fresh evidence?' said Ashley.

Dr McNiece shook his head decisively. 'There'd be no evidence to find. You see, gentlemen, Dr Lucas informed me privately that there had been talk about the case. I had the great advantage of examining the living patient with a view to discovering if there was any possibility of foul play. There wasn't. I would be prepared to testify as much in court, should it be necessary.'

'And that,' said Ashley once they were outside, 'seems to be that. I doubt if we'd get an exhumation order in any case, with Dr McNiece being so positive there wasn't any hanky-panky.' He sighed. 'I'm off to see the Vardons' solicitor. With any luck I might get something out of him that'll give us a lead.'

With Ashley departed to Gray's Inn, Jack and Bill paid a visit to the White Star Shipping office on Cockspur Street.

The White Star office couldn't be more helpful. Sir Thomas Vardon had been a first-class passenger on the *Olympic*. The ship had docked in Southampton at six thirty in the morning the previous Friday. By coincidence, the A deck steward was in the building. If Chief Inspector Rackham and Major Haldean would like a word . . .?

'Sir Thomas Vardon, sir?' said the steward. 'Yes, he was one of my passengers. He was a very quiet, pleasant gentleman and generous, too.' He looked at them anxiously. 'I do hope as how there's no trouble.'

'No, it's just a matter of routine,' said Bill easily. 'Well?' he asked Jack, once they were outside. 'Now you've proved what we knew already, what now? Simon Vardon's club?'

'I'm just dotting the i's and crossing the t's,' said Jack with a grin. 'As you said to the steward, it's a matter of routine. Considering the number of times you've grumbled that I don't know what routine police work is, you should be impressed. And yes, I think our next call should be to Simon Vardon's club.'

Simon Vardon's club, the Courtland, was on Dover Street, between Grafton Street and Piccadilly. Behind its Georgian frontage lay a world of solidly Victorian masculine comfort, with solid Victorian leather armchairs, solid Victorian mahogany furniture and, thought Jack, glancing at the menu in a frame outside the dining room, some very solid Victorian food.

Robert Hathaway, the secretary of the Courtland, met them at the porter's desk. 'Chief Inspector Rackham,' he said reflectively as he escorted them into his little cubbyhole of an office. 'It's not Captain Rackham, is it? Were you at Cambrai?'

'Yes,' said Bill in surprise. 'I was with the Cheshires.'

'I knew it!' said Hathaway, tapping his empty sleeve. 'That's where I lost my arm. I was with the Devonshires.' He grinned. 'You helped us pull a tank out of the mud.'

Bill snapped his fingers together. 'So we did! We shared a cigarette and two cold sausages on the strength of it.'

'Have another,' said Hathaway cheerfully, sitting down and pushing the box across the desk towards them. 'Cigarette, I mean, not sausages,' he added with a grin. 'Now, what can I do for you?'

'It's about one of your members. Simon Vardon.'

Hathaway grew suddenly wary. 'Vardon? What's he . . .?' He stopped short. Jack could've sworn he was going to say, What's he been up to? Hathaway pulled on his cigarette and started again. 'What's the problem?'

Bill had spotted the hesitation too. 'Have you read about the murder in Croxton Ferriers? The body in the church?' Hathaway nodded. 'I'm afraid the murdered man was Vardon.'

Hathaway gaped at them. '*Vardon*? Good God! Are you sure?'

'His brother identified him,' said Jack.

'His brother? I thought he was in Hollywood.' Hathaway broke off impatiently. 'Of course. I'm sorry, that was stupid of me. Vardon mentioned his brother was coming home to sort out the estate.' He looked at them in bewilderment. 'I can hardly credit it. It never crosses your mind, when you read about something like that in the papers that it's someone you know. So Vardon's dead, is he? Well, I'll be damned. The poor beggar. Fancy coming home to something like that.'

The 'poor beggar' Jack noticed, was Thomas, not Simon Vardon. 'Did you like Simon Vardon?'

Hathaway winced. 'You've just told me he was murdered. There's a certain decency in these things, Major Haldean.'

'I know,' agreed Jack. 'But an honest opinion as to Vardon's character may be very valuable.

209

His brother is obviously biased in his favour but we'd like to know what you thought of him.'

Hathaway pulled deeply on his cigarette. 'It's hard to say. He had a great sense of humour and was very easy to get along with, but I was on the verge of asking him to resign his member-ship.' He paused once more, clearly uncomfortable.

'Was it because he used drugs?' asked Bill, seeing Hathaway's unease.

Hathaway breathed a deep sigh of relief and leaned back in his chair. 'That's exactly it! More to the point, he brought them into the club. I had a complaint from two of our more crusty members who'd seen him in the Gents, trying to hide a syringe.' He paused awkwardly. 'As a general rule, I'd feel very sorry for someone caught up in that sort of thing, but he wasn't an injured innocent, by any means. When I did some delicate investigation, he'd offered to supply Jimmy Prideaux and Archie Layton with the filthy stuff, and I'm absolutely sure he kept that poor devil, Alan Leigh, fuelled up.'

'Alan Leigh?' repeated Bill.

'Yes. I don't know if you've run across him, but he could tell you more about Simon Vardon than I can. He's still officially a member, but I haven't seen him for a couple of months. There was some sort of family connection between him and Vardon and Leigh was Vardon's commanding officer in the war.' He sighed deeply. 'Leigh was a first-rate chap, a good scout. He suffered badly with shell shock after the war but recovered completely, until he was involved in a road accident last year. That broke him up, I'm afraid. He was prescribed morphine for the shell shock and it's my guess Vardon gave him something or other after his accident. To be fair to Vardon, I imagine Leigh was pretty insistent.'

'I suppose Vardon made a pretty penny out of Leigh, one way and another,' said Bill.

Hathaway shook his head. 'As a matter of fact, he didn't. Vardon was damn good to Leigh. He certainly paid Leigh's bills here and, from what I've heard, helped him out with rent and so on.' He looked concerned. 'Quite honestly, now Vardon's bought it, I'm not sure what Leigh's going to do. You need to find him, Rackham. The poor beggar will find it very hard to get along without Vardon.'

Isabelle, her eyes bright with indignation, was recounting Sue Castradon's woes.

Jack and Ashley had returned from London. Ashley had gladly taken up Isabelle's invitation to take pot luck with them and come to dinner. Now, dinner over, they were enjoying coffee and a nightcap in the sitting room.

'Honestly, Arthur, Sue was so *embarrassed*. It's the inquest tomorrow, which is horrible, and she wanted something nice to look forward to. She wanted to welcome Sir Thomas and his wife to the village and now Ned's made it virtually impossible for her.'

Arthur added a splash of soda to the tumbler of whisky and gave it to Ashley. 'To be fair to old Castradon, Thomas Vardon clearly admires Sue. I'm not surprised Castradon was bitten by the green-eyed monster.'

'That's true,' agreed Jack, sipping his whisky.

Isabelle turned on him. 'So Sir Thomas took to Sue. So what? You obviously noticed her, Jack. That was very clear.'

'I must learn to be more subtle,' he said with a grin. 'Yes, of course I noticed her, Belle. I'm not blind.'

'And admired her.'

'Oh, all right,' he agreed, flicking the ash off his cigar. 'So I did, but that's very different from being as smitten as Thomas Vardon clearly is.'

'Vardon will have to watch it when his wife arrives,' said Arthur, stretching himself out comfortably in an armchair. 'I can't imagine she'll be over the moon to find her husband making eyes at Sue Castradon.'

'That's what makes it serious,' said Isabelle. 'The situation with Thomas Vardon and his wife, I mean. According to Sue, Sir Thomas and his wife were on the verge of splitting up – that seems a lot easier in Hollywood – when he inherited the title and she was entranced by the idea of being Lady Vardon.' She shook her head impatiently. 'It's hard to believe that anyone could be so silly about a title.'

'That's because you've grown up in that world, Isabelle,' said Jack. 'A genuine title is hard to beat. It means you're someone to be treated with respect, with deference, even. What's Lady Vardon's background?'

'I'm not sure,' said Isabelle uncertainly. 'Her stage name is Esmé Duclair, but that's not her real name.'

'And being Lady Vardon is real. Depending on

circumstances, you've got to see how attractive that could be.'

'I still think it's all nonsense,' said Isabelle mutinously.

'How did you get on with the Vardons' solicitor, Ashley?' asked Arthur, changing the subject.

Under pledge of secrecy, Jack had brought them up to date over dinner with the news and the subject of gold mines had proved so enthralling that Ashley's investigations had been left to one side.

'I was greatly honoured,' said Ashley. 'I saw Mr Flood himself. He's a nice chap in a restrained, legal, without prejudice, sort of way. His firm has dealt with the affairs of the Vardon family for about the last hundred years. They never deal with criminal cases and he was appalled that one of his clients should go and get himself murdered. He couldn't tell me anything of the day-to-day dealings of either Sir Matthew or Simon Vardon, but he did tell me how everything works out with the various wills.'

'Do you think Simon Vardon was murdered for gain?' Isabelle asked, her brow wrinkling. 'Surely that's not the cause. He looked as if he'd been attacked by a lunatic. That's one reason why I was so upset. It all seemed so horribly violent and pointless.'

'I tend to agree, Belle,' said Jack, 'but now we've got a sniff of some real money in the case, we have to look at who gains what.'

'Absolutely,' Ashley agreed. He pulled out his notebook. 'I'll take Sir Matthew's will first. There's the house, of course, and a modest income from the let of the farms and cottages on the estate. That's entailed, so it goes to Sir Thomas. The income works out at about three thousand a year. The non-entailed property consists of Sir Matthew's share holdings and various mines in South America.'

'That includes *the* mine, does it?' asked Isabelle. 'The gold mine, I mean?'

Ashley nodded. 'Yes, it does. Now, the title to this property goes to Sir Thomas but Sir Matthew left his wife the income from investments, plus a small return on two iron mines in Peru and an amber mine in Bolivia, for her lifetime. If she re-marries, she loses the lot. Well, as you can imagine, I pricked my ears up at the mention of South American mines and did a little careful questioning. At the moment she has an income of something around a thousand a year. If the mine really does come good, the sky's the limit. She could be a very merry widow indeed.'

'Could she, by jingo?' murmured Jack. 'Lady Vardon, eh? I wonder . . .'

Ashley put his notebook down. 'Well, I don't know what you're wondering. Lady Vardon isn't a suspect. There'd be a bit of sense in it if she'd topped Sir Matthew, but there's no advantage to anyone in Simon being killed.'

'Lady Vardon might have seen off Sir Matthew, I suppose,' said Arthur, 'but I don't think she did. For one thing he seems to have died of natural causes and for another, she seems to have been really fond of him.'

'Never mind Sir Matthew,' said Isabelle. 'We know for a fact that Simon Vardon was brutally murdered. Lady Vardon thought the absolute world of him.'

'You're right,' agreed Jack. 'Sorry. I was just playing about with a few ideas. Go on, Ashley. Was there any provision for Simon in Sir Matthew's will?'

'Some. He was entitled to draw three hundred a year from the estate. If he predeceased his brother, the three hundred reverts to the estate. There's various provisions in the event of his marriage, but as we know, those don't apply. Lady Vardon has very little of her own to leave, apart from her diamonds, but she willed those to her son, Simon, together with a few other bits and pieces, amounting to a few hundred pounds in all.'

Ashley turned over the page of his notebook. 'Simon didn't make a will at all, and Sir Thomas made a very brief one on his marriage. He wrote to old Mr Flood leaving everything not covered by the entail to his wife. Mr Flood prepared the will, sent it to California and Sir Thomas returned it, all duly signed and witnessed.'

Haldean finished his whisky thoughtfully. 'Who gets the dibs if all the Vardons go west, as the Chessman's promising?'

'Good question. I thought of that myself. If they all die without issue, then the property goes to Sir Matthew's only surviving relative, a widowed aunt aged seventy-three by the name of Mrs Emily French of Budleigh Salterton, Devon. As things stand, the only item of any real value is Lady Vardon's diamonds. The joker in the pack is, of course, the gold mine. As we

215

know, it's owned by Antilla Exploration. Sir Matthew owned a third of the shares and bought Leigh's holdings, which gave him two thirds. However, a third of the mine is owned by Edward Castradon.'

'But he couldn't possibly know it was worth anything!' broke in Arthur.

'That's where you're wrong, Captain Stanton,' said Ashley gravely. 'By his own account, Edward Castradon didn't know when Simon Vardon asked to buy his shares, that they were worth anything. However, on the share folder we found in Vardon's flat, there was a note. It said, *Castradon knows.*'

Arthur drew his breath in. 'That's a bit of a facer,' he said uneasily, then shook his head impatiently. 'I don't believe it. Ned Castradon might have his problems, but he's all right. You've been talking about money and who would benefit from Simon Vardon's death. He didn't have any money to leave. He was going to inherit his mother's diamonds but, now he's dead, she keeps them. She had them anyway – or, at least, now they're recovered she has them – so there's no gain to anyone there. From what you've said, the only beneficiary is the estate, who gain the three hundred Vardon was entitled to under his father's will. That's what? Five pounds a week? That doesn't amount to anything, and it certainly doesn't benefit Ned Castradon. There's no *reason* to murder Vardon.'

'On the face of it, no financial reason, certainly,' agreed Jack. 'The mine makes a difference, though.'

'I want to know how Sir Matthew died,' said Isabelle. 'I know Dr Jacob McWhosits and Dr Lucas are certain Sir Matthew died from apoplexy, but the Chessman claimed to have killed him.' She put her head on one side and gazed at her husband. 'I hate to think Ned Castradon could be the Chessman, Arthur. For one thing, it would be so horrible for Sue, but *someone's* writing those letters and someone – someone who knows and hates the Vardons – murdered Simon Vardon.'

She looked at Ashley. 'You said that if all the Vardons died, then the only one to benefit is this aunt in Devon, but that's not true, is it? If all Vardons die, then Ned Castradon gets all the shares in Antilla Exploration.' She stubbed out her cigarette and sat back in her chair. 'He gets a gold mine.'

The moon scudded behind thin clouds as a triumphant howl reverberated across Southampton Water from the sirens of the Blue Riband holder, the liner *Mauretania*.

David Jordan glanced at his watch in the light from the deck lamps as the huge ship came to rest gently beside the quay. 'I reckon the Captain was right, Esmé. It's been a record-breaking run. I make it just over five days, six hours from New York to Southampton. Now all they have to figure out is a way of getting us through customs as fast and everyone'll be happy.' He paused. 'I don't suppose there's any chance of seeing you again, is there?'

Esmé Vardon smiled. 'I don't think that would be very wise, do you, David?'

'If you say so,' he agreed moodily. It had been a very pleasant shipboard romance. All his experience and instincts told him that Esmé wanted to take it further, but the title – she was very insistent on her title – held her back. She had an elevated and entirely erroneous opinion of the morals and accepted behaviour of English ladies. That, thought David Jordan cynically, would wear off as soon as she'd met some of Society's leading lights.

'I may run into you in London.'

'Perhaps,' she said. It wasn't a complete dismissal.

'I guess I can always look you up when you get back to the States.'

'I'll have Tom with me,' she said softly.

The presence of the husband, thought David, had never been an insurmountable problem. If anything, it added to the fun, but it wouldn't be politic to mention it.

'Point taken.' He raised his hat before walking up the deck. 'I've enjoyed the voyage.'

Politeness and restraint could be, he knew, a heady mixture. The next time they met, he thought, some of the novelty and glamour of playing the role of Lady Vardon would have rubbed off. Esmé Duclair would be herself again. She'd probably be disillusioned and, with luck, bored. That was a very promising combination.

The next time they met, in David Jordan's hopeful plans for the future, should have been a couple of months from now. Instead, although he'd made up his mind to avoid her, he found himself standing next to her, first on the quay and then funnelled together through the customs sheds.

Conversation was stilted to the point of

218

awkwardness. It was with unexpected relief that Jordan saw Esmé approach a man in the expectant crowd. He watched her walk over to him, then pause. The light caught his face as he bent his head towards her. 'Where's Tom?' she asked, her voice carrying clearly. 'I thought Tom would be here.' The man bent his head, his face catching the light, as he replied. There seemed to be an odd sort of shadow over him.

Esmé Vardon laughed and with a little toss of her head, took the man's arm. With a regretful sigh, David Jordan walked out into the warm Hampshire night.

Quarter of an hour later, lulled by the steady thrum of the engine and snuggled into the travelling rug, Esmé Vardon was half asleep in the comfortable seat of the big car. She smiled at the thought of David Jordan, then shook her head. A gentle flirtation, nothing more. She didn't want anything more, not with Tom waiting. 'How long will it be now?' she asked drowsily.

'Not long now,' said the man, with such an odd note in his voice that she turned to look at him.

He turned off the main road and the roughness beneath the wheels told her they must be on a cart track. The headlights showed black trees and a mud road closed in by hedges.

He switched the engine off and the headlights blinked out, leaving only the fitful moon. The wind stirred the leaves in a scarcely audible rustle, then that passed, leaving absolute silence.

She suddenly felt afraid. 'Is . . . Is Tom waiting for me?' she asked, a crack in her voice.

The man got out of the car and opened the door for her politely. 'He's waiting. We'll have to walk a little way, I'm afraid.'

His tone held nothing but polite regret and she consciously dampened down the apprehension that caught her. She got out of the car, then the moon came from behind the clouds again and she saw his twitching, waiting hands. Fear leapt again to be replaced by absolute terror as the hands shot out and fastened round her throat . . .

Fourteen

On the dark Hampshire road, Thomas Vardon heard the puttering of the motorbike before he saw it. He got out of the car and stepped into the road as the bike approached and drew to a halt beside the stationary Lanchester.

It was a motor breakdown mechanic. 'Thank goodness you're here,' said Thomas in relief. 'It's ages since I rang for help.'

Alfred Bourne, the Automobile Association scout, was not a man to be hurried. He dismounted, stood the bike on its stand, pushed up his goggles and unfastened his leather helmet. 'I'm sorry about that, sir. I came as soon as I got the call. What seems to be the problem with the car?'

'I haven't a clue,' said Thomas helplessly. 'She was going sweet as a nut and then she suddenly conked out on me. I tried to see what the problem was, but everything looks all right. I set off on foot, looking for a garage, when I saw the AA box a mile or so down the road.'

Alfred Bourne took his torch from his sidecar and shone the light over the raised bonnet, glancing to see that the AA membership badge was in place on the grille.

'Is there anything you can do?' asked Thomas Vardon, following the scout round the front of the car.

'I'll just check the petrol,' said Bourne in a maddeningly methodical way.

Thomas wriggled impatiently. 'It's not the petrol. I filled up before I set off. Look, I'd be awfully obliged if you'd hurry. I'm meant to be meeting my wife at Southampton. I'm horribly late already.'

Alfred Bourne unscrewed the cap and confirmed the tank was full with a flash of his torch. 'The tank might have been holed,' he explained. 'That happens far more than most people realize. Let's have a look at the leads.'

He spared a sympathetic look for the anxious man beside him. 'Why don't you sit down on the bank and have a cigarette, sir,' he said, indicating an overhanging oak by the side of the road. 'If the car was running fine before, I'm sure there's nothing I can't fix. Your wife is bound to be all right. She's probably having a nice cup of tea somewhere.'

'That doesn't seem very likely,' muttered Thomas, but it was obvious the AA man wanted him out of the way so he could look at the engine in peace.

He sat down on the grassy slope, lit a cigarette

and took a pull from his travelling flask as Bourne raised the bonnet.

Ten minutes or so passed, while Alfred Bourne worked in silence, broken by occasional comments. Thomas had taken another cigarette from his case and tapped it on the back of his hand, when Alfred Bourne raised his head and stood back from the car. 'If you'd just like to try her, sir, I think everything should be in order.'

Bourne stood back with a smile of satisfaction as the engine roared into life. He lowered the bonnet and stepped round to the driver's seat.

'It was a nut on the inlet—' he began, but Vardon cut him short.

'I really must dash. Thanks for everything you've done.' And with a flurry of dust and a blaze of red tail lights, the Lanchester was off.

Alfred Bourne stood back from the road and watched the disappearing car. 'I bet he's going to cop it from his missus,' he said to himself with a grin as he filled in his notebook. 'I wouldn't like to be in his shoes.' He climbed back on his bike and chugged away.

At the entrance to Pennyfold farm, three miles away, off the Titchfield Road, Esmé Vardon's twisted body lay beneath the stars.

Thomas Vardon went back in to the all-too-familiar Cunard office on the quayside. The shipping clerk looked up warily. This was the third time Sir Thomas had spoken to him that night. Sir Thomas, thought the clerk, looked dog-tired and haggard with worry.

'Have you had any luck, sir?'

Thomas shook his head. 'No. I've been to the principal hotels and contacted the hospital, too.' This had been the clerk's suggestion on Sir Thomas's previous visit. 'There's no sign of my wife. Are you certain she didn't leave a message?'

The shipping clerk looked at him helplessly. 'I'm sorry, Sir Thomas, but we checked the first time you called and no message has been received since.' He valiantly tried not to yawn. It was more than four hours since the *Mauretania* had docked and was now past five in the morning.

Vardon sunk his head between his shoulders and rested his arms on the desk. The clerk watched him sympathetically. 'Well,' he said eventually, 'I can't stay here all night. I'll be in the Palace Hotel. If, by any chance, my wife does get in touch with you, can you contact the hotel?'

'We'll certainly do that, Sir Thomas,' agreed the clerk, glad there was an instruction he could follow.

'Fine. I'll be round again later on. Good night.' With a weary sigh Vardon left the building and climbed once more into his waiting car.

Dawn comes early in July which, for the farmer, means that morning milking can, for a few precious weeks, be carried out in broad daylight. Percy Taston (known universally as 'Perce') liked this time of day. The sun dappled through the tracery of delicate green oak leaves and glinted on the dew of the grass beside the track up to Pennyfold farm. Fine morning, Taston thought.

The herd came to a shambling halt. 'Get along

there!' he called, slapping the rump of the reluctant cow in front of him. 'Drat that dog. What's he got now? Get out of it, Samson!' But Samson wouldn't get out of it. Taston squinted. There seemed to be some large grey animal lying huddled under the hedge.

The dog pawed and whined as Taston turned over the body, then, sensing his master's distress, sat on his haunches and howled.

The first Jack knew of Percy Taston's gruesome discovery was when the telephone rang at half eight that morning. Over a hastily snatched breakfast of a couple of rolls and the cup of tea Isabelle provided, he brought her up to date before calling for Ashley in the Spyker.

Ashley met him outside the police station. 'I'm sorry to get you up so early, Haldean,' he said as he climbed into the car. 'God help us, what a business.'

Jack put the car in gear and drove off. 'That's okay, Ashley. There's no doubt it's Esmé Duclair, is there?'

'None, I'm afraid. Her passport was in her handbag.'

'Does Sir Thomas know?'

'I imagine he will, by the time we get there. Apparently he drove down to Southampton last night to meet the ship. He must be in some hotel or other. It'll be an easy job for the Hampshire police to find him.'

'Poor beggar,' said Jack, as he slowed and manoeuvred the Spyker round a plodding horse and cart. 'Hell's bells! I've just remembered. We

224

should have had the inquest on Simon Vardon today.'

Ashley shook his head. 'I left a message for the coroner to adjourn the proceedings. We can't go ahead now a second murder has happened.'

Jack glanced at him. 'So there's no doubt in your mind the murders are connected?' he asked, gearing the car back up to fourth.

Ashley snorted. 'Is there in yours? No, I didn't think there was. We've got to get to the bottom of this, Haldean. We've just got to.'

It was a phrase Ashley repeated as he gently re-covered the dead woman's body with a blanket. The sight of the blue face and the blackened tongue made him first queasy, then angry.

The doctor, a small, competent-looking man, was briskly efficient. 'The cause of death is definitely asphyxiation caused by the crushing of the windpipe – or, to put it another way, strangulation. She's been dead for about nine hours, give or take an hour or so. Even at this time of year it can get very cold just before dawn, which can affect matters, but I don't think I'm far out, which gives us a time of death from two till four this morning.'

'We'll have to find out when the *Mauretania* docked last night, Haldean,' said Ashley.

Jack, a piece of paper in his hand, was holding the dead woman's handbag and seemed not to have heard him.

'Haldean?' repeated Ashley. 'What's the matter?'

Jack held out the handbag towards him. 'Look in there.'

Ashley took the bag with a frown, drawing in

his breath as he saw a familiar little box. Using his handkerchief he picked out the box and opened it. Inside, on a nest of cotton wool, lay a pink marble chess piece. A red rook ornamented with crystal chips.

Although he had been certain Simon Vardon's and Esmé Vardon's murders were conncctcd, Ashley felt his skin crawl.

'There's something else,' said Jack quictly. 'This paper,' he said, passing it over. 'I saw it under the hedge while you were looking at the body.'

It was a page torn from a magazine. The title, *Cinema Weekly*, was printed at the top of the page. The picture showed a girl with bare neck and shoulders smiling into the camera. She was just about identifiable as the same woman with the ghastly face under the blanket.

'"Esmé Duclair",' read Ashley, '"who appeared in *Eve's Daughters*, *The Twelve Caesars*, and *Victory Hill*, amongst others, is on her way to join her husband, Sir Thomas Vardon, in Sussex, England. It's to be hoped that the new Lady Vardon won't turn her back on Hollywood completely. Bon voyage, Esmé!"'

Ashley looked at the picture. 'Poor thing,' he said. 'She must've brought it with her.'

'It's not her's,' Jack said sharply.

'What?'

'It can't be hers. *Cinema Weekly* is printed on Fleet Street. It's an English magazine. There's only one reason why the Chessman should have it.'

'To make sure he recognized Lady Vardon at

Southampton.' Ashley bit his lip. 'But why should she go off with a man she didn't know? We've got some digging to do. We'll go to the Southampton police first and see what they've managed to get for us. With any luck they've found Thomas Vardon, poor devil. Let's start with him.'

Thomas Vardon was in the Palace Hotel. Unshaven and haggard, he could tell them little.

The *Mauretania* had docked at half one. His car had broken down on the main Arundel to Southampton road. He had called the AA – no, he didn't know the man's name, damnit, it hadn't been a social occasion – but it was, he thought, a few miles outside of Fareham. By the time he had got to Southampton docks it was about ten to three and his wife had long since vanished.

When asked why his wife should have driven off with a man she presumably didn't know, he looked horribly uncomfortable. When Jack suggested the man could have been dressed in chauffeur's uniform, he seized on the idea with an eagerness which Jack found oddly touching.

'That could be it,' he said. 'That could explain . . . Oh, hell. I'd been wondering if she'd just . . .' He broke off awkwardly. 'I suppose you'd better know. Things weren't all they could have been between us.'

Thanks to Isabelle, Jack did know, but said nothing.

'I wondered if Esmé had perhaps gone off with someone. It sounds crazy now, but I'd been to all the hotels I could think of last night and

227

couldn't think where she'd got to.' He looked at them in bewilderment. 'Why has this happened? This maniac, the Chessman, killed my brother. Could the Chessman have killed Esmé?'

Ashley swapped glances with Jack and nodded. 'Unfortunately, Sir Thomas, we believe that's exactly what happened.'

'My God.' Thomas Vardon sat very still for a moment, then looked up with a twisted smile. 'I'm next.'

'Don't you worry, sir,' declared Ashley with a lot more assurance than he felt. 'We'll get him before then.'

There was a distinguished visitor waiting for them at the police station. The Chief Constable of the county, Colonel Kimberly-West, had interested himself in the case.

'I want to know a bit more about this affair before I decide what action to take,' he said, smoothing out his moustache. 'I believe Lady Vardon was an American citizen, which makes me think we should call in Scotland Yard right away. I've already discussed the matter with them. Incidentally, Major, I believe you're associated with the Yard?'

'Sir Douglas Lynton will certainly vouch for me,' said Jack. Strictly speaking, he knew he had no right to be there, but he hoped the Assistant Commissioner's name would do the trick.

It did. The Chief Constable's face cleared. 'Sir Douglas? A very sound man and diplomatic, too. We have to be devilish careful with Americans. We can't afford to be seen shilly-shallying with the possibility of international repercussions at stake.'

A knock sounded on the door and the desk sergeant came in. 'Excuse me, sir, but a Mr Alfred Bourne's called. He's the AA scout who was called to assist Sir Thomas Vardon last night.'

'Send him in, man,' said Colonel Kimberly-West. 'We might as well hear what he has to say.'

Moments later a nervous-looking, middle-aged man was ushered into the room. 'Sit down, Mr Bourne,' said the Chief Constable with bluff geniality.

'Thank you, sir,' said Mr Bourne, perching uneasily on the edge of the proffered chair. 'I hope as how I'm not wasting your time. I only came because the office said I ought to.'

'Just tell us what happened, man,' said the Colonel.

'Well, sir, we had a call from the AA box two miles outside Fareham that one of our members had broken down and was in need of assistance. He was on the main Arundel Road four miles outside Fareham.'

Mr Bourne consulted his notebook. 'We received the call at two forty-five a.m., and I reached our member at ten minutes past three.' Ashley jotted down the times and places. 'I can show you the place exactly if you have a map,' added Mr Bourne helpfully.

A large-scale map was produced and after some slight hesitation, Mr Bourne put his finger on the spot. 'There we are, just about.'

Jack looked at the map. 'That's about two and a half miles from where the body was found. That's here, off the Titchfield Road. There's a minor road connecting the two places. I bet it's rotten.'

'It is that, sir,' agreed Mr Bourne, warmly. 'Shocking, some of these roads are. Anyway, the gentleman said he had been waiting for some time. He'd tried to mend the car himself before he walked on down the road and contacted us. He was in a rare hurry to get on. Well, I soon found what the problem was. I suspected it was a problem with the fuel and I was right. It was a 40 h.p. Lanchester. It's a lovely car and usually very reliable, but they have an autovac system which sometimes causes problems.'

Ashley and the Chief Constable looked blank.

'It's the way the fuel gets into the carburettor, you see. The petrol comes out of the main tank through a pipe to a small tank at the back of the engine drawn by the vacuum created. From there it's fed by gravity into the carburettor. Now, the vacuum intake pipe is joined to an inlet manifold on the engine, which is secured by a nut. If the nut works loose, then air gets in and the vacuum is broken, so the fuel stops. I tightened up the nut and everything was fine. It's simple enough, but it puzzles a lot of people who aren't used to an autovac.'

'How long did it take you to mend the car?' asked the Chief Constable.

'Oh, only about ten minutes or so. Once I'd found what was wrong it was no trouble. The gentleman was grateful enough, but he didn't stop to chat, like you get some gentlemen doing. As soon as the car was running again he was off like a flash. In a proper hurry, he was.'

'Could the damage have been caused deliberately?' asked Jack.

Mr Bourne looked startled. 'Why should anyone do such a thing?'

'Never mind why. Could the nut be loosened in advance so the car would break down mid journey?'

'I suppose so,' agreed Mr Bourne reluctantly. 'I still don't see why anyone should do that, though.'

'It's just an idea, Mr Bourne,' said Ashley with a smile.

The Chief Constable stood up. 'Thank you for your time, sir. I'd be obliged if you'd give your personal details to the sergeant at the desk for our records, but it's highly unlikely we'll have to call on you again.'

He waited until Mr Bourne had left the room, then turned to Ashley and Jack. 'Now, gentlemen, we can start to put some ideas together. I have the times from the Cunard office and the statement from Sir Thomas Vardon. I must say, in light of what we've just been told, it seems like a fairly straightforward case.'

He reached out for Ashley's notebook, frowning as he spoke. 'Look here. The ship docked at half one, near enough, and Lady Vardon should have had her luggage checked, delivered to a carrier, and been through customs in about an hour. We know she was murdered between two and four this morning. Vardon called the AA at two forty-five. Bourne turned up at ten past three, taking ten minutes or so on the job. Vardon first called at the shipping office at about ten to four.'

He tapped the map. 'There'd be nothing to stop Vardon meeting his wife at the docks, driving a few miles to deserted country, killing her and then driving off. All he'd have to do then is to stage a breakdown a couple of miles away – I appreciated your point that the breakdown could've been caused deliberately, Major – and Bob's your uncle.' He pointed to the thin lines of connecting roads. 'He could have done it.'

'He could, sir,' agreed Ashley cautiously, 'but there's more to this case than you realize. You've heard of the mutilated body found in the church in Croxton Ferriers?'

'Of course I have. What's that got to do with it?'

Ashley told him.

'Upon my soul,' muttered the Colonel. 'That's the most extraordinary thing I've ever heard. You say you found a chess piece in Lady Vardon's handbag?'

Ashley took Esmé Vardon's bag from his brief-case and, taking out the little box, opened it.

Colonel Kimberly-West gazed at the pink marble rook in horrified fascination. 'You're sure this is from the same set of chessmen as the one that was found with Vardon's body?'

'Absolutely certain, sir,' said Ashley.

'So Lady Vardon's murderer is this maniac, the Chessman,' said Colonel Kimberly-West slowly.

'It more or less has to be the Chessman, sir,' said Jack. 'Another point is the page torn from *Cinema Weekly* that we found. Thomas Vardon wouldn't need a picture to help him identify his wife.'

'But who is he?' demanded the Colonel. 'Damn it, you must have *some* idea!'

Ashley hesitated. 'Unfortunately, sir, our favourite suspect has an alibi for Simon Vardon's murder.'

Jack nodded. 'What we are certain of though, is that the Chessman is from Croxton Ferriers. That's what was actually in my mind when I asked Mr Bourne if Vardon's car could have been tampered with in advance. It's far too much of a coincidence to suppose that Vardon's car broke down by chance and the Chessman just happened to be around to meet Esmé Vardon. That breakdown was planned.'

A knock sounded on the door and the sergeant looked into the room. 'Superintendent Ashley, there's a telephone call for you. It's Chief Inspector Rackham of Scotland Yard.'

Nearly ten minutes had passed before Ashley rejoined them. 'Well, sir, we can scrub Vardon out for certain,' he said, addressing the Chief Constable. He looked at Jack. 'Your idea that the killer was wearing a chauffeur's uniform is a non-starter, too. We've had a statement from a Mr David Jordan, American citizen, currently residing at the Savoy. He read about the murder in the stop press of the lunchtime editions and came forward with his story. According to Rackham, he was horrified by the news. He travelled with Lady Vardon on the train from Chicago and sailed with her on the *Mauretania*. They parted at the exit to the customs sheds, but he saw the man who picked up Lady Vardon.'

The Chief Constable leaned forward eagerly. 'Did you get a description?'

'Yes . . .' said Ashley. His voice was abstracted.

'Well?' demanded the Colonel. 'Let's hear it, man!'

'The man was wearing an ordinary felt hat and trench coat, not a chauffeur's uniform. His height was about six feet or thereabouts. What Mr Jordan did hear was what Lady Vardon said. The man waved to her, she walked up to him and said, "Where's Tom? I was expecting Tom to be here." He can't swear to the exact words, but that was the gist of it. Then they walked off together.'

'There's something else, Ashley,' said Jack.

'Yes, there is. Mr Jordan thought there was something odd about the man's face, a sort of shadow. He's been puzzling about it ever since he read the news and thinks – this was completely unprompted, mind – that the man was wearing an eye patch.'

Fifteen

On his return from Southampton, Ashley asked Edward Castradon to come down to the police station.

Castradon arrived in a very unhappy mood, irritated at being called out of his office. His statement was short and to the point.

He hadn't killed Esmé Duclair or Lady Vardon or whatever the blessed woman was called. He was sorry she was dead, but he certainly had nothing – nothing whatsoever – to do with her death.

He didn't know why anyone, American or not, should say they'd seen him at Southampton docks last night. The fact that the presumed killer was wearing an eye patch seemed about as thin an identification as it was possible to have.

Lots of men wore eye patches. There had, if the Superintendent had noticed, been a fairly major war a few years ago. Eye patches were not uncommon. And no, he refused absolutely to give the police chapter and verse of the details of what he did last night. It wasn't any of their business. He was a perfectly innocent citizen carrying out his normal duties and pastimes in a perfectly innocent way. And no, he didn't want a lawyer present, damn it. He was a lawyer himself and perfectly capable of dealing with any nonsense, real or imagined, the police could dream up.

Ashley sighed. 'Please, Mr Castradon, I am trying to be fair about this.' He hesitated, finding the right words. 'We know that you resent the friendship that has sprung up between Sir Thomas Vardon and your wife. I believe your wife had invited Sir Thomas and Lady Vardon to dinner and you disliked the idea.'

Edward Castradon stared at him. 'Well, I'll be damned. Who the devil's told you that?'

Ashley didn't answer.

Castradon leaned back in his chair and gave a short laugh. 'Are you honestly suggesting I'd commit a murder to get out of a *dinner party*?'

'Not exactly, sir,' said Ashley evenly. 'But it's quite true that you don't care for Sir Thomas, isn't it?'

Castradon frowned. 'I don't think I want to answer that question.'

'In fact, you've never made any secret of the

fact you dislike the whole Vardon family. You disliked Sir Matthew Vardon and quarrelled with his son, Simon.'

'I quarrelled with him, yes. I told you as much. I threw him out the day he came to my office, attempting to bully me into selling him some shares my father left me.'

Ashley drummed a pencil on the desk. 'You told us those shares were worthless, Mr Castradon.'

'Well? So they are.'

Ashley shook his head. 'Apparently not. In fact, it appears they may be worth a great deal of money. But you knew that, didn't you?'

Castradon gaped at him. 'I knew no such thing. Look, what's all this about these shares? They were owned jointly and severally by my father, Matthew Vardon and Stamford Leigh. They haven't ever returned a dividend.'

'Alan Leigh, Stamford Leigh's nephew, sold his shares to Sir Matthew Vardon. If all the Vardons die, under the terms of the original agreement, you end up with all the shares. We know they're about to be very valuable indeed. They've found gold, Mr Castradon.'

Ashley picked up his pipe and, stuffing tobacco into it, struck a match and lit it, watching Castradon's reactions. 'Gold. Added to your dislike of the Vardons, I think that's a motive.'

Ned Castradon's jaw dropped. His eyes widened and for the first time he looked worried. 'Gold?' he repeated quietly.

Ashley nodded. Castradon reached for a cigarette and lit it absently. There was no doubt he was rattled.

'Look,' he said eventually, blowing out a mouthful of smoke. 'You'll have to take my word that I didn't know anything about these wretched shares. However, I can see, however fantastic it may appear, it does constitute a motive. What can I say? I know I've got a rocky temper. I admit that, but it falls far short of murder.'

'So can I ask you again, sir, what you were doing last night?'

Castradon nodded. 'All right. Look, I'm sorry I was shirty earlier on, but the whole thing struck me as utterly ridiculous and I resented it. All I did last night was have dinner with my wife, then go to the Red Lion for a meeting of the chess club. I had a couple of games, a short one with Tommy Martin and then a real ding-donger with Joe Hawley. We were the only two players left in the end, but some of the other men stayed to watch. That finished about eleven o'clock. It was past closing time, but Charlie Brandreth, the land-lord, treated us to a drink on the house. It must've been ten to twelve when I left the pub. Hawley walked across the green with me. I'd offered to lend him a book we'd been discussing, so I invited him in for a nightcap. I let myself in with my own latchkey. Sue was fast asleep and the girl had gone to bed long since.'

'What time did Mr Hawley leave, sir?'

Castradon shrugged. 'It must've been about half twelve or quarter to one, I suppose. I know it was late. I heard the church clock strike as I saw him out, but whether it was the half hour or the quarter, I couldn't say.'

Ashley steepled his fingers together in thought.

The *Mauretania* had docked at half one and David Jordan estimated it had been about half two by the time they were cleared through customs. If Castradon had left Croxton Ferriers at quarter to one, could he have reached Southampton in that time? It would be very tight. Tight enough, he decided, for him to want to investigate further.

He looked up with a smile. 'Thank you for your time, Mr Castradon. I very much appreciate it.'

'Blimey,' was Jack's comment, when he called in on Ashley at the police station. 'Croxton Ferriers to Southampton in under two hours? I could do it – just – in the time, but I've got both eyes and a rather better car than Castradon's Riley. If I really was going to do the journey, I doubt I'd be having nightcaps with old pals until half past midnight.'

'Joe Hawley left Castradon at a quarter to one,' said Ashley morosely. 'I've asked him. He checked his watch with the church clock as he left.'

He rubbed his hand disconsolately over his chin. 'I must say, Haldean, I was prepared to question everything Mr Hawley said, as his story gives Castradon an alibi, but I can't really say I doubted him. He struck me as absolutely honest and very circumstantial, too. He showed me the book Castradon had lent him – a chess thing called *Strategies of the Grand Masters* – and also mentioned that his wife was awake when he got in and asked him what time did he call this?'

Jack laughed. 'I imagine she did.'

'So you see, it's not a rock-solid alibi, but it's one that I think would carry conviction in court, which is why I didn't arrest Castradon on the spot. I really thought we had him this time.'

'You're certain he's our man?' Jack asked curiously.

Ashley put his hands wide. 'Who else *can* it be? Incidentally, I've had Constable Stock check if anyone answering to the description of Alan Leigh arrived in Croxton Ferriers last Wednesday. I'm afraid he drew a complete blank. The only place to stay is the Red Lion and they didn't have any guests at all.' He broke off as the telephone rang.

It was Bill Rackham from Scotland Yard. 'I've got some information about Alan Leigh,' he said. Jack could hear him clearly through the tinny speaker.

'We've just been talking about him,' said Ashley eagerly, picking up his pen and pulling his notepad towards him. 'There's no trace of him in Croxton Ferriers.'

'There's no trace of him in London, either. He left his lodgings a week ago, owing a month's rent, and no one seems to have seen him since. It's my guess that, with Vardon gone, Leigh's changed his name and the odds are that we'll never find him. I'll tell you something though. He fairly hated Sir Matthew Vardon.'

Ashley and Jack looked at each other sharply. This was something new.

'I spoke to a Dr Allerdyce, who occasionally attended Simon Vardon. Vardon called him out on the twenty-third of May to see Leigh, who was in a bad way from an overdose of heroin.

He pulled through, but told Dr Allerdyce his condition was due to Sir Matthew Vardon, who'd bullied him into selling him some shares, given him an overdose, and was quite happy to let him die. Vardon, who was with Leigh when the doctor saw him, agreed with Leigh's account of what happened. Well, strictly speaking, it wasn't any of the doctor's business. It's not against the law to take heroin, unlike some other drugs, but it is dangerous, and the doctor told him so. Leigh swore that when he had properly recovered, he'd make Sir Matthew pay for what he'd done. He wanted, according to the doctor, to make him feel what it was like to be really scared.'

Ashley whistled. 'And this is the man who's disappeared?'

Jack motioned for the phone. Ashley handed it over. 'Bill, I heard everything you've said. Can you dig out Alan Leigh's army record for me? And while you're about it, we might as well have Simon and Thomas Vardons', too.'

'All right, I can do that. Why d'you want them?'

Jack sighed. 'I can't really say at the moment, but at least army records are facts, and facts seem to be like hen's teeth in this case.'

He rang off.

'Alan Leigh,' said Ashley softly. 'He's someone I've never considered.'

The phone rang again. It was Sir Thomas Vardon. 'Mr Ashley? Could you come up to the house? I've got something I'd like you to see.'

Thomas Vardon greeted them with relief when they were shown into the drawing room. 'Thank

God you've come. It's my stepmother. She's had a letter from the Chessman. She's absolutely beside herself. The letter arrived by the afternoon post.'

'Can we see her?' Ashley asked urgently.

'Of course. She's in her sitting room. I wanted to see you before you spoke to her.' He looked utterly distraught. 'She hardly seemed to take on board the news about poor Esmé, but this has really rattled her.'

He paused before he opened the door into the hall. 'Is there any news about Esmé? Surely *someone* must've seen her at the docks.'

'Someone did see her, sir, but I'm afraid that what seemed like a very promising lead took us nowhere. We are trying very hard to get to the bottom of this case, sir. You mustn't doubt our efforts.'

'Esmé died, Superintendent,' said Thomas, his voice thin. He shuddered. 'Come and see my stepmother.'

Lady Vardon was lying on the couch in her over-furnished sitting room, a bottle of smelling salts and a glass of brandy and water on the table by her elbow. A small pile of letters were on the table. Jack could see the topmost was the familiar typed envelope. The Chessman.

'The police are here,' said Thomas.

Lady Vardon gave a little shriek. 'So *unfeeling,*' she muttered and struggled to sit up. Thomas helped her with weary patience.

'I can't understand why this is happening,' she said, her eyes round with fear. 'Why should anyone threaten me? I've asked the spirits for help and guidance. They know everything, absolutely everything. *They* give me words of comfort

241

and help,' she added, shooting a glance at Thomas, who she obviously thought was lacking in this respect. 'They tell me everything will be well, that peace and prosperity await, but now this!' Her pudgy cheeks trembled. 'It's evil. Why should I be threatened with evil?'

'If I could see the letter, ma'am . . .?' asked Ashley in the soothing tones suitable for a sickroom. Without waiting for permission, he picked up the envelope.

It was, as Jack had seen, typewritten, and obviously typed on the same Bartlett machine with a slipping 'e' and an elevated 'd'. It had been posted in Croxton Ferriers the previous day.

> So, Lady Vardon, you're looking for-
> ward to a new life? Count the minutes.
> They're all you have left. The end is
> very near. You are going to die.
> The Chessman.

'Why should anyone threaten me?' Lady Vardon wailed. 'I don't understand.'

'Actually,' said Jack, 'I don't know if this letter is meant for you.'

Lady Vardon stopped mid-sniff. 'What do you mean? That letter threatens *me*!'

Jack shook his head and turned to Sir Thomas. 'I think, Vardon, this was meant for your wife. After all, she's the one who was looking forward to a new life.'

'Esmé?'

Lady Vardon tossed her head impatiently. 'But she wasn't Lady Vardon.'

242

'Actually, Mother, she was,' said Thomas. 'We've had this discussion before.'

Lady Vardon sat up straighter. She sniffed again but when she spoke, her voice was stronger. 'I could never imagine a chit of a girl taking my place. It was inconceivable.' She looked at the letter and shuddered. '*Lady* Vardon,' she muttered. 'How could I have dreamt it was meant for anyone but me?' She took a deep breath and reached out for the brandy and water. 'I knew the spirits couldn't be wrong. Everything will be well. It's all for the best.' She closed her eyes as if summoning strength and muttered, 'Peace and prosperity' in the solemn tones of one uttering a prayer.

'For heaven's sake, Mother,' said Thomas Vardon. 'You can't think it for the best that Esmé was killed!'

A very shrewd, calculating look flashed into her eyes. 'Are you quite sure it wasn't?'

Thomas turned away, his shoulders rigid with anger.

Lady Vardon, who was recovering visibly by the second, finished her brandy and reached out for the rest of her letters.

She read through two quickly, discarding them on the table, then picked up the last. 'It's from Mr Flood, the solicitor,' she said in surprise and sighed. 'I think it's good news, but I can't really follow legal letters. They're always so complicated, but it's something to do with the estate.'

Thomas turned. 'Let me see it,' he said dully.

He took the letter and skimmed through it, then stopped and read it through once again. When he looked up his eyes were bewildered. 'Good news, Mother? I should say it is. The guv'nor's long shot has come home.'

'What is it, dear?'

'It's his mine, Mother. The Huánuco River mine. They've made a gold strike. A big one, by the sound of it.'

It came as something of a shock to Jack to realize that Sir Thomas didn't know about the papers they'd discovered in his brother's flat, or of Ashley's conversation with Mr Flood.

Thomas looked up from the letter. 'Old Flood is telling you that as you get the receipts from the mines under the guv'nor's will, you're going to be a very rich woman. Very rich.'

She snatched the letter back from him and read the paragraph he was pointing to. 'Rich?' she said faintly. 'Rich?' she repeated in a much firmer voice. 'I told you,' she said wildly. 'I told you what the spirits said! Peace and *prosperity*!'

Her plump little hands tightened on the letter and it suddenly seemed to Jack that they looked like claws.

Sixteen

Over a pint of home brewed in the Red Lion, Ashley was in serious need of consolation. It was five o'clock, tea time, but Ashley felt in need of something a bit stronger than tea.

'Every lead,' he said morosely, 'seems to disappear like water in the sand. Ever since hearing what Alan Leigh thought of Sir Matthew, I can't get it out of my mind that he might have something to do with it, but I can't see what. I can tell you something else, too. Lady Vardon's fond of money and no mistake. Did you see the way she held onto the solicitor's letter? She was absolutely cock-a-hoop.'

'Exultant,' agreed Jack.

'That too. It was heartless the way she reacted when she realized that Chessman letter wasn't meant for her. I mean, I'm not surprised she was relieved but she could have at least *pretended* to be sorry for the girl.'

He looked at Jack thoughtfully. 'How come the Chessman slipped up? He obviously intended to murder poor Esmé Vardon once she'd got to Croxton Ferriers, not before.'

'You can't really say he slipped up,' argued Jack. 'After all, Esmé Vardon is dead, which is what he wanted. He wrote that letter yesterday and, during the course of yesterday, saw an opportunity and took it.'

'You mean he saw a chance to tamper with Sir Thomas's car?'

'That, certainly, but he couldn't know his plan to meet Esmé Vardon was going to come off. He was just lucky.'

'Lucky,' repeated Ashley with a shudder. He looked round the dark, cool pub. They were alone in the saloon and couldn't be overheard. 'I don't know. Every single lead seems to point to Castradon and yet I can't make it stick.'

Jack walked across the green to where he'd left the Spyker parked on the road outside the Vicarage. This was where, he thought, Ned Castradon had his punch-up with Ryle. There had been a car parked there that evening too, the car Ryle had tried to drive off in. Who owned the car? It probably wasn't important, but it was odd, all the same, that no one had ever mentioned it.

He was about to climb into the Spyker when his name was called from the Vicarage garden.

It was Mrs Dyson. She straightened up with a hand on her back and waved a trowel at him in a cheery way. 'Do come in, Major, and give me an excuse to break off for a few minutes. Unless you're busy, that is?'

Jack went into the garden. 'I'm afraid I'm not,' he said with a smile. 'Busy, that is. As a matter of fact, I was just wondering who owned the car which was parked here the other Sunday.' He lowered his voice in deference to the fact that the Castradons lived next door. 'The night Castradon had his set-to with Ryle.'

Mrs Dyson stopped to think, unconsciously

246

rubbing her chin with the point of the trowel, leaving a smear of earth. 'D'you know, I don't know,' she said at last, in surprise. 'There aren't that many cars in the village and I thought I knew them all. For instance, I knew you were around, because I saw your car – it's a very handsome thing, isn't it, and so stylish – but I didn't recognize the car that was here that night. I haven't seen it since, either.'

She stooped and prodded viciously at an emergent dandelion that was sullying the path, then tossed the now defunct weed on a heap of garden rubbish. 'I really should do something about my poor lilies,' she said with a shudder. 'It's Tuesday, a week since they were taken. I intended to tackle them today, but when we heard the awful news about Sir Thomas's wife, all the heart went out of me.'

She looked at him, her honest, kindly face puzzled. 'People are saying the most awful things.' She lowered her voice. 'They say the most obvious person to have killed Esmé Vardon is her husband.'

'I can set your mind at rest, Mrs Dyson. Sir Thomas is in the clear.'

She looked relieved. 'Thank goodness for that. I know it shouldn't make a difference that he's so handsome, but it does.' She looked worried again and lowered her voice. 'On the other hand, Edward Castradon has come in for suspicion. It got around that he was called into the police station this afternoon and I'm afraid that's given rise to a lot of ill-natured gossip. It's not helped by the fact that the two families loathed each other.'

She smothered a yawn. 'I'm sorry. I didn't get

much sleep last night. Poor Frederick's been awake with toothache for the last couple of nights and he does hate suffering alone. If he wasn't such a baby about going to the dentist it would all be over before he knew it.'

'I don't suppose,' said Jack, struck by a sudden thought, 'you heard Mr Castradon getting his car out about one o'clock, did you?'

'I can't say I did,' she said after a few moments' thought. 'I was certainly awake at that time and so was Frederick. I think I would have noticed because the Castradons' garage door makes such a squeak and we had the windows open, naturally, because the nights have been so warm.'

She transferred another small portion of earth to her chin. 'But I wouldn't like to swear to it, Major Haldean. I wouldn't indeed.' She looked at him with concerned brown eyes. 'Is that important?'

'It might be . . .' began Jack, when a car horn sounded outside the gate. To Mrs Dyson's startled gaze, it seemed as if her visitor had been jerked backwards by invisible wires. He shot out of the gate and, when she joined him, was holding two wriggling small boys by their ears.

'Nathan and Ben Halford,' she said reprovingly. 'What are you doing to the Major's nice car?'

Jack released their ears and the boys stood, abashed, on the verge. 'Well?' he demanded, taking a swift glance at the immaculate blue-and-silver paintwork of the Spyker.

'We weren't doing nuffin,' said Nathan at length.

'Nuffin,' echoed Ben appointing himself as a sort of Greek chorus.

'We was just minding it. And the horn sort of went off.'

'By itself,' said Ben, with an air of gentle distance from the entire proceedings.

'Honest, Miss,' threw in Nathan, rubbing his ear.

Mrs Dyson resumed the attack. 'Why aren't you in school?'

'It's me jersey, Miss,' volunteered Nathan. 'Our mum said it wasn't fit to be seen and me other one's in the wash.'

Jack found himself agreeing with Nathan. The jersey presented for his inspection seemed to be a collection of holes.

Mrs Dyson looked at the offending garment and frowned. 'It's too bad, Nathan. I knitted that jersey myself at Christmas and look at it now. Why aren't you in school, Ben?' she asked, rounding on him.

'I can't go without Nathan,' said Ben, shocked to his very core. 'He'd be *by himself*!'

'And a good thing too,' said Mrs Dyson, briskly. 'Talk about double trouble! Have they done any damage, Major?'

'None,' answered Jack with a grin. 'But look here, boys, I can't have you climbing all over my car. If you see it parked, you can guard it, but you mustn't climb on it.' They nodded dumbly. 'Of course I'll pay you,' he said casually, with an eye on the future. 'What would you rather have? Sixpence each or a ride home?'

'Coo!' They said with one voice. 'A ride home, please, sir.'

'Climb in then. Carefully!' He turned to Mrs Dyson. 'I'll just run this pair of monkeys home.

If you do remember hearing anything last night, please let me know.'

Jack started the car and headed towards the cottages on the other side of the village, fending off innumerable questions as to the Spyker's speed, brake horsepower, age and endurance.

'We've got a car,' said Ben happily, ignoring his brother's signals to keep quiet.

This seemed monumentally unlikely to Jack, but he played along. 'Oh, really? What sort is it?'

'It's a Vauxhall with a roof on. It's *all right*, Nathan. He won't tell anyone, will you, sir? Our car won't go anywhere, but we're going to save up our pocket money and buy some petrol and then we can drive it. We're going to take it out on trips and go on adventures in it and do races in it. We've got it in a secret place until it can go. Morry Blandford's dad drives a van and he's always showing off about it but wait till he sees our car. Ours u'll be better'n any car in the world.'

''Cept this one,' said Nathan, politely.

'Even this one,' demurred Ben, with fewer social graces than his brother. 'This is our house, sir. I suppose we'd better get out now. Thanks a lot. It was smashing.'

Jack watched them run into the tiny terraced cottage, which was not, if he knew anything about it, tenanted by the car-owning classes. He briefly wondered what rusting heap the two boys had managed to find, then, dismissing the problem from his mind, abstractedly drove away.

Sue overheard the gossip as she went into the grocers. 'If you ask me, Mr Castradon knows more about it than he should. He was taken to the police station yesterday . . .'

Ned had said nothing. That was only what she'd learnt to expect, but she knew he was worried, desperately worried, about something. She stood to one side as Margaret Hernshaw and Jane Lawson came out of the shop, still chatting. They broke off abruptly as they saw her and smiled in an artificial way.

Sue forced herself to make some ordinary, commonplace remark and the two ladies walked on. 'Poor Mrs Castradon,' she heard as they walked away. 'I feel so sorry for her.'

Sorry for her? Why? Sue could have flared up or run away. Instead she went to the Vicarage, where she had gone once before when she wanted to know the truth about Ned. What Mrs Dyson told her didn't make for very pleasant listening and her advice, 'To go home, dear, and forget all about it,' was impossible to follow.

She went home but she couldn't think of anything else. Was it really possible that Ned should be suspected?

If only Ned had been like he used to be, she could talk to him, ask him why the police had this awful idea, asked him to explain things, but Ned wasn't like he used to be.

Could it be true? The thought came unbidden to her mind. She tried to dismiss it. Of course it wasn't true. Ned would never do anything like that. She wished she could talk to him. If only Ned was like he used to be . . .

It was with relief she heard the knock at the

door. At the moment she'd welcome anyone, even Margaret Hernshaw or Jane Lawson, to distract her from the thoughts – the awful thoughts – racing round her mind.

It wasn't Margaret Hernshaw or Jane Lawson; it was Thomas Vardon.

'Can I come in?' he asked. He seemed very shy, not his usual confident self.

She wasn't sure she wanted to be alone with Tom. She knew perfectly well that he liked her very much and she was guiltily aware of liking him, too. She was about to refuse, when she saw how haggard he looked. He'd just lost his wife, after all, lost her in horrible circumstances.

He saw her hesitation. 'Please? I – I need someone to talk to.'

Talk. The word chimed in with her own thoughts so exactly, she couldn't help feeling a surge of fellow feeling. And after all, talk was harmless enough.

'We'd better go into the garden.' She had a vague feeling the garden was a safer, more public place than the enclosed walls of the house. 'Would you like a drink?'

'No, nothing thanks.'

He followed her through the house, out of the side door to the sweet-scented garden, sank gratefully into a deck chair, and put his head in his hands.

'It's good to be here,' he said eventually. He wearily brushed the hair out of his eyes. 'The police suspect me. I suppose I'm the obvious suspect. I told them how things were between Esmé and me.'

'They don't suspect you,' she said. Sue was certain of that at least, after her talk with Mrs Dyson.

He looked up with sudden hope. 'Are you sure? How?'

Sue told him.

'My God,' he said softly. 'I don't believe it. You don't think your husband . . .'

He let the sentence trail off as Sue shook her head vigorously. Whatever her private nightmare was, she wasn't going to state it out loud. That would make it oddly real. 'I'm terribly sorry about your wife,' she said instead.

He nodded. 'It was pretty rough.' He relaxed back into the chair. 'I don't have to pretend with you. You know how things were, but to have it to end like that was foul.' His mouth tightened. 'She was so looking forward to being Lady Vardon. It was worse than anything I could imagine.'

'Poor Tom,' Sue said softly.

'I hate this country,' he said suddenly. 'I want to get away. Right away.'

She felt an unexpected pang at the idea. 'You can't leave now.'

He laughed bitterly. 'Why not? I can't bring Simon back, or Esmé. My stepmother doesn't want me around. Why should I stay?'

Sue clasped her hands together, picking her words carefully. 'We have to find who's doing these dreadful things. If you go now, it'll seem like running away.' Tendrils of her nightmare resurfaced. It *couldn't* be true about Ned, but . . .

'I might need you.'

The look on his face took her breath away.

'I like you to need me,' he said quietly. Their

eyes met for a second, then he dropped his gaze. 'Would it make much difference if I left? To you, I mean?'

There was a long pause. The gentlest of breezes stirred the tops of the trees and when her answer came, it was so quietly spoken it seemed like an echo of the wind. 'Yes.'

He started up and, kneeling beside her, caught her hands in his. 'Sue, I love you. You must know that. I've loved you since the moment I saw you. Come away with me.'

She drew back but he pulled her towards him. 'I want to take you to places you've only dreamed about. We can go anywhere. Paris, New York, Italy, Spain. Far away, in the sun. If you loved me, Sue, I'd do anything for you. Climb mountains, build bridges, even discover another gold mine! I'd spend every minute making you happy.' He reached up and touched her face with the palm of his hand. 'You deserve to be happy, Sue. Please.'

She didn't immediately pull away but looked at him with worried grey eyes. 'What about Ned?'

He shook his head impatiently. 'He's had his chance. It's time for your happiness now, Sue.' He stood up, holding her hands lightly. 'I know what it's like to be trapped with someone who doesn't care.'

'But I think he does care, Tom.' she said, half-fearfully.

'Then he's got a damn funny way of showing it,' said Thomas robustly. 'If you'd let me care for you, Sue, you'd know I loved you.' He slipped a hand under her shoulder and gently pulled her up beside him. He bent his head and kissed her.

She couldn't help it. For a split second she responded, then froze. 'Stop! I – I thought I saw someone in the house.'

He ignored her.

She put her hands on his chest, pushing him away. 'Stop it, Tom! It's no good, I tell you.'

He stepped back and bowing slightly, carried her hand to his lips. 'I'll go, if that's what you want. I'll do anything but hear you say no.'

She took him to the back gate but before she could open it he paused and, putting his hands on her shoulders, kissed her forehead lightly.

'I love you,' he repeated. 'I'll be back.'

The gate clicked shut behind him. Sue stood for a moment then walked slowly back to the house.

She went into the sitting room, wishing fervently that her thoughts would steady themselves. Did she love Tom? He was attractive, certainly, and it had been good – with a burst of guilt she realized how good – to be held like that and to feel she *mattered*.

But to leave Ned? She sat in the big armchair, hands clasped on her lap. If only she could believe that Ned still loved her, she would never dream of leaving him. But did he? There were times when she thought he hated her being there. And yet . . . And yet.

Their wedding photograph in its heavy silver frame stood on the mantelpiece. She picked it up. Ned had been so handsome then and so sure that life together would be wonderful.

She had thought so too. She had loved him the first time she'd seen him. Mr and Mrs Ansty had held a dance for the local young people and there was Ned, a godlike eighteen to her fifteen.

When he'd left to go to Cambridge at the end of the summer she'd wept buckets in the privacy of her bedroom. When she saw him the next year he seemed so much older and mature and hardly seemed to notice her. And then – her mouth lifted in an unconscious smile – it became obvious he *had* noticed her. 'We're getting up a party to go for a picnic. I wondered if you'd like to come? Do say yes.'

Going home in the twilight, the horse plodding patiently in front, the shafts creaking. The others, tired, quiet and happy and she, content beyond all measure, knowing that Ned was beside her. She shuddered. That was all so long ago. She had been little more than a child. Maybe – just maybe – it was time to put away childish things. She put back the photograph and sank into an armchair. She was so absorbed in her thoughts she didn't notice when a shadow fell across her.

'I saw you.'

She looked up with a startled gasp. 'Ned! I didn't know you were here.'

The oddest expression flickered across his face. 'Obviously.' It was almost as if he was satisfied. He turned away to the sideboard and poured himself a whisky, spilling some on the polished surface. 'Didn't you hear what I said? *I saw you.*' He leaned with his back against the sideboard. 'How long has it been going on?'

She looked up quickly. 'There's nothing going on.'

His hand tightened on the glass. 'Don't treat me like an idiot. I may be many things, but I'm not stupid.'

She jumped up and came towards him. 'Ned! It just happened. There's nothing going on.'

He flung up his arm, palm outstretched, to prevent her coming any closer.

She stopped, bewildered. 'Why won't you believe me?'

'Because I know what I saw.' He closed his eyes for a moment as if to shut her out. He opened his eyes again. 'I suppose you want a divorce?'

'No! No, I couldn't.'

'It's perhaps for the best, really,' he carried on, oblivious to her words. 'Anything's better than this constant pretence. I've known for a long time that all I have is your pity.'

She twisted her hands together. 'It's not *true*!'

He raised an eyebrow. 'So I've lost your pity as well now, have I? Well, it was a miserable little remnant, wasn't it? We should have admitted it was all a mistake years ago. Don't worry, Sue. You can have your divorce. God knows, it's not worth fighting over.' He gave her a death's head smile. 'Happy?'

'No!' The word was wrung out of her. 'I don't understand why you're talking like this.'

He shut his eyes again. 'Because I'm trying to salvage what's left of my self-respect. Do you want me to plead, to beg? Well, I'm damned if I will. And damn you, Sue. Leave me alone. Haven't you done enough?'

He snapped his eyes open and glared at her. 'I said I'd give you a bloody divorce. What more do you want?'

'I just don't understand.'

He laughed without a trace of humour. 'How

it's done? Do you really need the filthy details? I'll get a woman, go to a hotel, and arrange to be discovered.'

'It sounds so sordid.'

'It is. For God's sake, woman, will you go?' He put his hand to his face. 'Just go.'

She took a step towards him then, frightened by the look she saw, left.

For a few moments he stood rigidly, then drained his whisky. He walked to the mantelpiece and picked up the wedding photograph, looking intently at the faces in the picture.

He drew back his hand and smashed the heavy frame against the wall. The glass shattered and the frame fell to the floor. He made as if to kick it away then, with a sudden change of heart, snatched the picture up and held it close. Head cradled in his arms, he whispered her name, but she was gone.

When Jack arrived at Isabelle and Arthur's, he found a domestic crisis had occurred.

Sue Castradon had turned up in an awful state and Isabelle had invited her to stay. Sue was upstairs in the spare bedroom, getting ready for dinner. She hadn't wanted to eat anything, but Isabelle insisted she'd feel better for some food.

Arthur, who had given Jack a very biased account of the situation, raised his eyebrows at his wife as she came into the room. 'Well?' he demanded. 'Is she going to stay?'

Isabelle made sure the door was properly shut behind her.

'What else could I do but ask her?' she

258

demanded, flinging herself into a chair. 'For heaven's sake, give me a sherry, Arthur. I need a drink. Poor Sue was terribly upset.'

'I know,' replied Arthur.

'Ned's talking about a divorce.'

'I know.'

'He saw her kissing Thomas Vardon.'

'I know.'

'And wouldn't listen to a thing she said.'

'I *know,*' complained Arthur, passing her a sherry, 'but why did she have to come here?'

'Because there's nowhere else for her to go,' said Isabelle in exasperation. 'She's got no money of her own and no relatives to turn to. Not only that, but she's worried sick about Ned. She's got an awful fear he'll try and make away with himself or something. That's when she's not worrying that the police are going to arrest him for murder.'

Jack's eyebrows shot up. 'Does she think that's on the cards?'

'The entire village thinks it's on the cards, Jack. Everyone knows he was called into the police station this afternoon and it's obvious why. It's common knowledge that the tartan rug that Simon Vardon was wrapped in came from the Castradons' car and everyone knows that the Castradons and the Vardons loathed each other. It seems only too obvious to most people that Ned Castradon's carrying on the family feud. Everyone knows he had a violent argument with Simon Vardon and he really has got the most dreadful temper.'

'What do you think?' asked Jack curiously.

'Me?' Isabelle shrugged. 'I think the murderer,

the Chessman, to give him his own name, is insane. I don't want to think it is Ned Castradon, but it does seem possible.'

'He's got an alibi for Simon Vardon's murder.'

'A rock solid one?'

Jack was silent.

'I didn't think so,' said Isabelle.

'What about Thomas Vardon?' asked Arthur. 'I know he couldn't have committed the first murder, but couldn't he have taken advantage of the situation and bumped off his wife? After all, apparently it's no secret that they didn't get on and he's clearly smitten with Sue Castradon.'

Jack shook his head. 'Esmé Vardon was murdered by the Chessman. We found a chess piece in her bag and he wrote a letter into the bargain.'

'So why hasn't the Chessman attacked Thomas Vardon?' asked Arthur. 'I'd have thought he was the obvious target.'

'The Chessman wrote to him,' said Jack. 'He said he's saving Sir Thomas until the end.'

Isabelle winced and drank her sherry. 'As I said, he's insane.'

The telephone rang in the hall. Muttering an excuse, Arthur went to answer it. He returned with a wry expression. 'Speak of the devil,' he said. 'That was Thomas Vardon. Apparently the news has got round that Sue's left her husband and fetched up here. Can't you speak to the servants, Isabelle? They must've talked. I sometimes feel as if nothing's private.'

'We hadn't a hope of keeping this private, Arthur. She had to send for her things and it's only natural that the servants would talk. They're only human.'

'I suppose so,' he agreed glumly. 'Anyway, Vardon wants to see Sue. I can hardly stop him, even if I don't approve. What the devil was she doing, kissing Thomas Vardon in the first place?'

'Thomas Vardon kissed her, not the other way round,' said Isabelle sharply. 'It'd be much easier for poor Sue to know what to do if you'd only buck up and solve these murders, Jack.'

'What the devil d'you think I've been trying to do?' he asked, stung. 'I'm not a magician. If you've got any ideas, I'd love to hear them.'

Isabelle gathered herself up for a reply.

'If you ask me,' said Arthur hastily, anxious to stop a full-scale row between his wife and her cousin, 'the whole thing started with Sir Matthew Vardon. Are you sure he wasn't murdered? After all, the Chessman claimed him as a victim.'

Isabelle subsided. 'I don't see we'll ever know. Even if we guess and guess right, we can't prove it.'

'As a matter of fact,' said Jack, 'I don't know if it'd change anything even if he was bumped off.'

'I beg your pardon?' asked Arthur in surprise. 'Murders usually matter.'

'So they do, but think about it. Sir Matthew owned two thirds of a gold mine. Murdered or not, his death suddenly got all that potential wealth on the move.'

'I can't make up my mind between the two motives,' said Isabelle, her brow wrinkling. 'When you told us about the gold mine and how

Lady Vardon reacted, I wondered if she'd bumped him off.'

'She didn't know about the gold mine,' said Jack patiently.

'No,' agreed Isabelle discontentedly. 'And she certainly didn't kill Simon. Even if she wanted to, she wouldn't have the strength. Besides that, I'm certain whoever killed Simon Vardon was insane.'

'Maybe the Chessman knew Sir Matthew was dying,' suggested Arthur. 'Maybe he had intended to kill Sir Matthew but nature beat him to it. If only we knew who it was!' he exclaimed in frustration.

'Ned,' muttered Isabelle, with a defiant glance at her husband. She stopped short.

'Jack,' she said, in a different voice. 'If Ned really is the Chessman, then Sue's in danger. He's a very jealous man.'

Arthur looked at her, appalled. 'You can't honestly think he'd harm his own wife?'

'He's a jealous man, Arthur,' she repeated. She chewed her lip. 'If only there was somewhere for Sue to go, somewhere where she'd be safe.'

The words struck a chord with Jack. There was one place he always turned to when things got rough, somewhere that had always been home. Hesperus, with Isabelle's mother and father, his beloved Aunt Alice and Uncle Philip. 'What about asking your mother if Sue can stay with her, Isabelle?'

Isabelle breathed a sigh of relief. 'Of course! My mother won't mind a bit. That's the perfect solution.'

Seventeen

The next day Arthur drove Sue over to Hesperus, where she was warmly welcomed by Isabelle's mother.

Thomas Vardon missed her departure by an hour. 'Where is she, Haldean?' he demanded. He had walked up to the house and was dismayed to find Sue had gone. 'I need to see her.'

'I'm sorry, Vardon, but I really can't tell you. We thought – Sue thought – it would be better for everyone if she disappeared for a few days and the fewer people who know about it, the better.' He paused and added significantly, 'We thought it would be safer.'

'But that's ridiculous! Who on earth would harm Sue?'

Jack looked at him quizzically. 'Do you honestly need me to answer that? You, of all people, shouldn't need to be told. We've got a murderer on the loose.'

Thomas looked honestly puzzled. 'The Chessman, you mean?' Jack nodded. 'But the Chessman wouldn't harm Sue! It's my family he's after, God help us. My stepmother, poor soul, hasn't worked it out yet but I'm in no doubt that we're in danger. But Sue—'

'Don't be an idiot,' Jack broke in sharply. 'Mrs Castradon's left her husband. That's common knowledge. It's also common knowledge that the

263

reason she left him was *you.*' Sir Thomas still looked blank. 'For Pete's sake, join up the dots, will you?' said Jack, wearily.

Sir Thomas gazed at him uncomprehendingly, then his eyes widened. 'I see,' he said slowly. 'So what you're telling me is that until these murders are solved, Sue has to remain hidden?'

Jack nodded.

'Yes . . . perhaps it is safer that way.'

On Thursday Lady Vardon went to see Edward Castradon. Unlike her son, Simon, the previous week, she did make an appointment, but her presence was no more welcome.

Castradon regarded her with scarcely concealed antagonism as she was shown into his office. Henry Dinder, his clerk, took one look at his boss's face, drew a deep breath and was sincerely glad to escape back to the sanctuary of the outer office. He knew, as everyone in the village knew, that Mrs Castradon had bunked off. His wife had told him Mrs Castradon had been staying at the Stantons, but where she was now was anyone's guess.

What he didn't have to guess about was the effect Mrs Castradon's disappearance had had on the boss's temper. 'Walking on eggshells,' he muttered to himself. 'That's what we're all doing. Walking on eggshells.' Gladys, the office girl, gave her opinion that Poor Mr Castradon was heading for a nervous breakdown. The tension in the office was so great, Henry Dinder reckoned, it was only a matter of time to see if it was the boss or them that had the nervous breakdown first.

Edward Castradon was icily polite. 'How can

I help you, Lady Vardon?' he asked, sitting at the desk opposite her. 'I believe your legal affairs are dealt with by a London firm.'

'Yes, indeed,' she said. She was dressed in widow's black and sat ramrod straight in her chair, clasping her handbag like an offensive weapon. 'Newson, Harvey and Flood of Gray's Inn. I have not come here to consult you on a matter of business.'

'Really?'

'I have come here, Mr Castradon, because of this unfortunate situation that has arisen.'

Castradon said nothing. He picked up a pencil and rolled it in his fingers, the joints on his knuckles showing white.

'I would be paltering with the truth to say I was sorry that Esmé Duclair—' Lady Vardon sniffed as she said the name – 'is no longer with us, no matter how unsavoury the circumstances. With her background, there is no doubt she would have been a disruptive influence. However, her departure has left Sir Thomas open to *machinations.*'

'Machinations?' Castradon repeated bleakly. 'I'm afraid I don't quite follow.' There was a glint in his eye that would have warned a more sensitive listener to be careful.

'I mean entanglements, Mr Castradon. Romantic entanglements. Although I say it myself, to be Lady Vardon is to be a person of some importance. I can only think that the girl has been dazzled by what must seem to be a golden opportunity.'

'Lady Vardon!' Castradon's voice was biting. 'Do you honestly mean to tell me that *my wife* is responsible for Sir Thomas's behaviour?'

'If you do not know the truth of the matter, then it is my duty to inform you. Your wife has deliberately set her sights on becoming Lady Vardon and gone about it in the most shameless way. Whether you have aided and abetted her or not, perhaps with an eye to the future, I do not know, but this must stop! Divorce has become a mere matter of routine in our modern world, but I will not have my position usurped by a designing chit of a girl.'

The pencil in Castradon's hand snapped in half. 'My wife,' he said, standing up, 'is not open to criticism from you or anyone else. This interview is at an end.' He rang the bell. 'Dinder!' he snapped, as the luckless Henry Dinder came into the room. 'Show Lady Vardon out.'

'And really,' said Henry Dinder to his wife that evening, 'I don't know what that old trout said to the boss—'

'You mustn't call Lady Vardon an old trout,' said Corrie, shocked. 'It's disrespectful. She's posh.'

'Posh or not, the boss was like a bear with a sore head after she'd gone. He looked as if he wanted to murder her.'

'Don't say that, Henry,' said his wife, suddenly worried. 'You keep on the right side of Mr Castradon, d'you hear me? I wouldn't like you to go upsetting him. Not after all the talk there's been.'

The following lunchtime, Ashley telephoned Jack, asking him to call in at the police station. The army records he had asked Bill Rackham to dig up had arrived.

'You know, it's a week since Simon Vardon's body was found,' said Ashley, as Jack took the papers from the envelope. 'I wish we could make some progress with this case. I feel like we're on a knife-edge, waiting for the next ghastly outrage. You heard Lady Vardon called to see Castradon yesterday?'

'I did,' said Jack absently. He spread the records over the desk and started skimming through them. 'Castradon sent her off with a flea in her ear.'

'It wasn't the wisest thing she could've done, in my opinion. I wouldn't go out of my way to cross our Mr Castradon.'

Ashley inclined his head to see the records Jack was examining. 'Have you found anything significant? I've had a look already, of course. There's only one item of any interest as far as I can see, and that's the fact that Simon Vardon was wounded by a mine and sustained an injury to his right foot.'

'That's right,' said Jack, tapping the card. 'His little toe was amputated. Thomas Vardon and Alan Leigh ended the war with all their limbs intact.'

'It explains why Vardon's feet were removed,' said Ashley. 'That's been bothering me ever since I saw him. If you want to conceal a body's identity, you'd whip off his hands because of fingerprints and disfigure the face, but why bother with the feet unless there was something odd about them?' He paused. 'What's the matter? You don't look too pleased with yourself.'

'I can't say I am.' Jack sat quietly for a few moments and Ashley let him think in silence. 'I say, Ashley,' he said eventually, 'you haven't got a copy of Ryle's statement handy, have you?'

'*Ryle's* statement? Yes, I've got a copy here.' He searched in the drawer and produced a file. 'Here you are.'

Jack read through it quickly, then gave a little grunt of satisfaction. 'Would it be possible for me to see Ryle?'

'I suppose so,' said Ashley. 'Whatever for, though?' He looked at Jack hopefully. 'You haven't got one of your ideas, have you?'

Jack shook his head. 'I wouldn't put it as strongly as that, but like you, I wondered why Simon Vardon's body was so badly disfigured. After all, once Ryle was out of the picture, it didn't take us long to think of Vardon . . .'

The telephone rang. With a muttered excuse, Ashley answered it. As he spoke, his face became grim. After a brief conversation, he replaced the receiver.

'Come on, Haldean. We've got to get up to the Vardons, quick. Lady Vardon has committed suicide.'

The door was opened by the Vardons' butler, Mackay, who, pale and obviously very shaken, showed them into the dead woman's sitting room.

The last time they had been in this room, Jack thought, it had reeked with the pungent smell of brandy and Lady Vardon's smelling salts. Now, thank goodness, at least the air was fresh. The curtains stirred gently in the breeze from the open windows which looked out on to the garden. A rosewood bureau and chair stood against the far wall. The lid of the bureau was down, forming a desk with letters scattered across the top. The chair was overturned as if Lady Vardon had upset it when she had stood up. Jack took in these details almost unconsciously as he looked at the sprawled body on the floor.

Lady Vardon lay on the rug beside the sofa, one arm flung wide, Dr Lucas and Thomas Vardon beside her.

'What did she die of, Doctor?' asked Ashley, going down on one knee beside the dead woman.

'It's digitalis poisoning,' said Dr Lucas, pointing to a small, unstoppered medicine bottle, lying on the floor beside the desk. 'These are Lady Vardon's drops. It was a regular prescription of digitalis tincture. This bottle was delivered to her yesterday and it's now empty. I may say that the external signs are compatible with digitalis poisoning. Lady Vardon has been taking this prescription for over two years under my direction. She suffered from the heart condition known as auricular fibrillation and digitalis is the standard treatment in such cases.'

Ashley sat back on his heels. 'I wonder what made her do it.'

'I think the answer's over here, Ashley,' said Jack quietly. 'There's a letter from the Chessman on the desk. It's pretty vivid.'

Ashley strode across the room and read it silently.

Are you frightened yet? You should be. You will be the next to die. How shall I do it? With a knife or with my hands? I like using my hands. You can close the windows and lock the doors but I will come for you. Enjoy your life. You have very little of it left. I am looking forward to meeting you more than I can say. The Chessman.

'My God,' he muttered in disgust. 'When did this arrive?'

Thomas was ashen. 'I don't know. It certainly didn't come by the first post this morning. I'd have recognized the envelope. I'd never have let her see it.'

Ashley gingerly moved the envelope out from under the letter. 'It was posted at nine o'clock last night. Can you ring for Mackay, Sir Thomas? He might be able to tell us if it was in the mid-morning delivery.'

'It was, sir,' answered Mackay, when the question was put to him.

'I forgot about the second post,' said Thomas with a groan.

'Did you usually have morning coffee with your stepmother, sir?' asked Ashley.

'Yes, if I was in the house. This morning I stayed for about twenty minutes or so, then went into the garden.'

'What time did you clear away the coffee things, Mackay?' asked Ashley.

'It would have been about half past eleven, sir,' said the butler.

'So you were the last person to see her alive.'

Mackay looked at him anxiously. 'I never . . .' he began.

'Bear up, man,' said Ashley. 'We're not accusing

you of anything. Did Lady Vardon appear her usual self?'

Mackay hesitated. 'Well, yes and no, sir. She seemed perfectly well but very tired. I wondered if she'd had a disturbed night. Her Ladyship frequently suffered from sleeplessness.'

Dr Lucas nodded in agreement. 'She'd consulted me about it. It had become a real problem after Sir Matthew's death. I prescribed syrup of chloral which should have helped matters.'

Ashley turned to Mackay again. 'Did Lady Vardon always come in this room in the morning?'

'Oh, yes, sir. She'd have her breakfast, then come in here. She'd usually have a word with the cook about the meals for the day, then read her morning post. At eleven o'clock I would bring her coffee and any post from the second delivery. There were usually one or two letters. She'd spend the rest of the morning until lunch answering them. Lunch is always served at one o'clock and, when she didn't come, Sir Thomas asked me to see if her Ladyship would be joining him.'

His voice trembled. 'That's when I found her, sir. Just as she is now. I knew she was dead, sir, the minute I saw her. I went to get Sir Thomas straight away. He told me not to touch anything and to get Dr Lucas as fast as I could. I hope I've done nothing wrong, sir.'

'You seem to have acted very properly indeed,' said Ashley, soothingly. 'I suppose the coffee things have all been washed up now, have they? Ah, well, that can't be helped.'

He glanced down at the letter on the desk. 'Has anyone except Lady Vardon handled this?'

271

'I have, I'm afraid,' said Thomas. 'After Mackay called me, I came to see what was wrong. It seemed so unlikely but when I saw her, I realized she really was dead. The letter was on the floor by the desk.'

Ashley nodded his head. 'How was she when you saw her at eleven o'clock, sir? Was she in good spirits?'

'Mixed.' He hesitated. 'She wanted to go to London for a few days' shopping and she had an idea of wintering in Egypt. She was looking forward to spending some money on herself.'

He stopped, covering his mouth with his hand. Ashley waited patiently. 'I'm sorry. It suddenly got to me. Things have been pretty tight for the last couple of years. I hadn't appreciated how tight until I came home. After that, the conversation took a turn for the worse. She was trying to argue me out of something I'm going to do. A private matter.'

Ashley, who was perfectly well aware of what the private matter was, said nothing.

'I might have lost my temper a bit and said a few things I didn't mean. I didn't feel she had any right to interfere and said so. I'm afraid it ended with me striding off into the garden. If we hadn't quarrelled, she'd probably have shown me the letter. She must have been terrified. I wish I'd been here . . .' He tried to speak again, then shook his head and looked away.

Ashley looked at him with sympathy. 'It's only natural to feel like that, sir. Dr Lucas, can you give us an idea of what would have happened after Lady Vardon took the poison?'

'Individual reactions can vary greatly, but a

medicinal dose of digitalis makes the heartbeat regular and slower. An overdose has exactly the opposite effect. Breathing would become very difficult and she would probably have experienced convulsions, but I would hate to be dogmatic about it.'

'So it was as if she had a heart attack?' asked Ashley.

'She *did* have a heart attack, Superintendent,' said the doctor testily. 'That is the result of an overdose of digitalis. The effects would be noticeable immediately. She would become unconscious fairly quickly and, without any help, would die within an hour at the very outside. I arrived just on two o'clock, by which time I should say she had been dead for about an hour and a half. Maybe a little more. That means she died about half past twelve or shortly beforehand.'

He glanced at Thomas. 'Even if I had been at hand, it is unlikely that I could have done anything to save her.' Dr Lucas drew closer to Ashley and dropped his voice. 'Shall I arrange for the body to be taken away? That poor devil's really upset about this.'

'I want to get a photographer up here,' said Ashley after a few moments' thought. 'We wouldn't usually go to those lengths for a suicide but in the circumstances, I want as much evidence as I can gather.'

Thomas lit a cigarette with twitching fingers. 'This maniac is making a pretty efficient job of wiping out my family.'

Ashley felt as helpless as he had ever done in his life. 'We're doing all we can, sir,' he said, hiding behind the well-worn formula. 'Believe me, I wouldn't blame you for being scared.'

Thomas put a hand to his mouth. 'I am scared,' he said very quietly. 'But I wasn't thinking about myself.' He hesitated. 'Haldean, Mrs Castradon – Sue – she is safe, isn't she?'

'As long as she stays away, yes.'

Thomas took a deep breath. 'That's something.'

Dr Lucas gathered his things together. 'There's nothing more I can do here, Superintendent. I'll let you have a written report as soon as possible.'

Mackay showed him out of the room.

Thomas threw his half-smoked cigarette into the fireplace. 'Excuse me. I can't stay in here any longer.'

'It *is* suicide, isn't it, Ashley?' Jack asked quietly when they were alone.

'I'd say so.' Ashley puffed his cheeks out disconsolately. 'That letter's enough to frighten anyone. There was no doubt this time who it was meant for. If it wasn't suicide, then it was murder. I suppose Thomas Vardon could've killed her, but I doubt it. He couldn't have spiked her coffee with digitalis. Mackay saw her at half past eleven and she was all right then. She certainly wasn't having convulsions. If he did give her the digitalis, then he must have given it to her in something. There aren't any cups or glasses, so it would have had to have been in the coffee, which it can't have been.'

'No,' said Jack thoughtfully. 'Even the most obliging of women wouldn't knock back a straight dose of digitalis from the bottle simply to please their stepson.'

'You're right. Haldean, I suppose Mrs Castradon really is safe?'

'As long as she doesn't tell anyone where she is, yes. I just hope she remembers that.'

They didn't ring for Mackay to show them out, but made their own way to the Spyker which was parked in front of the house. The postman was coming up the drive. 'Let's wait,' said Jack, his hand on the car door. 'Call it caution, but I've become a bit twitchy about letters to the Vardons.'

Ashley hailed the postman. 'Can I see the letters?' he asked. The postman looked affronted. 'It's all right, I'm a police officer . . . Oh, my God!'

He stared at the small parcel in the postman's hand. It was addressed to Sir Thomas Vardon. It was from the Chessman.

Sir Thomas slit the parcel open. Inside were two little boxes. One contained a red marble queen with crystal chips, the other a black marble pawn. Jack frowned. *Two* chess pieces?

A letter was folded up with the box. Thomas winced and gave the letter to Ashley.

'You read it,' he said wearily. 'I know what it'll say. I can't bear him gloating over my step-mother's death.'

'He doesn't do that,' said Ashley, reading the letter. 'I'm afraid, Sir Thomas, this is a direct threat to you and . . .' He broke off, swallowed, then gave the letter to Jack.

'Bloody *hell*!' muttered Jack as he read it.

Well, well, Sir Thomas . . . And then there was one. I think you might go out

275

with a bang. By the time you read this, your dear stepmother will be dead. The red Queen suits her nicely. It goes well with the black King that was your late lamented father. Are you grief-stricken, I wonder, or privately relieved? She was getting in the way, wasn't she? Never mind; you haven't long to feel anything at all. You will be a black rook, a perfect partner to the red rook that was your dear wife. Soon it will all be over. I shall miss you all when you're gone.

By the way, I'm disappointed with our gallant detectives. Poor Alan Leigh. He wasn't rich, or important, just a cousin of yours. He had to go. He was far too nosy for his own good, but nobody noticed he'd gone. He only merits a pawn. That's all he ever was. Poor Alan. Maybe he'll turn up one of these days.

'Dear God,' said Jack. 'There's another body.'

Eighteen

Nathan Halford piled his mashed potato on top of his fishcake and ate it quickly. Then, with a nod to his brother, he carefully pulled back his chair so as not to grate on the stone flags of the kitchen floor, and crept quietly to the back door. Ben, less cautious than Nathan, squeaked his chair as he got down from the table, causing his elder sister to look up from where she was struggling with her homework.

'You'll catch it, you two, if Mum sees you. It's your turn to do the washing-up and she said you had to mind the baby after tea.'

His elder sister held no terrors for Nathan. Sticking out his tongue at her, he quietly lifted the latch and escaped to freedom, hotly pursued by Ben. As they ran through the back gate they could hear her voice uplifted in complaint. 'Mum! Nathan and Ben have gone out *again*!'

'Will we cop it, Nathan?' asked Ben anxiously, catching up with his brother.

'We might,' said Nathan. 'I don't care.'

They skirted round the village, leaving Walter Ribston's allotment worse off by four potatoes, relieved the Ansty orchards of a few handfuls of late cherries, muddied their boots in the river, and finally pulled aside part of the rickety fence which separated the old Cobden Heath branch line from the Arundel Road.

They could have got on to the old line by simply walking to the end of the cutting, where the road bridge had a flight of steps leading down to a tiny platform, but compared to climbing through the fence and scrambling down the embankment, that would have been unbearably tame.

Fifty years ago, this had been a halt station run up by a speculator from Hastings at the peak of the railway boom, but it had been quickly superseded by a proper station, at the other side of the village, built by the mighty London, Brighton and South Coast Railway.

The Halt stood, as it had for the last forty-six years, deserted and overgrown. The padlock and chains on the gates had long since rusted through. Tall grass grew between the steps of the abandoned signal box and such rails as were left were pitted with rust and red with age. All these things the boys ignored. They were heading for the tunnel.

The tunnel was not a popular place with the children of Croxton Ferriers. It wasn't that it was dark – that was to be expected – or that it was flooded and impassable a few hundred yards in. It wasn't even that it was a long walk out from the village, but rather that an unlucky reputation hung over it.

It wasn't ghosts; that would've been scary and exciting, but a sad atmosphere of failure and decay seemed to cling to the very walls. Nathan and Ben sensed the atmosphere and disliked it, but there was something in the tunnel that they loved with all the passion at their command. It was their secret, the secret that they thought about most of the day and dreamt about at night. The tunnel contained their car.

They looked at the Vauxhall saloon with swelling pride. They had stumbled on it nearly a fortnight ago whilst running away from an outraged Mr Ribston.

Ben, who was slightly more thoughtful than his brother, wondered how the car came to be in the railway tunnel, but Nathan had no doubts.

'I *wished* for a car when Albert Bennington found that dead cat at school. He said if you touched it your wishes come true.' Ben knew all about the dead cat. 'I wished for this 'xact same car. So it's mine.'

Ben wondered about this part of the story but Nathan could hit harder than he could and generously said he didn't mind sharing his car.

They wandered round the black Vauxhall, wishing for the hundredth time they could open the securely closed boot, took turns in the driver's seat and raised the bonnet to peer ignorantly but enthusiastically at the engine within.

'Let's pretend,' said Nathan, 'that we've driven across Africa and there's lions down in the dark and we have to light a fire to keep them off. You get the wood and I'll keep guard.'

'Why can't you get the wood?' asked Ben.

'I have to mind the car. It's our link between the darkest jungle and civilization. Hurry up. I can hear the lions roaring. And we can cook the potatoes too. It can be our frugal meal like real explorers have in stories.'

Ben got a mixture of grass and twigs and they started a smoky fire at the entrance to the tunnel. They put the potatoes in the fire, but were far too impatient to let them cook. The two little boys crunched into the smoky raw potatoes and were completely happy.

Nathan threw another handful of grass on the fire and stretched out with a sigh. 'The fire'll keep the lions away. If any come too close we'll shoot them with our trusty gun . . . *What was that?*'

For far beyond where the sunlight reached, in the dark and flooded depths of the tunnel, came not the imagined sounds of lions' paws, but the very real sound of a foot chinking against a stone.

Nathan gulped and sat up. 'Come out of there, Albert!' he called. Albert knew about the car.

He listened for Albert to start giggling. No giggles came. Instead another chink sounded, as if someone was coming quietly closer.

Ben, white-faced, jumped up and threw a stone into the blackness. It clattered into silence and then came the laugh. It was a man's laugh, a grown man's, not a boy's and it was caught, echoed and magnified by the tunnel. With a scream the two boys flung themselves away from the fire, along the old track and up the steps of the bridge – no fence this time – and away from that dreadful laugh.

They faced a grim Mrs Halford when they got home. 'Where have you been? Jean's had to mind the baby again and it was . . . What's the matter?' For Nathan and Ben had burst into tears. When she heard the story, Mrs Halford pinned on her best hat and took her sons by the hand.

'Where are we going?' sniffed Ben. There was a look on his mother's face that scared him. It was as if she was frightened too, but nothing ever frightened Our Mum.

'We're going to the police,' said Mrs Halford, taking a cloth and wiping most of the grime from his face. 'And you can tell them what you've told me. With all these goings-on lately, I think someone ought to know. If I've told you once I've told you a thousand times. You never know who's about.'

'And you see, Mr Stock,' said Mrs Halford after telling her story to the constable, 'I knows they shouldn't be playing in that old tunnel, but there's someone in there who shouldn't be, and with that awful thing in the church, there's something happening round here as should be stopped.'

Constable Stock nodded. Usually he would have dismissed the story as two kids whose imaginations had run away with them, but the Super was frankly worried that they had a lunatic at large. He brightened as the Super himself came out of his room with Major Haldean. 'There's something here I think you ought to know about, sir,' he started, but the two boys had run to Jack.

'You'll believe us, won't you? We're not making it up, honest.' And Jack and Ashley listened with serious faces as the children told of hearing that dreadful laugh.

'Nothing here, sir,' called Sergeant Haddon, coming out of the depths of the railway tunnel, torch in hand. 'If there was someone there, he's long gone.' He nodded towards the car, a substantial Vauxhall. 'That bit of the kids' story is true enough, though. Is there anything inside the car, sir?'

'It looks as if it's been recently cleaned,' said Ashley. 'The registration might tell us something but there's no papers in the car. There's some muddy marks on the seats, but that'll be from the boys. Major Haldean's gone to get a tyre lever from his car to prise the boot open.'

He looked up as Jack came back into the tunnel, holding a long iron bar.

'Here we are,' said Jack. 'Those kids told me they had a car. I thought they'd found an old wreck, but this Vauxhall is in perfectly good running order, I'd say.'

'Me, too,' agreed Ashley. 'It's far too good to be abandoned.'

Jack wedged the end of the tyre lever into the

rim of the boot. His mouth set in a grim line. This, he thought, might be very nasty. He heaved on the lever and the boot opened.

The smell hit him like a blow from a hammer.

He lurched back, a hand to his mouth. Beside him, Sergeant Haddon and Ashley choked, then all three of them ran for the open air.

Once back in the sunshine, all three men, pale and shaken, breathed again.

Jack thought there was every chance Sergeant Haddon was going to be sick. 'Have a cigarette, man,' he said, lighting one himself.

'Thank you, sir,' said the sergeant gratefully. 'I've never seen anything like that. And the smell!'

Ashley, pale and shaken, leaned against the wall. 'I reckon we've found Alan Leigh, but I'm not going near that car without the proper gear . . .'

He broke off. Jack wasn't listening. He was staring at the broken flight of wooden steps, leading up to the shabby old white hut of a signal box on the banking. There was mud on the steps and the grass stems were broken where they had grown up between the treads.

'There's a new padlock on the door,' Jack said quietly. 'Someone's been using the signal box.'

Ashley ran up the steps. 'This could be the break we've been waiting for! Bring that tyre lever, Haldean!'

Jack inserted the tyre lever in the clasp and splintered the lock away from the rotting door.

Inside, the dust which layered the room was broken by innumerable footmarks. Carefully avoiding the footprints as much as possible, the two men walked into the signal box. Light from the cobweb-covered window showed them a seized set of signal levers, an old-fashioned chair and a table, ringed with stains. A chess board, made of inlaid black and pink marble, stood on the table, garishly opulent against its grimy surroundings.

Jack knew that such a chess set must exist but, just for the moment, his eye was caught, not by the marble and crystal chess pieces, but by a small wooden crate that stood on the floor by the table, its lid askew. He had seen boxes like that before. Gesturing to Ashley to keep back, he walked very cautiously towards the crate, then breathed a sigh of relief.

'What is it?' asked Ashley.

'Gelignite.'

Ashley gave a startled yelp.

'It's all right,' said Jack with a grin. 'It's perfectly safe. It needs a detonator to set it off.'

He put his hand in the crate and pulled out something that looked like a sausage in greased paper. He unwrapped it. The gelignite was yellow, soft like marzipan and smelt of sickly grease. 'An engineer showed me how to handle this stuff in the war. I was looking for wires, as an electric current would set it off. A knife blade would do the trick too, as it can rasp on the grit inside.'

'For pity's sake, put it down, will you!' pleaded Ashley. 'I've got enough to worry about without you standing there, waving sticks of gelignite around. What the devil's it doing here? And where the dickens did it come from?'

Jack returned the gelignite to the box and wiped his hands on his handkerchief. 'There's tons of this stuff around, when you think of all the unused

283

munitions stores there are. As to what it's doing here, I don't know. It's a worrying find, though, isn't it?'

'Very,' agreed Ashley tightly. 'Let's see what else we can find. That chess set is familiar, isn't it?'

The chess set was laid out, as if for a game, but the black king, the black knight, the red rook, the red queen and a black pawn were missing. In the centre of the board stood the black rook. The Chessman had promised Thomas Vardon he would be the black rook, thought Jack with a shudder.

A Bartlett typewriter and a cardboard box containing a quire of paper stood on the table. On the wall was a rough chart with a series of names: *Matthew Vardon, Simon Vardon, Alan Leigh, Esmé Vardon, Adeline Vardon, Thomas Vardon* and then, scrawled in a different ink: *Sue?*.

The first five names were crossed out. 'It's his murder list,' said Ashley quietly.

Beside the typewriter was a manila folder. Jack opened it. There was a single sheet of typewritten paper inside. The edges were creased and the lines of type weren't level. It had been taken in and out of the machine many times.

Ashley held the paper up to the dim light from the filthy window and read it aloud. His voice was expressive.

'"Thursday, Nineteenth of June. I wanted to kill Matthew Vardon,"' he read, '"but he's dead. He was my black king. I should have killed Matthew Vardon. I will not be cheated again." My God! "Tuesday, Twenty-first of July. Today I will kill Simon Vardon." This next bit's on a different line, Haldean. "Simon Vardon struggled and paid the price. The black knight! The knife is good." There's a short sentence, added here,' he said. 'It's underlined. It says, "Job done!" Then we've got, "Wednesday, Twenty-second of July. Alan Leigh shouldn't have interfered. He went the same way as his friend. The knife is very good. He was just a pawn." The next sentence is underlined again. "Job done!"'

Ashley breathed deeply, then went on reading. '"Monday, Twenty-seventh of July. Today I will kill Esmé Vardon. If not today, then soon, very soon." Then, underneath, he's added, "Esmé, beautiful Esmé, the red rook, doesn't look so beautiful now. My hands are even better than the knife." This bloke's a monster! "Job done! And enjoyed." Then we've got, "Today I will kill Adeline Vardon. She is my red queen. I want to use my hands." Then there's a gap and . . .' He was silent for a moment.

'What is it?' asked Jack urgently.

'It's the next entry. "Thomas Vardon, the black rook, will be utterly destroyed. Gelignite in his car? I will enjoy that."' Ashley put down the paper. 'Haldean, he's written the date. Friday, Thirty-first. It's going to happen today!'

Leaving Sergeant Haddon guarding the Vauxhall, they scrambled up the steps and into the Spyker.

How they escaped an accident, Jack didn't know. All he knew was that he came near to overturning the car as they raced along the narrow country lane, back up to the village.

'Go to the police station,' shouted Ashley above

the noise of the engine. 'We'll telephone Vardon from there.'

Jack had to slow down as they came over the humpbacked bridge and into the village, but instead of making for the police station, he brought the car round in a long swoop around the green.

'Vardon's car!' shouted Jack in explanation. 'It's parked in front of the Vicarage!'

He screeched to a halt some way in front of the Lanchester and, swinging himself out of the Spyker, set off running.

Thomas Vardon, who had evidently just driven up, sat in the driver's seat, looking at Jack in amazement as he pelted towards him.

'Get out of the car!' yelled Jack. Panting, he slammed his hands down on the rim of the driver's door. 'Vardon! Get out! We've got a message from the Chessman. He's put a bomb in your car!'

Thomas's eyes widened and he flung open the door. Together he and Jack hurtled themselves onto the green. Ashley stood in the road, his arms wide, forcibly preventing two women, one with a pram, from coming any closer. Jack caught his shouted words.

'Unexploded bomb!'

Then, with a deep boom, the Lanchester blew up.

Jack slapped a hand on Thomas's back, forcing him to the ground. They lay flat on their faces while glass and metal crashed down onto the road behind.

Thomas craned his head to look at the Lanchester. 'My car,' he said shakily. 'My God, it's my car! I could've been in that.'

Jack caught his breath. 'Ashley,' he called

286

unsteadily, scrambling to his feet. 'Is everyone okay?'

Ashley was comforting the two women. The baby in the pram was crying. 'It's all right here, Haldean,' he called and turned to the women. 'There, Missus, don't upset yourself. There's no harm done. Why don't you go and have a sit-down and a nice cup of tea?'

Ashley came back to the twisted metal shell that was the wreck of the Lanchester. The car was still more or less intact outside, but the interior was completely destroyed. Broken glass and bits of metal littered the road.

'Thank God you got out of there, Sir Thomas,' he said. 'You wouldn't have stood a chance.'

Thomas, white-faced, nodded. 'I got a message from Sue, asking to meet me at the Vicarage,' he said. 'It was a note delivered by hand. I should've realized there was something wrong.' He laughed, a little choking, humourless sound. 'I don't suppose it was from Sue, was it?'

'No,' agreed Ashley. 'It was from the Chessman. We stopped him this time. And,' he added grimly, 'with any luck, we'll soon have him stopped for good.'

Nineteen

Jack drove Thomas Vardon home, leaving Ashley and the police to deal with the destroyed Lanchester. He wanted a hot bath – the smell from the tunnel seemed to linger on his clothes – a hot meal with Isabelle and Arthur, and a peaceful night.

Ashley telephoned halfway through dinner. The grisly contents of the Vauxhall in the tunnel had been brought out and, according to Ashley, the remains were as gruesome as the smell.

That wasn't all; deep within the tunnel they found undeniable evidence that the tunnel wasn't just a tomb but was the scene of the actual murder. There were the remains of a fire with calcified remnants of human bones.

The body, who, as Ashley said, more or less had to be Alan Leigh, had been stabbed then mutilated in the same way as Simon Vardon. The only difference was that the left arm, where Simon Vardon had carried his telltale tattoo, was untouched.

'That,' said Jack to Arthur and Isabelle as he resumed his interrupted dinner, 'was only to be expected, you know. The Chessman said in that ghastly note – I suppose you could call it a diary entry – which we found in the old signal box that Leigh, the poor devil, went the same way as his friend.'

'But who is this maniac?' demanded Arthur, finishing the last of his pork chop.

'Sue's name was on that list,' said Isabelle significantly.

Arthur squared his shoulders defiantly. 'It's not Ned Castradon. I won't believe it until I absolutely have to. Ned's got a dickens of a temper but he's not insane.'

'Do you think the Chessman is insane?' asked Jack thoughtfully.

'There's no other explanation,' said Isabelle. 'He's just playing chess with people, and as for all the horrible things he does to them afterwards . . .' She shoved her plate away. 'I'm sorry. I don't think I'll ever forget what we saw in the church. Why treat someone like that?'

Jack, knife and fork in hand, stared at her.

'Don't look at me like that, Jack,' she said uncomfortably. 'I can't help being upset.'

'No, of course you can't,' he said absently. 'It's just what you said rang a bell. I said as much to Ashley earlier on. *Why treat someone like that . . .?*'

He sat silently for a few moments, then pushed his chair back from the table. 'Excuse me a moment, will you? I need to talk to Ashley again.'

He came back a few minutes later, looking cheerful. 'It's all right,' he announced. 'Ashley's promised to square it with the authorities for me. I'm going to see Jonathan Ryle in the morning.'

'Jonathan Ryle?' repeated Arthur blankly. 'The chauffeur, you mean? What's he got to do with it?'

'I'm hoping,' said Jack, 'I'll find out in the morning. Don't ask any questions just at the moment. I need to work something out.'

'Well,' said Ryle. 'This is a pleasure. There's one thing about being a guest of His Majesty's, and that's the butler doesn't need to enquire if you're at home.'

Jack grinned and took a carton containing a hundred Gold Flake from his case. 'Are these any use to you?'

Ryle's eyes gleamed but he hesitated before he picked up the cigarettes. 'What's the game, squire? I mean, I'm lagged up in here safe and sound, just waiting to do my bit of time like a good boy. I've told you everything I know. You can't pin anything more on me.'

Jack leaned back in his chair. 'I don't want to pin anything more on you, Mr Ryle. Do take the cigarettes, by the way, they're yours. What are the charges against you?'

'Assault, blackmail and larceny,' muttered Ryle. 'It isn't *fair,* I tell you. Yes, I had a pop at that bugger, Castradon. He'd been asking for it and no mistake, but all the rest I did for the boss. He was my old man, after all. I had to do what he said, didn't I? He was family.'

Leaving aside this perhaps skewed notion of family values, Jack moved on. 'That's quite a collection of charges.'

Jack's voice sounded admiring and Ryle couldn't help but preen himself. 'Now, it's possible,' Jack went on, 'not to put it any stronger, that things might be easier if you helped the police. I'm not offering anything. I'm just pointing out the obvious.' Jack pushed his cigarette case and a box of matches across the table. 'Have one of those and think about it.'

'I don't need to think about it,' said Ryle, striking a match. 'Strewth, guv, the nick's all right but you don't want to go overdoing it.' He grinned and the astonishing likeness to Sir Matthew and Thomas Vardon flared out. 'But you haven't come to tell me this out of the kindness of your heart. I'll ask you again. What's the game?'

For an answer Jack drew a sheet of paper out of his case. 'This is a copy of the statement you made to Superintendent Ashley concerning your fight with Mr Castradon. As a writer of fiction myself, I appreciated it. But that's what it is. Fiction.'

'What d'you mean?' blustered Ryle. 'Every single word of that is God's truth.'

Jack shook his head. 'Oh no. Like all good stories it has large slices of truth in it, but that's not the same thing at all. For instance, this part here, where you say after fighting with Mr Castradon you ran across the road, climbed into a car, got it to start, but fell into the back and abandoned the car when Mr Castradon caught up with you.'

Jack put the statement down. 'Mr Dyson and Mr Castradon, the other two witnesses, both stated that you leapt out of the car with a shriek, and ran off, yelling, down the road. What sort of car was it, by the way?'

'How the hell should I know? I was trying to escape in it, not buy the ruddy thing.'

'Fair enough,' Jack acknowledged with a grin. 'I wondered if it was a Vauxhall.'

'How the hell . . .?' began Ryle again, then stopped. 'No. No, I don't think it was, guv. I couldn't say what it was, but I don't think it was a Vauxhall.'

'In any case, you say you ran away because, "I had Castradon after me." That's not true.'

Ryle blenched. 'It is.'

'I think not, Mr Ryle. What did you see in the back of the car?'

'Oh, God.' The nicotine-stained fingers started to shake. 'Nothing. I saw nothing. They'd only twist it. They'd make out it was me. Once you get a record, guv, everyone's after you, and it wasn't me. I had nothing to do with it.'

'I know that, man. This isn't official, remember. There's only the two of us here. No one's listening and as far as the authorities are concerned, what you said in your statement is the truth. But I know it's not true and you know it's not true, so why don't you tell me what really happened?'

Ryle shook his head. 'Catch me! They've got a down on me, I tell you. Sorry, squire, I can't do it.'

Jack drew back his chair. 'Pity.' He examined his fingernails. 'You saw a body in the back of the car, didn't you? A body with a disfigured face and its feet and hands cut off.'

Ryle jumped to his feet. 'If you know that, why're you asking? God 'elp, it was too. I fell right on top of it. Horrible, it was. The arms sort of jumped up and came round me. It had a coat over it but it was mother-naked underneath. If I say I seen it, they'll have me strung up before you can say knife.'

'Calm down, Mr Ryle. We're alone, remember? As far as you're concerned, this hasn't changed a thing. Perhaps you'd consider changing your statement once we've caught the murderer?'

Ryle relaxed. 'Well, that'd be different, wouldn't it? You catch him, squire, and I'll sing for you. But you've got to get him first.'

* * *

292

Jack stopped for a late lunch on the way back from Lewes. It was nearly four o'clock when he arrived back in Croxton Ferriers, a hot, quiet, sleepy afternoon, with few passers-by in the village. Even the geese on the green were roosting placidly under the shade of the willows by the river.

He pulled up outside the police station and walked in to the back room to find Ashley on the telephone. Correctly interpreting Ashley's silent gestures, Jack sat down and waited without speaking. Judging from the amount of times Ashley said 'sir', he was talking to someone important.

He was. Ashley put the phone down, stretched back in his chair, reached for his pipe and lit it with a broad grin. 'I've been trying to reach you this afternoon,' he said. 'That was the Chief Constable on the phone.' He couldn't help but pause. 'He was telephoning with his congratulations.' Ashley beamed at him. 'We've cracked it, Haldean! It's all over.'

Jack looked at him sharply. 'What d'you mean, it's over?'

'Just that. The case is solved. We've got the evidence and we've got the man.'

'You've got the man! Who is it?'

'Castradon.' Ashley drew out the syllables of the name. 'Edward Castradon.' He jerked his thumb at the door leading to the corridor. 'He's banged up nice and tight in the cell at the back until the van comes to take him to Lewes. He's the Chessman.'

'But he can't—' began Jack when Ashley silenced him with a wave of his hand.

'There's no doubt about it. He came quietly enough when we arrested him. All he said was, "I've been expecting this," when I read him the charge. He came as meekly as a lamb, with all the fight knocked out of him. I think,' said Ashley, tamping down the tobacco in his pipe, 'that we might find that he's one of these Jekyll and Hyde personalities. I always did think we were looking for a lunatic.'

'But what evidence have you got?' demanded Jack.

'It's all from the Vauxhall. He made one crucial mistake. He forgot the number plates on the car.'

'The Vauxhall's registered to *him*?' Jack asked in astonishment.

'Not exactly. The last registered owner is a Gerald Randall of the Pioneer Garage, Pevensey Road, Eastbourne. He always has a few second-hand cars at fairly knock-down prices. He sold the Vauxhall to a man who gave his name as John Smith and paid the cash price of forty-five pounds for it. The description Randall gives fits Castradon to a T. In the boot of the car we found a wrench and a small axe – you remember a wrench and an axe were missing from Castradon's garage – and we also found Castradon's knife. It's very distinctive. Henry Dinder, the clerk, recognized it as one he'd seen Castradon use as a paper knife and Castradon acknowledged the knife was his. He didn't seem to *care,*' added Ashley in an aggrieved voice.

'He could be reserving his defence,' suggested Jack. 'He is a solicitor, after all.'

'True, but he appeared completely indifferent.

Anyway, at least we know what that farrago with the false telegram was about. You remember he said he had a telegram from Sir Arnold Stapleton from Eastbourne on Tuesday evening? There was no telegram sent from any of the Eastbourne offices on Tuesday.'

'We thought,' said Jack mildly, 'that it was an alibi. The fact that he wasn't here, I mean.'

'He must've got round it somehow, that's all I can say. After all, it was never impossible, only unlikely. I'm not sure how he did it, but he managed it somehow. After all, there's only Mrs Dyson's word for it that the lilies were taken from her garden on Tuesday night. They could've easily have been taken earlier in the evening. He dropped his silver matchbox while he was carrying the body around. He could have easily got the church key and copied it at any time. He only lives next door to the Vicarage, after all.'

'It's possible, I suppose,' said Jack doubtfully.

'Absolutely it is. After all, Castradon's local, he's notoriously bad-tempered, he suffered from shell-shock or its first cousin, his family had a grudge against the Vardons, he's got no alibi worth tuppence, he lied about the telegram, his property was found at the scene of the crime and there's a clear connection between him and the Vauxhall. I just don't know where Alan Leigh fits in to the picture, but we know from that revolting diary entry that he was the next in line. Maybe Leigh saw him and Castradon realized he had to act, otherwise his alibi would be blown sky high. We might very well find that he bought

295

the Vauxhall with the express intention of meeting Leigh and seeing him off.'

'Why leave the body in the car?'

Ashley shrugged. 'Why not? He might have intended to move it or dispose of the car and body together. Perhaps he always intended to abandon the body in the car. The railway tunnel was a good hiding place. It was only because of those scamps of kids that we found it, after all.'

'Speaking of the boys, what does Castradon say he was doing when they heard the man in the tunnel? He should've been at work, surely.'

'He wasn't. He says he'd gone for a walk. Apparently he's hardly been in the office all week and when he was there he didn't do much. Henry Dinder, the clerk, was worried that Castradon was heading for a breakdown or, as he delicately put it, "problems with his nerves". That sounds like the understatement of the year.'

'What about Esmé Vardon's murder? I just don't see how he could have got from Croxton Ferriers to Southampton in time. Certainly not in that Riley of his.'

'Maybe that's it,' said Ashley. 'If he bought one car, the Vauxhall, what's to stop him buying another? A car that's a damn sight faster than the Riley. Again, to refer back to the diary, he didn't *know* that murder was going to come off. He chanced it, and it did.'

'As a matter of fact,' Jack said slowly, 'there is another car involved.'

He told Ashley the gist of what Ryle had seen on the Sunday night. Ashley was horrified.

'You mean there's yet *another* body, Haldean?'

'That's what Ryle said, and I believe he's telling the truth. He didn't want to admit it. He's convinced that we'll try and pin the murder on him.'

'Idiot,' muttered Ashley. 'Didn't you tell him we were after a madman? Ryle's as sane as you and me. I suppose I'd better get him to amend his statement. Now we've got Castradon under lock and key, he might be a bit more forthcoming.'

Jack ran his thumb round his chin. 'I did wonder if there was a simpler explanation. I might be wrong, but I can't help thinking we've been led up the garden path by this idea that the killer's a lunatic. There's one way of looking at things which makes the killer horribly sane.'

Ashley looked at him blankly. 'And what's that, when it's at home? And why are you saying *the killer*? We know who the killer is. It's Castradon.'

'Perhaps not.'

There was a frozen pause.

'*Not* Castradon?' demanded Ashley. 'If it's not Castradon, then who the hell is it?'

He broke off in irritation as a high-pitched woman's voice, punctuated by the low rumble of Constable Stock's replies, sounded in the outer room. 'What the dickens is going on out there?' he muttered, rising to his feet.

The door was abruptly flung back and Sue Castradon erupted into the room, Constable Stock, red-faced and apologetic behind her. 'I couldn't stop her, sir,' he said heavily.

'Mr Ashley!' yelped Sue. 'Isabelle Stanton telephoned to say my husband had been arrested. Is that true?'

'Quite true, I'm afraid, Mrs Castradon.'

Sue's mouth quivered and she swayed on her feet. Jack caught hold of her arm and guided her into a chair.

'Thank you,' she muttered absently, then took in who he was. 'Mr Haldean? It can't be true, can it? Not Ned. Surely not *Ned.*' She reached out and clutched his chest. 'Isabelle swore you'd find the truth. She knows it can't be Ned who's done these dreadful things. She told me you'd find out the truth and set him free.'

Considering what he'd heard Isabelle say on the subject of Ned Castradon, that seemed a bit rich, but Jack wasn't going to argue. He gently covered her hand with his. 'We'll find the truth, Mrs Castradon.'

She gave a long shuddering sigh. 'Let me see him! Is he here?' She read the expression in his face. 'He is here!'

Ashley was a kind-hearted man and couldn't resist that look. 'You can see him if you like, but I'm afraid I'll have to be there, too.' He nodded at Jack. 'You'd better come too.'

Her eyes widened but Jack knew the reason for Ashley's caution. Sue's name had been on the Chessman's list.

'All right,' she said unsteadily. 'Anything, as long as I can see him.'

The tiny cell at the back of the police station was a stone-built room with a solid door with a peephole, a barred window, a shelf and a plank bed, which usually housed drunks and petty thieves.

Jack stood for a moment in awkward silence,

looking at the man sitting on the plank bed.

Sue pushed past and flung herself down beside her husband. Castradon looked at his wife. Jack saw his expression, an expression of bewildered, delighted hope. Despite Ashley's warning movement, Castradon held out his arms and Sue clung to him, her breath coming in little gasping sobs.

'I came as soon as I could, Ned. I know it's not true. It's not you. Why don't you tell them it's not you?'

He kissed her hair, oblivious to the presence of the two men. 'Do you care?'

She drew back. 'Care? Of course I care!'

'I thought you wanted to be free. If I was out of the way you'd be free.'

She looked at him steadily. 'Ned! Tell me you're not guilty.'

'Of *course* I'm not guilty,' he said with a spark of his old self. 'I thought it would be better for you if I was.' His mouth twisted. 'I was going to end it, anyway.'

Her eyes sparked grey fire. 'No you damn well don't! Now stop feeling so *bloody* sorry for yourself and fight!'

'But . . .'

'Do you love me?' she demanded.

Jack touched Ashley's arm and the two men withdrew tactfully round the corner and out of sight. That, thought Jack, was more to spare his feelings than Ned or Sue Castradons'. Although their voices were clear, he didn't want to witness such raw emotion.

In the cell, Ned stood up. 'Do I love you?' He covered his face with his hands. 'I love you more

299

than I can say, but I can't see why you should give a damn. Knowing I've got a foul temper and how I look and all the—'

She interrupted him indignantly. 'Will you stop being so *bloody* silly? I couldn't give a . . . a *bugger* what you look like!'

Castradon blinked. 'Sue! I've never heard you use language like that before.'

'Well, you're hearing it now. And I'll use a bit more language if you don't stop being so stupid. What the . . . the . . .'

'Careful!' he warned, his mouth starting to lift at the corners.

'What on earth,' she amended, 'does it matter if you have got a few scars? It's been hell, Ned, trying to get you to believe it. Because I loved you I stuck it for so long until you finally managed to convince me you didn't give a damn.'

'Oh, hell.' He sat down heavily on the bed, holding her hands in his. 'I've been every kind of fool I can think of. After the war I was so ill and useless. I'd wanted to make things wonderful for you. All I did was bring one worry after another. And then – I know this is horrible – I convinced myself that you didn't love me, that you couldn't love me and I hated you for pretending. I wanted you to get it over with and go. Prove me right.' His voice trailed off to a whisper. 'And you did.'

She squeezed his hands. 'Do you care?'

He looked up quickly. 'I care.'

Jack stepped outside the police station. He wanted fresh air and he wanted to think.

He was surprised to see Isabelle and Arthur sitting in their car.

'I telephoned Sue,' Isabelle explained, 'and we picked her up from the train.' She looked at him with that determined expression he knew so well. 'Jack, Ned's innocent.'

'You've changed your tune,' he couldn't resist saying.

She gave a little toss of her head. 'That's before I saw how Sue reacted. She *couldn't* be so wrong about him, Jack. She's lived with him for years. She'd know if he was the Chessman.'

'I never thought Castradon was guilty,' said Arthur.

'I told Sue you'd sort it all out, Jack,' said Isabelle with complete conviction.

Jack winced. 'Thanks. How the dickens am I meant to do that? There's evidence against him, Belle. Good evidence.'

She looked at him shrewdly. 'I thought you had an idea. Did you see Ryle?'

'Yes, I did,' he said slowly.

'I knew it!' said Isabelle triumphantly. 'You're on to something.' She reached for his hand. 'Jack, you've got to *do* something. What's the problem?'

'A total and complete lack of evidence,' he said glumly. He lit a cigarette and flicked the match onto the green. 'I have an idea but not a shred of proof. I need facts and facts don't grow on blackberry bushes. I have to show Ashley something concrete.' He broke off, staring into the middle distance. 'We need another body,' he said quietly. 'We need another murder.'

'For God's sake, Jack,' cried Arthur, seriously alarmed. 'That's about the last thing we need.'

Jack grinned. 'Don't worry. The next victim will be me.'

'That's not a terribly good idea—' began Arthur, when Jack cut him off impatiently.

'I don't intend to actually die. That's taking devotion to the cause a little too far.' He bit his lip thoughtfully. 'Where's Sue Castradon staying tonight?'

Isabelle shrugged. 'I was going to ask her to stay with us.'

'Don't do that,' said Jack quickly. 'She can stay in her own house. She strikes me as a very honest sort of person and I don't want her to give the game away.'

'What game?' demanded Arthur. 'Come on, Jack. Tell us what you've got in mind.'

'Take Sue home, then meet me back here,' said Jack. 'Isabelle, you can stay with Sue for a time if you like, but Arthur and I need to have a word with Ashley. You can be as sympathetic as you like to Mrs Castradon but don't, for heaven's sake, let her know I've got an idea. For one thing, I might be wrong – I really might be, you know – in which case it's cruel to offer false hope and, for another, we don't know who she'll talk to. One hint that anyone, bar Sue, thinks that Castradon's not guilty could really upset the apple cart.'

Twenty

Edward Ashley looked at Arthur and Jack in stupefaction. They were in Ashley's office and Jack had made sure that the windows and door were shut. He didn't want anyone to overhear what they were saying.

'*Thomas Vardon*,' said Ashley disbelievingly. 'You think *Thomas Vardon* is the Chessman? But he can't be! Damn it, it was only yesterday we saved him from being blown to smithereens.'

'He could've easily planted that bomb himself,' said Jack. 'All he needed to do is to wait until we came running up to him like a pair of maniacs and bingo! He sets off the bomb and bang!'

'I don't believe it,' said Ashley, his voice rich with scepticism. 'He can't be guilty.' He ticked the points off on his fingers. 'One, he was on the *Olympic* when Simon Vardon and Alan Leigh were murdered; two, Esmé Vardon would've recognized him; three, he's not a local and wouldn't know where anything was, such as the keys to the church and so on; and four – and most important of all – he's not a lunatic.'

'As a matter of fact, I'm not so sure about that,' said Jack.

'But where's your evidence?'

Jack put his hands wide. 'That's the snag. I haven't got any.'

Ashley rolled his eyes heavenwards. 'I need a damn sight more than your hunch.'

'I know,' said Jack in a placatory way. 'Don't get so agitated, old thing. It's to get some evidence that I've asked Arthur to come along. Now, this is what I've got in mind . . .'

That evening Jack drove himself and Arthur up to London. He saw Arthur off on a train north from King's Cross, garaged his car, and went home to his rooms in Chandos Place.

The next morning, he packed a suitcase for a few days and augmented his travelling wardrobe with his old service Webley. Silverthorne's, he thought, as he pocketed the pistol. Silverthorne's should do it nicely.

Silverthorne's in Vigo Street (established 1793) no longer sells the sword-sticks and life-preservers referred to in the flowing eighteenth-century gilt script on the window; instead its steel and glass cabinets gleam with creations of burnished blue metal and polished wood that epitomize the very zenith of the gunsmiths' art. Jack's requirements were modest but precise; and Silverthorne's met those requirements exactly.

There were two letters for Sir Thomas Vardon. One was local, one was postmarked Matlock, Derbyshire. Vardon opened the local letter with a twisted smile. He could guess what it contained. He was right.

. . . and so I think you'll agree, Tom, that in the circumstances we had better see as little of each other as possible. I shall always value your friendship and I am more sorry than I can say that I allowed you to believe your feelings were returned.

It was a confused and unhappy time when I thought the best thing would be for me to make a complete break. I hope you will understand when I tell you that is no longer so. This has been a horribly difficult letter to write. Please try to forgive me.

Sue.

Vardon rested his head in his hands. Sue! He could visualize her so clearly that it filled him with a sick hunger. He knew this would be a difficult time but after the trial was over and the inevitable verdict returned, she would find her way back to him. All he had to do was wait. He knew that patience wasn't his strong point, but Sue was worth waiting for.

He idly slit open the second letter and read it with growing surprise.

Dear Tom,

First let me say how sorry I and everyone else was to hear about Esmé. [Stacks more about Esmé]

I realize this is a bad time, but I have to see you about the contract we had with Lord Evedon. Thanks to you, he's agreed to let us use the Priory for filming and the really good news is that Doug Fairbanks and Mary Pickford are signed and secured. Old Burnford is excited about the gross on this one! Lord Evedon wants to see you, though. I guess, as you did all the preliminary work, he thinks he can trust you and, as you're now a real English aristocrat, the studio are keen for you to wrap it up.

I got into Liverpool last night and I'm travelling down through England, seeing some of your country on the way. It looks just like the movies! I know you asked me to stay, but it might not be convenient for you right now, as the house will still be mourning for Esmé, so I suggest that we meet at Upper Eadsley, Sussex, the village near Lord Evedon's place on Wednesday 3rd.

I'll be staying at the hotel there, the Bull's Head. Sounds cute. You can write to me at the Old Fleece at Stratford-upon-Avon. I'll be there on Monday. Can you let me know in your letter if you want to go ahead with the Mayer contract? We could do with a definite answer. Let me know and I can cable him right away. Those were the only two bits of unfinished business you left but the Mayer contract is urgent. If I don't hear from you, I'll come to Croxton Ferriers directly, as we originally arranged. See you soon. Luke Vettori.

Vardon put down the letter and frowned. This was all he needed! He sat down at the desk and pulled a sheet of notepaper towards him, then, changing his mind, reached for a telegram form.

Telegram from T. Vardon, Croxton Ferriers, West Sussex to L. Vettori, C/O Old Fleece, Stratford-Upon-Avon, Warwickshire. Meet six o'clock Wednesday, Bull's Head, Upper Eadsley stop Yes to Mayer stop

'There's a telegram for you, Mr Vettori,' said Mrs Knowle who, as well as owning the Old Fleece, combined in her ample person the offices of receptionist, barmaid, part-time cook and occasional chambermaid.

Mrs Knowle liked Mr Vettori. You'd expect him to be foreign with a name like that, but he was as English as she was. He was a nice-looking man with a high forehead, curly brown hair and a hesitant manner. 'Since the war, I always worry so about telegrams,' she said. 'Is is good news?'

'Yes, it is. Is there a telephone I can use?'

'It's in the hall, sir.'

Passing through the hall minutes later with some cutlery for the dining room, she heard Mr Vettori on the phone. It was none of her business, of course, but she did wonder why Mr Luke Vettori had said, 'Hello, Jack. This is Arthur.'

In the Residents' Lounge of the Bull's Head, Upper Eadsley, Ashley introduced the two men who had accompanied him to Jack and Arthur.

'This is Sergeant Thurrock and Constable Birch,' he said, sitting down. 'I thought it best to have two trustworthy witnesses with me.'

Jack liked the look of the two policemen. They were sturdy, intelligent-looking men who managed to wear their dark suits without making it obvious they were in plain clothes.

'I wanted witnesses,' continued Ashley, 'and some support should anything go wrong,' he added, with a meaningful look at Jack. 'Why don't you bring Thurrock and Birch up to date? They know,' he said, lowering his voice, 'we're after Sir Thomas Vardon.'

'Okay,' said Jack obligingly. 'If Sir Thomas is guilty, he's a very dangerous and a very clever man. In order to draw him out, Captain Stanton travelled to Derbyshire to post a letter I'd written in the name of his colleague, Luke Vettori, asking Sir Thomas to meet Mr Vettori here.'

Arthur nodded. 'As soon as I had the reply, I telephoned, and here we are.'

'Sir Thomas is due at six,' said Ashley. 'He'll ask for Mr Vettori and be shown up to his room.' He raised an eyebrow at Jack. 'What d'you think he'll do when he finds out it isn't this American chap waiting for him, but you? He'll know you're not Vettori straight away.'

'I'm hoping,' said Jack, 'he'll go off pop. The discussion should prove interesting, to say the least. You'll be in the next room, together with Captain Stanton, listening to every word we say. I'll rely on your discretion to step in should it seem necessary.'

The two policemen nodded. 'Is the landlord all

right?' asked Sergeant Thurrock. 'He won't speak out of turn, I mean?'

'He won't say a word,' said Arthur. 'I've known him for years. My old home, the Priory, is nearby. I suggested meeting here.'

'The room's fine, too,' Ashley said. 'There's an adjoining door. We won't have any trouble hearing what's being said – or intervening, if we need to.'

'We need to keep out of sight before the kick off,' said Jack, glancing at his watch. 'We've got over two hours to fill. I'm blowed if I'm going to be cooped up in my room all afternoon. I'm going for a walk. D'you fancy coming, Arthur? We could revisit some of your old haunts.'

For a moment Arthur looked tempted, then he shook his head. 'I think I'd better have a word with Jim in the garage,' he said. 'I didn't like the feel of the brakes when I drove over this morning.'

'Well, keep an eye on the time,' said Jack, standing up. 'We all need to be in position by quarter past five at the latest.'

Jack swung his legs over the top of the stile and jumped down to the dried mud of the lane. Long ago this had been the main road up to the quarry where the stones of the Priory had come from. The house itself was invisible behind a rise of ground and the quarry belonged to the birds and rabbits, undisturbed amongst the stones. Jack lit his pipe and strolled down the track.

Arthur Stanton found Jim in the garage, only too willing to help with his brakes.

'I haven't seen you for a long time, Captain,'

Jim said, from under the car. 'I heard as how you'd got married. It's the cable,' he added. 'This shouldn't take long.'

A conversation, mainly about brakes and the smooth running of cars followed, interspersed with biographical details.

His brakes now performing to his satisfaction, Arthur returned to the Bull's Head. Mr Woods, the landlord, was in the lobby. 'Did you get your brakes fixed, Captain?'

'Yes, it didn't take long. Has my friend come in? Mr Vettori?'

'Mr Vettori?' said Mr Woods, glancing at the board where the keys hung. 'No, he hasn't. He mentioned he'd probably stroll over to the old quarry. That's what I told the gentleman who called for him.'

Arthur stopped dead. 'The gentleman?' he repeated.

Mr Woods nodded. 'That's right. He asked for Mr Vettori . . .'

Arthur swore, turned, and hurtled out of the building. The 'gentleman' could be one man only. He remembered Jack's smile as he said they needed another murder. His stomach churned. It seemed as if they might have one.

Thomas Vardon shielded his eyes from the sun. There was the fellow. He noticed with grim satisfaction that the quarry was completely bare. There were some caves in the cliffs that rose to the overhang of trees. They could be useful later on. The man, a black solid against the dazzling white of the chalk slope, hadn't seen him.

Vardon walked purposely forward. 'Vettori!' he called again. He slowed as he got nearer.

Jack froze as the voice rang across the open ground. His hand instinctively tightened on the comforting bulk of the pistol in his pocket. A fat lot of good that would do him! He was viciously angry with himself. All their preparations were useless because Vardon had arrived early. He should have known that's what the man would do. He should have *known*.

Vardon was nearly level with him now. 'Vettori! I came a bit . . . Haldean! What the hell are you doing here?'

'Waiting,' said Jack, as urbanely as he could, 'to meet a murderer.' He didn't want Vardon to guess how frantically his mind was racing. 'Waiting, in fact, to meet you.'

Vardon frowned. 'What on earth are you talking about? I've come to meet a colleague, Luke Vettori.'

'I know,' agreed Jack with a smile. 'It's me.'

Vardon's face darkened. 'You! You mean to tell me that you've dragged me all this way on a wild goose chase?' Jack could see he was thinking fast. 'I wondered who the devil this Vettori could be, so I came to see for myself.'

'Of course,' said Jack smoothly. 'Does that also explain why you sent a telegram agreeing to a contract you knew not to exist?'

Vardon took a quick look round and sprang. He was the heavier man and Jack staggered back under his desperate rush. He twisted out from under the clutching hands and brought his knee up sharply. Vardon grunted and fell away, pulling

Jack with him, rolling so he was on top.

Dust gritted against Jack's face and he shut his eyes as Vardon landed a hammer blow on his chest. Winded, he opened his eyes as Vardon's hand clutched his throat and saw the glint of a knife. Desperately he hit upwards and was rewarded with the solid thump of fist against flesh. Vardon grunted and Jack, with a convulsive jerk, got to his knees, leaving Vardon sprawling.

As Vardon got up, Jack pulled the pistol from his pocket. Vardon stopped warily, holding his knife loosely.

'Drop the knife,' Jack commanded.

Vardon wiped his mouth and laughed. 'You daren't use that gun. Who'd be a murderer then?'

'It'd be self-defence,' said Jack curtly. The man was going to spring. He could see it in his eyes.

'Oh yes? Your word against mine, remember.' Vardon brought the knife up and tested the blade with the ball of his thumb. 'Now I, on the other hand, have done this before. Quite a few times before.'

'Drop the knife!' snarled Jack and, deflecting the gun, fired.

Vardon crouched as the shot reverberated round the quarry. 'You *bloody* idiot!' he yelled and jumped. The knife came out, slashing, and Jack flinched back as Vardon's foot, with all the weight of his body behind it, smashed into his weak leg.

The gun flew out of his hand and clattered against the rocks. Blackness with dancing lights flared in front of his eyes. Through a red-speckled mist he saw Vardon scramble for the gun.

312

Jack forced himself to his knees as Vardon whirled and took aim.

'Talk yourself out of this one,' Vardon crowed and, pointing the gun directly at Jack's chest, pulled the trigger. The gun exploded in a shattering roar. Jack was flung back and keeled over, face down.

The cliffs caught the noise in a series of reverberating echoes, which whispered into silence.

Vardon approached the limp body. He stooped down with a grunt, then, holding Jack's shoulder, rolled him over.

Jack's clenched fist came up and twisted in below his left ear where the carotid artery runs up the neck.

There was a sound as if a wet towel had been smacked against a wall. Vardon rolled his eyes and fell, completely unconscious.

Jack lay still, Vardon's body across his. A vast silence descended which was broken by the sound of shouts and pounding feet thudding across the stones. Wearily Jack got up and started to dust himself down.

Arthur Stanton's arm came round his shoulders, holding him up. 'Jack! Thank God you're all right! When I saw him with the gun I thought . . .' He gulped. 'I thought . . .'

'We thought you were a goner,' said Ashley. 'I don't know how you got out of it, but you were damn lucky.'

Jack leaned against Arthur. 'I'd loaded the gun with blanks, of course,' he said, irritated at having to explain. 'I bought them in Silverthorne's.' His leg was on fire. 'I'd have been really up the creek if I had shot him, wouldn't I? Besides that – oh, hell, this *leg!* – I thought if he saw a gun he would use that to try and get me.'

Arthur produced a handkerchief and a small silver flask of brandy. Jack wiped the grit off his face and took a cautious sip of brandy. 'Whew, that's better.'

Ashley bent down beside the unconscious man. Producing a set of handcuffs, he snapped them round Vardon's wrists. 'I wonder how long he'll be out for? That was a meaty crack you gave him.'

'If I'd hit him properly, it would be twenty minutes or so, but I couldn't get my strength behind it,' said Jack, resting his head on his crooked knees.

'I'd hate to see someone you did hit properly,' muttered Ashley. 'It's a great pity we didn't manage to get Sir Thomas's confession.'

'It doesn't matter,' said Jack, groggily. 'Now we know, we'll have enough evidence to hang him five times over without it.'

Vardon stirred and groaned. He tried to move his hands and stopped as he felt the handcuffs. Sergeant Thurrock helped him sit up.

Vardon's eyes rested warily on Jack. 'He attacked me,' he said to the policemen. 'He lured me here and attacked me without warning. He's mad, I tell you.'

'Drop it, Vardon,' said Ashley curtly. 'We know what really happened.'

'This is an outrage—' he began when Jack interrupted him.

'We *know*. We know you murdered your brother and quite a few others.'

'I did no such thing!' Vardon's eyes gleamed brightly. 'It was Castradon, I tell you! He did it. How dare you accuse me of such a thing? I couldn't have killed my brother. I wasn't *there*. I'm Sir Thomas Vardon.'

'Oh no, you're not,' said Jack, leaning forward. 'You murdered Sir Thomas. You're *Simon* Vardon.'

Simon Vardon gazed at him, then his face subtly changed. He seemed smaller somehow, dangerous yet pathetic like a cornered, injured rat.

'There's men who know you well and, what's more, knew your brother well. They know who you are. Take off your shoe and we'll see you've got a toe missing. Thomas didn't. You not only murdered your brother,' went on Jack, 'you killed your best friend, the man who saved you, the man who trusted you. You murdered Alan Leigh.'

Vardon's lip quivered. 'Alan . . .' he whispered, and covered his face with his hands. 'You don't understand. I had to do it. It wouldn't work without Alan. I had to kill him. I didn't want to, but I *had* to.'

'Because you wanted the gold.'

'It was my idea! I knew there was gold there. It was my idea to have the survey. It was *my* idea, I tell you. My father was going to share it with me and then he died. It wasn't fair! Tom wouldn't share. Tom never liked me. Why should Tom have it?'

'Simon Vardon,' began Ashley heavily. 'I charge you with the murders of—'

But Simon Vardon wasn't listening. 'Alan

315

would want me to do it,' he said. He looked up and smiled brightly, his eyes wet with tears. 'Alan would do anything for me. He told me so.'

'And you took him at his word,' said Jack.

Simon Vardon nodded enthusiastically. 'Alan wanted me to be happy. He told me so.'

Jack glanced up at Ashley. 'I didn't think he was completely sane.'

Ashley and the two policemen took Simon Vardon away in the police wagon.

Jack telephoned Isabelle from the Bull's Head. 'You'd better,' she said, after he had finished his very brief explanation, 'come back straight away. I want to hear the full story. And Jack – can I invite Jerry Lucas for the evening? He's been to see Ned Castradon and he's got some wonderful news.'

Twenty-One

'So what's this wonderful news?' asked Jack.

It was a lovely evening, warm and rich with the scent of the roses and honeysuckle that cascaded over the sun-soaked stones that sheltered them. Jack, Isabelle and Arthur, together with Jerry Lucas and Ned and Sue Castradon, were on the terrace in Isabelle and Arthur's garden.

'I'll let Jerry tell you,' said Sue. 'Jerry's been marvellous.'

Jerry Lucas, whisky and soda in hand, grinned. 'It wasn't anything much, you understand. Any doctor worth his salt would have seen it.'

316

'Ned wouldn't go to a doctor,' said Sue, reprovingly.

Ned drew a deep breath. 'I was scared,' he admitted. 'It was getting worse. I forgot things, had blank periods, would arrive somewhere and not know why I was there, but worst of all, I couldn't control my temper.'

'And you had headaches,' put in Sue.

Ned nodded. 'Funnily enough, it was the headaches that saved me in the end, wasn't it, Jerry?'

Jack looked a question.

'I had a dreadful headache,' continued Castradon. 'I suppose it was made worse by being in prison, but it really was unbearable. Constable Stock, who's a decent chap, called for the doctor and Jerry turned up.'

'Not that you were particularly pleased to see me,' said Jerry Lucas with a laugh. 'However, you agreed to let me have a look at you.' He laughed once more. 'You very nearly took a swing at me when I examined you.'

Ned held his hands up. 'I'm sorry! But you can't imagine what it felt like.'

'To cut a long story short,' said Sue, her eyes shining, 'Jerry discovered that Ned's had – what did you call them? Congestion headaches?'

'It was a souvenir of the war, apparently,' said Ned soberly.

Jerry nodded. 'The bone hadn't set properly. It will be, once you've seen the surgeon.' He looked at Castradon in sympathy. 'You must be in nearly constant pain. It's not surprising your temper was affected.'

'You are a stubborn idiot, Ned,' said Sue. 'You

literally had to be locked up before you'd let a doctor near you.'

Castradon gave a crack of laughter and sat back with a delighted smile. Jack realized with a shock that he'd never seen him look genuinely happy before.

'Tell us what happened this afternoon, Jack,' said Isabelle. 'Actually, don't start there. Tell us the whole story. It started when Sue and myself discovered that hideous body in the church, but I don't understand *why* it all happened.'

'As a matter of fact,' said Jack, taking a cigar from the box on the table and lighting it, 'it started long before. Sir Matthew Vardon, as we know, had, together with his cousin, Stamford Leigh and your father, Castradon, explored the wilds of South America together.'

'They quarrelled on that trip,' said Castradon. 'I wouldn't be surprised if that cock-and-bull story Simon Vardon tried to blackmail me with was part of his father's reminiscences.'

'You might well be right,' agreed Jack. 'But they formed a company, Antilla Exploration. The shares were split equally between all three. From what he said, Simon Vardon knew an American company had made a strike further up the river, so had a survey carried out on the land owned by Antilla. As we know, they struck gold. Sir Matthew, according to Simon, was going to share the profits with Simon, but he suffered an apoplectic stroke and died. Incidentally, Castradon, we found a note in Simon Vardon's flat that said you knew Antilla Exploration had found gold.'

318

He raised an eyebrow. 'I don't suppose you did?'

'*Gold*!' repeated Ned incredulously. 'Of course I didn't know.'

'I don't understand,' said Sue. 'Why go through all this elaborate charade? Why not – it sounds horrible, I know – just kill his brother? Then he'd have been Sir Simon and inherited the estate.'

Jack shook his head. 'He didn't want the estate, he wanted the gold mine. Sir Matthew might have rewritten his will if he'd lived, but as things stood, Lady Vardon had the income from all Sir Matthew's holdings for her lifetime. Those holdings, which included the Antilla gold mine, were bequeathed to Sir Thomas. Sir Thomas had willed all his possessions to his wife, Esmé Duclair. If Simon had merely bumped off Thomas, then Lady Vardon and Esmé Duclair would benefit but Simon would be left with nothing.'

'How did Vardon hope to get away with it?' asked Arthur.

'He took me in,' said Sue regretfully. 'Even though he'd shaved off his moustache and darkened his hair, I thought he resembled his brother, but I never dreamt they were the same man.'

Jack nodded. 'All the Vardons had a marked family likeness – it's startling when you see it in Ryle – and Simon resembled his brother enough to make the impersonation credible. All he had to do was avoid Hollywood and stay out of London for a couple of years. After that time he'd be so well-established as Thomas Vardon that anyone who questioned him would have to be very sure of their ground. Simon knew enough about Thomas to see him through most situations that would crop up.'

319

Jack took a sip of his whisky. 'Let me take you back to the Sunday you had your fight with Ryle, Castradon.'

'Do you have to?' said Ned, reluctantly. 'I'd rather forget it.'

'It's important,' said Jack with a grin. 'Ryle tried to get away from you in a car.'

'He didn't get very far. He leapt out of it, yelling his head off, as I recall.'

Jack flicked the ash off his cigar. 'That's because there was a body in it.' He looked at Isabelle. 'I guessed as much and Ryle confirmed it when I asked him.'

'A body?' questioned Isabelle. 'Whose body, Jack?'

'Alan Leigh. He was the first one to be killed, despite the evidence Vardon manufactured to the contrary, and the one murder that Simon Vardon was upset by. He really did seem to have cared about Leigh. When he saw the body – Leigh's body – in the mortuary, he was grief-stricken, but it was Alan Leigh he was grieving for, not his brother.'

Isabelle shuddered. 'But why kill him?'

'Because Simon Vardon wanted an alibi. A cast iron, twenty-four caret, hundred per cent alibi. Not only that, but he knew that where there's a murder, there's a murderer, and the police never give up. He created the character of the Chessman and, Castradon, tried his level best to pin it on you. After all, the feud between your two families was well known and you stood to gain a gold mine if all the Vardons died.' His gaze slid to Sue. 'But perhaps, most importantly of all, you had something he wanted very much indeed.'

Ned reached out to Sue in a protective gesture.

'I knew he was sincere,' she said thoughtfully, squeezing Ned's hand. 'I trusted him because of that. I felt sorry for him, too.' She paused a moment. 'When did he come up with this dreadful plan?'

'Before his father died. Incidentally, I don't believe that Simon Vardon knew Ryle was his half-brother or that Ryle had conspired with his father to steal his mother's diamonds. His father might have been going to tell him about the robbery but from what I've gathered of Sir Matthew's character, I think he'd have kept that knowledge to himself.'

'I think you're probably right,' said Ned. 'He was a selfish, secretive devil, who wouldn't give away anything without a good reason. I wouldn't like the Vicar to hear me say as much, but I wasn't sorry when I heard he'd died.'

'No,' agreed Jack. 'He wasn't a nice man, was he? Anyway, Lady Vardon got the first of the Chessman letters before Sir Matthew died. Sir Matthew was clearly on the way out and, looking back, it all seemed very much part of a pattern, that some lunatic had a grudge against the entire Vardon family. Simon Vardon saw you, Mrs Castradon, at his father's funeral and the identity of the Chessman, which he had probably decided anyway, was assured. He knew his brother was coming back from Hollywood, so he had to act.'

'And this is where that poor beggar, Leigh, comes in?' asked Arthur.

'Exactly. On the Sunday, he doped Leigh up, drove him to Croxton Ferriers and killed him.

321

His plan was to leave Leigh in the church, but he wanted to sneak into your garage, Castradon, and steal something – anything – that would point to you. He chose the tartan rug, the axe and the wrench. He used that tartan rug to lay a nice little trail of evidence back to your garden gate.'

'The devil,' growled Ned. 'Was he there, d'you think? Near the car on Sunday night, I mean?'

Jack nodded. 'I bet he was. It must've been a nasty moment for him when Ryle actually tried to drive off in the car but, fortunately for him, Ryle made a run for it instead. It could've all gone wrong then, but Ryle was so shaken by what he'd seen, it was quite a job to get him to admit it. After leaving Alan Leigh in the church, Vardon had one last job, late on Sunday evening, and that was to post a letter that would be collected and therefore postmarked on the Monday, addressed to himself in London. It was from the Chessman, warning Simon Vardon to stay away from Croxton Ferriers.'

'Hang on,' said Ned slowly. 'You say the murder happened on Sunday? But we know it was *Tuesday* the body was left in the church.'

Jack shook his head. 'No. You remember the lilies that were stolen from the Dysons' garden and left on the corpse?'

'Don't,' said Sue. 'I'll never forget it. It seemed such a mockery of the dead man.'

Jack shook his head. 'The lilies were taken for one purpose only, to make us think the body had been left there on Tuesday. Simon Vardon had a busy day on Tuesday. First of all he left that note in the flat, purporting to come from Alan Leigh.

That made us think that Leigh had been alive on the Wednesday. Then Vardon left his car at London Bridge station and came, quite openly, to Croxton Ferriers.'

'That's the day he called at my office,' said Ned.

'Exactly. I remember you said he was waiting for you when you arrived.'

'That's right. I found him with his feet on my desk. The clerk swore he hadn't admitted him.'

'He didn't,' said Jack. 'Vardon watched his moment and sneaked in. He needed a few minutes alone in your office.'

'Is that when he stole my paper knife?' asked Ned.

Jack nodded. 'And your silver matchbox, I imagine. He was setting you up, remember, so he deliberately forced a quarrel with you, knowing it would count against you, but what he was really after was the name of one of your clients. Anyone would do, as long as they lived some distance away and preferably in or near a large town. He wanted to make sure that you'd be away the following day.'

'Hang on,' said Ned. 'Is this where the telegram comes in? The one from Sir Arnold Stapleton?'

'That's right.'

'Sir Arnold's file was on the desk,' said Ned, his eyes narrowing. 'But Haldean, I really *did* get a telegram, you know. I was told it couldn't be traced at Eastbourne.'

'No more it could,' said Jack with a grin. 'That was a very black mark against you. I worked that one out. He actually sent it from a village called Easebourne. It's not far away – just outside Midhurst – and easy to get to. When we traced the telegram, it convinced Ashley I wasn't just clutching at straws.'

Ned whistled. 'It's such a little thing.'

'It showed you were telling the truth though, and that's what Ashley needed.'

'Why was Vardon so anxious to get me to Eastbourne?'

'He wanted to buy a car – or, rather, he wanted *you* to buy a car, the Vauxhall we found in the railway tunnel. To anyone working from a police description alone, you're an easy man to impersonate. You and Vardon are about the same build and, with an eye patch and a greasepaint scar, it's no wonder the man in the garage at Eastbourne identified you as the John Smith who'd bought the car. Vardon then returned to Croxton Ferriers and, when it was dark, stole the lilies from the Dysons' garden and placed them on the corpse in the church.'

'Where did he get the key to the church, Jack?' asked Arthur. 'Come to that, why put the body in the church at all?'

'He must've taken an impression of the key at his father's funeral. It's hung up in the vestry and it's easy to find. He put the body in the church because he wanted the body discovered on Friday. The rota for the various church duties is in the parish magazine and pinned up on the noticeboard at the back, so he would have known that the body was safe, barring accidents, until Friday. He must've known that for most of the year the

324

only time that cupboard was ever opened was on Fridays to get the flower things out.'

Sue Castradon stirred. 'When I spoke to Simon Vardon after Sir Matthew's funeral, he asked me about the flowers, and who did them and where we kept the things and everything. I thought he was just being polite.'

'It's natural enough to talk about flowers at a funeral,' agreed Jack. 'That conversation could have given him the whole idea.'

'But why Tuesday?' demanded Isabelle. 'Why did he want to make us think the murder had happened on Tuesday?'

'Because, Belle, on Tuesday he had, as Simon Vardon, had a row with Castradon and then, to all intents and purposes vanished off the face of the earth. He intended to re-appear – as he did – as Thomas Vardon on Friday, fresh off the boat and obviously innocent of any murder that had happened earlier in the week when, as could be later proved, Thomas Vardon was in the middle of the Atlantic.'

'So what happened to Thomas Vardon?' asked Ned. 'The real Sir Thomas, I mean.'

Jack ran his forefinger across his throat in a significant gesture. 'Simon knew when his brother was due to arrive at Southampton. Thomas had sent him a cable from the boat. Simon must've met him at the docks in the Vauxhall, murdered him and abandoned the body in the car in the tunnel.'

'That's the body you thought was Alan Leigh,' said Arthur.

'That's the body we were *meant* to think was Leigh's, certainly. Simon Vardon wanted it to be

325

left for a good few days. By that time it would be impossible to say with any certainty when the poor beggar had been killed. Naturally, he confused matters as much as he could by making the bodies practically unidentifiable. That worried me, you know. Why, if the Chessman was perfectly happy to crow about Simon Vardon's murder, had he taken such pains to disfigure the body?'

'I thought it was because he was a lunatic,' said Isabelle.

'Yes, and that's what we were meant to think. Now we come to what I'm sure was supposed to be the last murder, that of Esmé Duclair.'

'Why d'you say that was supposed to be the last?' asked Ned.

'Because, old son,' said Jack, 'you only escaped being arrested for it by the skin of your teeth. Vardon had done such a good job of casting suspicion on you for the first murder, we were bound to think of you. If you hadn't had a nightcap with your chess pal that didn't break up until quarter to one in the morning, you'd have been for it. Simon Vardon wore an eye patch to meet Esmé. That was seen, as it was meant to be seen. Naturally Simon couldn't allow Esmé to live; she'd rumble him right away. In fact, that's precisely what she did do. He was sufficiently like Thomas for her to walk up to him, and sufficiently unalike for her to say "Where's Thomas? I expected Tom to be here," or words to that effect. He must have been kicking himself when you had enough of an alibi to make it very improbable, if not impossible, for you to have killed Esmé. However, he turned

326

that mistake to his advantage, when he decided to murder his mother.'

'His mother!' said Isabelle, shocked. 'But she committed suicide.'

Jack shook his head. 'I don't think so.'

'Actually,' said Arthur, 'I was going to ask you about Lady Vardon. She must've known Simon was Thomas all along.'

'Yes,' said Jack in an odd voice. 'She must have done, mustn't she?'

'I told you!' said Isabelle. 'I told you Lady Vardon resented Thomas.'

'You were obviously right,' said Jerry Lucas dryly.

'So why did he kill her?' asked Arthur.

'She was getting to be a nuisance. She was a greedy woman, and she owned the income from the gold mine. I don't think she knew Simon was the Chessman, but she knew a great deal about Simon – a dangerous amount – and she knew how he felt about you, Mrs Castradon. She resented it bitterly.'

'I'll say she did,' agreed Ned. 'She called on me to say as much.'

Isabelle nodded. 'Everyone heard about that. I think she was the sort of woman who'd always resent their son's wife, Jack. There are mothers like that. They want to be the only one who matters.'

'But, damn it, Jack, she got a letter from the Chessman,' said Arthur. 'Surely her natural reaction wouldn't be to kill herself but to ask him what the devil was going on?'

Jack shook his head. 'I don't think she ever saw that letter. An envelope from the Chessman certainly arrived with the second post, but I bet the original contents were innocent enough. Simon must have planted the letter we found afterwards. I can't prove this, but what I think happened is that Simon doped her coffee with choral, which made her sleepy. The butler said she was tired. After the butler had cleared away the coffee things, Simon came back through the window and injected her with digitalis. By the time he killed her, she must have been fast asleep. He'd leave the bottle to allow us to reach the obvious conclusion. She was a plump little woman, and one little pinprick from a hypodermic wouldn't be noticed.'

'You're probably right,' said Jerry Lucas. 'As it was classed as suicide right away, there wouldn't be a post-mortem and, even if there was, I doubt if a single pinprick would be noticed. Doctors are as guilty of having preconceptions as anyone else. I suppose once Lady Vardon was dead, Simon Vardon thought it was all over.'

'More or less. He had the gold mine and now it was time for him to lead us to the car, the body and the things in the old signal box. He must have known roughly what time those two little scamps of Halfords came to the tunnel – they went nearly every day, apparently – and so he contrived to frighten the living daylights out of them, knowing that they were bound to tell someone. I must say, Castradon, it did look black for you. Arthur never believed for a moment you were guilty.'

Ned reached across the table and clasped Arthur's hand. 'Thanks,' he said simply.

'I think a celebration is in order,' said Isabelle.

Jack glanced at her suspiciously. There was a look in her eye that he knew only too well. She was planning something.

Isabelle got up and, going into the house, returned a few minutes later, accompanied by Mabel, who was carrying a tray containing six champagne glasses and an ice bucket from which protruded a gold-topped bottle.

Mabel, who was clearly on her very best behaviour, put the tray on the table. 'I've put the other bottles to chill, ma'am, just as you said.'

'Thank you,' said Isabelle.

Arthur took out the bottle from the ice. 'Isabelle,' he said weakly, 'this is my 1906 Dom Perignon! I was saving this for a special occasion!'

'Isn't this special enough?' asked Isabelle wickedly and giggled. 'I told you there was some wonderful news,' she said, her eyes shining. 'Arthur, you don't know, but Jerry does. Jack, open the champagne and pour a glass for everyone, will you?'

Jack, very conscious of Arthur's bewildered consternation, opened the champagne.

'Tell them, Jerry,' said Isabelle happily.

Jerry laughed. 'All right.' He stood up. 'Could you all raise your glasses to the new father – and mother – to be.'

Arthur, glass in hand, looked thunderstruck. 'A baby? We're going to have a baby?'

'Congratulations,' said Jack, kissing Isabelle. 'That's the best news yet.'

They had talked long into the night, and the night was mild and welcoming, as only a summer night in Sussex can be. Ned and Sue Castradon, refusing all offers of cars, walked home hand in hand, seeing their way by the light of the moon.

'Sue . . .' Ned suddenly looked very awkward. 'If Lucas really can cure my headaches and I can stop being so – so difficult – are you absolutely sure it won't matter what I look like?'

She squeezed his hand. 'Ned. Don't be so *bloody* silly.'

He laughed. 'Don't start swearing again! All right. I promise. A baby,' he said softly. 'Isabelle will be a wonderful mother. Arthur Stanton will be a great father, too.'

'I always thought you'd be a wonderful father,' she said thoughtfully.

He stopped and kissed her. 'Now that,' he said eventually, 'is a really good idea.'

P CH